ALIEN CRIMES

ALIEN CRIMES

Edited by
Mike Resnick

SCIENCE
FICTION

First Science Fiction Book Club printing April 2007

Published by Science Fiction Book Club, 401 Franklin Avenue, Garden City, New York 11530.

Visit the SF Book Club online at www.sfbc.com

Book design by Christos Peterson

ISBN: 978-1-58288-223-9

Printed in the United States of America

❖ CONTENTS ❖

Introduction
  by Mike Resnick vii

Nothing Personal
  by Pat Cadigan 3

A Locked–Planet Mystery
  by Mike Resnick 55

Hoxbomb
  by Harry Turtledove 115

The End of the World
  by Kristine Kathryn Rusch 173

Dark Heaven
  by Gregory Benford 271

Womb of Every World
  by Walter Jon Williams 345

❖ INTRODUCTION ❖

Two years ago I edited *Down These Dark Spaceways,* an anthology of six hard-boiled science fiction detective novellas, for the Science Fiction Book Club. It was pretty well received: Robert J. Sawyer's novella was nominated for a Hugo and a Nebula, Catherine Asaro's was nominated for a couple of awards, others appeared in various Best-of-the-Year anthologies.

So last year I approached the book club and suggested we do another. They agreed, with the stipulation that *this* book of alien crimes not contain any hard-boiled mysteries, that we show that the infinitely adaptable field of science fiction is able to encompass *all* kinds of mysteries. After all, Alfred Bester's *The Demolished Man* and Isaac Asimov's *The Caves of Steel,* the two archetypal science fictional mysteries, weren't hard-boiled novels.

Hence, *Alien Crimes.* Once again I chose some of the very best writers in the field and put the challenge to them: give me a science fiction mystery, make it novella length, play fair with the reader, and this time let's have no genuflecting to the Hammett/Chandler school of writing. In due time they delivered their stories, and I think you'll find the broad range of approaches and subject matter as interesting as the mysteries themselves. Hugo winner and best seller Harry Turtledove examines the odor of crime in *Hoxbomb;* I bring back my *Down These Dark Spaceways* detective Jake Masters, but this time he's working for the police and trying to solve *A Locked-Planet Mystery;* Hugo winner and Edgar nominee Kristine Kathryn Rusch demonstrates that things are not always what they seem in *End of the World;* Hugo nominee and Clarke winner Pat Cadigan gives us an interesting lady investigator with a unique problem to solve in *Nothing Personal;* Nebula winner Gregory Benford seems to be telling a contemporary mystery in *Dark Heaven,* and then proves that appearances can be deceiving; and finally, in *Womb of Every World,* Nebula winner Walter Jon Williams brings you a story that . . . well, whatever you think it is, it's almost certainly not.

I think, like its predecessor, this book proves that science fiction can always bring something fresh and new to other forms of fiction—especially the mystery story.

—Mike Resnick

ALIEN CRIMES

❖ NOTHING PERSONAL ❖

Pat Cadigan

DETECTIVE RUBY Tsung could not say when the Dread had first come over her. It had been a gradual development, taking place over a period of weeks, possibly months, with all the subtlety of any of the more mundane life processes—weight gain, graying hair, aging itself. Time marched on and one day you woke up to find you were a somewhat dumpy, graying, middle-aged homicide detective with twenty-five years on the job and a hefty lump of bad feeling in the pit of your stomach: the Dread.

It was a familiar-enough feeling, the Dread. Ruby had known it well in the past. Waiting for the verdict in an officer-involved shooting; looking up from her backlog of paperwork to find a stone-faced Internal Affairs Division officer standing over her; the doctor clearing his throat and telling her to sit down before giving her the results of the mammogram; answering an unknown trouble call and discovering it was a cop's address. Then there were the ever-popular rumors, rumors, rumors: of budget cuts, of forced retirement for everyone with more than fifteen years in, of mandatory transfers, demotions, promotions, stings, grand jury subpoenas, not to mention famine, war, pestilence, disease, and death—business as usual.

After a while she had become inured to a lot of it. You had to or you'd make yourself sick, give yourself an ulcer, or go crazy. As she had grown more experienced, she had learned what to worry about and what she could consign to denial even just temporarily. Otherwise, she would have spent all day with the Dread eating away at her insides and all night with it sitting on her chest crushing the breath out of her.

The last ten years of her twenty-five had been in Homicide and in that time, she had had little reason to feel Dread. There was no point. This was Homicide—something bad *was* going to happen so there was no reason to dread it. Someone was going to turn up dead today, tomorrow it would be someone else, the next day still someone else, and so forth. Nothing personal, just Homicide.

Nothing personal. She had been coping with the job on this basis for a long time now and it worked just fine. Whatever each murder might have been about, she could be absolutely certain that it wasn't about her. Whatever had gone so seriously wrong as to result in loss of life, it was not meant to serve as an omen, a warning, or any other kind of signifier in her life. Just the facts, ma'am or sir. Then punch out and go home.

Nothing personal. She was perfectly clear on that. It didn't help. She still felt as if she had swallowed something roughly the size and density of a hockey puck.

There was no specific reason that she could think of. She wasn't under investigation—not as far as she knew, anyway, and she made a point of not dreading what she didn't know. She hadn't done anything (lately) that would have called for any serious disciplinary action; there were no questionable medical tests to worry about, no threats of any kind. Her son, Jake, and his wife, Lita, were nested comfortably in the suburbs outside Boston, making an indecent amount of money in computer software and raising her grandkids in a big old Victorian house that looked like something out of a storybook. The kids e-mailed her regularly, mostly jokes and scans of their crayon drawings. Whether they were all really as happy as they appeared to be was another matter but she was fairly certain they weren't suffering. But even if she had been inclined to worry unduly about them, it wouldn't have felt like the Dread.

❖

Almost as puzzling to her as when the Dread had first taken up residence was how she had managed not to notice it coming on. Eventually she understood that she hadn't—she had simply pushed it to the back of her mind and then, being continuously busy, had kept on pushing it all the way into the *Worry About Later* file, where it had finally grown too intense to ignore.

Which brought her back to the initial question: when the hell had it started? Had it been there when her partner, Rita Castillo, had retired? She didn't remember feeling anything as unpleasant as the Dread when Rita had made the announcement or later on, at her leaving party. Held in a cop bar, the festivities had gone on till two in the morning and the only unusual thing about it for Ruby had been that she had gone home relatively sober. Not by design and not for any specific reason. Not even on purpose—she had had a couple of drinks that had given her a nice mellow buzz, after which she had switched to diet cola. Some kind of new stuff—someone had given her a taste and she'd liked it. Who? Right, Tommy DiCenzo; Tommy had fifteen years of sobriety, which was some kind of precinct record.

But the Dread hadn't started that night; it had already been with her then. Not the current full-blown knot of Dread, but in retrospect she knew that she had felt something and simply refused to think about the bit of disquiet that had sunk its barbed hook into a soft place.

But she hadn't been so much in denial that she had gotten drunk. You left yourself open to all sorts of unpleasantness when you tied one on at a cop's retirement party: bad thoughts, bad memories, bad dreams, and real bad mornings-after. Of course, knowing that hadn't always stopped her in the past. It was too easy to let yourself be caught up in the moment, in all the moments, and suddenly you were completely shitfaced and wondering how that could have happened. Whereas she couldn't remember the last time she'd heard of anyone staying sober by accident.

Could have been the nine-year-old that had brought the Dread on. That had been pretty bad even for an old hand like herself. Rita had been on vacation and she had been working alone when the boy's body had turned up in the Dumpster on the South Side—or South Town, which was what everyone seemed to be calling it now. The sudden name-change baffled her; she had joked to Louie Levant at the desk across from hers about not getting the memo on renaming the 'hoods. Louie had looked back at her with a mixture of mild surprise and amusement on his pale features. "South Town was what we always called it when I was growing up there," he informed her, a bit loftily. "Guess the rest of you finally caught on." Louie was about twenty years younger than she was, Ruby reminded herself, which meant that she had two decades more history to forget; she let the matter drop.

Either way, South Side or South Town, the area wasn't a crime hotspot. It wasn't as upscale as the parklike West Side or as stolidly middle/working class as the Northland Grid but it wasn't East Midtown, either. Murder in South Town was news; the fact that it was a nine-year-old boy was worse news and worst of all, it had been a sex crime.

Somehow she had known that it would be a sex crime even before she had seen the body, lying small, naked, and broken amid the trash in the bottom of the Dumpster. Just what she hadn't wanted to catch—kiddie sex murder. Kiddie sex murder had something for everyone: nightmares for parents, hysterical ammunition for religious fanatics, and lurid headlines for all. And a very special kind of hell for the family of the victim, who would be forever overshadowed by the circumstances of his death.

During his short life, the boy had been an average student with a talent for things mechanical—he had liked to build engines for model trains and cars. He had told his parents he thought he'd like to be a pilot when he grew up. Had he died in some kind of accident, a car wreck, a fall, or something equally unremarkable, he would have been remembered as the little boy who never got a chance to fly—tragic, what a shame, light a candle. Instead, he would now and forever be defined by the sensational nature of his death. The public memory would link him not with little-kid stuff like model trains and cars but with the pervert who had killed him.

She hadn't known anything about him, none of those specific details about models and flying when she had first stood gazing down at him; at that point, she hadn't even known his name. But she had known the rest of it as she had climbed into the Dumpster, trying not to gag from the stench of garbage and worse and hoping that the plastic overalls and booties she had on didn't tear.

That had been a bad day. Bad enough that it could have been the day the Dread had taken up residence in her gut.

Except it wasn't.

Thinking about it, remembering the sight, the smell, the awful way it felt when she had accidentally stepped on the dead boy's ankle, she knew the Dread had already been with her. Not so cumbersome at the time, still small enough to snub in favor of more immediate problems, but definitely there.

Had it been Ricky Carstairs, then? About a month before the nine-year-old, she had been on her way out of the precinct house when she had passed two uniformed officers bringing him in and recognized him immediately. She had no idea how she had managed that mental feat—he had been skinny, dirty, and obviously strung out, and she hadn't seen him since he and Jake had been in the seventh grade together but she had known him at once and it hadn't been a good moment.

"It's just plain wrong," she had said when Rita asked her why she looked as if she had just found half a worm in the middle of an apple. "Your kid's old school friends are supposed to go away and live lives with no distinguishing characteristics. Become office workers in someplace like Columbus or Chicago or Duluth."

"And that's just plain *weird*," Rita replied, her plump face wearing a slightly alarmed expression. "Or maybe not weird enough—I don't know. You been watching a lot of TV lately? Like the Hallmark Channel or something?"

"Never mind," she said, making a short dismissive wave with one hand. "It made more sense *before* I said it out loud."

Rita had burst into hearty laughter and that had been that; they'd gone with the rest of the day, whatever that had involved. Probably a dead body.

The dismaying sight of one of Jake's old school friends sweating in handcuffs had lodged in her mind more as a curiosity than anything else. Uncomfortable but hardly critical—not the fabled moment of clarity, not a short sharp shock or a reality check or a wake-up call from Planet Earth. Just a moment when she hoped that poor old Ricky hadn't recognized her, too.

So had the Dread already been lodged in her gut then?

She tried but she honestly couldn't remember one way or the other—the incident was just that too far in the past and it had lasted only a minute, if that—but she thought it was very possible that it had.

It was unlikely, she realized, that she would ever pinpoint the exact moment when something had shifted or slipped or cracked—gone faulty, anyway—and let a sense of something wrong get in and take root. And for all she knew, it might not even matter. Not if she were in the first stage of one of those on-the-job crack-ups that a lot of cops fell victim to. Just what she needed—a slow-motion train wreck. Christ, what the hell was the point of having a breakdown in slow motion unless you could actually do something about it, actually prevent it from happening? Too bad it didn't work that way—every cop she knew who had come out the other side of a crash described it as unstoppable. If it had to happen, why couldn't it be fast? Crack up quick and have an equally rapid recovery, get it over with. She pictured herself going to the department shrink for help: *Overclock me, Doc—I got cases to solve and they're gaining on me.*

Ha-ha, good one; the shrink might even get a chuckle out of it. Unless she had to explain what overclocking was. Would a shrink know enough about computers to get it? Hell, she wouldn't have known herself if she hadn't picked things up from Jake, who had blossomed into a tech head practically in his playpen.

Her mind snagged on the idea of talking to the shrink and wouldn't let go. Why not? She had done it before. Granted, it had been mandatory, then—all cops involved in a shooting had to see the shrink—but she'd had no problem with that. And what the hell, it had done her more good than she'd expected it to. She had known at the time that she'd needed help and if she were honest with herself, she had to admit that she needed help now. Going around with the lead weight of the Dread dragging on her wasn't even on the extreme ass-end of acceptably screwed up that was in the range of normal for a homicide detective.

The more she thought about it, the more imperative it seemed that she talk to the department shrink, because she sure hadn't talked to anyone else about it. Not her lieutenant, not Tommy DiCenzo, not even Rita.

Well, she wouldn't have talked to Lieutenant Ostertag—that was a no-brainer. Throughout her career, she had always had the good sense never to believe any my-door-is-always-open bullshit from a superior officer. Ostertag hadn't even bothered with the pretense.

Tommy DiCenzo, on the other hand, she could have talked to and counted on his complete confidence. They'd gone through the academy together and she'd listened to plenty from him, both before and after he'd dried out. Tommy might even have understood enough to tell her whether she was about to derail big time or was just experiencing another side effect of being middle-aged, overworked, and underpaid. But every time she thought about giving him a call or asking him to go for coffee, something stopped her.

Maddeningly, she couldn't think of a single good reason why. Hell, she couldn't even think of a crappy reason. There was no reason. She simply could not bring herself to talk to him about the Dread and that was all there was to it.

And Rita—well, there had been plenty of reasons not to talk

to her. They were busy, far too busy to devote any time to anything that didn't have a direct bearing on the cases piling up on their respective desks. Not that Rita wouldn't have listened. But whenever she considered bringing it up, saying, *You know, Rita, lately I've had the damnedest feeling, a sense of being in the middle of something real bad that's about to get a whole lot worse,* the image of the nine-year-old boy in the Dumpster would bloom in her brain and she would clench her teeth together.

Of course, she could go to Rita now. She could trot on over to her neat little fourth-floor condo, sit out on the balcony with her amid the jungle of plants with a few beers, and tell her all about it. Only she knew what Rita would probably say, because Rita had already said it. That had been the night before she had put in her retirement papers; she had taken Ruby out to dinner and broken the news to her privately.

"I always planned to put in my twenty and get out while I was still young enough to enjoy it," she said, cheerfully sawing away at a slab of bloody steak. "You could have done that five years ago. Do it now and you'll be in good shape all the way around. Maybe you want to get in thirty but is putting in another five years really worth it?"

"Five years"—Ruby had shrugged—"What's five years? Blink of an eye, practically."

"All the more reason to get out," Rita had insisted. "Before it's too late to get a life."

Bristling inwardly, Ruby had looked down at her own steak. Why she had ordered that much food was beyond her. The Dread didn't leave anywhere nearly enough room for it. "I have a life."

"The job is *not* a life," Rita said, chewing vigorously and then dragging her napkin across her lips. "The job is the job. What do you do when you're not on the job?"

"Talk to the grandkids on e-mail. Shop. Rent DVDs—"

"You ever go *out* to a movie? Or out to dinner—with anyone *other* than me?" Rita added quickly before she could answer. "Hell, girlfriend, when was the last time you got laid?"

Ruby blinked at her, startled, unsure whether it was by the question itself or by the fact that she didn't know the answer.

"I don't know if you've heard"—Rita leaned over the table and lowered her voice confidentially—"but there are more alternatives for people our age than the cone or the rabbit."

"Yeah, but my idea of sex doesn't involve *typing*." Ruby looked at her sidelong.

"Keeps the fingers nimble." Rita laughed. "No, I wasn't referring to chat room sex. I'm talking about going out and meeting people."

"Dating sites?" Ruby made a pained face.

"*Please,*" Rita mirrored her expression. "Social groups. Meetups for people with similar interests. Hobbies, film festivals, shit like that. You know I've got a boyfriend?" Pause. "*And* a girlfriend."

"Sounds exciting," Ruby told her. "But I don't know if that's really for me."

"I didn't know either," Rita said. "I sure didn't go looking for it. It just happened. That's how it is when you have a life—things happen. You ought to try it."

"Yeah? Well, what I really want to know is how come I haven't gotten to meet these people you've been seeing." Ruby folded her arms and pretended to be stern.

"Well, for one thing—and I've got to be perfectly honest here"—Rita put down her knife and fork—"I wasn't sure how you'd react."

Ruby's eyebrows went up. "What? All this time we've worked together and you don't know I'm not a homophobe?"

"I was referring to the guy," Rita said, deadpan.

"Damn. And I thought I hid it so well," said Ruby, equally deadpan.

Rita gave a laugh and picked up her knife and fork again. "So pull the pin with me. You won't have to hide anything you don't want to."

"I'll give it some thought," Ruby lied.

"I'm asking you again—what're you waiting for?" Rita paused, regarding her expectantly. When she didn't answer, she went on. "They're not gonna promote you, you know. You *do* know that, don't you?"

Ruby dipped her head noncommittally.

"I sure knew they weren't gonna promote *me*. I knew that for a goddamn *fact*." Rita took a healthy swig of wine and dragged her napkin across her mouth again.

"So is that why you decided to retire?"

Rita wagged her head emphatically. "I told you, it was my plan all along—get in my twenty and get the hell out. They'd have had to come up with a pretty hefty promotion to make me want to stay."

"Yeah? Like what—chief? Commissioner?"

"Supreme dictator for life. And I'm not so sure I would have said yes." Rita sighed. "What are you holding out for—lieutenant?"

"I passed the exam."

"So did I. So did umpty-hundred other cops ahead of us both and they ain't moving up, either." Rita's expression abruptly turned sad. "I never figured you for a lifer."

"Or maybe you hoped I wasn't?" Ruby said. "Personally, I never thought about it. I just get up and go to work every day."

"Think about it now," Rita said urgently. "Think about it like you've never thought about anything else. Get serious— you're topped out. Whatever you're waiting for, it isn't coming. All you can do is mark time."

"I work on solving murders and putting away the guilty parties," Ruby said, an edge creeping into her voice. "I wouldn't call that marking time."

"For you personally, it is," Rita insisted, unapologetic. "And in case you forgot, you count for something."

"I'm a good cop. That counts for a lot."

"That's not all you are, though. Do you even know that anymore?"

Ruby shifted in her seat, more than a little irritated. "Retiring young isn't for everybody, even if you think it is. When all you have is a hammer, everything looks like a nail."

"Oh, for chrissakes, already—" Rita blew out a short breath. "That's what *I've* been trying to tell *you*."

They sat looking at each other for some unmeasured time and Ruby realized that her soon-to-be ex-partner was just as irritated with her, possibly more. She tried to come up with something to say to defuse the situation before a serious quarrel developed but the Dread sitting large and uncomfortable in the middle of her body was eating her brain. The Dread was actually all she ever thought about now, like a pain that never went away, she realized, and there was barely room for anything else anymore.

Then Rita had sat back in her chair, dismay in her plump, round face. "Shit, what the hell am I doing? I'm sorry, Rube."

Ruby stared at her, baffled.

"I'm telling you you don't have a life and I'm browbeating you like I'm trying to get a confession." She shook her head as if trying to clear it. "I think I'm getting out just in time."

"Well, I *was* gonna lawyer up," Ruby said, laughing a little. "Forget it. It's a touchy thing when a partner leaves, we both know that. Things can get a little weird, blown out of proportion."

They had finished their dinner—or rather, Rita had finished hers while Ruby got a doggy bag—and called it a night early, smiles all round, although the smiles were slightly sad.

That was how things still stood between them: smoothed over but not actually resolved. If she went to Rita now and told her about the Dread, growing a little bit bulkier, a little heavier, and a little more uncomfortable every day with no end in sight, Rita would only take that as further proof that she was right about retirement.

And she really did not want to have that conversation with Rita because she had no intention of retiring. Because she knew, deep in her core and in her bones, that even if she did take Rita's advice to pack it all in, even if she took it a step further, sold everything she owned and went off to a luxury beach condo in the Caribbean to laze around in the sun all day, indulge in fancy food and drink, and get thoroughly, perfectly laid every night by a series of gorgeous men and women, separately and together—despite all of that and a billion dollars besides, she knew with no uncertainty at all that she would still wake up every morning with the Dread that much larger and heavier and unrelenting than it had been the day before.

If she went to Rita, she would have to tell her that and she didn't want to because she really didn't think Rita would understand. And if she didn't tell her, then Rita would only start harping again on the question of what she was waiting for. Probably accuse her of waiting for the Dread to go away.

Then she would have to confess: *No. I'm waiting to find out. I'm waiting for whatever it is I've been Dreading to show up.* Which was something she hadn't quite admitted to herself yet.

"Coffee?"

The voice cut through the combination of Ruby's usual morning haze and the constant overriding pressure of the Dread, startling her and making her jump a little. She looked up from the open folder she had been staring at unseeingly to find a young guy standing next to her desk, holding out a large cup that definitely had not come from any of the precinct machines.

"I didn't know you guys delivered," she said, smiling as she took the cup from him.

"Don't let it get around," the guy said, "or I'll have to do it for everybody." He was about thirty, just a little too dark to be called olive-skinned with a sprinkling of freckles across the bridge of his nose and a head full of honey-colored dreadlocks that had the potential to become unruly. He was only a couple of inches taller than Ruby herself—five-eight, five-nine at the most—and slightly husky.

"It'll be our secret," she assured him, taking the lid off the cup. A dark roast aroma wafted up with the steam; not her favorite but she wasn't inclined to find fault. "Am I supposed to know you?"

"When the lieutenant comes in, he'll introduce me as your new partner."

"I see." Ruby studied him. "Transfer from vice?"

He shook his head.

"Narcotics?"

"Ah." He smiled with half his mouth. "Must be the dreads."

Ruby barely managed not to flinch at the word; it took a quarter of a second before she realized what he was referring to. "Well, it was some kind of undercover work, though. Right?"

"Fraud and cybercrime. Rafe Pasco." He held out his hand and Ruby took it. It was strong and square but as smooth and soft as a woman's.

"Portuguese?" she guessed.

"Filipino, actually. On my father's side." He grinned and half-sat on the edge of her desk. "Though as you can see, that's only part of the story. Even on my father's side." His grin widened a bit. "Like you, maybe."

Ruby shrugged. "Everybody had a story in my family and none of them could ever keep them straight. My father claimed they almost named me Kim Toy O'Toole. And I didn't even have freckles."

"Then you grew up deprived." He tilted his head to look at the file on her desk. "What are you working on?"

She had to glance down to remind herself. "Ah. Suspicious drowning. Wife reported her husband missing. Three days later he turns up on the rocks under the Soldiers Road bridge. Coroner says he's pretty sure the guy didn't just happen to wash up there, that someone must have pulled him out and then just left him."

"Anonymous call tipping you off where to find him?"

Ruby shook her head. "Couple of kids found him and told their parents. Can't figure why someone would pull a corpse out of the river and then just leave him."

"The killer?"

"Then why pull him out at all?"

"Well, the wife couldn't collect on any insurance without a body. For instance."

"Could be." Ruby made a face. "But I don't think she killed him. I think he's a suicide and she's trying to make it seem like a murder so she doesn't lose the insurance. The payout isn't much—twenty-five thousand dollars. Not enough to inspire murder but not a sum you'd want to have to give up, either."

Pasco nodded, looking thoughtful. "Is she a hardship case?"

"Why?" Ruby asked, frowning.

"Maybe she really needs it."

She gave a short laugh. "Hey, man, who *doesn't* need twenty-five thousand dollars? Especially if it's on the verge of dropping right into your lap."

"Yeah, but if she's got kids or she's gonna get evicted or something, it'd be too bad to take it away from her."

Ruby leaned back in her chair and gave him a searching look. "Are you kidding?"

"I'm just saying."

"That's a whole lot of *just saying* about a case I only just now told you about. You always get so deeply invested on such short notice?"

He looked slightly embarrassed. "I'm not invested. This is just something we do in fraud—think about all the angles. Try to get into the mind-set of the people we're investigating, try to figure out where they're coming from—are they desperate or do they feel entitled for some reason. Stuff like that."

Ruby had to bite her tongue to keep from making an acid remark concerning the mass media image of criminal profiling and other extraordinary popular delusions and the madness of crowds. It wouldn't do any good. Pasco would only get defensive and then expend a lot of effort trying to prove she was wrong instead of just working the cases. In the end, he'd flounder, trying to adapt the job to his methods rather than the other way around.

Abruptly she realized that she had been staring at him in silence for more than just a moment or two. Before she could think of some neutral comment, Lieutenant Ostertag came in and waved them into his office.

"I know, I know—he's a geek," Ostertag said to Ruby after he had waved Pasco out of his office again. "He's got, I dunno, two, three degrees, maybe four. He's been in fraud and cyber-crime since he joined the department about five years ago."

Ruby nodded. "And somebody thinks he'd make a good homicide detective."

"Apparently he already is. In the course of his last two cases he cleared up two murders, one of which nobody even knew about at the time."

"Good for him," said Ruby. "Has anyone told him that he left all the criminal masterminds back in cybercrime?"

"He's working another case right now. I'll let him tell you about it." He got up and opened the door for her by way of de-claring the meeting over, then caught her arm before she could leave. "You OK?"

Ruby drew back slightly, giving him a surprised look. "Sure I'm OK. Why wouldn't I be?"

Ostertag's mouth twitched. "You OK with getting this guy as a partner so soon after Rita leaving?"

She laughed a little. "Rita retired, she didn't die. I'm not in mourning."

The lieutenant nodded a bit impatiently. "This guy's pretty different than what you're used to."

Ruby tilted her head and frowned. "Are you asking me if I'd rather work with someone else?"

Ostertag's face turned expressionless. "No."

"What I thought," Ruby said good-naturedly and went back to her desk.

She decided to give Pasco a little while to organize his desk, maybe meet a few of the other detectives, and then go over to ask him about his case. Instead of taking over Rita's old spot, he had opted for the vacant desk by the blocky pillar that served as an unofficial bulletin board for less-than-official notices and items, usually cartoons (which were usually obscene). It was a strange choice; Ruby had never seen anyone actually opt for that particular desk if there was anything else available and there were two others empty at the moment. It was badly positioned—you had to sit either facing the pillar or with your back to it. Turn the desk sideways and it would obstruct the aisle. The previous lieutenant had tried switching the desk with a set of filing cabinets but that had been no solution at all and they'd switched things back before the day was up. Moving the desk out altogether would have made more sense but there were no city employees anywhere who would have been so foolish as to voluntarily give up anything. Someone at City Hall could get the wrong idea, start thinking that if there was no room for a desk in your area, there were probably other things you could do without as well.

Rafe Pasco obviously had no idea he had picked the lousiest spot in the room, Ruby thought. Maybe he'd had a similar spot in cybercrime, wherever that was headquartered. Spending all his time on a computer, he might not have noticed or cared where he sat.

"So you get the new guy." Tommy DiCenzo sat down in the chair beside her desk, a bottle of Coke Zero in one big paw. He tilted it toward her, offering her a sip.

She waved it away. "Rafe Pasco. From cybercrime."

"I heard." Tommy glanced over his shoulder. "What'd you do, tell him to keep his distance?"

"Didn't get a chance to," she said. "He picked it out himself." From where she was sitting, she could actually see him quite well. She watched as he took a shiny black laptop out of a bag and set it on the desk. "I see he brought his own hardware. Maybe he figures he'll have more privacy over there. No one'll be able to see when he's playing solitaire."

Tommy followed her gaze. "Guy's a geek. No offense," he added quickly. "How is Jake, anyway?"

Ruby laughed. "Fine. And he'd take offense if you *didn't* call him a geek. As would he, I imagine." She jerked her chin in Pasco's general direction.

"It's a different world," Tommy said, affecting a heavy sigh. Then his face grew suddenly serious. "You OK?"

"Damn." Ruby gave a short laugh. "You know you're the second person to ask me that today?"

Tommy's steely gray eyebrows arched. "Oh? Must be something going around." He gazed at her thoughtfully. "So, *are* you OK? Anything bothering you?"

The Dread seemed to reawaken then; it shifted inside of her by way of reasserting itself, reminding her that it was there and it was in charge. "Like what?" she said, hoping the casually off-hand tone in her voice didn't sound as forced as it felt.

"Well, like Rita pulling the pin."

She let out a long breath. "It'll take some getting used to. I keep looking around for her. Which is only normal, I guess."

"You weren't prepared for her leaving, were you." It wasn't really a question.

"No," she admitted. "But I'm OK with it."

"I'm sure you are." Tommy's smile was knowing. "But it still took you by surprise. You never thought about her retiring."

"I was busy," she said and then winced inwardly. Had she ever said anything lamer? "But you know, things, uh, change." Now she had.

"They do that." Tommy pushed himself to his feet. "It's not a steady-state universe."

"No, I guess not." Ruby stared after him as he ambled over to introduce himself to Rafe Pasco, wondering why his words seemed to hang in the air and echo in her brain. Maybe having him and Ostertag ask her if she was OK within a few minutes of each other had put a whole new level of odd over the day.

The call came in about twenty minutes before Ruby had tentatively planned to go to lunch. Which figured, she thought as she and Pasco drove to the East Midtown address; it had been a quiet morning. Any time you had a quiet morning, you could just about count on having to skip lunch. Of course, since the Dread had moved in on her, it hadn't left much room in her stomach. Not a whole lot of room in her mind, either—she missed the turn onto the right street and thanks to the alternating one-ways, had to drive around in a three-block circle. If Pasco noticed, he didn't say anything. Maybe she would let him drive back to the station.

She was a bit surprised to see that patrol cars had almost half the street blocked off, even though there were very few curious onlookers and not much in the way of traffic. The address in question was a six-story tenement that Ruby had visited with Rita a few times in the past.

"Is this an actual residence or a squat?" Pasco asked her as they went up the chipped concrete steps to the front door.

"Both," Ruby told him. She wasn't actually sure anymore herself.

The uniform standing at the entrance was a young guy named Fraley. Ruby thought he looked about twelve years old, despite the thick mustache he was sporting. He opened the door for them as if that were really what he did for a living.

The smell of urine in the vestibule was practically a physical blow; she heard a sharp intake of breath from Pasco behind her.

"Straight from the perfume counter in hell," she said wryly. "Ever wonder why it's always the front of the building, why they don't take a few extra seconds to run to the back."

"Marking their territory?" Pasco suggested.

"Good answer." Ruby glanced over her shoulder at him, impressed.

There was another uniformed officer in the hallway by the stairs, a tall black woman named Desjean whom Ruby recognized as a friend of Rita's. "Sorry to tell you this," she told them, "but your crime scene's on the roof and there's no elevator."

Ruby nodded, resigned. "Do we know who it is?"

Desjean's dark features turned sad. "Girl about twelve or thirteen. No ID."

Ruby winced, feeling acid bubbling up in her chest. "Great. Sex crime."

"Don't know yet," the uniform replied. "But, well, up on the roof?"

"Local kid?" Ruby asked.

Desjean shook her head. "Definitely not."

Ruby looked at the stairs and then at Pasco. "You can go first if you think you might go faster."

Pasco blew out a short breath. "I'm a geek, not a track star." He frowned. "Ostertag did tell you that, didn't he?"

"Uh, yeah," Ruby said, unsure as to whether he was kidding around or not. "Before we go up, one thing."

"Don't talk to you on the way?" He nodded. "The feeling's mutual."

She felt a brief moment of warmth toward him. Then the Dread overwhelmed it, crushing it out of existence, and she started up the stairs.

A uniformed sergeant named Papoojian met them just outside the door on the roof. "Kid with a telescope spotted the body and called it in," she told them as they stood catching their breath. "I sent a couple of officers over to get a preliminary statement from him and his very freaked-out parents."

"Kid with a telescope." Ruby sighed. "I don't know if that's an argument for closed-circuit TV surveillance or against it."

The sergeant looked up at the sky worriedly. "I wish the lab guys would hurry up and get here with a tent or we're gonna have regular TV surveillance to deal with. I'm surprised the news helicopters aren't buzzing us already."

As if on cue, there was the faint sound of a chopper in the distance. Immediately, one of the other three uniformed cops on the roof produced a blanket and threw it over the body, then turned to look a question at Papoojian. Papoojian nodded an OK at him and turned back to Ruby. "If the lab has a problem with that, tell them to get in *my* face about it."

Ruby waved a hand. "You got nothing to worry about. No ID on the body?"

The sergeant shook her curly head. "Except for a charm on her bracelet with the name *Betty* engraved on it." She spelled it for them.

"There's a name you don't hear much these days." Ruby looked over at the blanket-covered form. She was no longer panting from the long climb but for some reason she couldn't make herself walk the twenty feet over to where the body lay on the dusty gravel.

"Hey, you caught that other case with the kid," Papoojian said suddenly. "The Dumpster boy."

Ruby winced inwardly at the term. "Yeah."

"They dumping all the murdered kid cases on you now?"

She shrugged, taking an uncomfortable breath against the Dread, which now seemed to be all but vibrating in her midsection.

Was this what she had been dreading, she wondered suddenly—murdered children?

It almost felt as if she were tearing each foot loose from slow-hardening cement as she urged herself to go over and look at the victim, Pasco at her elbow with an attitude that seemed oddly dutiful.

"Ever see a dead kid?" she asked him in a low voice.

"Not like this," Pasco replied, his tone neutral.

"Well, it's gruesome even when it's not gruesome," she said. "So brace yourself." She crouched down next to the body and lifted the blanket.

The girl was lying faceup, her eyes half-closed and her lips slightly parted, giving her a sort of preoccupied expression. She might have been in the middle of a daydream, except for the pallor.

"Well, I see why Desjean was so sure the girl wasn't local," Ruby said.

"Because she's Japanese?" he guessed.

"Well, there are a few Japanese in East Midtown, not many, but I was referring to her clothes." Ruby shifted position, trying to relieve the pressure from the way the Dread was pushing on her diaphragm. It crossed her mind briefly that perhaps what she thought of as the Dread might actually be a physical problem. "That's quality stuff she's got on. Not designer but definitely boutique. You get it in the more upscale suburban malls. I have grandchildren," she added in response to Pasco's mildly curious expression.

She let the blanket drop and pushed herself upright, her knees cracking and popping in protest. Pasco gazed down at the covered body, his smooth, deep-gold face troubled.

"You OK?" Ruby asked him.

He took a deep breath and let it out.

"Like I said, kids are gruesome even when they're not—"

"I think this is related to this case I've been working on."

"Really." She hid her surprise. "We'll have to compare notes, then. Soon."

He didn't answer right away, looking from the blanket to her with a strange expression she wasn't sure how to read. There was something defensive about it, with more than a little suspicion as well. "Sure," he said finally, with all the enthusiasm of someone agreeing to a root canal.

Ruby felt a mix of irritation and curiosity, which was quickly overridden by the Dread. She couldn't decide whether to say something reassuring or simply assert her authority and re-assure him later, after she knew she had his cooperation.

Then the crime lab arrived, saving her from having to think about anything from the immediate situation. And the Dread.

At the end of the day, Pasco managed to get away without talking about his case. It was possible of course that he had not been purposely trying to elude her. After spending most of the day talking to, or trying to talk to, the people in the building, checking on the results of the door-to-door in the neighborhood, looking over the coroner's shoulder, and through it all pushing the Dread ahead of her like a giant boulder uphill, she was too tired to care.

She made a note about Pasco in her memo book and then dragged herself home to her apartment where she glanced at an unopened can of vegetable soup before stripping naked and falling into bed, leaving her clothes in a heap on the floor.

3:11.

The numbers, glowing danger-red, swam out of the darkness and into focus. It was a moment or two before she realized that she was staring at the clock radio on the nightstand.

Odd. She never woke in the middle of the night; even with the Dread pressing relentlessly harder on her every day, she slept too heavily to wake easily or quickly. Therefore, something must have happened, something big or close, or both. She held very still, not even breathing, listening for the sound of an intruder in the apartment, in the bedroom.

A minute passed, then another; nothing. Maybe something had happened in the apartment next door or upstairs, she thought, still listening, barely breathing.

Nothing. Nothing and more nothing. And perhaps that was all it was, a whole lot of nothing. It could have been a car alarm out on the street, an ambulance passing close with its siren on, or someone's bassed-out thumpmobile with the volume set on stun. Just because she didn't usually wake up didn't mean that she couldn't. She took a long deep breath and let it out, rolling onto her back.

There was something strange about the feel of the mattress under her and she realized that she wasn't alone in the bed.

Automatically she rolled onto her right side. Rafe Pasco's head was resting on the other pillow. He was gazing at her with an expression of deep regret.

Shock hit her like an electric jolt. She jumped back, started to scream.

In the next moment she was staring at the empty place next

to her in the bed, her own strangled cry dying in her ears as day-light streamed in through the window.

She jumped again and scrambled out of bed, looking around. There was no one in the room except her, no sign that anyone else had been lying in bed with her. She looked at the clock. 7:59.

Still feeling shaky, she knelt on the bed and reached over to touch the pillow Pasco's head had been resting on. She could still see him vividly in her mind's eye, that regretful expression. Or maybe apologetic was more like it. Sorry that he had showed up in her bed uninvited? *Hope you'll forgive the intrusion—it was too late to call and there wasn't time to get a warrant.*

The pillow was cool to her touch. Of course. Because she had been dreaming.

She sat down on the edge of the bed, one hand uncon-sciously pressed to her chest. That had been some crazy dream; her heart was only now starting to slow down from double time.

She stole a glance over her shoulder at the other side of the bed. Nope, still nobody there, not nobody, not no how, and most especially not Rafe Pasco. What the hell had that been all about, anyway, seeing her new partner in bed with her? Why him, of all the goddamn people? Just because he was new? Not to mention young and good-looking. She hadn't thought she'd been attracted to him but apparently there was a dirty old woman in her subconscious who begged to differ.

Which, now that she thought about it, was kind of pathetic.

"God or whoever, please, save me from that," Ruby mut-tered and stood up to stretch. Immediately, a fresh wave of the Dread washed over her, almost knocking her off balance. She clenched her teeth, afraid for a moment that she was going to throw up. Then she steadied herself and stumped off to the bath-room to stand under the shower.

Pasco was already at his desk when Ruby dragged herself in. She found it hard to look at him and she was glad to see that he was apparently too wrapped up in something on his notebook to pay attention to anything else. Probably the mysterious case he was working on and didn't seem to want to tell her about. *Shouldn't have slipped and told me you thought it might be related to the one we caught yesterday,* she admonished him silently, still not looking at him. *Now I'll have to pry it out of you.*

Later. She busied herself with phone calls, setting up some witness interviews, putting in a call to the medical examiner about getting a preliminary report on the Japanese girl, and re-questing information from Missing Persons on anyone fitting the girl's description. It wasn't until nearly noon that it occurred to her that he was working just as hard to avoid catching her eye as vice versa.

She drew in an uneasy breath and the Dread seemed to breathe with her. *Maybe he had the same dream you did,* suggested a tiny voice in her mind.

As if he had sensed something, he looked up from his note-book at her. She gave him a nod, intending to turn away and find something else that had to be done before she could talk to him. Instead, she surprised herself by grabbing her memo book and walking over to his desk.

"So tell me about this case of yours," she said, pulling over an empty chair and plumping down in it. "And why you think it might have something to do with the dead girl from yester-day."

"Do we know who she is yet?" he asked.

Ruby shook her head. "I'm still waiting to hear from Miss-ing Persons. I've also put a call in to the company that makes the charm bracelet, to find out who sells it in this area."

Pasco frowned. "She could have bought it on the Internet."

"Thanks for that," she said sourly. "You can start with the auction sites if I come up empty."

He nodded a bit absently and then turned his notebook around to show her the screen. The dead girl smiled out from what seemed to be a formal school photo; her eyes twinkled in the bright studio lights and her lips were parted just enough to show the thin gold line of a retainer wire around her front teeth.

"Where'd you get that?" Ruby demanded, incredulous.

"It's not the same girl," he told her.

"Then who is it—her twin?"

"Can't say at this point." He smiled a little. "This girl is Alice Nakamura. I was investigating a case of identity theft involving her parents."

"Perps or victims?"

"To be honest, I'm still not clear on that. They could be either, or even both."

Ruby shook her head slightly. "I don't get it."

"Identity theft is a complex thing and it's getting more complex all the time."

"If that's supposed to be an explanation, it sucks."

Pasco dipped his head slightly in acknowledgment. "That's putting it mildly. The Nakamuras first showed up entering the country from the Cayman Islands. Actually, you might say that's where they popped into existence as I couldn't find any record of them prior to that."

"Maybe they came from Japan via the Caymans?" Ruby suggested.

"The parents have—had—U.S. passports."

Ruby gave a short laugh. "If they've got passports, then they've got Social Security cards and birth certificates."

"And we looked those up—"

" 'We?' "

"This task force I was on," he said, a bit sheepishly. "It was a state-level operation with a federal gateway."

Here comes the jargon, Ruby thought, willing her eyes not to film over.

"Anyway, we looked up the numbers. They were issued in New York, as were their birth certificates. There was no activity of any kind on the numbers—no salary, no withholding, no income, no benefits. According to the records, these people have never worked and never paid taxes."

"Call the IRS, and tell them you've got a lead on some people who've never paid taxes. That'll take care of it."

"Tried that," Pasco said, his half smile faint. "The IRS records show that everything is in order for the Nakamuras. Unfortunately, they can't seem to find any copies of their tax returns."

"That doesn't sound like the IRS *I* know," Ruby said skeptically.

Pasco shrugged. "They're looking. At least, that's what they tell me whenever I call. I have a feeling that it's not a priority for them."

"But what about the rest of it? The birth certificates? You said they were issued in New York?"

"They're not actually the original birth certificates," Pasco said. "They're notarized copies, replacing documents that have been lost. Some of the information is missing—like, where exactly each of them was born, the hospital, the attending physician, and, except for Alice, the parents' names."

Ruby glanced heavenward for a moment. "What are they, in witness protection?"

"I'll let you know if I ever get a straight answer one way or another on that one," Pasco said, chuckling a little, "but I'd bet money that they aren't."

"Yeah, me too." Ruby sat for a few moments, trying to get her mind around everything he had told her. None of it sounded right. Incomplete birth certificates? Even if she bought the stuff about the IRS, she found that completely implausible. "But I still don't understand. Everything's computerized these days, which means everything's recorded. Nobody just *pops* into existence, let alone a whole family."

"It's not against the law to live off the grid," Pasco said. "Some people do. You'd be surprised at how many."

"What—you mean living off the land, generating your own electricity, shit like that?" Ruby gave a short, harsh laugh. "Look at that photo. That's not a picture of a girl whose family has been living off the grid. She's got an orthodontist, for chrissakes."

"I'm not so sure," Pasco said. "We had the Nakamuras on our radar, so to speak, when they entered the state. However they had been covering themselves before they left the Caymans, whatever they'd been doing to stay invisible, they weren't doing it anymore. They left an easy trail to follow. I found them in a Northland hotel near the airport. They were there for a week. At the same time, the task force was investigating some fraudulent activity elsewhere in the same area. It seemed that the Nakamura case was going to converge with it."

"What was it, this other activity?" Ruby asked.

Pasco made a face. "More identity theft. I can run you through the long version later if you want but the short version is, be careful what you do with your utility bills after you pay them, and if you insist on paying them over the phone, don't use a cordless phone or a mobile." He paused. When she nodded, he went on. "Anyway, we had enough evidence for a warrant. But when the police got there, the house was abandoned. The only thing they found was the body of Alice Nakamura in one of the bedrooms. Her birth certificate, school photo, library card, and passport were lying next to her on the floor."

"How did she die?"

"Natural causes. Heart failure. I forget what the condition's called but the coroner said that a lot of kids on the transplant lists have it. Alice Nakamura wasn't on any of those. There are no medical records for her anywhere, in fact. And it turned out that her passport was a forgery."

Ruby blinked. "So much for homeland security."

"It was an excellent forgery, but a forgery nonetheless, as there was no record of her ever applying for a passport, let alone receiving one. Unlike her parents."

"If this is some kind of conspiracy, it's the most random and disorganized one I've ever heard of," Ruby said, frowning. "Not to mention that it doesn't make any sense. Unless you've actually been speaking a language that only sounds like English but all the words mean something entirely different and I haven't really understood a single thing you've said."

Her words hung in the air between them for a long moment.

Pasco's face was deeply thoughtful (not deeply regretful; she stamped down on the memory again), practically contemplative, as if she had set out a significant issue that had to be addressed with care. Inside her, the Dread pushed sharply into the area just under her breastbone.

"I'm sure that's how everything probably looks when you see it from the outside," he said finally. "If you don't know a system, if you don't understand how things work or what the rules are, it won't make any sense. The way a foreign language will sound like gibberish."

Ruby grimaced at him. "But nothing's that strange. If you listen to a foreign language for even just a minute, you start picking up some sense of the patterns in it. You recognize it's a system even if it's one you're not familiar with—"

"Oh?" Pasco's half smile was back. "Ever listened to Hungarian?"

She waved a hand at him. "No, but I've listened to Cantonese and Mandarin, simultaneously at full volume when my grandparents argued. You know what I mean. For a system—or anything—to be completely incomprehensible, it would have to be something totally"—she floundered, groping for a word—"it would have to be something totally alien. Outside human experience altogether."

Her words replayed themselves in her mind. "Christ," she said, massaging her forehead. "What the hell are we talking about and why?"

Pasco pressed his lips together briefly. "You were saying that there are a lot of things about my case that don't make any sense."

"You got *that* right, my man," she said feelingly and then let out a long sigh. "I suppose that's the human element at work."

"Pardon?" Now he looked bewildered.

"People are infinitely screwy," she said. "Human beings can make a mess out of chaos."

He surprised her by bursting into loud, hearty laughter. She twisted around in her seat to see that the whole room was staring at them curiously. "Thanks, I'll be here all week," she said a bit self-consciously and turned back to Pasco, trying to will him to wind down fast. Her gaze fell on the notebook screen again.

"Hey, what about her retainer?" she asked, talking over his guffaws.

"Her what?" Pasco said, slightly breathless and still chuckling a little.

"On her teeth." Ruby tapped the screen with her little finger. It felt spongy. "Were you able to trace it to a particular orthodontist?"

"She wasn't wearing a retainer and they didn't find one in the house," Pasco said, sobering.

"And what about her parents?"

"The Nakamuras have dropped out of sight again."

"*Popped out* of existence?"

"I thought so at first," he said, either oblivious to or ignoring her tone of voice. "But then that girl turned up on the roof yesterday, which leads me to believe they were still around. Up to that point, anyway. They might be gone by now, though."

"Why? You think they had something to do with the girl's death?"

"Not intentionally."

Ruby shook her head. "Intentionally, unintentionally—either way, why? Who is she to them—the long-lost twin of the girl who died of heart failure?" Abruptly the Dread gave her stomach a half twist; she swallowed hard and kept talking. "How long ago was that anyway, when you found Alice Nakamura?"

Pasco hesitated, his face suddenly very serious. "*I* didn't find her. I mean, I only pinpointed the address. I wasn't there when the police entered the house. The Geek Squad never goes along on things like that. I think the other cops are afraid of geeks with guns."

"But you're cops, too."

"Exactly. Anyway"—he swiveled the notebook around and

tapped the keyboard a few times—"that was about five and a half weeks ago, almost six." He looked up again. "Does that suggest anything special to you?"

Ruby shook her head. "You?"

"Just that the Nakamuras have managed to lay pretty low for quite a while. I wonder how. And where."

Ruby wanted to ask him something about that but couldn't quite figure out how to word the question. "And you're absolutely sure that girl—Alice Nakamura, I mean—died of natural causes?"

"Absolutely. Also, she wasn't abused or neglected in any way before she died, either. She was well taken care of. She just happened to be very sick."

"Uh-huh." Ruby nodded absently. "Then why would they just go off and leave her?"

"If they didn't want to be found—and judging from their behavior, they didn't—then they couldn't carry her dead body along with them."

"All right, *that* makes sense," Ruby said. "But it still leaves the question of why they don't want to be found. Because they're in on this identity theft thing, conspiracy, whatever it is?"

"Or because they're victims of identity theft who have to steal a new identity themselves."

Ruby closed her eyes briefly. "OK, now we're back to not making sense again."

"No, it's been known to happen," Pasco insisted. "For some people, when their identity gets stolen, the thief does so much damage that they find it's virtually impossible to clear their name. They have to start over."

"But why steal someone else's identity to do that?" Ruby asked. "Why not just create an entirely new identity?"

"Because the created identity would eventually trace back to the old one. Better to get one with completely different connections."

Ruby shook her head obstinately. "You could still do that with a brand-new identity."

Pasco was shaking his own head just as obstinately. "The idea isn't just to steal someone's identity—it's to steal their past, too. If I create a new identity, I really do have to start over in every way. That's pretty hard. It's easier if I can, say, build on your already excellent credit rating."

"Obviously you've never tried to steal my identity," Ruby said with a short, humorless laugh, "or you'd know better than to say something like that."

"I was just giving an example."

Ruby let out a long breath. "I think I'll pay the coroner a visit, see if there's anything he can tell me about how Alice Nakamura's twin died. Maybe it'll tell us something about—oh, I don't know, *anything*. In a way that will make sense." She stood up to go back to her desk.

"Hey"—Pasco caught her wrist; the contact startled her and he let go immediately—"what if she died of natural causes?"

"Jesus, you really can dream things up, can't you." Ruby planted her fists on her hips and gave him a hard look. "That would be entirely too much of a coincidence."

"Natural causes," said the coroner's assistant, reading from a clipboard. Her ID gave her name as Sheila St. Pierre; there was a tiny Hello Kitty sticker under the St. She was a plump woman in her mid-twenties with short, spiky blond hair and bright red cat's-eye glasses and, while she wasn't chewing gum, Ruby kept expecting to hear it pop every time she opened her mouth. "Aneurysm. Tragic in one so young, you know?"

"You're sure you have the right chart?" Ruby asked tensely.

"Unidentified Oriental adolescent female, brought in yesterday from a rooftop in East Midtown, right?" Sheila St. Pierre offered Ruby the clipboard. "See for yourself."

Ruby scanned the form quickly several times before she was able to force herself to slow down and check each detail. "How can a thirteen-year-old girl have a fucking *aneurysm*?" she said finally, handing the clipboard back to the other woman. "The coroner must have screwed up. Where is he? I want to make him do it again."

"There's no do-overs in postmortems," Sheila St. Pierre said, making a face. "What do you think we're working with here, Legos?" She shifted her weight to her right side and folded her arms, hugging the clipboard to her front. "How about a second opinion?"

"Great," Ruby said. "Where can I get one?"

"Right here. I assisted Dr. Levitt on this one and I saw it myself firsthand. It was an aneurysm. Case closed. You know, an aneurysm is one of those things anybody can have without even knowing it. You could have one, or I could. We just go along living our lives day in, day out, everything's swell, and suddenly— boom. Your head blows up and you're history. Or I am. Or we both are. Most people have no idea how thin that membrane between life and death can be. But then, isn't it really better that way? Better living through denial. Who'd want to go around in a constant state of dread?"

Ruby glared at her but she was turning away to put the clipboard down on a metal table nearby. "At least it isn't all bad news," she said, holding up a small plastic bag between two fingers. There was a retainer in it. "We did manage to identify the girl from her dental records."

"I didn't see that on that report!" Ruby snapped. "Why wasn't it on there? Who is she? When were you going to fucking tell me?"

Sheila St. Pierre tossed the bag with the retainer in it back on the table. "Which question would you like me to fucking answer first?"

Ruby hesitated and then looked at the retainer. "Where did that come from, anyway? I didn't see one at the scene."

"Well, it was there. Nobody looked close enough till we got her on the table. Her name is Betty Mura—"

"What's her address?" Ruby demanded. "And why didn't you call me?"

"I did call you," Sheila St. Pierre said with exaggerated patience. "You weren't at your desk so I left a message."

Ruby had to force herself not to lunge forward and shake the woman. "When was that?"

"As near as I can tell, it was while you were on your way over here."

"Give me that information *now*!" Ruby ordered her but she was already picking up the clipboard. She slid a piece of paper out from under the form on top and handed it over.

"Thank you," she prompted politely as Ruby snatched it from her.

"You're welcome," Ruby growled over her shoulder, already out of the room.

There was a ticket on her windshield; another skirmish in the struggle to keep the area in front of the municipal complex a strict no-parking zone, this means you, no exceptions, especially cops. Ruby crumpled it up and tossed it in the backseat as she slid behind the wheel. She clipped Betty Mura's home address to her visor. A West Side address, no surprise there considering the girl's clothes. But what had she been doing on a roof in East Midtown? What had she been doing *anywhere* in East Midtown, and how had she gotten there? She might have died of natural causes but there had definitely been something unusual going on in the last hours of her life.

She went to start the car and then paused. First she should call Rafe Pasco, tell him she had the girl's name and address and she would pick him up.

The image of his head resting on the pillow beside her flashed in her mind; irritation surged and was immediately overwhelmed by the Dread in a renewed assault. She had a sudden strong urge to close her eyes and let her head fall forward on the steering wheel and stay that way until the next ice age or the heat death of the universe, whichever came second.

She took a steadying breath, popped her cell phone into the cradle on the dashboard, put it on speaker, and dialed the squad room. Tommy DiCenzo answered. She asked him to put her through to Pasco.

"Can't, Ruby. He's not here. He left."

"Where'd he go?" she asked, but as soon as the words were out of her mouth, she knew the answer.

"Coroner's office called—they identified your rooftop girl from her dental records. He took the name and address and left."

"Did he say anything about coming to get me first?" Knowing that he hadn't.

Tommy hesitated. "Not to me. But I got the impression he thought you already knew, since you were on your way over to the coroner's anyway."

"*Shit,*" she muttered and started the car. "Hey, you wouldn't happen to know Pasco's cell phone number, would you? I don't have it with me."

"Hang on—"

"Tommy—" But he had already put the phone down. She could hear the tanky background noise of the squad room: footsteps, a phone ringing, and Tommy's voice, distant and indistinct, asking a question. A few seconds later he picked up the phone again.

"OK, ready?"

"Wait"—she found a pen, looked around hurriedly and then held the point over the back of her other hand—"go."

He dictated the number to her carefully, saying it twice.

"Thanks, Tommy," she said, disconnecting before he could say anything else. She dialed the number he'd given her, then pulled away from the curb as it began to ring.

To her immense frustration, it kept on ringing for what seemed like a hundred times before she finally heard the click of someone picking up.

"Rafe Pasco speaking—"

"Goddamnit, Rafe, why didn't you call me before—"

"I'm in the Bahamas for two weeks," his voice went on cheerfully, cutting into her tirade, "and as you can see, I didn't pack my cell phone. Sorry about that. But you can phone my house sitter and talk to her if you want. It's *your call.*" There was another click followed by a mechanical female voice inviting her to leave a message after the beep.

Ruby stabbed the disconnect button and redialed. The same thing happened and she disconnected again, furious. Was Pasco playing some kind of mind game or had he really just forgotten to change his voice mail message after his last vacation? Either way, she was going to have a hard time not punching him. Weaving in and out of the traffic, she headed for the freeway.

She was merging into traffic from the entrance ramp when all at once she found herself wondering what she was so frantic about. Pasco had been inconsiderate, even rude, but he must have figured she'd get the same information from the coroner. Possibly he had assumed she would head over to the Mura house directly from the coroner. He was her partner, after all—why should she be concerned about his going to the girl's house without her?

The Dread clutched her stomach like a fist and she swerved halfway into the breakdown lane. Behind her, a horn blared long and hard. She slowed down, pulling all the way into the breakdown lane to let it pass; it whizzed by a fraction of a second later. The Dread maintained its grip on her, flooding her system and leaving no room for even a flash of fear at her close call. She slowed down intending to stop, but the Dread wouldn't let her step on the brake.

"What the *fuck*," she whispered as the car rumbled along. The Dread seemed to have come to life in her with an intensity beyond anything she had felt in the past. The maddening, horrible thing about it, however, was that it had not tipped over into terror or panic, which she realized finally was what she had been waiting for it to do. She had been expecting that as a logical progression—apprehension turned to dread, dread became fear. But it hadn't. She had never suspected it was possible to feel so much dread—Dread—without end. It shouldn't have been. Because it wasn't a steady-state universe.

So what kind of universe was it, then?

This was it, she thought suddenly; this was the crack-up and it was happening in fast motion just like she had wanted. The thing to do now was stop the car, call Tommy DiCenzo, and tell him she needed help.

Then she pressed the accelerator, put on her turn signal, and checked the rearview mirror as she moved back into the travel lane.

The well-groomed West Side houses slid through the frame of the car windows as Ruby navigated the wide, clean streets. She didn't know the West Side quite as well as the rest of the city and the layout was looser than the strict, organized Northland Grid or the logical progressions of Midtown and the South Side. Developers and contractors had staked out patches of the former meadowlands and put up subdivisions with names like Saddle Hills and Wildflower Dale and filled them with split-level ranches for the young middle-class and cookie-cutter mansions for the newly affluent. Ruby had taken small notice of any of it during the years Jake had been growing up. The idea of moving from downtown to the West Side held no appeal for her—it would have meant two hours of sheer commuting every day, time she preferred to spend with her son. The downtown school district had not been cutting edge but it hadn't been anywhere near disastrous, either—

She gave her head a quick shake to clear it. Get a grip, she ordered herself, and tightened her hands on the steering wheel, as if that would help. She checked the address clipped to her visor again, then paused at the end of the street, craning her neck to read the road sign. It would solve a lot of problems, she thought, if the cheap-ass city would just put GPS navigation in all the goddamn cars. She turned right onto the cross street and then wondered if she had made a mistake. Had she already driven along this street? The houses looked familiar.

Well, of course they looked familiar, she realized, irritated— they were all alike. She kept going, watching the street signs carefully. Christ, it wasn't only the houses themselves that were all alike—it was also the cars in the driveways, the front lawns, even the toys scattered on the grass. The same but not the same. Like Alice Nakamura and Betty Mura.

She came to another intersection and paused again, almost driving on before she realized that the street on her left was the one she wanted. The Dread renewed its intensity as she made the turn, barely noticing the woman pushing a double stroller with two toddlers in it. Both the woman and her children watched her pass with alert curiosity on their unremarkable faces. They were the only people Ruby had seen out walking but the Dread left no room for her to register as much.

The Mura house was not a cookie-cutter mansion—more like a cookie-cutter update of the kind of big old Victorian Jake and Lita lived in with the kids. Ruby pulled up at the curb instead of parking in the driveway where a shiny black SUV was blocked in by a not-so-shiny car that she knew had to belong to Rafe Pasco.

Ruby sat, staring at the front of the house. It felt as if the Dread were writhing inside her now. The last thing she wanted to do was go inside. Or rather, it should have been the last thing she wanted to do. The Dread, alive everywhere in her all the way to her fingertips, to the soles of her feet, threatened to become even worse if she didn't.

Moving slowly and carefully, she got out of the car and walked up the driveway, pausing at Pasco's car to look in the open driver's-side window. The interior was impossibly clean for a cop or a geek—no papers, no old sandwich wrappers or empty drink cups. Hell, even the floor mats were clean, as if they had just been vacuumed. Nothing in the backseat, either, except more clean.

She glanced over at the glove box; then her gaze fell on the trunk release. If she popped it, what would she find in there, she wondered—a portable car-cleaning kit with a hand vac? A carton of secret geek files? Or just more clean nothing?

There would be nothing in the trunk. All the secret geek files would be on Pasco's notebook and he probably had that with him. She considered popping the trunk anyway and then moved away from the car, stopping again to look inside the SUV. The windows were open and the doors were unlocked—apparently the Muras trusted their neighbors and the people who came to visit them. Even the alarm was off.

There was a hard-shell CD case sitting on the passenger seat and a thin crescent of disk protruding from the slot of the player in the dash. A small string of tiny pink and yellow beads dangled from the rearview mirror along with a miniature pair of fuzzy, hot pink dice. Ruby wondered if Betty Mura had put them there.

She turned toward the front door and then thought better of it. Instead, she made her way around the side of the garage and into the unfenced backyard.

Again she stopped. The yard was empty except for a swing set and a brightly painted jungle gym. Behind the swings was a cement patio with a couple of loungers; under one of them was an empty plastic tumbler lying on its side, forgotten and probably considered lost.

The sliding glass patio doors were open, Ruby realized suddenly, although the screen door was closed and the curtains were drawn. She edged her way along the rear of the garage and sidled up next to the open door.

". . . less pleading your case with me," she heard Pasco saying. "Both girls are dead. It ends here."

"But the other girls—" a man started.

"There are *no* other girls," Pasco told him firmly. "Not for you. They aren't your daughters."

Ruby frowned. Daughters? So the girls really had been twins?

"But they *are*—" protested a woman.

"You can't think that way," Pasco said. "Once there's been a divergence, those lives—your own, your children's, everyone's—are lost to you. To act as if it were otherwise is the same as if you went next door, to your neighbor's house, and took over everything they owned. Including their children."

"I told you, we didn't come here to kidnap Betty," the man

said patiently. "I saw her records—the man showed me. He told us about her aneurysm. He said it was almost a sure thing that it would kill her before Alice's heart gave out. Then we could get her heart for transplant knowing that it would be a perfect match for Alice—"

"You heartless bastard," said a second male voice identical to the one that had been speaking. How many people were in that room, Ruby wondered.

"She was going to die anyway," said the first man. "There was nothing anyone could do about it—"

"The hell there wasn't. If we had known, we could have taken her to a hospital for emergency surgery," a woman said angrily. "They can fix those things now, you know. Or aren't they as advanced where you come from?"

"It doesn't matter anymore," Pasco said, raising his voice to talk over them. "Because Alice died first after all."

"Yes," said the woman bitterly, speaking through tears. It sounded like the same woman who had been talking so angrily a few moments before but Ruby had a feeling it wasn't.

"And do you know why that is?" Pasco asked in a stern, almost paternal tone of voice.

"The man was wrong," said the tearful woman.

"Or he lied," said the angry one.

"No, it was because you came here and you brought Alice with you," Pasco said. "Once you did that, all bets—as they say here—were off. The moment you came in, it threw everything out of kilter because you don't belong here. You're extra—surplus. One too many times three. It interrupted the normal flow of progress; things scattered with such force that there were even natural-law anomalies. This morning, a very interesting woman said to me, 'Human beings can make a mess out of chaos.' I couldn't tell her how extraordinarily right she was, of course, so I couldn't stop laughing. She must have thought I was crazy."

Ruby pressed her lips together, thinking that he couldn't be any crazier than she was herself right now; it was just that she was a lot more confused.

Abruptly, she heard the sound of the front door opening, followed by new voices as a few more people entered the house. This was turning into quite a party; too bad Pasco had left her off the guest list.

"Finally," she heard him saying. "I was about to call you again, find out what happened to you."

"These West Side streets are confusing," a woman answered. This was a completely new voice but Ruby found it strangely familiar. "It's not a nice, neat grid like Northland, you know."

"Complain all you want later," Pasco said. "I want to wrap this up as soon as possible."

"I don't know about that," said another man. "Have you looked out front?"

Pasco groaned. "What now?"

"There's a car parked at the curb, right in front of the house," the man said. "I don't think that's a coincidence."

"Oh, hell," Pasco said. She heard his footsteps thumping hurriedly away from the patio door—probably going to look out the window at the car—and then coming back again. She straightened her shoulders and, refusing to give herself time to think about it, she yanked open the screen door and stepped into the house, flinging aside the curtain.

"I'm right h—" Her voice died in her throat and she could only stand, frozen in place, one hand still clutching the edge of the curtain while she stared at Rafe Pasco. And a man who seemed to be his older, much taller brother. And two identical Japanese couples sitting side by side on a long sofa with their hands cuffed in front of them.

And, standing behind the couch, her newly retired ex-partner Rita Castillo.

"Now, don't panic," Pasco said after what might have been ten minutes or ten months.

"I'm not panicking," Ruby managed in a hoarse voice. She drew a long, shaky breath. Inside her, the Dread was no longer vibrating or writhing or swelling; it had finally reached full power. This was what she had been Dreading all this time, day after day. Except now that she was finally face-to-face with it, she had no idea what it actually was.

"I can assure you that you're not in any danger," Pasco added.

"I know," she said faintly.

"No, you don't."

"OK," Ruby said. Obviously he was in charge so she would defer willingly, without protest.

"The sensation you're feeling right now has nothing to do with your actual safety," Pasco went on, speaking carefully and distinctly, as if he were trying to talk her down from a high ledge. Or maybe a bad acid trip was more like it, she thought, glancing at the Japanese couples. The Muras and the Naka-muras, apparently. She wondered which was which. "What it actually is is a kind of allergic reaction."

"Oh?" She looked around the room. Everyone else seemed to understand what he was talking about, including the Japan-ese couples. "What am I allergic to?"

"It's something in the nature of a disturbance."

Oh, God, no, she thought, *now he's going to say something about "the force." I'll find out they're all actually a lunatic cult and Pasco's the leader. And I'm trapped in a house with them.* Her gaze drifted over to Rita. No, Rita would never have let her-self get sucked into anything like that. Would she?

Rita shifted, becoming slightly uncomfortable under Ruby's gaze. "Do I know you?" she asked finally.

Ruby's jaw dropped. She felt as if Rita had slapped her.

"No, you don't," Pasco said over his shoulder. "She knows someone like you. Where you come from, the two of you never met. Here, you were partners."

"Wow," Rita said, shaking her head. "It never ceases to amaze me, all that what-might-have-been stuff." She smiled at Ruby, giving an apologetic shrug.

"And where does she come from?" Ruby wanted to know. Her voice was a little stronger now.

"That doesn't matter," Pasco told her. "Besides, the less you know, the better you'll feel."

"Really?" She made a skeptical face.

"No," he said, resigned. "Actually, you'll feel not quite so bad. Not quite so much Dread. It may not be much but any relief is welcome, isn't it?" He took a small step toward her. "And you've been feeling very bad for a while now, haven't you? Though it wasn't quite so awful in the beginning."

Ruby didn't say anything.

"Only you're not sure exactly when it started," Pasco continued, moving a little closer. Ruby wondered why he was being so cautious with her. Was he afraid of what she might do? "I can tell you. It started when the Nakamuras arrived here. Ostensibly from the Cayman Islands. When they stepped out of their own world and into this one. Into yours."

Ruby took a deep breath and let it out, willing herself to be less tense. She looked around, spotted an easy chair opposite the couch, and leaned on the back of it. "All right," she said to Pasco, "who are you and what the hell are you talking about?"

Pasco hesitated. "I'm a cop."

"No," Ruby said with exaggerated patience. "*I'm* a cop. Try again."

"It's the truth," Pasco insisted. "I really am a cop. Of sorts."

"What sort?" Ruby asked. "Geek squad? Not homicide."

He hesitated again. "Crimes against persons and property. This includes identity theft, which is not a geek squad job in my line of law enforcement."

Ruby wanted to sit down more than anything in the world now but she forced herself to stay on her feet. To make Pasco look at her on the same level, as an equal. "Go on."

"It's my job to make sure that people who regret what might've been don't get so carried away that they try to do something unlawful to try to rectify it. Even if that means preventing a young girl from getting the heart transplant that will save her life."

Ruby looked over at the people sitting handcuffed on the sofa. They all looked miserable and angry.

"An unscrupulous provider of illegal goods and services convinced a couple of vulnerable parents that they could save their daughter's life if they went to a place where two other parents very similar to themselves were living a life in which things had gone a bit differently. Where their daughter, who was named Betty instead of Alice, had an undetected aneurysm instead of a heart condition."

Light began to dawn for Ruby. Her mind returned to the idea of being trapped in a house with a bunch of lunatic cultists. Then she looked at Rita. *Where you come from, the two of you never met.*

"Many of my cases are much simpler," Pasco went on. "People who want to win instead of lose—a hand of cards, a race, the lottery. Who think they'd have been better off if they'd turned left instead of right, said yes instead of no." He spread his hands. "But we can't let them do that, of course. We can't let them take something from its rightful owner."

"And by 'we' you mean . . . ?" Ruby waited; he didn't answer. "All right, then let's try this: you can't possibly be the same kind of cop I am. I'm local, equally subject to the laws that I enforce. But you're not, are you?"

"I wouldn't say that, exactly," Pasco replied. "I have to obey those laws. But in order to enforce them, I have to live outside the system they apply to."

She looked at Rita again. Or rather, the woman she had thought was Rita. "And what's your story? He said you're from a place where we never met. Does your being here with him mean you don't live there anymore?"

Not-Rita nodded. "Someone stole my identity and I couldn't get it back. Things didn't end well."

"And all you could do was become a sort of a cop?" Ruby asked.

"We have to go," said Pasco's taller brother before the woman could answer. He could have been an alternative version of Pasco, Ruby thought, from a place where she hadn't met him, either. Would that be the same place that Not-Rita came from? She decided she didn't want to know and hoped none of them would feel compelled to tell her.

"We've still got time," Pasco said, looking at his watch, which seemed to be a very complicated device. "But there's no good in pushing things right down to the wire. Take them out through the garage and put them in the SUV—"

"Where are you taking them?" Ruby asked as taller Pasco and not-Rita got the Japanese couples on their feet.

Pasco looked surprised by the question; it was a moment or two before he could answer. "To court. A kind of court."

"Ah," Ruby said. "Would that be for an arraignment? A sort of arraignment?"

He nodded and Ruby knew he was lying. She had no idea how she knew but she did, just as she knew it was the first time he had ever lied to her. She let it go, watching as the other two herded the Japanese couples toward the kitchen.

"Wait," she said suddenly. Everyone stopped, turning to look at her. "Which ones are the Nakamuras?"

Judging from the group reaction, she had definitely asked the wrong question. Even the couples looked dismayed, as if she had threatened them in some fashion.

"Does it matter?" Pasco said after a long moment.

"No, I guess not."

And it didn't, not to her or anyone else, she realized; not now, not ever again. When you got caught in this kind of identity theft, you probably had to give identity up completely. Exactly what that meant she had no idea but she knew it couldn't have been very pleasant.

Pasco nodded and the other two escorted the couples out of the room. A few moments later, Ruby heard the kitchen door leading to the garage open and close.

"How did you know the Nakamuras would come here?" Ruby asked Pasco.

"I didn't. Just dumb luck—they were here when I arrived so I took them all into custody."

"And they didn't resist or try to get away?"

"There's nowhere for them to go. The Nakamuras can't survive indefinitely here unless they could somehow replace the Muras."

"Then why did you arrest the Muras?"

"They were going to let the Nakamuras supplant them while they moved on to a place where their daughter hadn't died."

The permutations began to pile up in Ruby's brain; she squeezed her eyes shut for a moment, cutting off the train of thought before it made her dizzy.

"All right," she said. "But what about this master criminal who convinced the Nakamuras to do all this in the first place? How could he—she—whatever—know about Betty Mura's aneurysm?"

Pasco's face became thoughtful again and she could practically see his mind working at choosing the right words. "Outside the system, there is access to certain kinds of information about the elements within it. Features are visible outside that can't be discerned inside.

"Unfortunately, making that information available inside never goes well. It's like poison. Things begin to malfunction."

"Is that really why Alice Nakamura died before the other girl?" Ruby asked.

"It was an extra contributing factor but it also had to do with the Nakamuras being in a world where they didn't belong. As I said"—Pasco crossed the room to close the patio door and lock it—"what I was referring to were certain anomalies of time and space."

Ruby shook her head, not understanding.

"It's how Betty Mura ended up on a rooftop in Midtown," he clarified. "She just *went* there, from wherever she had been at the time. Undoubtedly the shock blew out the weakness in her brain and killed her."

"Jesus," Ruby muttered under her breath. "Don't think I'll

be including that in my report—" *Abruptly, the memory of Rafe Pasco lying in bed with her, his head resting on the pillow and looking at her with profound regret, lit up in her mind. So sorry to have dropped in from nowhere without calling first.* Not a dream? He might tell her if she asked him but she wasn't sure that was an answer she really wanted.

"That's all right," Pasco said. "I will. Slightly different case, of course, and the report will go elsewhere."

"Of course." Ruby's knees were aching. She finally gave up and sat down on the edge of the chair. "Should I assume that all the information you showed me about the Nakamuras—passports, the IRS, all that—was fabricated?"

"I adapted it from their existing records. Alice's passport worried me, though. It's not exactly a forgery—they brought it with them, and I have no idea why they left it or any other identifying materials behind."

"You don't have kids, do you?" Ruby said, amused in spite of everything.

"No, I don't," he said, mildly surprised.

"If you did, you'd know why they couldn't just leave her to go nameless into an unmarked grave."

Pasco nodded. "The human factor." Outside, a horn honked. "It's time to go. Or do *you* want to stay here?"

Ruby stood up, looking around. "What's going to happen to this place? And all the other things in the Muras' lives?"

"We have ways of papering over the cracks and stains, so to speak," he told her. "Their daughter was just found dead. If they don't come back here for a while and then decide not to come back at all, I don't think anyone will find that terribly strange."

"But their families—"

"There's a lot to take care of," Pasco said, talking over her. "Even if I had the time to cover every detail for you, I would not. It comes dangerously close to providing information that doesn't belong here. I could harm the system. I'm sure I've told you too much as it is."

"What are you going to do?" she asked. "Take me to 'court' too?"

"Only if you do something you shouldn't." He ushered her through the house to the front door.

"OK, but just tell me this, then." She put her hand on the doorknob before he could. "What are you going to do when the *real* Rafe Pasco comes back from the Bahamas?"

He stared at her in utter bewilderment. "What?"

"That is what you did, isn't it? Waited for him to go on vacation and then borrowed his identity so you could work on this case?" When he still looked blank, she told him about listening to the message on his cell phone.

"Ah, that," he said, laughing a little. "No, I *am* the real Rafe Pasco. I forgot to change my voice mail message after I came back from vacation. Then I decided to leave it that way. Just as a joke. It confuses the nuisance callers."

It figured, Ruby thought. She opened the door and stepped outside, Pasco following. Behind his car was a small white van; the print on the side claimed that it belonged to Five-Star Electrical Services, Rewiring Specialists, which Ruby thought also figured. Not-Rita was sitting in the driver's seat, drumming her fingers on the steering wheel. The tall guy was sitting in the SUV.

"So that's it?" Ruby said, watching Pasco lock the front door. "You close down your case and I just go home now, knowing everything that I know and that's all right with you?"

"Shouldn't I trust you?" he asked her.

"Should I trust you?" she countered. "How do I know I'm not going to get a service call from an electrician and end up with all new wiring, too?"

"I told you," he said patiently, "only if you use any of what you know to engage in something illegal. And you won't."

"What makes you so goddamn sure about that?" she demanded.

Forehead creasing with concern, Pasco looked into her face. She was about to say something else when something happened.

All at once, her mind opened up and she found that she was looking at an enormous panorama—all the lost possibilities, the missed opportunities, the bad calls; a lifetime of uncorrected mistakes, missteps, and fumbles. All those things were a single big picture—perhaps the proverbial big picture, the proverbial forest you sometimes couldn't see for the proverbial trees. But she was seeing it now and seeing it all at once.

It was too much. She would never be able to recall it as an image, to look at it again in the future. Concentrating, she struggled to focus on portions of it instead:

Jake's father, going back to his wife, unaware that she was pregnant—she had always been sure that had been no mistake, but now she knew there was a world where he had known and stayed with her, and one where he had known and left anyway—

Jake, growing up interested in music, not computers; getting mixed up with drugs with Ricky Carstairs; helping Ricky Carstairs straighten out; coming out to her at sixteen and introducing his boyfriend; marrying his college sweetheart instead of Lita; adopting children with his husband, Dennis; getting the Rhodes Scholarship instead of someone else; moving to California instead of Boston—

The mammogram and the biopsy results; the tests left too late—

Wounding the suspect in the Martinez case instead of killing him; missing her shot and taking a bullet instead while someone else killed him; having the decision by the shooting board go against her; retiring after twenty years instead of staying on; getting fed up and quitting after ten; going to night school to finish her degree—

Jury verdicts, convictions instead of acquittals and vice versa; catching Darren Hightower after the first victim instead of after the seventh—

Or going into a different line of work altogether—

Or finding out about all of this before now, long before now when she was still young and full of energy, looking for an edge and glad to find it. Convincing herself that she was using it not for her own personal gain but as a force for good. Something that would save lives, literally and figuratively, expose the corrupt and reward the good and the worthy. One person *could* make a difference—wasn't that what everyone always said? The possibilities could stretch so far beyond herself:

Government with a conscience instead of agendas; schools and hospitals instead of wars; no riots, no assassinations, no terror, no Lee Harvey Oswald, no James Earl Ray, no Sirhan Sirhan, no 9/11—

And maybe even no nine-year-old boy found naked and dead in a Dumpster—

Abruptly she found herself leaning heavily against the side of the Mura house, straining to keep from falling down while the Dread tried to turn her inside out.

Rafe Pasco cleared his throat. "How do you feel?"

She looked at him, miserable.

"That's what makes me so certain," he went on. "Your, uh, allergic reaction. If there's any sort of disruption here, no matter how large or small, you'll feel it. And it won't feel good. And if you tried to do something yourself"—he made a small gesture at her— "well, you see what happened when you only thought about it."

"Great," she said shakily. "What do I do now, spend the rest of my life trying not to think impure thoughts?"

Pasco's expression turned sheepish. "That's not what I meant. You feel this way because of the current circumstances. Once the alien elements have been removed from your world"— he glanced at the SUV—"you'll start to feel better. The bad feeling will fade away."

"And how long is that going to take?" she asked him.

"You'll be all right."

"That's no answer."

"I think I've given you enough answers already." He started for his car and she caught his arm. "Just one more thing," she said. "Really. Just one."

Pasco looked as if he were undecided whether to shake her off or not. "What?" he said finally.

"This so-called allergic reaction of mine. Is there any reason for it or is it just one of those things? Like hayfever or some kind of weakness?"

"Some kind of weakness." Pasco chuckled without humor. "Sometimes when there's been a divergence in one's own line, there's a certain . . . sensitivity."

Ruby nodded with resignation. "Is that another way of saying that you've given me enough answers already?"

Pasco hesitated. "All those could-have-beens, those might-have-dones, and if-I-knew-thens you were thinking."

The words were out of her mouth before she even knew what she was going to say. "They all happened."

"I know you won't do anything," he said, lowering his voice and leaning toward her slightly, "because you have. And the conscience that bothered you still bothers you, even at long distance. Even in the hypothetical."

Ruby made a face. "My guilty conscience? Is that really what it is?"

"I don't know how else to put it."

"Well." She took a breath, feeling a little bit steadier. "I guess that'll teach me to screw around with the way things should be."

Pasco frowned impatiently. "It's not *should* or *shouldn't*. It's just what *is*."

"With no second chances."

"With second chances, third chances, hundredth chances, millionth chances," Pasco corrected her. "All the chances you want. But not a second chance to have a first chance."

Ruby didn't say anything.

"This is what poisons the system and makes everything go wrong. You live within the system, within the mechanism. It's not meant to be used or manipulated by an individual. To be taken personally. It's a system, a process. It's nothing personal."

"Hey, I thought it was time to go," the man in the SUV called impatiently.

Pasco waved at him and then turned to Ruby again. "I'll see you tomorrow."

"You will?" she said, surprised. But he was already getting into his car and she had no idea whether he had heard her or not. And he had given her enough answers already anyway, she thought, watching all three vehicles drive away. He had given her enough answers already and he would see her tomorrow.

And how would that go, she wondered, now that she knew what she knew? How would it be working with him? Would the Dread really fade away if she saw him every day, knowing and remembering?

Would she be living the rest of her life or was she just stuck with it?

Pasco had given her enough answers already and there was no one else to ask.

Ruby walked across the Muras' front lawn to her car, thinking that it felt as if the Dread had already begun to lift a little. That was something, at least. Her guilty conscience; she gave a small, humorless laugh. Now that was something she had never suspected would creep up on her. Time marched on and one day you woke up to find you were a somewhat dumpy, graying, middle-aged homicide detective with twenty-five years on the job and a hefty lump of guilty conscience and regret. And if you wanted to know why, to understand, well, that was just too bad because you had already been given too many answers already. Nothing personal.

She started the car and drove away from the empty house, through the meandering streets, and did no better finding her way out of the West Side than she had finding her way in.

❖ A LOCKED–PLANET MYSTERY ❖

Mike Resnick

He looked exactly like a purple beachball with legs. I've seen stranger, but not many.

He waddled into my office and stood there, swaying slightly as if waiting for someone to come over and bounce him.

"Mr. Masters?" he said.

I did a double take at the sound of his voice. Almost all alien races use a T-pack that translates their native language into a cold, emotionless Terran, but this beachball had evidently learned Terran, and even two words into it I could detect not only a thick accent but also a sense of urgency.

"Yes?" I said, leaning my elbows on my desk, interlacing my fingers, and trying to look confident and impressive.

"I require your help, Mr. Masters," he said.

"That's what I'm here for," I replied, trying to make it sound like I said it a dozen times a week. "What can I do for you?"

"A murder has been committed on Graydawn."

"Graydawn?" I repeated. "I don't believe I've heard of it."

"It's in the Alpha Gillespie system," said my visitor.

"That's forty light-years from here," I noted.

"Forty-two, to be exact."

"Okay, a murder's been committed on Graydawn," I said. "What has that got to do with me?"

"I just told you: I need your help."

"I'm a private investigator working on Odysseus," I said. "You need to talk to the Graydawn police force."

"There isn't one."

"On the whole damned planet?" I said, frowning.

"May I sit down?" he said. "I can see that this will require an explanation."

"Be my guest," I said, wondering how he was going to fit into one of my office chairs.

He lowered himself gently to the floor. I couldn't see him over the desk, so I walked around and perched on the front of it.

"I suppose I should introduce myself first," he said. "My name is Mxwensll."

"I think I'll just call you Max, if it's all the same to you."

"That is acceptable," said Max. He paused, as if trying to order his thoughts. "I live on Alpha Gillespie III."

"Graydawn?" I asked.

"No. Graydawn is the seventh planet in our system."

"Okay, you're from Alpha Gillespie III. I assume you have a catchier name for it?"

"Yes, but that's not important," said Max. "The important thing is that there's been a murder on Graydawn."

"So you said."

"And I'm in charge of it."

"Why?" I asked. "You already said you don't live there."

"No one does."

"Then how could there be a murder there?"

He made sort of a face and snorted little blue puffs of vapor. "I'm not saying this well."

"Just calm down and try to put your thoughts in order," I said. "I'm going to pour myself a drink while you do." I paused and stared at him. "I don't suppose you . . . ah . . . ?"

"No, thank you. My metabolism cannot handle human stimulants."

I poured a short one into a plastic cup, then sat back down on the edge of the desk. "It might work better if I could ask you a few questions, Max," I suggested.

"Please do," he said gratefully.

"Let me make sure I've got this straight. For starters, is Graydawn inhabited?"

"Not exactly."

"Max, either it is or it isn't."

"It depends."

"Okay, so much for me asking questions. Maybe you should go back to explaining."

"Graydawn is an uninhabited chlorine world, by which I mean it possesses no native life-forms. But at the chairman's request, the Braaglmich Cartel built a domed corporate retreat there about ten years ago."

"For oxygen breathers?"

"Yes." He shifted uncomfortably, and I couldn't tell if it was because he was sitting on the floor or because of what he was about to tell me. "The chairman was about to retire. He had chosen his successor, and he invited the cartel's five vice presidents to the cartel's Graydawn retreat to meet and become acquainted with their new chairman. Evidently everything went well for the first two days. On the morning of their third and final day there, the retiring chairman took them out beyond the dome to see some unique rock formations. While they were out in the chlorine atmosphere, he collapsed, seemingly from a heart attack or stroke, and was dead before they could carry him back into the dome." He stared at me. "Have you any questions yet?"

"Not yet," I told him.

"His health had been deteriorating, so it was not a surprise to his companions. For the past few years he has always had a doctor in attendance, and it seemed a mere formality for the doctor to examine him and determine the cause of death."

"Let me guess," I said. "It wasn't his heart or a stroke."

"How did you know?" asked Max.

"You wouldn't be here if it was."

He sighed. "It was death by asphyxiation. We assumed that there was a mechanical malfunction to the protective suit he was wearing outside the dome . . ."

"You said 'we' "—I interrupted him—"Could you explain that, please?"

"My world is the only inhabited planet in the system," said Max. "At least when no one is at the retreat on Graydawn. So we are responsible for all the planets."

"Okay," I said. "They reported an unusual death to you and you went there to investigate. Then what?"

"Then we asked the vice presidents and the newly anointed president to remain on the planet until we could certify that the suit's malfunction was accidental."

"Which you couldn't do?"

"It had been tampered with."

"No question about it?" I said.

"None." He made another face. "My world doesn't even have a police force. I am one of the Order Keepers, but crime is very rare among my race and homicide is all but unknown. We have not had a murder in a hundred and eighty-nine years, Mr. Masters, and that one had mitigating circumstances. We simply have no experience in dealing with this type of situation."

"What about the muscle?"

"I beg your pardon?"

"You said the new chairman and the five veeps were on the planet. Now, even *I* have heard of the Braaglmich Cartel. It's huge. You can't tell me that each of those executives didn't come equipped with his own security force."

"At the request of the retiring chairman, they remained in orbit during the meeting," answered Max. "Only the six principles were allowed to land. A private shuttle transported each of them from their ship to the surface. Then, once I was informed of the murder, I knew I had to lock down the crime scene preparatory to bringing in an expert such as yourself, so I ordered them to remain in orbit and not to land."

"It sounds like you've got your hands full," I said, trying my best to sound sympathetic. "But why seek me out? Why not just go to the Odysseus cops? I guarantee *they* know a little something about murder."

"That was the first place I went," answered Max. "But Alpha Gillespie is a neutral system, and your Democracy is at war with the Thrale Coalition."

"So?" I said, wondering what his point was.

"We trade with both sides, and the Coalition has threatened military action against us if we have dealings with any branch of the Democracy's government—and they define the police as such. I explained my plight to the police, and they recommended you." He looked at me hopefully. "They said you used to work in their homicide division before you became an independent contractor."

"Yeah, I worked homicide, and vice, and robbery," I replied.

"So will you help us?" asked Max. "We will put ourselves at your disposal and do whatever you tell us."

"Not interested," I said.

"Is there a reason?"

"Lots of them," I replied. "First, I hate chlorine worlds. Second, one of my specialties is finding missing persons, which occasionally takes me into the Thrale Coalition's territory; I don't need them mad at me for helping you. Third, you don't know it yet, but all you really need is a good forensics team. With the equipment they've got these days, they'll take a microscopic bit of DNA or the alien equivalent, or maybe some trace elements taken from the crime scene, and ninety-nine times out of a hundred they'll identify the killer before the day's over."

"They work for the government," said Max glumly.

"Not all of them," I replied. "I'll give you some names."

"*You're* what we want!" insisted Max, looking like he half-thought I might take a swing at him for his outburst but determined to get what he came for.

"I'm sorry," I said, "but I'm still not interested."

Max stood up, looking for all the world like he was getting ready to run, or at least duck, if I lost my temper. "We checked you out after the police recommended you," he said in an unsteady voice. "You are 13,407 credits in debt. If you will accept the assignment, we'll pay off all your debts *and* give you four thousand credits more." He studied my face. "Are you getting interested?"

I did some quick mental math to see how soon they'd be throwing me out of my office and canceling my vidphone ad.

"Make it five thousand and you pay my own forensics expert and it's a deal."

"Done!" said Max.

I reached out to shake on it. He stared at my hand as if it might bite him, and then he reached out his own three-fingered hand. It trembled when I grabbed it, but he didn't pull it away.

Max had been so certain he was going to hire *some* human that he'd retrofitted his ship with a pair of very comfortable human chairs and programmed his various computer systems to speak Terran.

We'd just taken off from Odysseus when the navigational computer announced that the trip would take seven hours if we made use of the MacNaughton Wormhole, or 183 hours without. Max insisted that I was in charge of all aspects of the investigation, including captaining the ship, so I told it to enter the wormhole and get us to Alpha Gillespie III as fast as possible. (Well, first I told it to get us to Graydawn, but like most unofficial names, it wasn't in the data bank.)

"All right, Max," I said, swiveling my chair and turning to him. "Time to fill me in."

"I thought I did."

I shook my head. "All you did was tell me what happened. Now I need some details. Who's alive? Did anyone show up much earlier than the others? Are they all oxygen breathers? Do they have names?"

"Oh," he said. "I guess you need to know all that, don't you?"

"Well, there's always a chance the killer won't run up to me and confess the second I get there."

"That is sarcasm, is it not?" asked Max. "I mean, killers are not inclined to run up to policemen and confess, are they?"

"Wrong time of year," I said.

"But you don't know what time of year it is on Graydawn."

"That was more sarcasm, Max," I told him. "Give me the details, please."

"Yes, Mr. Masters."

"And call me Jake."

"Isn't that too informal?"

"I'm an informal kind of guy," I replied. "Now how about some details, Max? For starters, what exactly does the Braaglmich Cartel do? I know they make spaceships, and I know they own about a quarter of the Democracy's pharmaceutical industry, and I've seen their name a bunch of other places."

"They also dominate a number of retail industries, dealing in basic human needs—soap, foodstuffs, things like that."

"They must do pretty well," I offered. "Not everyone needs a spaceship, but two trillion men and women need to eat and wash. Now tell me about the suspects."

"The five vice presidents are each in charge of the cartel's operations in major areas of the galaxy: the Rim, the Inner Frontier, the Outer Frontier, the Democracy, and the Thrale Coalition."

"So one of them is a human and one is a Thrale?" I asked.

"Yes, Jake."

"And the other three?"

"They, plus the new chairman, are all members of the Gaborian race, which is native to Beta Sanchez IV." I didn't say anything, and he stared at me for a moment. "Don't you find it unusual that four of the six executives are Gaborians?"

"Only if the late chairman wasn't a Gaborian. People—*beings,* make that—tend to associate with their own kind. And to hire their own kind as well."

"He was a Gaborian," Max confirmed.

"Figures," I said. "And I assume that Beta Sanchez IV is neutral?"

"Yes, Jake."

"Okay, so which one's the new head honcho?" I asked.

"I beg your pardon?"

"A vice president got elevated to the chairmanship. Which territory was his and who replaced him?"

"She was elevated over all five vice presidents, Jake."

"Sleeping with the chairman?"

"The chairman is dead."

I sighed. "Was she having an affair with him?"

"An affair?" he asked, frowning. "You mean a public celebration?"

"I mean did they indulge in a sexual liaison?"

"I have no idea," answered Max. "But I do know some things about Gaborians. They are not as neurotic about sex as humans. A sexual liaison would hardly constitute a killing offense."

"Would it constitute a reason for promotion?" I asked. "In other words, if the new chairman achieved her position through sexual rather than business skills . . ."

"I hadn't thought of that, Jake," admitted Max. "But it is an invalid premise. Her rise through the corporation has been meteoric, and justified by her record wherever she has been. She has been innovative, creative, and, above all, wildly successful."

"Okay, it was an idea," I said. "Have any of these executives got names?"

"Certainly."

"Are they an official secret?"

"I thought I would wait to introduce you, and that way you could associate the name with the being."

"Max, we're going to be stuck on this ship for six more hours. If you haven't got six hours of details to give me, let me have their names."

"The Thrale is Toblinda, the human is Malcolm Shea, the three Gaborian vice presidents are Kchang, Ktee, and Kmorn, and the new chairman is Ktamborit."

"She's got extra syllables," I noted.

"I gather she just added them," replied Max. "She was Ktam, but her new position allowed her to add to her name."

"Strange custom," I said, ignoring our own custom of sharing surnames after marriage. "How about the victim?"

"It gets confusing," said Max. "He was Kdineka, but now that he's dead and no longer in a position of power he's once again Kdin."

"And that's everyone who's on the planet?"

"No, there's also Kdin's physician."

"Another Gaborian, I presume?"

"Yes. His name is Bdale."

"With a B, not a K?" I asked.

"He's a doctor," said Max, as if that explained it.

"All right," I said. "So we've got seven suspects."

"I thought we had five."

"You think a doctor has never committed a murder?"

"Doctors *save* people," said Max sincerely.

"Doctors are subject to the same greed and fear and lust and out-and-out stupidity that affects non-doctors."

"I see," said Max, who sounded like he didn't see at all. "But surely Ktamborit is not a suspect."

"She was there. He was killed. She's a suspect."

I'd never seen a beachball shrug before. "Well, that's why we hired you. We know nothing about murder and the motivations that would lead someone to such a heinous crime."

"Of course you do," I said. "You just haven't been asked to apply what you know."

Another shrug. "Probably you are right."

"Now tell me about the crime scene. Have you cordoned it off?"

"The crime scene?" he repeated in puzzled tones.

"The place where Kdin was killed."

"It will be of no use to you, Jake," said Max.

I grimaced. "You've walked all over it."

"Certainly not. But he collapsed and died almost six hundred meters beyond the dome. Visibility on Graydawn is extremely limited, and the winds whip across the surface at an average of

forty kilometers per hour, often double that at night. And he has
been dead for almost three days. There will be nothing to discover there, Jake," he concluded apologetically.

"All right," I said. "There's a second crime scene."

"There is?" he asked, surprised.

"If we can't learn anything from where Kdin died, maybe we
can learn something from where his protective suit was tampered
with—or at least, at the most likely place for it to have been tampered with."

"Ah! The area where they keep the protective suits!"

"Why are you smiling?" I asked.

"I left a team of Order Keepers on Graydawn, and I instructed one of them to guard the suits and let no one near them.
I did something right!"

"I'm sure you've done a lot of things right," I said. "Keeping
the muscle in orbit was probably the most important of them."

"Really?" Max's alien smile got bigger.

"One of these seven is a killer. Six of the seven employ armed
bodyguards whose loyalty is more likely to be to them than the
law. We don't need them bucking for promotion once we make
an arrest."

"I *knew* it was a reasonable thing to do!" said Max, looking
as proud of himself as an animated beachball *can* look.

"You're not stupid, you're just inexperienced," I said.

"Yes," he agreed. "I acknowledge the truth of that."

"Sometimes the quickest way to solve a crime is with a pair
of fresh eyes that don't know what to look for, that bring a
new perspective to the problem," I said. "Any time you have an
idea, don't be afraid to come to me with it. I can use all the help
I can get."

"I will, Jake." He extended his hand, and this time when I
took it it wasn't trembling. "I've never had a partner before. This
is going to be most exciting."

"If we both live through it," I said.

The trembling started again.

❖

We emerged from the wormhole and reached Graydawn an hour after that. The whole planet was shrouded in a chlorine fog that looked more green than gray. I didn't want to chance an instrument landing with no spaceport helping us out with coordinates, so I radioed the retreat and told them to send up the shuttle.

While we were waiting for it, our sensors spotted the other ships in orbit, and a thought occurred to me.

"Max," I said, "there aren't too many places a legitimate executive is going to find his muscle. Check and see if any of them ever worked homicide or forensics."

"I thought you'd contacted your forensic expert," he said.

"I did. But he'll be another day, and he won't show up here first anyway. I sent him to your world, where they've stashed the body and the suit. Who knows? There might be something here your people have missed. The sooner we look for it, the better."

"I'll get right on it," said the rotund alien.

He began contacting the ships, while I had the computer transfer all the information we had on the cartel and its veeps to a small glowing cube that I put in a pocket. I had it make a second one, and handed it to Max. He looked up after a few minutes. "There are three former police officers," he announced. "But none of them ever worked homicide."

"Any telepaths?"

"No."

"Too bad," I said. "We could have used a mind reader."

"I suppose we could send for one," offered Max.

I considered it, then shook my head. "No. There are only a handful of telepathic races in the galaxy, and everyone knows what they look like."

"What difference does that make?" asked Max. "I mean, if I was a telepath, I would be able to read your thoughts whether you knew what I was or not."

I couldn't repress a smile. "I can tell you haven't had much crime on your world."

"I don't understand, Jake."

"Unless we can get a telepath who works for the cops, whose loyalty is unquestioned, he could look into the killer's mind and see a silent offer of five million credits to finger someone else—after all, five million is probably just pin money to these six. Or he could see an image of himself being dismembered by the killer's muscle the second he leaves the planet if he tells what he knows." I shook my head. "No, if his integrity isn't already established, we can't take the chance."

"I think I chose the right person to head the investigation," said Max admiringly. "You don't trust anyone, do you?"

"That's probably why I've lived so long in this goddamned business." I lit a smokeless cigarette. It tasted sour—the first few drags always do—and looked around the ship. "Is there anything else we have to do before the shuttle arrives?"

Max uttered the code for the armory in his native tongue. The door irised and he reached in, found a pair of burners and a pair of screechers. They were made for alien hands, but I decided I could use them, and I took one of each, while he appropriated the other two.

"How about a pulse gun?" I asked.

He looked. "There aren't any."

"Five'll get you ten they were sold on the black market by an underpaid civil servant."

"No member of my race would do that," he assured me.

"You'd be surprised what members of *any* race will do when they get the chance," I said.

"I don't imagine we'll need all this firepower anyway," said Max. "I ordered my assistants to confiscate all the weapons in the retreat."

I just stared at him.

"All right," he said uneasily. "What did I miss, Jake?"

"This didn't start out as a murder investigation," I explained. "Everyone but the killer thought it was a heart attack or something similar. Your people took the body away for a quick autopsy and kept the six execs on Graydawn just as simple routine. No one knew until a couple of hours later that it was murder."

"Of course!" he said suddenly. "The killer knew what the medical examination would show, and he had plenty of time to hide a weapon!"

I nodded approvingly. "You're learning."

What passed for his chest puffed out until I thought he might explode. "Thank you, Jake." He stared at me thoughtfully. "Is there any way to codify the basic rules of your trade, some list I can refer to?"

"There's nothing official, but I'll give you some rules, and if you always keep them in mind, you should do okay."

"Fine!" he said eagerly. "What are they?"

"Rule Number One is that everyone lies; guilty or innocent makes no difference. Rule Number Two is that nothing is ever as simple as it seems. And Rule Number Three is that the odds are always against the killer."

"Why?"

"Most killers are new to murder. They've never done it before, and they tend to make beginner's mistakes. Homicide cops deal with murder every day of the year. It's old hat to them. They've seen it all, and they know how to spot those mistakes."

"But *I* don't."

"You'll learn," I said. "In the meantime, that's why you've got me along."

Max stared at me with a typically inscrutable alien expression. Finally he said, "Did anyone ever take a shot at you, Jake?"

"From time to time."

"No one ever shot at me," he said. "I don't know what I'd do if someone did."

"Relax," I said. "It'll probably never happen."

"But it's happened to you," he said nervously.

"It goes with the territory when you're private," I explained, trying to ease his fears. "No one cares if you kill a private eye, but kill a cop and they'll turn the galaxy inside out hunting you down. People think twice before they shoot a cop."

Max sighed, and little blue puffs of vapor shot out of his nostrils. "When I listen to you, I feel so overmatched."

"If I didn't think you'd pull your weight, I'd leave you on the ship," I said.

"Thank you, Jake," he replied. "You just told me that everyone lies, but it is a lie that I appreciate."

I was about to reply when the shuttle arrived, reached a long arm out to our hatch, and gave us a protected walkway so we didn't have to get into our spacesuits.

"Wow!" I exclaimed as we entered the shuttle. "Kdin knew how to treat his guests, didn't he?"

"It's quite impressive," said Max, surveying the chairs that could change shape to accommodate almost any race, the plush carpet, and the gleaming bar.

"I'll bet you he's got gold fixtures in the head," I said. "This is some shuttle. I've had apartments that were smaller, and I've seen five-star hotel lobbies that weren't as well-appointed."

"Smooth, too," added Max. "You can barely feel the G's as it enters the stratosphere."

"I'll bet it's got so much protection that its nose doesn't even glow when we hit the atmosphere," I said.

"Excuse me," said a mechanical voice. "May I offer you a drink?"

"Not for me," I said. I hate drinking when a ship is decelerating. "How about you, Max?"

"What have you got?" Max asked the ship.

"I cannot identify your race," replied the ship. "Therefore, I do not know what to offer you. What is your planet of origin?"

"Bramanos," answered Max.

"I have no such planet listed in my data bank."

"Official name, Alpha Gillespie III," responded Max.

"I have no record of a sentient race in the Alpha Gillespie system," said the ship.

"Some programming!" snorted Max contemptuously. "You're in the Alpha Gillespie system right now! You ply your trade here."

"May I have a blood or saliva sample, please? That will help me to classify you."

"Forget it," said Max disgustedly.

"Bad choice of words," I said in amusement.

He gave me a puzzled look.

"You just ordered it to forget that there's a sentient race in the system."

"Let the next member of my race worry about it."

The shuttle offered us a series of holographic entertainments, and by the time we'd said no to each of its offerings we had touched down.

"Please wait," announced the shuttle. "I am making sure my bond with the dome's airlock is fully sealed." A pause. "It is now safe to leave me and enter the retreat."

"Thanks," I said, walking to the hatch.

Max fell into step behind me, and a moment later we entered the dome, walked past a trio of small outbuildings, and came to an imposing structure that made the governor's mansion on Odysseus look like a cave.

"Isn't it impressive?" asked Max, surveying our surroundings as we entered the building.

"I don't even like art, and I'm impressed."

"You don't like art?" he asked, as if no one had ever said that before.

"Well, except for naked women," I qualified.

We were standing in a long corridor with high ceilings. It was lined with exquisitely framed paintings and holos, any one of which probably cost ten times more than I'll make in a lifetime. The plush carpet seemed to be in motion, anticipating our steps and thickening itself before we put our feet down. And somehow you knew that no germ would dare to show its face (or whatever it is germs show) anywhere inside the retreat or any of the outbuildings inside the dome.

"So where are they?" I asked.

"I told my agents to have them all assembled in one of the main rooms," said Max. "I know you'll want to question each one individually, but I thought you might like to meet them all first, put names with faces, see if anything about any of them strikes you as strange."

"Good thinking, Max," I said, mostly to encourage him. "I assume there's a private room where I can question each of them?"

"There are seventy-three rooms," he answered. "Most of them will suit your needs." He shuffled his feet nervously, which made it look like he was about to fall over. "Could I . . . may I observe while you question the suspects?"

"You're paying for it," I said. "You can do whatever you want."

"Thank you," he said gratefully. "I'm sure there is much I can learn from an experienced interrogator like yourself."

"Hell, we might even do a little good cop–bad cop," I added.

"That is not a term with which I am familiar," said Max.

I explained it to him, and if a beachball can look shocked, then that's what Max looked.

"Jake," he said, "we cannot intimidate the suspects. We are bound by ethical considerations and I am personally constrained by the tenets of my religion."

"What was the killer bound by?" I asked.

"We cannot pattern our behavior on that of a killer."

"You know why I quit the force and went private?" I said. "It's because I hated regulations and I hated regular hours and I hated having to salute my superiors, but mostly I quit because I hated treating criminals better than they treated their victims. If I have a credo, it's that showing any sympathy to a killer is an in-sult to his victim."

"Jake, five of the six people we will be questioning are *not* killers. We must treat them all with courtesy."

"You're making it harder to nail the Bad Guy," I said.

He was shaking like a leaf, but he wasn't going to back down. "Nevertheless," he said adamantly.

"Okay, it's your party," I said.

"Are you mad at me?"

"No," I said. "As a matter of fact, I envy you."

"You do?" said Max, surprised. "Why?"

"You haven't seen enough crimes to hate the criminals. Probably you never will." I figured I might as well be totally honest. "I also admire you."

It was unnerving to see a beachball do a double take. "What for?"

"Because you're afraid of me, but even so you stick to your guns."

"My guns?"

"Figure of speech. Your principles. I admire that. Not many beings of *any* race are willing to meet their fears head-on and stare them down." I gave him a pat on what passed for his shoulder. "We're going to get along fine, Max."

He didn't say anything, but he positively glowed with pride. I got the distinct impression that either he'd never heard a compliment before, or else that his race was so damned polite that he heard them all the time and didn't believe any of them.

We soon reached the end of the corridor and found ourselves in a room that was probably smaller than a murderball field and may have had a few less windows than the Church of the Nine Worlds on Jefferson II. There was more artwork, of course; a stone fireplace wall some sixty feet wide that was a work of art in itself; furniture that read your race and size and instantly adjusted if you got within ten feet of it; and a dozen other luxuries that were beyond the experience of private eyes or almost anyone else. Five Gaborians, a Man, and a Thrale were sitting in various chairs and couches. A dozen gleaming metallic robots were posted around the room, and I was sure there were robot chefs, robot maids, robot valets, and maybe even a robot bedmate or two; I assumed that, like the ones I could see, they were all shaped like Gaborians.

Four members of Max's race, all armed, stood at the four corners of the room, probably at attention though with beachballs it's difficult to tell. A fifth approached us, held out a hand, palm up. Max waved his fist over it. I took it to be their equivalent of a salute, or maybe even a handshake.

"Have there been any problems?" asked Max.

"No." The voice came out dull and unaccented through a T-pack. "But they each keep asking when they can leave."

"I'll answer that," I said, stepping forward.

"Who are you?"

"Ask Max," I said, walking into the room. "May I have your attention, please?" I said, raising my voice.

All seven of the suspects turned to me.

"My name is Jake Masters. I am not an employee of any department of the Democracy. I am a freelance investigator who has been hired to solve the murder of your late chairman. If you have any questions regarding my authority, check with my friend here," I said, gesturing to Max.

"Mr. Masters has been employed by the government of Alpha Gillespie to take charge of the investigation," he confirmed. "Jake, these are the executives of the Braaglmich Cartel, and the late chairman's personal physician." He introduced each by name. The Thrale, tall, angular, and covered with brown fur, glared at me with open hostility, either because I was a Man or because I was investigating a murder. Malcolm Shea was pudgy, nervous, and apprehensive. I couldn't tell the squat tripodal Gaborians apart except for their clothing.

"I'm sure we'll all get to know each other better very shortly," I said when Max was finished. "I understand that some of you have asked how long your presence here will be required. The answer is simple enough: you will be free to leave when we have identified and arrested the killer."

The six executives leaped to their feet and began protesting, while the doctor sat where he was and looked bored. I was actually grateful that five of them wore T-packs; it cut down on the volume and the vitriol.

"Max," I said, "do I have the right to detain them?"

"For a reasonable period of time," he confirmed.

"Good," I said. I turned back to the executives. "How I define 'reasonable' will depend on the level of cooperation I receive. In the meantime, let me remind you that one of you is a murderer, and far from resenting our presence you should be grateful for it."

"What makes you think any of us is in any danger?" demanded Malcolm Shea, who was so overdressed and coiffed that he looked like he was planning to pose for a fashion holo.

"I can answer that," said Max. "Kdin had already named Ktamborit as his successor—so we know this murder wasn't committed to create an opening at the top of the corporate ladder, an opening the killer might hope to fill. That was the most likely motive, and barring that, we not only do not know who the killer is, but *why* the murder was committed. And until we do know, you are all at risk."

"Nice answer," I whispered to him, then turned back to the execs. "I'll be questioning each of you individually. I see all of you except Mr. Shea are wearing T-packs. Even if you speak Terran, I want you to keep them on; I don't want anything anyone says or hears to be subject to misinterpretation. We'll start in a few minutes."

"Why not now?" demanded Ktamborit.

"Because there are other things I need to check first," I said. "Max, come back into the corridor with me. I need to consult with you." I turned to the agent who had approached us before. "Nobody leaves this room until I get back."

"But what if . . . ?"

"If they have to answer a call of Nature, one of your people goes with them."

"Understood."

We left the room and walked down the corridor past dozens of priceless paintings, Max at my side, until I was sure we were out of earshot, then stopped.

"Where do they keep the protective suits?" I asked. "The ones you wear when you're going outside the dome?"

He described what sounded like a luxurious locker room—

actually a locker *building*—right next to an airlock that led to the dome's exterior.

"Fine. Now, if the suit was tampered with, it wasn't done outside, in front of five witnesses, no matter how poor the visibility was. So it stands to reason it was rigged right where the suits are stored."

"I agree."

"A luxury retreat like this has got to have a state-of-the-art security system."

"We checked, Jake," he said. "But the system—"

"—was disabled in the building that houses the protective suits," I concluded for him.

"How did you know?"

"If it hadn't been, you wouldn't have come all the way to the Iliad system looking for a homicide cop," I said with a smile. "Also, we're not dealing with a spur-of-the-moment killing here. Someone planned this very carefully, and if you're bright enough to be a vice president in charge of a fifth of the galaxy, you're bright enough to know you have to disable the security system while you're doing your dirty work."

"Would you like me to show you the building, Jake?"

I shook my head. "There won't be anything for me to see. But when my forensics guy shows up tomorrow, that's the first place I want you to send him."

He nodded his agreement—as much as a beachball *can* nod, anyway. "Is there anything else?"

"No," I said. "We might as well go to work." I turned and headed back the way we'd come. "Let's start with the new boss."

"Ktamborit?"

"Whatever."

"Is there some reason you chose her?"

"Since she'd already been announced as the new chairman, she figures to be less likely than the others to be carrying a grudge," I answered. "Let's get her interview over with and concentrate on the others."

"All right," he said. "Where do you wish to conduct your interrogations?"

"How many floors in this palace?"

"There are three levels."

"Are all the executives housed on the second floor?"

"The first and the second, yes."

"The top level, then," I said, stopping at one of the half-dozen airlifts. "I'll find a room; you bring her along in a few minutes."

"Is there a reason why you wish to be so far from the others?" asked Max.

"There is."

"May I ask what it is?"

"Why don't you tell me?"

He lowered his head in thought, then looked up. "It will prevent the others from overhearing."

"Closing the door would do that. Come on, Max—why would I want to get a suspect so far from his comfort zone?"

He smiled. "You have just said it: you want the suspects to be on unfamiliar terrain, so to speak. If you question them down here, you are the intruder. On the third level, *they* are the intruders."

"Good for you," I said. "It's a tiny advantage, microscopic really, but we need any edge we can get. After all, the murderer knows who we are; we don't know who he is."

"It seems so simple when you explain it," said Max. "I suppose you will adjust the heat and light, too?"

"Not bad," I said approvingly. "Yeah, I noticed those big eyes on the Gaborians. We'll make the room a little too bright for them. Not blindingly so, just uncomfortable. The Man will be wise to that, and besides, human pupils adjust very fast, so we'll make him either too hot or too cold, so he becomes increasingly anxious to leave the room. I'm sure you've had more experience with Thrales than I have, so before I question our Thrale, let me know what you think might put him on edge."

"On edge?"

"Make him uncomfortable."

"A very interesting term," opined Max. "Shall I get Ktamborit now?"

"Give me a minute to find an office," I said. Then: "Make it five minutes. I want to set it up to be as uncomfortable as possible."

Max smiled. I had a feeling he'd call me a devious son of a bitch if he wasn't afraid I'd get offended and take a poke at him.

I stepped into the airlift, rode a cushion of air up to the third level, stepped out, and found myself at the juncture of four corridors, with half a dozen robots standing by, waiting to cater to my needs. I'd have liked to take a room at the far end of the longest corridor, but I wasn't sure Max would be able to find me, so I picked one right next to the airlift. It was an elegant little parlor with a few chairs, a couch, and a phony fireplace.

"Hey, you!" I said.

"Yes, sir?" said the robots in unison, responding in the same language they'd been addressed in.

"Move all this furniture except for one chair into some other room," I said. "Then find me a desk and move it in here as fast as you can."

The robots fell to work instantly, and had the room set up the way I wanted it in less than three minutes, while I busied myself adjusting the light and the temperature.

"Thanks," I said. "Now go back to your stations."

They silently walked out of the room and returned to where I'd first encountered them. A moment later Max appeared in the doorway with Ktamborit in tow.

"Are you ready for us, Mr. Masters?" he asked politely.

"Yeah, come on in." I nodded to Ktamborit. "I'm sorry, but there was only this one chair in the room. I hope you won't be too uncomfortable."

She gave me a look that said it was beneath her dignity to respond to such a transparent lie. "I will stand."

"Fine," I said. "Max, if you want to sit down, go right ahead."

He lowered himself to the floor, as he had done in my office back on Odysseus, and I turned back to Ktamborit. "What can you tell me about Kdin's death?"

"You already know how he died," she said through her T-pack.

"That's true," I acknowledged. "But I don't know *why* he died. I thought you might be able to help me out with that."

"You thought incorrectly. I have no idea why anyone would want to kill him."

"That's odd," I said. "I can think of four or five reasons, and I never even met him."

She stared at me and made no reply.

"Let's try again," I said. "Can you tell me why one of the vice presidents would want to kill him?"

"No. I had already been named chairman. The position was not open, so why should they kill him?"

"Anger," I suggested. "Bitterness. Hatred. I'm sure every one of them thinks he's more qualified to run the cartel than you are."

"That is not so," she replied. "My record is unsurpassed. I was promoted over all the others for valid reasons."

"Let's get back to the morning Kdin died. All seven of you went outside the dome, right?"

"That is correct."

"He led you to a spot about three hundred meters away?"

"Farther than that," she said. "Perhaps five hundred."

"To look at rocks?"

"To look at a unique rock formation, towering some sixty meters high on an incredibly narrow base."

"All right, you all went there and looked. What happened then?"

"Then he died."

"Right away?"

"Within a few seconds of reaching the formation."

"He just keeled over?" I persisted.

"He collapsed and died."

"Did he say anything?"

"No."

"Did he try?"

"I have no idea," she said. "I was standing behind him."

"And then the six of you carried him back to the dome?"

"Malcolm Shea and Toblinda carried him," she replied. "They are larger and stronger than we Gaborians, and speed was of the essence. We were not sure he was dead, and even if he was, we felt if we got him back inside the dome quickly enough there might be a chance of reviving him." She paused. "It was too late."

"When did Kdin announce that he had chosen you as his successor?" I asked.

"Twenty-two . . . no, twenty-three Standard days ago."

"And when did he ask you and the five vice presidents to come here to Graydawn?"

"Last week."

"I guess that'll be all for now," I said. "I'll want to speak to you again later, and if you should need any help or have anything to tell me, however trivial, please feel free to come to me with it."

"I require no help," she said coldly. "I just want to get back to work."

She turned and left the room.

"Well?" I said to Max.

"She was remarkably uncommunicative."

"That's understandable," I said. "She's anxious to get out of here and start running her empire. Did you learn anything else?"

"You seem to think I should have," he said.

We were silent for long moment.

"It's not fair," I said at last. "You don't have the experience to see it."

"To see what?"

"Look," I said. "She told us that she was promoted three weeks ago."

"Twenty-three days," he corrected me.

"Three weeks, three months, it makes no difference. The important thing is that she was promoted *before* Kdin decided to invite everyone to Graydawn."

"But we already knew that."

"Think it through, Max," I said. "There are a lot of reasons for killing Kdin, but the likeliest is anger or resentment at being passed over for the top spot. Would you agree?"

"Yes, certainly."

"What does that imply to you?"

He was silent for a moment as he considered the question. "That sooner or later the killer will realize that getting rid of Kdin didn't solve his problem. If he wants to control the company, he'll have to kill *her*."

"That's right," I said. "Now, we've been told that she's brilliant, creative, innovative, imaginative, everything a successful and ruthless executive is supposed to be. If you and I can see that, don't you think she can?"

"And yet she doesn't seem worried or apprehensive!" he said excitedly.

"Okay, you've got it," I said. "Now try not to get too excited about it."

"But—"

"You figured out what you were supposed to figure out," I said. "But that doesn't mean you should jump to conclusions. Consider: she could simply have total confidence in her ability to protect herself. She could have a pretty good notion about who killed Kdin, and will make sure she's never alone with him. She could *know* who killed Kdin, and told him he'll be exposed if he harms her. She could know that the motive had nothing to do with business. She could think we're not able to protect her; she wouldn't be the first. She—"

"Enough," said Max. "I understand." Then: "What do we do now?"

"We interview the other five and hope we can catch one or more of them contradicting her or each other."

"She didn't tell us anything. How could anyone contradict her?"

"What if the Thrale says he cried out, 'I can't breathe!'?" I said. "What if Kbing says Kbang told her he wanted to kill him?"

"Kbing? Kbang?" he repeated, confused.

"I don't know their names," I said. "What if one contradicted her statement about not knowing why anyone would want to kill Kdin?"

"I see," said Max.

"Remember, no one's going to walk up to us and confess. We'll build a case one tiny brick at a time. No matter how trivial it is, if it's an inconsistency or a contradiction, it could lead to bigger ones."

"It's fascinating, Jake," said Max, his enthusiasm returning.

"It can be," I said. "Usually it isn't. Usually the forensic boys come in and an hour later they tell you who the killer is, and all you have to do is hunt him down. This kind of detective work was obsolete a few millennia ago." I grimaced. "Except when the corpse and all the suspects were wearing full-body protective suits, and the wind and the chlorine destroyed every clue that might have been left behind." I sighed deeply. "Oh, well, bring in the next one."

"Have you any preference?"

"Yeah. Let's have the human. Maybe I can sympathize with his being passed over for a Gaborian, and we can bond a bit."

"If he's the killer, are you sure you want to bond with him?" asked Max.

"He's probably not," I said. "Neither is the Thrale."

"Why do you say that?"

"They're aliens in a Gaborian-owned and -dominated cartel. They've risen as high as they're going to. I can't imagine there's as much bitterness and jealousy there as among the Gaborians." I shrugged. "Still, I could be wrong. Let's see if I can get him talking, and then we'll know a little more."

"You want me to bring him up here now?"

I thought about it for a moment. "No," I said. "I'm a human, he's a human. Anything that makes him uncomfortable is going to make *me* uncomfortable, too. And as long as I'm going to be uncomfortable, I might as well kill two birds with one stone."

"There are no birds on Graydawn," said Max.

"That must depress all the cats," I said.

"There are no cats on—"

"Never mind," I cut him off. "Sooner or later I have to look at the murder scene, even if we both know it'll be useless. Have Shea meet me in the building that holds the protective gear."

"Do you want me to come along, too?" he asked.

"I can't imagine it'll do any good," I said, and his face fell— well, about as much as a beachball's face *can* fall. "What the hell," I added quickly. "Sure, come along. Maybe you'll spot something everyone else has been missing."

"Thank you, Jake."

He left to get Shea, and I snapped my fingers to get the robots' attention.

"Sir?" they said in unison, reentering the room.

"This will be my room for as long as I'm on the planet," I said. "During that time, I don't want anyone making any changes in it without my permission. Do you understand?"

"Yes, sir," they all said. I thought for a minute that they were going to salute me, but they just went back outside the room and then stood motionless.

I took the airlift down to the main floor, then walked out of the retreat, crossed the lawn of alien grass that scrambled to get out of my way, and entered the outbuilding that held the protective suits. Max and Malcolm Shea were already there, getting into their gear.

"You're not going to learn much," announced Shea. "You'll be lucky if the wind doesn't blow you over. And the visibility is wretched."

I was surprised he didn't tell me I'd get warts too.

"I just need a brief look at it," I said. "I can question you while we're walking there and back and get it over with."

"I hope you have a lot of questions saved up," he said. "It could take me hours to locate the formation."

"I thought it was just a quarter mile away."

"It is—but visibility's about five or six meters, tops. And I've only been there once."

"Max," I said, "find a robot that can lead us to the spot."

"Yes, Jake," he said, scurrying off.

"So who do you think did it?" I asked Shea.

He shrugged. "Beats me. Doesn't make much sense, does it? I mean, if I wanted to be chairman, I'd kill the current one, not the former one."

"I agree," I said. "So who had a grudge against Kdin?"

"Everybody except Ktamborit, I imagine," he said. "We were all passed over for the job."

"You never seriously expected to get it, did you?"

"No, not really. And while I hate to say anything to remove suspicion from a Thrale, Toblinda didn't expect it any more than I did."

"So why are you working for an organization where you can't rise to the top?"

"I'm the cartel's top executive in the Democracy," said Shea, not without a touch of pride. "I have more power, more people under my command, than almost any governor, admiral, or general. I couldn't spend my annual salary in a couple of lifetimes, and in fact I have so many perks that I don't spend much of it."

"Okay," I agreed with a smile. "Those are pretty good reasons."

"I have fourteen million good reasons a year, plus stock options," he said, returning my smile.

"So you think it was one of the Gaborians?"

"It seems likely. Except . . ."

"Except?"

"Except that I can't see what could be gained from it," he said, frowning. "Maybe we're all bitter that Kdin chose Ktamborit rather than one of us, but killing him doesn't change anything."

"Maybe it makes the killer feel better."

"On the one hand is the ability—maybe—to feel better for a while," he said. "On the other is losing everything you've got if you're caught. It's a piss-poor business proposition, and we're all businessmen."

Max returned with a gleaming silver robot that was shaped exactly like a Gaborian. We finished getting into our gear. Then I walked out of the building and to a hatch about fifteen meters away, and stepped into the airlock, followed by Shea, Max, and the robot. Once the hatch was secure, the outer door opened and we stepped out into the swirling chlorine fog.

"Lead the way," I said to the robot.

A glowing light indicated that he'd received my transmission, and he began walking very slowly to the northwest, calling out the hazards—large rock, small depression, slippery rocks, sharp incline, whatever—and it took us about eight minutes to cover the quarter mile. I was surprised that none of us tore our suits on the razor-sharp rock formations we had to pass.

"Why the hell would someone build a retreat *here*?" I mused.

"No visitors," said Shea.

"I suppose so," I agreed. "If there's a second reasonable answer, I can't come up with it." Then: "Max, you're from this system. Has Graydawn got any natural resources worth anything on the open market?"

"No, Jake."

"Any native life-forms?"

"No."

"I didn't think so. It's a pretty inhospitable place." I looked around. "Robot, where did Kdin fall?"

"I was not here, sir," answered the robot. "You asked me to take you to the spot where he often viewed his favorite rock formation. This is that spot."

I looked around. "I don't see any rock formation."

"It's there, all right," said Shea. "Wait until the wind stops blowing all this chlorine around."

And sure enough, no sooner had he spoken the words than the atmosphere stopped swirling and I could see a strange structure about ten yards ahead of me: a thin rock, maybe five inches around, extending straight up about fifty feet, with a huge circular slab of stone, maybe eight feet in diameter, balanced precariously atop it.

"Why doesn't the wind blow it over?" I asked.

"Beats me," said Shea. "From what Kdin told us, it's been like that ever since he built the place."

"Maybe the needlelike structure is piercing the circular one so it *can't* blow off," suggested Max.

"I suppose that's as good an answer as any," I said. "So you seven were looking at this thing, and Kdin fell over dead?"

"He clutched at his face mask first," said Shea. "Clawed at it like he was in a panic."

"Did he say anything?"

"Not that I recall."

"And you picked him up immediately and carried him back?"

"No," said Shea. "Two of the Gaborians knelt down next to him to see what had happened. There was a powerful wind, and it was possible he'd just been blown over. Then they announced that they couldn't see any signs of life, so the Thrale took one end, I took the other, and we carried him back to the dome."

I looked around. Visibility hadn't increased since we'd come out onto the surface. "How did you find the dome?" I asked. "I couldn't."

"Ktamborit and Ktee had been here a number of times before. *They* knew the way, or we might all still be out here."

"When you got him back, what then?"

"We called Bdale as soon as we reached the dome. He showed up a minute later and tried to revive Kdin, but he was past it." He paused. "Just as well. There hadn't been any oxygen to the brain for ten, maybe eleven minutes. If Gaborians are anything like us, he'd have been a vegetable anyway."

"Then what?"

"We put his body in a refrigerator bag to keep it fresh, and loaded him and his suit in the shuttle, which we sent to Bramanos."

"And then?" I said.

He looked confused. "That's it."

"Did any of the executives want to leave?"

"We all did," said Shea. "But Ktamborit ordered us all to stay here until the authorities confirmed that it was death from natural causes."

I thought about his answers on the way back to the dome. Once we'd entered it I told him that I was through questioning him for the time being and sent him back to the retreat.

"Aren't we going inside, Jake?" asked Max.

"In a minute," I said, fascinated as the grass kept ducking away from my feet. "We want to think first."

"What are we thinking about?"

"We're not sure," I said. "But something is bothering us."

"What?"

"I don't know," I said. "Everything Ktamborit and Shea said makes sense, but there's something wrong, something I can't quite put my finger on."

Five minutes later I still hadn't spotted it, so I finally gave up teasing the grass and walked back into the retreat with Max.

The next one I questioned was Kchang. He seemed genuinely distressed over Kdin's death, and didn't like Ktamborit at all . . . but in the next breath he admitted that she was the proper choice for the job, that her skills and intellect dwarfed everyone else's.

Ktee struck me as a good company man—or a good company Gaborian, as the case may be. He'd been with the cartel for thirty-four Standard years, never made waves, and seemed animated only when describing the business and his role in it. Was he pissed off at being passed over? Not at all. He loved what he was doing, and as chairman he'd be doing too many things he didn't like as well. Or so he said.

Kmorn was the third of the Gaborian vice presidents. He seemed the dullest, but he had an advantage the other two lacked: he was family. He tried to explain Gaborian bloodlines to me; the closest I could figure was that he was the equivalent of Kdin's cousin. He was more upset over Kdin's death than the others, but then, if he was as slow as I suspected, he'd just lost his protector, and his days of power and luxury might be numbered. Of them all, he had the least reason to want to see Kdin dead.

I figured that as long as I was questioning Gaborians I might as well work my way through them. Besides, I had an innate dislike of Thrales after what they did to a few outlying worlds I used to visit, so I decided to put off talking to Toblinda a little longer and sent for Bdale, the doctor.

Max ushered him into the room a few minutes later. He walked up to me, made some kind of obeisance that looked for all the world like a curtsy—it was a gesture none of the high-powered executives had felt obligated to make—and then waited patiently for me to start questioning him.

"I won't be long," I assured him. "How long were you Kdin's physician?"

"Just over ten Standard years," said Bdale.

"How was his health?"

"Not good. He suffered many of the problems of aging, exacerbated by the enormous pressure he worked under. His heart especially was not in good condition. That is why he decided to step down and turn the company over to Ktamborit."

"Did you feel any apprehension when he left the dome?"

"No, he did it almost every day, usually alone, though occasionally I or a visiting executive would accompany him. Exploring the area was physically taxing, but paradoxically it seemed to relax him. He had taken me to the structure a few times, so I knew he wasn't going far afield, and of course he was in the company of friends."

"Did you recommend that he take a robot along?"

Bdale smiled a Gaborian smile. "Kdin was the one who programmed the robots, Mr. Masters. He could find his way around the area as quickly and easily as they did."

"I assume his failing health was not a closely kept secret?"

"No, he had given it as his reason for retiring."

"Since all the executives knew he was in poor health, did any of *them* suggest that a robot come along?"

"No," he said. "I don't suppose it occurred to any of them."

"What did you think when they brought his body back?"

"That he had finally overtaxed his heart," answered Bdale.

"I gave him a perfunctory examination and pronounced him dead."

"Why was the body shipped to Bramanos as opposed to being buried or disposed of either here or on Kdin's home world?" I asked.

"When someone who wields that much power dies, even from what appear to be natural causes, it is essential to have an autopsy, just to ease everyone's mind," answered Bdale. "I don't have all the necessary equipment to perform one here, so his body was sent to Bramanos, with the stipulation that the autopsy be performed by a member of the Gaborian race, who would be conversant with his physiology."

"You had no reason to suspect foul play?" I persisted.

"None. As I said, the autopsy was routine."

"What was your initial diagnosis?"

"Heart failure. There were no discernible signs, and in such instances heart failure is usually the case."

"What are the signs of asphyxiation in a Gaborian?" I asked.

"They are all internal," replied Bdale. "If chlorine had somehow entered his protective suit, I would have spotted the signs instantly. But with simple asphyxiation, the Gaborian lungs collapse and the pulmonary artery often ruptures—but it takes an autopsy to discover that."

"What was your reaction when the results of the autopsy came back from Bramanos?"

"I was shocked," said Bdale.

"One last question," I said. "Did anyone suggest that the body *not* be shipped to Bramanos for a postmortem?"

"No."

"Thank you," I said. "I'll want to speak to you again later."

"I am at your disposal," he said, curtsying again and leaving the room.

I decided to take a break when I finished with Bdale. I wasn't tired; I just wasn't looking forward to even talking to a Thrale. And something was nagging at me; it was nothing I could put my finger on, but in this job you learn to trust your instincts, and

my instincts told me I'd already heard some things that didn't
add up.

Max was pretty sensitive to my mood. I could tell he wanted
to talk, to discuss the various statements we'd heard, but he kept
quiet and waited for me to work things out. It looked like it was
going to be a long wait; the more I tried, the more things kept
slipping away from me.

Finally I pulled a smokeless cigarette out of a pocket and lit
it up.

"Well, what do you think, Max?" I said.

"Me?" he asked, surprised.

"You heard everything I heard."

"Everything seemed logical. I know it's early in your investigation, but I would say we could probably eliminate Kmorn from
consideration."

"Kmorn," I repeated. "That's the cousin?"

"Yes."

"Every company's got a cousin or a brother or a nephew," I
said. "Most of them have a lot in common with Kmorn."

"They do?"

I nodded. "Most of them would still be in the shipping department if they weren't related to someone who could get them
out of there." I paused. "Yeah, if I were making book, he's the
long shot."

"What about the physician?" asked Max.

"Bdale?" I said. "If he was going to kill his boss, he'd have
enough brains to make sure it couldn't be spotted too easily in an
autopsy. Still, it wouldn't hurt to find out if he's mentioned in
Kdin's will, always assuming Gaborians *have* wills—and if so,
did he know about it? Also, will he become Ktamborit's physician now, and if so, is that part of the job description?"

"I don't understand."

"Was he Kdin's personal physician, or the chairman's official
physician?"

"Ah," said Max. "I see. If he was hired by the cartel rather
than Kdin, then he will probably retain his position with Ktam-

borit. And if he had a falling-out with Kdin, or if Kdin threatened to fire him for some reason, he had everything to gain by eliminating Kdin."

"Good for you, Max," I said. "Right on every count. Can I depend on you to find exactly who hired Bdale and what his duties were or are?"

"I shall do so before the day is over," Max promised. He paused uncomfortably. "I have a question, Jake."

"What is it?"

"You seemed lost in thought for a few minutes, and your expression was troubled. If you will confide in me, perhaps I can be of some help."

"I can't put my finger on it," I said.

"If you will give me some of the details . . ."

"I don't know them," I said. "I know it sounds like I'm ducking your question or hiding things from you, but I'm not." I tried to think of an example. "Did you ever go to the zoo world of Serengeti, over in the Albion Cluster?"

"No, though I've heard of it."

"It's a planet-wide game park," I said. "You drive through it and view animals from maybe two hundred worlds in their natural habitats. The first thing you learn is that animals are pretty good at concealment. You could be twenty yards away from a three-ton herbivore that's standing in the bush. His outline is broken up by trees and shrubs, and he's the same color as his surroundings, and you stare for two minutes, then three, and you'd swear there's nothing there. Then he flicks an ear or a tail, and suddenly you can see the whole beast, just because of that."

"So you know something's there, something wrong, and you're just waiting for the equivalent of an ear flick to bring it into focus," said Max.

"Exactly," I said.

"I heard the same things as you did, and I can't find anything wrong with them."

"That's because you're new to the game," I said. "If it was anything obvious, I'd have spotted it right away." I finished the cigarette, toyed with lighting another, and decided not to. "We'll just keep plugging away until something clicks. I'm going to question the Thrale now. The odds are he didn't do it for the same reason that Malcolm Shea doesn't figure to have done it. You can sit in on the interview if you want, but you'd be a lot more useful hunting up a computer or whatever else you need and finding out about Bdale."

"I'll send Toblinda up to you, and get busy learning what I can about the doctor," he said, walking to the door.

"Thanks," I said. "And Max?"

"Yes."

"Find out when they eat in this place. I haven't had anything since a couple of hours before we left Odysseus."

"I will do that, too, Jake," he said, and walked to the airlift.

Even before I spoke to him, I was pretty sure Toblinda wasn't the killer. He was in the same position as Shea; no matter who lived or died, he was as high up the corporate ladder as he was going to get. Not only did Kdin seem to have a predilection for his own kind, but for a cartel that traded with the Democracy *and* the Coalition it made sense not to offend a sizeable portion of its market by elevating an enemy of one side or the other to the top position.

Toblinda showed up about ten minutes later. I'm sure Max approached him before he did anything else, and I'm sure the Thrale could have made it seven or eight minutes earlier, but our races were mortal enemies—we'd been friends a century ago and we'd be friends a century in the future—and he wasn't about to make my job any easier or any more pleasant.

He took one look at the room, stepped out into the corridor, and ordered a robot to bring him a chair. It didn't respond until I okayed the command. It was only then that I realized that no one else had thought of it. These were the top executives in one of the most powerful cartels in the galaxy. They should have been used to snapping their fingers and having flunkies fight for the privilege of catering to their needs and even their whims.

"That's better," said Toblinda when he finally sat down. I noticed he was using a T-pack, though most Thrales spoke Terran. In fact, the Thrale Coalition had been part of the Democracy before it became independent, and Terran is the Democracy's official language. I guessed it was his way of showing me that no trace of the Democracy remained to stain his person.

"I have some questions to ask you," I said.

"And if I choose not to answer them?"

"That's your privilege," I said. "Of course, I'll have to arrest you and incarcerate you until you decide to honor me with your answers, but as far as I'm concerned, I'll be just as happy if you take twenty years to get around to it."

He grinned an alien grin. "I'll bet you would, too."

"You'd win," I answered, returning his grin.

"All right, Mr. Masters," he said. "Ask away."

"Damn!" I said. "And here I'd gotten my hopes up."

He laughed, a throaty, guttural alien laugh. "I like you, Masters. It is a shame we're on opposite sides."

"Not in this instance, Toblinda," I said. "I want the crime solved and you want it solved."

"Why should I care?" he said. "We both know it wasn't committed by Shea or myself."

"We both think it's highly probable that it wasn't either of you," I agreed. "But the sooner we can solve it, the sooner the lot of you can go back to work, and the less chance there is that word will get out that your executives are killing each other. I don't think any of the financial markets would respond favorably to that."

"You have a point," he admitted. "We shall set our enmity aside until the killer is apprehended. Ask your questions. I will answer them completely and truthfully."

"Fine," I said. "I saw the spot where Kdin collapsed. What indication did you have that he was in distress?"

"Almost none," answered the Thrale. "He clutched at his neck, or maybe it was the tubes leading from his oxygen tank to his face mask. I think he tried to say something, but nothing came out. Then he fell to the ground. My guess is that he was dead less than a second after he hit it."

"That pretty much agrees with what the others said. Who was the first one to suit up before you all went out?"

He frowned, which didn't look quite as menacing as I'd thought it would. "I can't remember," he said. "I think we all changed into our protective gear at the same time."

"Are you sure?"

"No, I could be mistaken," he said. "Why don't you just check the security system?" Suddenly he grinned again. "It was disabled, wasn't it?"

"You're quick on the uptake, I'll give you that," I acknowledged. I was getting the feeling that this was one sharp sonuvabitch, maybe the only one who could have given Ktamborit a run for her money if he hadn't had the misfortune to be born a non-Gaborian. "Let me try another one. Who got to Graydawn first?"

"That's easy. Ktamborit was invited a few days earlier, so Kdin could acquaint her with the subtleties of her new position. He probably also gave her some highly classified information, so secret that even the vice presidents were not allowed to share it."

"Okay, so Kdin and Ktamborit were waiting for the five vice presidents. Who was the first to land?"

"Kchang."

"How do you know?"

He smiled again. "Because I was the second, and Kchang was already here. Malcolm Shea showed up next, and then the other two Gaborians."

"I gather you were all here for two full days, and then Kdin took you outside the dome on the morning of the third day."

"Yes, that's right."

"If his suit wasn't tampered with on the day of the murder, it had to be tampered with earlier. Did you notice anyone's absence during those two days?"

"That's a silly question, Mr. Masters," he said. "Gaborians, humans, and Thrales all require some personal privacy. It's a huge house; we were often out of each other's sight. And of course, different executives retired at different times."

"You're right, Toblinda," I acknowledged. "It *was* a silly question. But I had to ask it anyway. Did anyone go outside the dome before that third morning?"

"No."

"So no one had a reason or an excuse to be in the building that holds the suits?"

"No."

"That figures," I said, as much to myself as to him. "We're not dealing with a stupid killer. It's obvious that no one else was going to become chairman after Ktamborit was elevated to that position, so the killer probably had what he thought were sufficient reasons to murder Kdin even with no possibility that it would lead to the chairmanship. You know all of them. Who had a reason?"

He thought for a moment, then shook his head. "I know business relationships, and we both agree they're probably meaningless in this case. You want information on personal relationships, and of these—except for my own, of course—I know nothing."

"All right," I said. "Tell me about your own."

"I met Kdin—it still feels strange not to call him Kdineka, the name by which we all knew him—exactly four times. Until I came here I had probably spent less than six hours in his presence. To the best of my recollection, we were never alone together, and while we may have disagreed about certain aspects of company policy—who doesn't?—it was never acrimonious, and in fact he usually gave in to me."

I stared at him, trying to think of what to ask next, and finally decided the interrogation was over. "That's it," I said. "Thank you for your help. I'll probably want to speak to you again."

"I'd enjoy that," he said. "I could probably be arrested for saying this in the wrong venue, but I like you."

"I like you, too," I said. "It's a dumb war."

"But even a dumb war does wonders for the economy," he said with a final smile. Then he was on his feet and out the door.

Max showed up about fifteen minutes later. "Dinner will be in half an hour," he announced. "Do you want to join the others in the dining room or have it brought to you here?"

"Here," I said. There was no sense letting the suspects know how little progress I'd made. "What about the doctor?"

"Bdale was Kdin's personal physician, and was paid from Kdin's personal account."

"Do Gaborians make wills, and is he in it?"

"They have extremely rigid inheritance customs. I have not spoken about it to a Gaborian lawyer, but from what I was able to glean from a brief search with my computer, the likelihood is that Bdale will not inherit a thing."

"Not even any severance pay?"

"I don't think so, but I'll still have to check and make certain."

"I assume Ktamborit has her own physician?"

He looked blank. "I have no idea."

"It wouldn't hurt to find out."

"I will, Jake."

"Has my forensics guy checked in yet?"

"Not personally, but one of my Order Keepers got a message from his office that he'll arrive at Bramanos sometime tomorrow morning, and then come here when he's done."

"Pity he's not going to find a goddamned thing," I said.

"Explain, please?" said Max.

"You saw the spot where Kdin died," I said. "Even if the killer left a clue, it's blown halfway around the world by now. And it didn't have to. If it blew thirty yards away, that'd be enough. We'd never find it."

"But perhaps in the building that houses the protective suits . . ." he suggested hopefully.

I shook my head. "The killer had enough brains to deactivate the security system, Max. He's got to be smart enough not to leave anything behind." I stopped and just stared ahead.

"What is it, Jake?" asked Max after a moment.

I sighed deeply. "I don't know. Something was on the edge of my mind, knocking to get in, but"—I shrugged—"nothing."

"Shall I contact the forensics expert and cancel his visit?" asked Max.

"No," I said. "We might as well let him go through the motions. Maybe God will drop everything else and leave us a clue. But I'd bet everything you're paying me that my man doesn't turn anything up."

"Is there anything else we can do while we're waiting for him?"

"Yeah, I suppose so," I said. "It's a zillion-to-one shot, but at least it'll keep your agents busy. When everyone's having dinner, have a couple of them search every room in the retreat."

"What are they looking for?" asked Max.

"Someone with a grudge against Kdin who thought if he killed him this week we'd be up to our ears in suspects and never look past the obvious ones."

"You think someone might be hiding in an unused room?" asked Max excitedly.

"No. I just believe in being thorough. You might run a quick test or two on the robots and make sure they haven't been programmed to lie, and then"—I stopped to consider—"then find out if they saw anyone sneak out to the suit building, or if they know of anyone who's been inside the dome the past few days besides Bdale, Ktamborit, and the veeps."

"That sounds promising, Jake," said Max.

"It's busywork, Max. It'll stop us from getting too bored, but it's not going to turn up a killer."

"If this won't, and your expert won't, then . . ." he began.

"Don't ask."

"Are you saying that we've been here just a few hours and you've decided we can't solve it?" he persisted.

"No. I'm just saying we're not going to solve it by the usual methods. But we might as well try them all, just so we can say we did." I paused. "Maybe you'd better get back down to the main level, so you can give your agents their instructions."

"All right, Jake." He walked to the door, then turned to me. "Don't get discouraged. I have faith in you."

"I can't tell you how comforting that is," I said. He never spotted the sardonic tone, and walked away with a happy smile on his face.

A robot showed up with my dinner a few minutes later. It looked and smelled exactly like a steak with mashed potatoes in gravy, but while the galley robots could make soya products look and smell like real food, they still tasted like soya products. Still, I hadn't eaten in maybe twenty hours, and it sure as hell wasn't the first soya meal I'd had—or the hundredth, or the thousandth, for that matter—and I decided I'd had worse. Plenty of them.

I spent the next hour going over all the interviews I'd conducted. There were some discrepancies—one said Kdin collapsed like a stone, one said he banged his hand on his face mask, one said he tugged at the hoses leading to his helmet—but that was absolutely standard. No two people ever saw or remembered an incident exactly the same. If one of them had said he collapsed and another had said he'd run fifty feet first, that would be worth another pair of interrogations, but that wasn't the case.

I suppose the biggest problem was that I just couldn't come up with a motive. Ktamborit had been publicly anointed as the new chairman. If someone had killed *her* I'd have something I could sink my teeth into; but there just wasn't any sense killing Kdin once he'd named his successor. He was just a civilian again; why risk all the power and money each of them controlled to kill someone who was no longer a player?

Could the killer have thought he could talk Kdin into changing his mind about his successor? Out of the question. It was too late; Ktamborit was already the chairman. Could the killer have been promised the chairmanship, and killed Kdin for breaking his word? There were three problems with that. First, it wasn't worth the risk. Second, he couldn't know that Kdin was going to take them out on the surface. (Or could he? I made a mental note to find out.) Third, there were five Gaborians. How could he be sure he was rigging the right protective suit?

I thought about that last point for a minute, and started getting excited. If the killer didn't know which suit was Kdin's, could he have been trying to kill Ktamborit? Now, *that* would be a murder with an obvious motive.

But if he couldn't tell one suit from another, he had to figure the odds were four-to-one he'll kill the wrong Gaborian. And if he was a Gaborian, as seemed likely, he also had a one in five chance of donning the rigged suit himself.

Well, there was an easy way to find out. I walked to the door and ordered the nearest robot to tell Bdale I wanted to speak to him right away.

The doctor entered the room a minute later and treated me to another curtsy.

"You sent for me?" he asked.

"Yeah," I said. "It won't take long. What was your first reaction when they brought the body into the dome?"

"That Kdin's heart had finally given out."

"You were summoned from the retreat, right, and they were coming in through the hatch that was closest to the rock structure?"

"That's right."

"So when you saw them you were, what, maybe forty meters away?"

"Thirty or forty."

"Could you see his face from that distance?"

"No, not the way they were carrying him."

"Okay, doctor, here's my question: how did you know it was Kdin?"

"The gold suit."

"Gold suit?" I repeated.

"He'd had his suit and helmet colored gold, so it would be easier for me or a guest to follow him in the low visibility of the planet's surface. I don't know if it actually worked, but he thought it did, and who would contradict him over such a trivial matter?"

"Thank you, Doctor," I said.

"That's all?"

"That's all."

Suddenly he smiled. "You thought maybe the killer tampered with the wrong suit."

"It was a possibility." I grimaced. "It isn't anymore."

He seemed about to say something else, changed his mind, curtsied, and left.

Well, I told myself, no one ever said it was going to be open and shut. Forensics labs identified killers in the early hours of a case. It took detectives a lot longer.

I was still pondering the situation when Max entered the room maybe an hour later.

"Well?" I said.

"It was as you predicted," he reported. "We went through the house with state-of-the-art sensors and couldn't detect any life-forms. I had one of my Order Keepers test all the robots, and they cannot lie. And finally, none of the robots saw anyone enter the building that holds the suits."

"Does your agent know enough about robotics to tell if they have been given false information without knowing it?"

"I don't understand."

"Can your agent tell if the robot saw someone enter the suit house and was later programmed to forget it, so when he says he never saw anything he checks out as being truthful?"

"That's very complex, Jake. I think we'll need a robotics expert for that."

"It's a long shot anyway," I said. "What are the odds that anyone in the retreat could pull off that kind of tampering? Still, if we're not making any progress in a few days, we'll call in a robotics expert. I assume your supply of money is endless?"

"We will spend whatever it takes to bring the killer to justice," he assured me.

"It may take a while," I said.

"What makes this case so unusual?" he asked. "The lack of clues?"

"That's part of it."

"What else?" he asked. "I'm not trying to by pushy, Jake," he added apologetically. "I'm trying to *learn*."

"Okay, Max, no offense taken," I said. "The traditional way of solving a murder is to examine motive, means, and opportunity. That's where the problems begin. I can't find a motive for killing Kdin. A year ago, absolutely. But once he'd stepped down and named his successor, no. As for means and opportunity, everyone had the same: they all are capable of tampering with the suit, and they all had the same two days at the same location in which to do it."

"That's not exactly true, Jake," said Max. "Ktamborit was here for a few days before the others arrived."

"Yeah, but the security system was working then. If she'd tampered with the suit before the system was deactivated, we'd know it."

"Yes, that's true," he agreed.

"So I keep returning to motive, and I may never be able to come up with one."

"Surely you're not suggesting that it was a motiveless murder," said Max.

"No, of course not. But the only thing all the suspects have in common is that they work for a cartel that functions in a capitalistic system, so I keep assuming that money and power are the motives, because they would be the motives in *my* society. But except for Shea, these are aliens, and while they've been interacting with Men for years and know how to comport themselves, I don't know what makes them tick."

"*I* am an alien in your eyes, too," he said gently.

"Damn it, Max," I said irritably, "every last one of them is more alien to you than to me. At least I come from a world where murders get committed; you come from one where no one kills anyone no matter how many valid motives they have. If I can't understand them, neither can you."

"But we *do* understand them," he persisted. "I was there when you interrogated them. Their answers all made sense."

"Because I asked what I know about, Max," I said. "I see that they're all executives in the same company, so I think that must have something to do with it. But for all I know, Kdin didn't laugh at one of Kchang's jokes thirty years ago, and to a Gaborian that's a perfect justification for murder. Maybe he accidentally brushed against Toblinda's uncle during a visit to his Thrale headquarters, and Toblinda thinks *that's* a killing offense. Maybe he didn't kill and eat a pet that Ktee gave him for his birthday. I could be ten lifetimes just figuring out what the Gaborians and Thrales think *is* a killing offense."

"Then are we defeated already?"

"No. We just have to be a little more creative than usual."

"How?"

I couldn't repress a chuckle. "Max, if I had a ready answer, it'd be routine and not creative. We'll just keep plugging away until we find a flaw and work from there."

"Do you want to question them again tonight?" he asked.

"Not really," I said. "I can't think of anything else to ask. Let me sleep on it."

"You are going to sleep now?"

"In another hour or two," I said. "I've been up a long time."

"Will you be sleeping here?"

"No, this is my interrogation room," I said.

"Well, wherever you choose to sleep, let me know, so we can monitor you on the security system. I know you feel you're not in any danger . . ."

"I'm not."

"Nevertheless, I think we should keep a watch on you."

"Forget it," I said. "I don't like being watched."

"But Jake—"

"I'm not kidding," I said. "I want you to promise you won't spy on me while I'm sleeping, or I'm going to spend the night in the suit house, where you *can't* watch me."

"Of course we can. We got it working again."

"How?"

"I had my Order Keepers contact the manufacturer, and once he'd checked our credentials, he gave us the proper codes to activate it again."

There was a big mental *click!* as the pieces suddenly fell into place. I toyed with pulling out a cigarette, but this time I decided I deserved the one smokeless cigar I'd brought along.

"What is it, Jake?" said Max anxiously. "You've got the strangest expression on your face. Are you all right?"

"Never been better," I assured him.

"Then what—"

"I know who did it," I said.

"Then let's make the arrest!" he said excitedly.

"It's not that easy," I replied. "I know who did it, sure as you're standing there—but I don't have any proof that would stand up in a court of law."

"Who was it?"

"Ktamborit."

He frowned. "But she had less reason to kill him than anyone else."

"Like I said, she's an alien. I could be half a dozen lifetimes learning and understanding her motives. But a lot of little things didn't add up."

"I didn't notice anything untoward."

"Hang around the homicide bureau for a few years and you will," I said. "For example, she had to know Kdin's health was suspect. After all, that's why he was stepping down. So why didn't she insist that a robot accompany them outside the dome?"

"But they found their way back without one," said Max.

"Yeah . . . and it took them ten minutes to cover a quarter mile, more than enough time to make sure he was dead when he got there. Maybe a robot could have led them back in four minutes; maybe Bdale could have revived him if he'd gotten to him soon enough."

"But by the same token, any one of them should have thought of having a robot accompany them," noted Max.

"That's why I didn't say anything at the time. But there was more. Why didn't she contact Bdale on her suit's radio when they were carrying Kdin back to the dome? Why wait until they got there?"

"I never thought of that," said Max. "But again, it applies to all of them."

"I agree. I knew *something* was wrong, but I still had six suspects." I paused, ordering my thoughts. "I also thought it was strange that she didn't insist that her security team come down to the dome. I mean, hell, she's the boss, no one could stop them, and there was no logical reason for anyone to kill Kdin once he'd retired. There was at least a chance that *she* was the target, but she didn't do anything about it."

"You're right, Jake," he said, his enthusiasm waning. "That will never hold up in a court of law. Even *I* am not convinced."

"Neither was I. I knew all that hours ago. And like I said, I knew something was wrong, but I didn't know what. I began homing in on her when Bdale told me that she insisted that all the executives stay on Graydawn until the autopsy was performed on Bramanos. Why? Kdin's own physician said he had died from natural causes. The only reason for the postmortem is that it's standard when someone worth billions dies. But the killer would know that if the executives left, they'd just be called back for questioning."

"Ah!" said Max, his eyes widening. "I see. And based on that . . ."

I shook my head. "Based on that, I thought she was the likeliest suspect, nothing more. I didn't know for sure until you gave me the information I needed."

"*I* did?" he said, surprised.

"That's right."

"When?"

"Just now."

Max frowned, and I could see him trying to replay our conversation in his mind. Finally he gave me that beachball shrug I was getting used to. "I give up, Jake. What was it?"

"You told me you could monitor me even if I slept in the suit house."

"But we can."

"*Why* can you?" I asked.

"Because we activated the security system," said Max.

"How?"

"We fed it the proper codes to get it up and running again."

I just smiled at him.

He stared back at me, and suddenly his eyes got wider and wider. "Of course!" he exclaimed excitedly. "This isn't Kdin's private house. It's a corporate retreat. He would know all the codes, and Ktamborit arrived a few days early so that he could instruct her and turn over classified material to her. The security system in the suit house wasn't broken; it was deactivated by someone who knew the code!"

"Give the boy a cigar," I said.

"No, thank you, Jake," said Max. "I do not smoke."

"It's just an expression," I said. "Anyway, Ktamborit's the killer, but we can't go into court with what we have. We'll say she knew the codes, she'll say Kdin never gave them to her, and we won't be able to prove otherwise. In fact, a good lawyer will put the blame on Bdale: he had ten years to spy on his boss and learn the code."

"*Could* he have done it?" asked Max.

"No," I said. "If he did, he'd never have claimed Kdin died from natural causes. He'd have known the postmortem would prove otherwise. And he wouldn't kill him here on Graydawn, where he was one of seven suspects. He'd wait until Kdin was at a convention or a business meeting, surrounded by rivals. It'd be nothing to slip some poison in a drink, examine the corpse, announce that he'd been murdered, and let the police spend the next decade trying to sort out the two or three hundred people who had motive, means, and opportunity. Take my word for it, it's Ktamborit."

"How can we prove it?"

"We'll need some help," I said.

"Whose?"

"Ktamborit's."

"I don't understand."

"You will," I promised.

I considered the Gaborians, but except for Bdale they hadn't made much of an impression on me, and if I could see what a lawyer could do with Bdale, he could, too, and was probably too busy planning his own defense to be of any use to me. That left Malcolm Shea and Toblinda. Shea was a Man, but he wasn't a very impressive one, and I didn't know how he'd perform under pressure. Toblinda's race may have been this year's mortal enemy, but I thought he was worth more than the other five put together. I was only going to have one shot at this, and I decided he offered me my best chance of success.

"Max, have Toblinda come up here."

"Shall I tell him that—?"

"No"—I cut him off—"we'll tell him in private, so that if there's any reaction, no one but you and I see it."

"And my Order Keepers?"

I shook my head. "Not a word. They're probably all trustworthy, but if they don't know, they can't inadvertently give it away."

"I'm confused, Jake," he said. "I thought the whole purpose of this investigation was to identify the killer."

"I've identified her," I told him. "Now the purpose is to come up with something that she won't be able to explain away in court."

He left to find Toblinda, and while he was gone I had the robots bring another chair into the room. Then he was back, accompanied by the Thrale.

"Have a seat," I said. "You, too, Max."

They sat down.

"Something's changed," said Toblinda.

"What makes you think so?" I asked.

"You don't mind my being comfortable this time," he said

with an alien grin. "And your friend here seems a little less nervous than usual."

"Okay, something's changed," I said. "I have a proposition for you."

"I'm listening," said the Thrale.

"What would you say to declaring a temporary truce between Men and Thrales, and helping me nail a killer?"

"You know who it is?"

I nodded.

"Well?" he said expectantly.

"Do we have a deal?" I said.

"Of course we have a deal. Every member of the Democracy and half the neutral planets will be sure I did it if we don't catch the real killer." He grinned again. "And everyone else will think it was Malcolm Shea."

"It's neither of you," I said. "Ktamborit killed him." I gave him the same explanation I'd given Max, and as I did so his expression changed from disbelief to anger.

"I guess gratitude is not in the Gaborian lexicon," he said. "He made her one of the six or seven most powerful corporate heads in the entire galaxy, and this was how she thanked him."

"I don't know her motive, and neither do you," I said. "Maybe we never will. But that won't stop us from incarcerating her if we play our cards right."

"Cards?" interjected Max, puzzled.

"Another figure of speech," I said. "Since I can't come up with enough proof to please a court, we're going to have to make her incriminate herself."

"I love the devious human mind," said Toblinda. "How do you plan to do this?"

"I'm working on it. I'd be happy to consider suggestions from either of you. What we have to do is convince her that there's evidence that can convict her, something she overlooked. Then we sit back and wait for her to go looking for it, and we've got her."

"We could say that there was a secondary security system that she missed," offered Max.

"She'd know it's a lie," I said. "Remember, she couldn't have deactivated the system if Kdin hadn't shown her where it was and how to shut it off. Why would he do that and then not tell her about a second system?" I looked from one to the other. "Remember, we've only got one shot at this. Once she knows we're trying to trap her, she'll sit there like a statue and take her chances in court."

"Let's look at it logically," said Toblinda. "If she were to leave a clue, the most logical place for it is in the outbuilding that holds the suits. She knows the security system was off, so whatever she did isn't recorded, and she knows the Order Keepers came up with nothing when they searched the building. So there is probably no way she can be enticed back there to look for incriminating evidence. And she knows that no one will ever find a clue outside the dome."

"I agree."

"Then we're defeated and she goes on to run the cartel for the next thirty years," said Toblinda.

"Come on," I said. "If the Thrales gave up that easily, our war would have been over in a week."

He smiled. "I will take that as a compliment to my race, if not myself. But I still say that the only place to look for a clue is the outbuilding."

I shook my head. "No. You're right: it's not likely that we can trick her into going back there."

"Then what's left?"

"Only one thing," I said.

"The body?" he asked.

"No," I said. "She never touched the body."

"The suit!" shouted Max.

"The suit," I agreed.

"But they've examined it on Bramanos," said Toblinda.

"I know," I said. "They didn't find anything." I paused. "I've got my own expert arriving on Bramanos tomorrow morning.

He won't find anything either—but what if we say he landed a few hours ago, and what if we hint that he *did* find something?"

"Hint?" repeated Toblinda. "Why not just *say* it?"

"Because if we say *what* he found, she'll know we're lying," I answered. "Let's let her worry about it."

"All right. She's worried. Now what?"

"Now Max, who is the inexperienced member of the team, lets slip what it is that we're looking for. We'll have to dope out what it is, but Max will tell her that they found some microscopic trace elements on the suit where it had been tampered with. If she was a human, I'd say it could be something as tiny and easy to overlook as a flake of dandruff. But whatever it is, it'll be something that she'll believe will clearly identify her as the killer."

"So she'll have to get rid of it!" exclaimed Max.

"Right," I said. "But once she knows they found one trace of something, she can't be sure they won't find traces of something else tomorrow or next week or next month. So we're going to bet the farm—no, Max, I don't own a farm; it's another figure of speech—that she'll try to foist the incriminating evidence off on another executive rather than destroy it. Once we have a killer in custody, it stands to reason that we'll stop looking for another."

"Why are you looking at me with that expression on your face?" asked Toblinda.

"Max is going to blurt out to her that we think you're the killer, and we hope to be able to prove if before long. Then you're going to have a public blowup with me and Shea—you hate Men, remember?—and stalk off to spend the night in the suit house. Max and his agents and I are all going to spend the night on the main floor, waiting to hear the latest news from my forensics expert."

"And sometime during the night she plants the evidence in my room?" said Toblinda.

"Right. You're the only one who could spend the night in an outbuilding and make it believable; my race isn't at war with anyone else. I'll have Max and at least two of his agents make a complete inventory of your room before we have our little scene, so they can testify that you didn't possess whatever it is that she's going to plant there."

"She'll just say someone else planted it."

"She can say anything she wants," I replied. "The house's security system isn't disabled."

"Yet," said the Thrale.

"Yet," I agreed. "But I'll post one of Max's agents by the computer that runs the house and the system, and if she tries to disable it in front of a witness, that ought to be enough to convict her."

"If anything goes wrong, you'll testify that this was your scheme and I merely agreed to follow your orders?" demanded Toblinda.

"I'll put it in writing or state it for your personal computer, whichever you prefer," I said.

"Both," he answered.

"Agreed," I said. "Now all we have to do is figure out what she's got that could leave a microscopic trace, and yet wouldn't seem totally out of place in a Thrale's room."

"That requires us to enter her room and examine it," said Max.

"Why?" I said. "*She's* made use of the security system. Why shouldn't *we*? There has to be a control room for the computer that runs the retreat and the security system. Take Toblinda there and scan her room until he finds something that fits our needs."

"You'll stay here?" asked Max.

"No, I'm going down to socialize." They both looked at me like I'd lost my mind. "I've been cooped up here all day, questioning them one at a time. I just spoke to Toblinda a second time. If I go down to the main level now, it may lend the impression that I've found what I'm looking for."

"You are as devious as a Thrale!" said Toblinda with a laugh. "And that is a high compliment."

"Thanks. I think."

We all left the room and took the airlift down to the main level. They turned one way and headed toward the control room, while I joined the five Gaborians and Malcolm Shea in the huge room where I'd first met them.

I hate small talk, but I made my share of it for the next few minutes. Once I awkwardly let slip that I didn't trust Toblinda any farther than I could spit with my mouth closed, and if things worked out the way I anticipated he was going to be sorry he'd ever met me.

Then Max and Toblinda joined us. I didn't know if they'd found what they were looking for, but after a few minutes the Thrale picked a fight with Shea and me and then stalked off in a fury, announcing that he wouldn't spend the night under the same roof as any Man, and he was going to the suit house.

I kept talking for another fifteen minutes while Max and a pair of his agents made their inventory of Toblinda's room. When he returned I announced that I was going into the pantry kitchen to find something to drink, and he knew enough to follow me.

"Okay," I said. "What was it?"

"We made an educated guess," answered Max. "The robots sterilize the rooms every day, and the residue of their chemicals causes some very minor discomfort, especially for the Gaborians. They have each been supplied with a small vial of powder that, when opened, eliminates the discomfort. Thrales do not suffer from the affliction, or perhaps it is a weakness. At any rate, Toblinda does not have such a vial. That seemed to be the only thing in her room that was not in his."

"I don't like it," I said. "This is our only shot at her, and it requires her to think this powder leaves some residue on her hands or gloves, whatever she was wearing, and she also has to think that it wouldn't be out of place in a Thrale's room when Toblinda tells you it would."

"We don't have to tell her anything, Jake," said Max. "We can wait and try something else."

I shook my head. "How many times can Toblinda stalk off and sleep in another building?" I said. "Besides, I've already dropped a hint that I think he's the killer. No, we'll have to go with it, but I sure have bad vibes about it."

"Vibes?"

"Never mind. Just find a way to clumsily impart the information to her."

"Yes, Jake." Then: "I'm sorry if I've made it more difficult."

"It's not your fault," I said. "You found the only difference in the two rooms. You were just doing what I told you to do."

I poured myself a glass of water, then went back to the main room. After a few minutes Ktee and Kchang announced they were going to bed, and Malcolm Shea followed suit a minute later. Bdale was the next to leave. Then, when Kmorn went into the kitchen to hunt up a snack, I followed him and engaged him in some meaningless conversation, leaving Max alone with Ktamborit. I kept Kmorn in the kitchen for a good ten minutes. When I came back, Max actually winked at me to show me he'd dropped the info on Ktamborit.

I explained that Max, the Order Keepers, and I were all staying by the subspace radio, waiting for definitive word from my expert on Bramanos, and that should any of us feel the need to sleep, we'd hunt up empty rooms on the main level so as not to disturb any of the executives, who were all housed on the second level.

Ktamborit went off to bed about five minutes later, and Kmorn followed suit a few minutes after that.

"All right, Max," I said. "All the groundwork has been laid. There's only one more thing for you to do."

"What is that?"

"At some point Ktamborit is going to come back down to this level, ostensibly to get something from the kitchen, or to retrieve something she left down here. And then she is going to very quietly sneak off to the computer room and deactivate the retreat's security system, with the intention of coming back down in another hour or two to reactivate it. I want you to keep all your agents in the main room and let her do it."

"And that's all?"

"Almost," I said, giving him his final instructions.

I waited until all the executives were in their rooms, then

went to the computer room, made a quick adjustment, and took the airlift up to the second level. I tiptoed down the corridor to Toblinda's room, waited for the door to iris and let me pass through, then ordered the lights on just long enough to find a nice comfortable corner and sit down with my back propped against the wall. I pulled my burner out, laid it in my lap, ordered the lights out, and waited.

I was afraid I might fall asleep before anything happened. I'd been up a long time, and there aren't many things duller than sitting on a plush carpet in a dark room when it's been a day and a half since you had any sleep. In fact, I think I did nod off once or twice, but each time my body would start to relax I'd wake up with a start.

And then, finally, the door irised again, and I saw the figure of a Gaborian silhouetted against the light in the corridor. It walked over to a small table. I couldn't see or hear what it was doing, but it didn't matter. My hand closed on the burner, and when I sensed the Gaborian started to walk back to the door, I said, in a loud, clear voice, "That's far enough, Ktamborit. Lights on."

It took both of us a few seconds to adjust to the flood of light. I'd expected her to panic, or at least look surprised, but nothing affected her calm.

"What are you doing here?" she demanded coldly.

"Waiting for you."

"It will do you no good," she said. "It is just your word against mine, and I am the Chairman of the Braaglmich Cartel."

"For another few weeks," I said. "Then you're just another inmate."

"I heard you moving around in here. I know that Toblinda is in one of the outbuildings, so I entered to see what was happening, and I came across a common thief."

"Sounds good," I said. "But I don't think it'll play in court."

"Oh?" she said with an expression that was as close to a smug smirk as a Gaborian can come. "Why not?"

"It's not your word against mine," I said. "It's your word

against everything that was captured by the infrared holo camera."

"That camera is not working," she replied.

Suddenly Max's image appeared before us. "Oh yes it is," he said.

"Damn," I said apologetically. "I guess we forgot to tell you that we got the security system codes from the manufacturer."

"It makes no difference," she said, still cold as ice. "The record will show that I have transported nothing lethal or criminal to this room."

"It doesn't matter what you brought," I answered. "Your presence here is enough to incriminate you."

"Your case will never hold up," she said.

"Ready to bet your empire on it?" I asked.

A long pause. "Name your price," she said. "We can deal."

"Before or after we turn off the camera?"

She uttered some obscenity that the T-pack couldn't translate, as we both realized she'd blown it, that beneath the icy calm exterior she'd been caught so off guard that she forgot the security system was capturing everything.

I contacted Malcolm Shea's security team, which was orbiting the planet, deputized them—it was probably illegal, since I myself wasn't an officer—and had them transport Ktamborit and a pair of Max's agents off to Bramanos for trial.

Then we brought Toblinda back to the retreat and told him what had transpired while the other executives and Bdale, all of whom had been awaked by the commotion, gathered around and listened.

"Did she really think that anyone would believe a Thrale would use that disgusting powder?" asked Toblinda.

"You know," I said, "I was so concerned about taking her into custody that I never even looked. Max, was she planting the powder?"

"No, Jake," he answered. "Actually, she planted a form of hand cleanser."

"You mean like a bar of soap?" I said, surprised.

"The equivalent. Evidently each room has its own distinctive cleanser—different color, different scent—"

"And of course different chemical makeup," added Toblinda.

"So she probably disabled the suit with her bare hands," I said, "or at least some bare flesh may have touched it, or she *thought* something may have touched it, and she figured *that* was what our expert had found or would find."

"She appropriated Toblinda's cleanser and replaced it with her own before you turned the lights on," said Max, "but of course we captured it all on infrared holo."

"Well, when you get right down to it," I said, "I don't suppose a bar of soap is any dumber than a tube of powder. If she'd just sat still and not worried about it, we'd never have nailed her."

"She could have doubled the size of the company," said Kchang bitterly. "Kdin was on his way to the grave anyway." He glared at me. "Why did you have to ruin everything?"

"It's my nature," I said. "I can't stand rich executives."

I think my sarcasm was lost on the Gaborian, because he began calling me every obscene name the T-pack could translate and more than a few that had never been programmed into it.

I've been cussed out by experts, so I just let it roll off my back, but I could see Max getting more and more upset, and finally he took a swing and decked the executive.

"Don't you ever speak that way to my friend again!" he bellowed. In just a day and a half he'd come a long way from the nervous little alien who shook like a leaf at the mere thought of contradicting someone.

We stuck around another day, did some paperwork—I don't know why we call it that, since no paper was involved—and finally boarded Max's ship (but not before I'd made arrangements to meet Toblinda for drinks once a year on a neutral planet).

Max was silent, even morose, for the first couple of hours. Finally, just after we entered the MacNaughton Wormhole, I asked him what was bothering him.

"I should never have struck Kchang," he said.

"Feeling guilty?" I asked, amused at his discomfiture.

"Certainly not!" he replied heatedly. Then he seemed to collapse within himself. "But it was reported to my superiors, and I have been terminated."

"They sacked you for hitting the little sonuvabitch?" I demanded.

"Yes," he said with a heavy sigh. "I loved my work, and the past two days have been the most fascinating of my life. Now I shall have to learn another trade."

I stared at him for a moment. "Maybe not," I said.

"What do you mean?" he asked.

"You didn't hit the Gaborian because of what he was saying about *you*," I said. "I could use a partner I can trust, one who isn't afraid to back me up."

His alien face lit up. "Do you mean it, Jake?"

"I only lie to the Bad Guys," I said, extending my hand.

He took it, and this time he didn't tremble a bit.

❖ HOXBOMB ❖

Harry Turtledove

THEY MET by twilight.

The hours when day died and those when night passed away were the only ones humans and Snarre't comfortably shared. Jack Cravath thought it was a minor miracle humans and Snarre't shared anything on Lacanth C.

You had to try to do business with them. Everybody said so. Everybody, in this case, was much too likely to be right. If the two races didn't get along, they had plenty of firepower to devastate a pretty good stretch of this galactic arm. Black-hole generators, ecobombs, Planck disruptors, tailored metaviruses . . . The old saying was, they'd fight the war after this one with rocks. Not this time around—there'd be nobody left to do any fighting, and the rocks would be few and far between, too.

By one of those coincidences that made you think somebody had it in for both species, they'd found Lacanth C at the same time 150 years earlier. They'd both liked the world. What was not to like? It was a habitable planet, as yet unscrewed by intelligent life of its own. They both wanted it. They both needed it, too. In lieu of a coin flip, stone-paper-scissor, or that spiral-arm-wrecking war, they decided to settle it jointly.

Codominium, they called it. On Earth, such arrangements went back to the seventh century CE—ancient days indeed—when the Byzantines and Arabs shared Cyprus for a while. The

Snarre't had precedents of their own. Jack Cravath didn't know the details about those; he just knew there were some.

And he knew codominium worked—as well as it worked, which often wasn't very—only because all the alternatives that anybody could see were worse. His own alternatives were none too good right this minute, either. By choice, he would have closed his scooter dealership when the sun set and gone home to dinner with his newly pregnant wife. But that would have shown interspecies insensitivity. You didn't do such things on Lacanth C, not if you had anywhere close to your proper complement of marbles you didn't.

He sat in his office instead, while darkness deepened around him. The ceiling lights began to glow a dull, dim orange. As far as anybody could tell, that amount and shade of illumination annoyed both races equally.

In a little more than an hour, when it was full dark outside, he could legitimately close. Then he could use his IR goggles to get out of the interspecies business district in Latimer and back to the human residential zone, where such perverse curiosities as streetlights were allowed. His stomach growled. Beverly's good chicken stew tonight. He was hungry, dammit.

He could watch the street from his dealership. Humans went by on scooters or, occasionally, on Snarre'i drofs or caitnops. Far more Snarre't rode their beasts, but some of them sat on scooters. That was why—aside from law and custom—he kept the dealership open into their hours. Every so often, he did business with them. He wasn't allergic to fattening up his credit balance, not even a little bit.

That wasn't the only reason he was always happy when he unloaded a scooter on a Snarre'. Drofs and caitnops creeped him out. They looked like nothing so much as Baba Yaga's house, only with most of the house part gone: oversized yellow scaly legs with a platform for the rider and handholds through which he controlled his drof. Press here, and it went forward. Press *here,* and it stopped. Press here, and it turned right. Press *here*—left. Press here and *here,* and it opened its mouth so you could give it some yummy drof treats.

He shivered. The Snarre't had a technology that mostly matched and sometimes outdid humanity's. But theirs was biotech from the ground up, with mechanical gadgets as relatively recent high-tech innovations. It wasn't the way humanity had done things, but it worked.

Caitnops and drofs did what they did about as reliably as scooters did the same thing. Human programmers and engineers had loudly insisted biocomputers could never come close to electronic gadgets . . . till the Snarre't showed they were talking through their hats.

For their part, the Snarre't thought the idea of the Turing test was the funniest thing they'd ever heard. Of course computers were intelligent, as far as they were concerned. How not, when they were built from neurons? And the Snarre't had left in the pain response, even amplified it, to make sure their servants didn't turn into masters. Jack shivered again.

He looked at his watch. Half an hour till he could bail out. He thought about chicken stew, and about Bev, and about the baby due in 270 days or so (talking about months was pretty silly on a world without a moon—Lacanth C's year was divided into neat, tidy tenths). Beverly'd found out within hours that she'd caught. That was a Snarre'i-derived test; humanity's reagents weren't nearly so sensitive. He smiled. The baby would be their first.

The door opened. Two Snarre't walked in. Jack muttered under his breath. Bev wouldn't be happy if he came home late. But she would be if he made a sale. "I greet you," he called to them in Snarre'l.

"Hello," they chorused in English. Using the other race's language first showed you had manners.

Returning to English himself, Jack asked, "What can I do for you today?"

Both Snarre't showed their teeth in the gesture that meant they were amused. They had more teeth, and sharper ones, than humans. Their noses were three vertical slits in their round faces, their eyes enormous and reflective, as suited nocturnal creatures. They had big ears that twitched, ears that put the legendary

Alfred E. Newman to shame. They didn't wear clothes; they had
gray or brown pelts. All in all, they looked more like tarsiers than
any other earthly beasts . . . but they didn't look a hell of a lot
like tarsiers, either.

"We would like to buy from you some meat," the taller one
said in—probably—her own language. The babelfish in Cravath's
left ear translated the word. The wider rictus on the other Snarre's
face translated the sarcasm.

Thinking of Beverly, Cravath answered, deadpan, "I can give
you a good deal on chicken stew."

He didn't know exactly how the Snarre't turned English into
their tongue. Maybe a worm in their brains—and, with them, it
would be a literal worm, not a gadget—did the translating.
Maybe . . . Well, since he didn't know, what point to worrying
about it?

The shorter Snarre' said, "We are interested in trying the
Model 27 two-seater. If we like it, perhaps we will also get from
you some chicken stew."

They both thought that was pretty funny. Jack Cravath duti-
fully smiled. Were they a mated pair? Jack thought so, but he
wasn't sure. Among Snarre't, females were usually taller than
males, but not always. Their sex organs were neatly internal unless
they were mating, and females had no boobs: despite the fur, they
weren't mammals, but fed their young on regurgitated food like
birds.

"A Model 27, you say?" the dealer echoed. Both Snarre't
splayed their long, spindly fingers wide, their equivalent of a nod.
Cravath went on. "Well, come with me, and I'll show you one.
What sort of payment did you have in mind?"

There was the rub. Humans had a burgeoning economy, and
the Snarre't had a burgeoning economy, and the two were about as
much like each other as apples and field hockey. Each species' notion of what constituted wealth seemed strange, stranger, strangest
to the other. That turned every deal into a barter—and a crap-
shoot.

"Knowledge, perhaps," the taller alien said. "We have a

brain that is getting old but is not yet foolish with age. This might be a good enough price, yes?"

"It might, yes." Jack tried not to sound too excited. How much good did that do? If they got a whiff of his pheromones, they'd know he was. Snarre'i brains intrigued human scientists the same way human electronics fascinated the aliens. Different ways of doing the same thing . . . He was pretty sure he could get more for even an old one than a Model 27 was worth. "Step into the showroom with me, why don't you?"

"We will do that," the taller one said, and they did.

He made his best pitch for the Model 27. He talked about its speed, its reliability, and its environment-friendly electric motor. "You don't have to clean up after it, either, the way you do with your drof."

"We don't mind. Drofshit is for us pleasant—more than pleasant—to eat," the shorter Snarre' said. Jack kept his face straight. You couldn't expect aliens to act like people: the oldest cliché in the book, but true. They weren't asking *him* to eat candy turds. *A good thing, too,* he thought. But they'd bred their animals to do that, which was not the sort of thing people would ever have thought of . . . he hoped.

"May we test drive?" the taller one asked.

"Sure," Jack said. "Let me check the headlight to make certain it's not up too bright." In the human part of Latimer, people needed headlights when they drove at night. The kind of light levels humans preferred would have blinded Snarre't, though. When the aliens had to go out by day, they wore sun goggles even more elaborate than the IR jobs humans needed to see at night without raising havoc among the Snarre't.

"Thank you for your courtesy," both aliens chorused, and he could hope they meant it.

The headlight was okay. Cravath asked, "Whichever one of you is driving is allowed to use a scooter? You are of the proper age and know-how?"

"Oh, yes," the Snarre't said together. The taller one pulled what looked like a caterpillar out of its fur and breathed on the

thing, which glowed a faint pink. "You see?" When a Snarre'
asked if a human saw, the alien always sounded doubtful. To
them, humans *didn't* see very well, and being adapted to do best
in daylight didn't count.

But Jack Cravath nodded. That response on that thing meant
the same as a green light on a human computer reader scanning
a driver's license. He didn't know why, but he knew it did.

"Shall we try it, then?" the shorter one said. "Our drof is
yours if we fail to return the scooter."

Jack wanted a drof like a hole in the head. But what could he
say? "Go ahead," he answered. "Come back in twenty minutes."

"Agreed," the two Snarre't said. The taller one got on the
scooter in front. The shorter one sat behind. Jack held the door
open for them. Out they went. They turned the headlight on. The
orange glow was just bright enough to warn humans who
weren't wearing IR goggles. That was what interspecies law required, and they lived up to it . . . barely.

Out on the street, the drof's big eyes—much like those of the
Snarre't themselves—swung to follow the scooter as it purred
away. How smart *were* drofs? Humans had acquired a good many,
just as the Snarre't had a fair number of scooters by now. It remained an open question, though. Some scientists maintained they
were only bundles of reflexes; others insisted more was going on.

As for the Snarre't, they weren't talking. Nobody human was
even sure the question meant anything to them.

Jack pulled his phone off his belt to warn Bev he'd be late.
"What? You've got Furballs in the office?" she said.

"Well, they're taking a test-drive now." Jack was glad the
two Snarre't were, too. If their translator picked up what his wife
said, they could nail her on a racism charge—or threaten to, and
screw him to the wall on the scooter deal. The two races sharing
Lacanth C didn't have to love each other, but they did have to
make nice where the other guys were listening. Cravath continued, "Anyway, I'll get back as soon as I can. Go ahead and eat.
I'll nuke mine when I come in."

"Okay," Beverly said. She was so freshly pregnant, she hadn't even started morning sickness yet. Her appetite was still fine. "Don't be too long."

"I'll try not to. It isn't just up to me. Love you, babe. 'Bye." Jack stowed the phone.

He looked at his watch. Naturally, the Snarre't didn't use hours and minutes; they had their own time units. Translators were usually pretty good about going back and forth with those. But if this one had screwed up . . .

Nineteen minutes and forty-one seconds after they left, the two aliens drove back into the showroom. "It is a very different sort of conveyance," the taller one said. "Less responsive than a drof—you cannot deny that."

"But peppier," the shorter one said. "Definitely peppier."

The taller Snarre's big googly eyes swung toward its partner or friend or whatever the shorter alien was. Jack didn't know for sure, but he guessed that meant the same it would have with people. *Don't praise what we're shopping for. You'll run up the price.*

If the shorter one noticed, he—she?—didn't let on. "The price we proposed before is acceptable?" the Snarre' asked Jack. "For the scooter, our aging but still functional brain?"

The babelfish translation made that sound pretty silly, as if the aliens would open up their heads and pour out whatever was inside. But Jack Cravath spoke formally: "Yes, the price you proposed before is acceptable."

"Draw up the contracts, then," the taller one said.

"How old is the brain you want to trade for the scooter?"

"Six years. Six years of Lacanth C."

"Okay." Jack spoke into the office business system. It spat out contracts in English and in Snarre'l. Jack reviewed the English versions to make sure they had the deal straight. He signed all the copies, thumbprinted them, and added a retinal scan to each one. The aliens also signed in their angular squiggles. They pressed a special area on each contract to an olfactory gland under the base of their stumpy tails. Those chemical signatures were supposed to be even more distinctive and harder to counterfeit than retinal scans.

"I will get the brain." The smaller Snarre' went out to the drof and stroked it. A pouch opened. If Baba Yaga's house were a kangaroo instead of a chicken . . . But the edge of the pouch had teeth, or something an awful lot like them. The Snarre't discouraged drof thieves.

Back came the alien. He—she?—put the brain on the counter. It looked up at Jack out of disconcertingly Snarre'-like eyes. *Have to keep it in the dark,* he thought. A tagline floated through his mind: *and feed it bullshit.* It was about the size of a basketball, with two little arms and four little legs. Its fur was molting here and there. It looked like something that had seen better days.

"What *do* I feed it?" Jack asked.

"Here is about ten days' worth of brain food." The Snarre' set a membranous sack on the counter by the brain. "You can get more from any of our merchants." Another, smaller, sack went by the first one. "And here, because you have shown yourself to be congenial, are some spices for flavoring your food. They are not harmful to your kind. It is likely—not certain, for taste is never certain—you will find them flavorsome. They are a gift. We ask nothing in return for them."

That was also polite. Even so, Jack said, "Well, thank you very much. Let me give you my stapler here." It was the first thing he saw on his desk. He showed them what it was for, and threw in a box of staples.

They seemed happy enough with the theoretically optional return gift. He wondered how they held papers together. Pointy twigs? Bugs with sharp noses? Something biological—he was sure of that.

They took their copy of the contract. One of them got on the scooter. The other tethered the drof to the new purchase. Away they went. Jack got on the phone. "Made the sale. On my way. See you soon."

"Oh, good," Bev said. "I didn't start after all, but I was going to pretty soon."

"Back as quick as I can," Jack told her. " 'Bye."

His own scooter was parked out front. He eyed the brain,

which was sitting on the counter. It looked back at him. Did it know it belonged to him now? If it did, what did it think of that? Rather more to the point, how was he supposed to get it home without hurting it?

He found a cardboard box and put the brain into it. To his relief, it didn't kick up a fuss. It said something in Snarre'l. The babelfish gave Jack gibberish. "It'll be okay, honest," he said in English, and hoped he wasn't lying. Did the brain understand? Whether it did or not, it kept quiet. That would do.

Jack set the box between his knees as he got on the scooter. That was the best way he could think of to keep it safe. As soon as he put in the key, the scooter's electric motor whispered to life. Getting home to Bev made him want to speed up. Protecting the brain made him want to slow down. He probably ended up somewhere in the middle.

He could tell the second he left Latimer's mixed-race central business district and got back to the human-settled east side of town. Streetlights became bright enough to be useful. He turned the rheostat on the headlight switch and lifted his goggles onto his forehead. Now he could really see where he was going. The Snarre't might be nocturnal, but he wasn't.

The brain was. As the lights brightened, it made a small, whimpering noise. It was taking in more glare than it could handle. He put his riding jacket over the top of the box. The brain stopped whining, so he supposed he'd done the right thing.

He stopped at a traffic light—one more reminder he was in the human part of Latimer. Another scooter pulled up alongside his. "Hey, Jack!" the man on it said. "How you doing?"

"Oh, hello, Petros," Jack answered. Petros van Gilder lived around the corner from him. He sold a rival firm's scooters. They forgave each other their trespasses. Jack went on, "I'm tolerable. How's by you?"

"Fair to partly cloudy," van Gilder answered. "What's in the box?"

"Snarre'i brain. I sold 'em a two-seater, and this is what I got for it."

"Not too shabby." Petros stuck out his hand, which he'd kept in the pocket of his riding jacket. "Way to go. I had a near miss with the Furballs the other day, but I couldn't close the deal. Congrats."

"Thanks." Jack shook hands with him. "Yeah, that ought to make the firm a tidy little profit once I sell it to the right people. Some left over for me, too."

"There you go," Petros said. The light turned green, and he zoomed off. Jack would have, too, if not for the brain in the box. He followed more sedately. Van Gilder would get home ahead of him tonight.

He parked in front of the house when he did arrive. One of Lacanth C's big selling points for human colonists was that it was roomy enough for every family to enjoy its own house and lot. That was one more thing the Snarre't didn't grok. Most of them lived in apartment warrens. They liked crowding together. Smells meant more to them than they ever would to humans.

Come on now, dear. Let's sniff the Hendersons' butts. To humans, the talking dogs made a classic T-shirt. The Snarre't wouldn't have got the joke, because they really did stuff like that.

Cravath carried the box to the house. He kept his jacket over it, because the lights were bright—if you were something (someone?) the Snarre't had bioengineered. He unlocked the front door and let himself in. "Hi, hon!" he called. "I'm home!"

"What have you got there?" Beverly asked. She was short and blond and plump, and worked for a quantum-mantic outfit that would have to learn to do without her before too long.

He explained about the brain again. She was suitably impressed. He told the house to turn down the lights. "Now I can uncover it without hurting its eyes," he said.

He tossed the jacket on a chair. Bev peered down at the brain. "It looks so sad," she said.

"I thought the same thing. I'll give it some food. Maybe that'll perk it up. Would you get some water for it, too, please?"

Bev did, in a plastic cup. The brain ate and drank. It still looked sad after it finished. Jack was happy after chicken stew and a bottle of beer. He tried some of the Snarre'i spices in the stew. He liked them. Bev stayed away from them even so, for fear that anything alien wouldn't be good for a rapidly growing fetus. She didn't drink any beer, either, and she liked it.

They celebrated the sale of the scooter back in the bedroom. The brain stayed in its box in the kitchen. Did it know what was going on at the other end of the house? If it did, it couldn't do a damn thing about it. *Poor thing,* Jack thought.

Did brains mate with other brains to make more brains? Or did the Snarre't clone them one at a time from a genetic template marked *brain*? Cravath had no idea. Was the brain in the box male or female? Or, if it was a clone, had the Snarre't bioengineered all the complications of sexuality out of it? If they had . . . *Poor thing,* Jack thought again.

Well, he was going to sell it to the humans best equipped to take care of it. How well would the Snarre't have cared for an aging indoor cat? That comparison didn't occur to Jack, or he probably would have thought *Poor thing* one more time.

He got almost as much for the brain as he hoped he would. The retail price for which he would have sold the scooter to humans went into the firm's account. The rest went into his. Were the tall Snarre' and the shorter one making similar arrangements? Had they bought the scooter for themselves, or were their engineers tearing the tires and the powerpack to pieces, trying to figure out how they worked?

That wasn't his worry. Neither was the brain, not anymore.

He and Bev used the extra credit in his account to take a South Coast vacation. They lay in the sun and swam in the sea. He drank drinks with plastic rocketships in them. She stuck to fruit nectars and occasional sips stolen from his mugs. She was being good for the baby's sake. He admired her for that.

When they got home, a genetics scan showed that it was a boy, and that it suffered from none of the four hundred commonest genetic syndromes. That scan came free with their medical coverage. If they wanted to check for the next four hundred, they would have to pay for the test. Beverly looked up the incidence rate of syndrome 401. It was named for four twenty-first-century doctors, and occurred, the data net said, once in every 83,164,229 births.

"What do you think?" she asked Jack.

"Your call, babe. We can afford it if you want to do it," he said. If, God forbid, anything really rare was going on, he didn't want her blaming him for not looking into it.

But she smiled and shook her head. "If you worry about odds like that, you probably snap your fingers to keep the elephants away." Jack snapped his. They both laughed. The closest elephants to Lacanth C were a lot of light-years away, so snapping your fingers worked like a charm there.

And that secondary scan wouldn't have picked up what was going on, anyhow. Neither would a tertiary scan, or a quaternary . . .

The ultrasound very clearly showed the baby's heart. As for the rest . . . The tech examining the image frowned a little. "You've got a wiggly kid," she said. "He twisted himself into a really funny position."

"Is everything all right?" Bev asked.

"Yeah, I think so," the tech answered. "Maybe you want to come in for another check a little closer to term."

"Well, maybe I will," Beverly said. But she didn't. The tech didn't make it sound like a big deal, and so she didn't worry about it. Her OB seemed to think everything was fine. The fetal heartbeat came in loud and clear. Junior—she and Jack were going to name him Sean—sure kicked like a soccer player.

Both new parents were as ready as new parents could be when labor started. It took a long time, but they were braced for that. It hurt, too, but Bev knew ahead of time that it would, which made a lot of difference. When she finally got the urge to push, the OB told her to go ahead.

"Won't be much longer," the woman said cheerfully from behind her mask. Bev made a noise somewhere between a grunt and a squeal—she might have been trying to lift a building off her toe. The OB nodded approval. "That's good! Do it again!"

Jack thought his wife would explode if she did it again. But then, that was the point.

Bev bore down once more. Her face turned a mottled purple. That couldn't be good for her . . . could it? The obstetrician seemed to think so. "The baby's crowning," she said. "I can see the top of its head. Push hard. One more time!"

And Beverly did, and the baby came out, and that was when the screams in the delivery room started.

Sergeant John Paul Kling was in the shower when the telephone rang. Swearing under his breath, he turned off the water and plucked the phone out of the soap dish. "Exotic Crimes Unit, Kling here," he said.

"This is Dr. Romanova. I'm at Tristar Hospital." The woman on the other end of the line sounded like someone biting down hard on hysteria. *And she's a doctor,* Kling thought. *Whatever this is, it isn't good.*

"Go ahead," he said out loud, while water dripped from the end of his nose and trickled through the mat of graying hair on his chest.

"I think . . ." Dr. Romanova had to pause and gather herself. "I think we've had a hoxbomb here." There. She'd said it.

"Good Lord!" Kling didn't know what he'd expected, but that wasn't it. "Are you sure?"

"I'll send you the image," she said, and she did.

For a few seconds, Kling thought he was seeing what he was seeing because his phone screen had drops of water on it. He wiped it clear with his thumb, and what he saw then was even worse.

It was a newborn baby. Well, it couldn't be anything else, but whoever'd put it together hadn't looked at the manual often enough. Parts sprouted from places where they had no business being. He'd heard of sticking your foot in your mouth. Now he saw it—either that or the kid's tongue had toes. Which would be worse? He had no idea.

"Sergeant? Are you there, Sergeant?" Dr. Romanova asked. "They put me through to you, and—"

"I'm here." Kling got rid of the photo, but it would haunt him forever. And he was going to have to see the model in a few minutes. "Tristar Hospital, you said? I'm on my way. Shall I notify the Snarre't, or do you want to do it?"

"You're the police officer in charge," she answered, which was a polite way of saying, *You're stuck with it, buddy.* "A hoxbomb *could* be purely human, of course."

"Yeah. Right," John Paul Kling said tightly. He was a cop. Like any cop with two brain cells to rub against each other, he went with the odds, not against them. A hoxbomb didn't have to mean the Furballs were involved, but that was sure as hell the way to bet. They were the ones who really knew how to do that stuff: a lot better than humans did, anyhow.

He got out of the shower, put on his clothes, and called headquarters. He would have to show them visuals, and naked just didn't cut it. Lieutenant Reiko Kelly took the call. "I thought it would be you, John Paul," she said. "A hoxbomb, the doctor told me."

"Uh-huh. I'm about to head for Tristar now. Reason I'm checking in is, I want to involve the Snarre't." He was doing things by the book. Being only a sergeant, he needed formal permission before taking care of what everybody—even the doctor, or maybe especially the doctor—could see he had to take care of.

Lieutenant Kelly sighed, but she nodded. "Yes, go ahead. With a hoxbomb in the picture, you don't have much choice. If it turns out they aren't involved, we can always peel them out of the investigation later."

"Okay. We're on the same page, anyhow," Kling said. "I'll make the contact. Boy, that'll be fun. Fun like the gout, is what it'll be. So long, Reiko. Talk with you later." He hopped on his scooter and headed for the hospital.

The Snarre'i investigator's name was a collection of screeches and smells that don't translate well into human-style phonemes.

We can call her Miss Murple. The name is similar but not identical to that of a legendary human investigator. What she did was similar but not identical to what a human investigator might do, too, so Miss Murple works well enough as a handle.

She didn't want to be investigating just then. She was right in the middle of an exciting lifey. Again, the name is approximate, but it will do. Since it was daytime out, she'd told her windows to exclude most of the ambient light. She sat in her darkened living room, her eyes closed, her brain's little hand wrapped around her left index finger.

A special nerve patch there connected with the brain. The genetically engineered creature spun out the story, which was set in the Era of the Three Queendoms. They hadn't known much about biology back then, but they'd had amazing adventures. She was living this one, with all her senses involved. When the character from whose viewpoint she was experiencing the action walked across the grass, she smelled it and felt it on the bottoms of her feet. When the character got hurt, she felt that, too. And when the character mated, it was as good as the real thing—better, if you'd run into some of the clumsy males Miss Murple had met lately.

She had to deliver the spice package before sunup if she wanted her love interest to keep blinking when . . . "I'm sorry," the brain said as it abruptly returned Miss Murple to the mundane world. "You have an urgent message from Investigation Thumb."

"A stench!" she said. Of course the brain stayed connected to the rest of the neural net while it entertained her. But why did Thumb have to come in right at the most exciting part of the lifey? She was an investigator. She knew why. Because things worked that way—that was why. Hadn't she already seen it too many times? "Connect," she told the brain resignedly.

Instead of the trees of the home world, she saw the unlovely offices of the gripping organ of the Snarre'i self-protection agency. Her superior's name was as unpronounceable as hers, so we can call him Sam Spud. "A Baldy requires communication with you," he said without preamble.

"A Baldy!" Miss Murple said in dismay. That was too much! The aliens *didn't* communicate, not at any truly important level. That was a big part of what was wrong with them. "What's this about?"

Sam Spud's pupils narrowed to slits, even though the offices were also darkened against the day. "A hoxbomb," he answered grimly. "You'd better talk to the human, sweetheart. That's trouble with a capital T." Not quite the idiom he used, but humans don't have the odor receptors they'd need to appreciate his to the fullest.

"A hoxbomb? Used on the Bald Ones? Is someone out of her mind?" Miss Murple said. Antagonizing weird, dangerous aliens had to be a maniac's game . . . didn't it? She hoped so. Humans could do things with ordinary, boring inorganic matter that the Snarre't had never imagined possible. They could blow up a world. They could, very possibly, blow up a star.

Sam Spud waggled his ears to show he wasn't kidding. The brain in his office caught the scent of his agitation and relayed it to Miss Murple through the neural net. "Yes, a hoxbomb. No possible doubt. I've seen the image. That's one scrambled baby Bald One."

It showed up in his mind, which meant it showed up in Miss Murple's. She winced. He wasn't wrong. A baby that distorted was good for nothing but euthanasia. "A hoxbomb," she agreed. "All right, we need to get to the bottom of this before the humans break out in assholes." A Snarre' who said something like that meant it literally. Reluctantly, Miss Murple went on. "I will activate my telephone. You may—I suppose you may—give the code to the Bald One investigating."

"Right." Sam Spud would have given it to the human anyhow. Miss Murple knew that. And he would have overridden her if she tried to keep the telephone inactive. He was her boss, so he had the right. And he was a son of a bitch, so he would have used it without compunction. He broke the connection.

A very little while later, the telephone made a horrible noise. Gingerly, Miss Murple picked it up. It didn't quite fit her hand. It felt unnaturally smooth and slick. It smelled funny, to say nothing of nasty. Even with shielding, its little screen lit up too bright to suit her.

The human who appeared on the screen was, like any human, a bad caricature of Snarre'kind: bare face, tiny eyes, pointy beak with only two round breathing orifices, small mouth with niggardly teeth. "I greet you," it said in Snarre'l.

"Hello," Miss Murple replied in English. How were you supposed to get anything important across when all you could use were sound and sight? She didn't know, but she'd have to try. Returning to her own language, she said, "A hoxbomb?"

His translator—a mechanical thing, cousin to the mechanical thing she was holding—must have worked well enough, for he said, "That's right." That was what *her* translator said he said, anyhow. It gave his impoverished speech all the overtones it would have had in Snarre'l. Whether those overtones were really there in English was a question for another time. The human went on. "The victim's mother and especially father dealt with Snarre't about the time the pregnancy began."

"You don't know one of us used the hoxbomb," Miss Murple protested.

"I didn't say I did," the human replied. "But that's more your kind of weapon than ours. And even if it was one of our people who did it, you're liable to be better than we are at tracking it down. And I hope you want to help, because you know our news media will start screaming it was all your fault."

He might be ugly—he *was* ugly. He might—he *did*—speak an impoverished language. Impoverished or not, he made too much sense in it. From everything Miss Murple knew of human news reporters, they were at least as simplistic and sensational as those of her own folk. She couldn't think of anything worse to say about them, especially when their yattering might help uncoil an interstellar war.

She sighed. Another Snarre' would have smelled the resignation coming off her. Not only would she *not* have a chance to finish the lifey any time soon, but she *would* have to work with this alien. For its benefit, she had to put what she was feeling into plain old ordinary words, too: "I'll do what I can."

Miss Murple wanted to put on eyecovers and go out by daylight the way she wanted to come down with the mange. What choice did she have, though? Crime happened when it happened, not when it was convenient. More resignation poured from her, not that the human could notice. "I'm coming," she said, and hung up. She didn't deactivate the telephone, though. She knew she would have to keep using the stinking thing.

Hospitals gave John Paul Kling the willies. Maternity wards were supposed to be better than the other units. Happy things happened there. Mostly healthy women went in, and they mostly came home with healthy babies.

Yeah, mostly. Not this time, though. Tristar was treating the birthing room as a crime scene. Kling didn't tell the doctors and nurses not to. But this was only where the crime was discovered, not where it had happened. Kling didn't know where that was yet. But he could make a damn good guess about when: just about 280 days earlier.

He talked with the victims. Mrs. Cravath was in no condition to help yet. It wasn't only that she was devastated by what had happened. Going through labor made her look as if she'd just stepped in front of a truck. Kling couldn't really question her.

Her husband wasn't in much better shape. "Why would anyone do this to us?" he asked.

"I don't know, sir," Sergeant Kling answered. "That's one of the things we have to look into. Do you have any personal enemies? Any business enemies? Did you ever do anything to offend the Snarre't?" *Did you ever do anything to really, really piss off the Furballs?* was what he wanted to ask, but this was being recorded, so he didn't.

Jack Cravath just looked bewildered. "I sell scooters. What kind of business enemies am I going to have, for crying out loud? I'm not important enough to have enemies like that. I haven't been in a fight with anybody since the fourth grade, and I lost then. The

Snarre't buy scooters from me every once in a while. You never can tell for sure, but I don't think I ever got 'em mad at me."

"Okay," Kling said, a little wearily. Cravath sounded as ordinary as he looked. But he wasn't, not to somebody—not unless the perpetrator hoxbombed his wife for the hell of it. *Isn't that a lovely thought?* Random criminals were a lot tougher to catch.

"Detective Sergeant Kling, please report to the reception desk. Detective Sergeant John Paul Kling, please report to the reception desk," came from a speaker on the wall.

Kling jumped out of the uncomfortable hospital chair on which he'd perched. "Excuse me," he said. Getting away from what should have been a proud new papa was nothing but a relief.

Going out by day, going into the human part of town, Miss Murple felt as if she'd fallen into a lifey of light. Back when lifeys were fairly new, those had been all the rage for about twenty years. Ambitious directors still turned one out now and then, but the modern imitations didn't come close to the originals.

Part of the allure about lifeys of light was the seamy side of things they portrayed. The other part was the way they portrayed it. As their name implied, they were *daytime* dramas, showing what went on while honest, ordinary Snarre't slept. They blasted you with light, and you couldn't even squeeze your pupils into tight slits against it, because it was *inside* your head. And all that light didn't just wash out the details of what you saw. It somehow mashed down smells, too, and made hearing seem less distinct. Part of that was the director's postproduction work, of course. But part of it was the endless, inescapable, brutal glare.

Humans live this way all the time. It's as natural to them as night and shadow are to us, Miss Murple reminded herself. Another thought followed hard on the tail of that one. *No wonder humans are so stinking weird.*

Her eyecovers and her narrowed pupils warded her from the worst of the daylight. A human with a machine would have insisted that the light level Miss Murple actually experienced was only very slightly higher than it would have been in the middle of the night. But the Bald Ones, again, were stinking weird. The human and the machine wouldn't have understood about the heat of the sun on her fur, or about the way the air felt and smelled when she breathed it, or the simple fact that she was up and about and doing things when she should have been asleep. A lifey of light, all right.

Street signs in the human part of town were also lettered in Snarre'l characters, just as those in the Snarre'i area had transliterations—of a sort—in the odd letters humans used. Most human buildings weren't marked in any way that made sense to her, though. Humans assumed no Snarre' would want anything to do with them . . . and the humans were likely to be right.

Tristar Hospital was an exception. *Area for the Infirm of Three Stars,* read the Snarre'l translation of the English name. No olfactory cues or anything, but what could you expect from humans? At least they made some effort, anyhow. Only in the direst of emergencies would Miss Murple have wanted a bungling, ignorant human physician—but she repeated herself—coming anywhere near her, but the possibility of such an emergency was there.

Another sign in Snarre'l got her to the reception desk. A human behind a machine—one of the devices that were a little like a brain—said, "I greet you," and then, still in Snarre'l, "How may I help you?"

Miss Murple needed a few heartbeats to realize this human actually did speak some of her language. That was a nice touch. "I am looking for Detective Sergeant John Paul Kling," she said, hoping she wasn't mangling the name past comprehension. "It told me we were to meet here."

"One moment, please," the human said, again in Snarre'l. The Bald One spoke in English into something that looked a little like a telephone: "Detective Sergeant Kling, please report . . ." The human looked at something Miss Murple couldn't see, then reported. "He is on the way."

So this Kling was a male. Well, it could only matter to another Baldy. Miss Murple wondered how the functionary knew

Kling was coming. Did the humans have something like Snarre'i hearers that could pick out the male's footsteps from among all the others. Or did they . . . ? Miss Murple's fur rippled in a gesture of uncertainty. When it came to inorganic technology, she knew how little she knew.

Hoxbombs were a different story. The Snarre't had used them for thousands of years, and hadn't needed long to discover they worked on humans, too. It made sense that they should. Even humans understood how tightly biochemistry constrained biology. If things were going to work at all, they needed to work within certain narrow limits.

Creatures with front ends and back ends, for instance, needed hox genes to order their endedness. If you scrambled the sequence of those genes and added a couple in places where they didn't belong . . . If you did something like that, you got a monstrosity like the one that had been born here.

Easy to make hoxbombs—too stinking easy. All you needed was a little technique and a whole lot of malice. Sometimes ideology would do in place of malice. If you wanted to grab attention, not much worked better than a hoxbomb.

"I greet you," said a human with a voice of familiar timbre.

"Hello," Miss Murple replied, glad to get jolted out of her gloomy reverie. She returned to Snarre'l: "You are the human detective, aren't you?"

"That's right. Easier for me to recognize you here than the other way around. I wouldn't have such an easy time in your part of town."

"No, I suppose not." Miss Murple thought telling her own folk apart the easiest thing in the world. Why were humans so inept? That she'd also had trouble recognizing him never crossed her mind.

"I talked to the couple who had the damaged baby—mostly to the father, because the mother's still wiped out," the human said.

Miss Murple had heard somewhere that delivering a baby was difficult and unpleasant for a human female. She'd never expected to *need* to know that, but life was full of surprises. "Any leads?" she asked.

"No known enemies or business rivals. No known trouble with the Snarre't," the other detective replied. "They got blind-sided, in other words."

She heard the human idiom as *The sun rose in their faces.* "That doesn't make this any easier," she said.

"Tell me about it!" the human replied. "It'll take lots of leg-work, trying to nail down everybody they dealt with around the time she got pregnant."

"That may not have anything to do with it," Miss Murple said. "Some hoxbombs are planted in a parent's genes years be-fore the affected offspring are born."

"Oh, my aching back!" the human detective said. "How do you ever catch a perp in a case like that?"

"You said it yourself," Miss Murple replied. "A lot of leg-work—and a lot of lab work."

"This is a mess, Kling," Reiko Kelly said. "You've got to pin it on somebody, or there'll be hell to pay."

"Okay," Kling said obligingly. He stabbed out a forefinger at the lieutenant. "Why'd you do it?"

"What?" Then Lieutenant Kelly got it. "Oh. Funny. See? I'm laughing. How about nabbing the bastard who really did it?"

"Yeah. How about that?" John Paul Kling was not a happy man. "From what the Furball says, it could be anybody who ever had anything to do with the Cravaths. That's sure what it sounded like, anyhow. Happy day, happy day."

"It could be anybody, uh-huh. It could be, but it isn't. It's *somebody,* somebody in particular. Who had a reason to give them grief? Grief!" Kelly shook her head. Long auburn hair flipped back and forth. "What do you do with a kid like that? What do you do *for* a kid like that? You know the worst part? No matter how scrambled it is, it's pretty much healthy. It could be around for a lot of years. How would you like to be Mommy and Daddy, knowing what Junior's like all that time?"

"How's it supposed to eat or talk? You see that thing it's got for a tongue?" Kling said.

"I saw." The lieutenant shuddered. "But surgery can probably fix that. Surgery can fix . . . quite a bit, maybe." She sounded like someone trying to make herself believe it.

John Paul Kling *didn't* believe it, not for a minute. "And all the king's horses and all the king's men / Couldn't put Humpty Dumpty together again," he quoted grimly.

"Yeah, well, if we don't solve this one, that's what Lacanth C is liable to be like," Kelly said. "Plenty of humans will want to pay the Snarre't back for this. Then they'll have an excuse for paying us back, and then . . ." She spread her hands.

"We don't even know they did it," Kling pointed out.

"No, but everybody human here will sure think they did. A hoxbomb? My God!" Kelly rolled her eyes. "Do you want to risk escalation?"

"Nope. If this is such an important case, how come a dumb sergeant catches it?" Kling asked.

"So I can cut your nuts off if you screw up," his superior said brutally.

"You sure know how to pump a guy up so he'll work hard," Kling said.

"What? You think my nuts—well, my tits—aren't on the line, too? Get real," Kelly said.

"Happy day," Kling said again. "Okay, I'll start the legwork. I'm going to assume Beverly Cravath caught the hoxbomb around the time she got pregnant—"

"What if she didn't?" Kelly broke in.

"Then either we're screwed or the case takes a lot longer to solve unless we get lucky," Kling answered. "But I can get a pretty good handle on who all they both had anything to do with from surveillance cameras and stuff. I'll do that first, check those people out, and see what the lab can figure out about the hoxbomb. Maybe they'll be able to work out if it's one of ours or straight from the Snarre't, and how long it was in Mrs. Cravath and Junior." He flinched. No, he didn't like thinking about Junior. Who would?

Grimacing, the lieutenant nodded. "Yeah, go ahead. That's about all you can do, I guess. You think the Snarre't will really help, or are they just blowing smoke?"

"Well, they sent a Furball over in the middle of the day, so that's something," Kling replied. "He—she—it—whatever—didn't seem to like the idea of a hoxbomb much. I sure hope like hell they help. Their genetics labs beat ours six ways from Sunday."

"You're not supposed to say stuff like that," Kelly told him.

"Why not? Isn't it true?" Kling made as if to spit in disgust. "You didn't see us inventing goddamn hoxbombs, did you?"

"We're as smart as they are," Lieutenant Kelly insisted.

"Sure we are. Who says we're not? We do some stuff better than they do. But they do some stuff better than we do, too. Electronics? Yeah, we wallop the snot out of them. Biotech? You know the answer as well as I do."

Reiko Kelly didn't argue with him. Maybe that meant he was unquestionably right. Maybe it meant he'd stuck himself in deep kimchi. Maybe it meant both at once. Sergeant Kling was mournfully certain which way he'd bet.

Miss Murple managed to obtain a tissue sample from the baby human who'd been hoxbombed. The human doctors wouldn't let her take the sample herself—as if she could do anything to the baby now that hadn't already happened to it! She wasn't happy when they did it. Bald Ones knew about as much about genetics as Snarre't knew about popup-blocking software. She only hoped they wouldn't mess up the sample.

She rode her caitnop—a faster though slightly stupider beast than a drof—back to the Snarre'i side of town with nothing but relief. The laboratory, of course, stayed open all hours of the day and night. She turned over the sample to the chief technician on duty: we can call him Louie Pasture. He smelled unhappy when she told him the provenance of the sample.

"Why didn't you take it yourself, so we'd know it was done right?" Louie demanded.

"Because I damn well couldn't," Miss Murple answered. "It

was their jurisdiction. It was their chemical-stinky, glareblind hospital. One of their physicians did it. They don't like us any better than we like them."

"Chemical-stinky is right," Louie Pasture said scornfully. "They try to do analysis like that, you know? With machines and electricity and I don't know what. They make everything as complicated as they can. Amazing they ever got anywhere, when they don't understand bacteria at all."

The Snarre'l word for *bacteria* actually meant something more like *one-celled chemical factories you can train to do your work for you.* That's a lot to pack into one word, but the Snarre't packed a lot into the technology. Bacteria, on their home planet and on Earth, were much more versatile biochemically than plants or animals or fungi or slime molds. From a bacterium's point of view, all the bigger, more highly organized forms of life represented a couple of boring variations on a theme. Either they photosynthesized or they ate things that photosynthesized. But there were more tricks in heaven and earth than were dreamt of in their philosophies.

Some varieties of bacteria used oxygen. Some got along without it very nicely. Quite a few preferred temperatures close to that of boiling water. Those were some of the most valuable, because their biochemistry was so robust. If it weren't, they would have cooked. When you used enzymes and other proteins derived from them down at room temperature, those were often much more potent than the ones taken from less thermophilic beasties.

Miss Murple's race had understood that for a lot of years, and centered an elaborate technology of selective breeding and deliberate mutation on it. Human DNA analysis had scratched the surface of such techniques. From a Snarre' perspective, that was about all humans had done along those lines.

"Well, we'll see what we've got," Louie Pasture said, and placed the sample in a preliminary checking bath, one that searched for contaminants. His nostril slits widened as he sniffed the bath. "Not . . . too bad." His voice was grudging. "And they gave you a big enough sample, didn't they?"

"They measured it by their standards," Miss Murple answered. "If they need this much to know anything—"

"Then they aren't likely to find much no matter what kind of sample they take," Louie finished for her. "Makes it easier for us, though."

He prepared several more baths. Each was a culture of a bacterium primed and tweaked to react to the genetic presence of a particular hoxbomb that hit humans. Miss Murple didn't know whether the bacteria were originally from her own home world or from Earth. For all she cared, some could have come from one planet and some from the other. The only thing that mattered was what they told her—or rather, told Louie Pasture.

The lab tech muttered to himself as he diluted some of the tissue sample from the victim and put a small amount in each bath. "How long do we have to wait for results?" Miss Murple asked. She didn't have much experience with hoxbomb labwork.

"Depends," Louie said. "If it's a common one, we'll find out right away. If it's not one I'm set up for with these baths, we'll have to try some others."

He passed a sniffer over each bath in turn. Its nostril slits were vastly more sensitive than his own—for this purpose. The little animal was bred to detect the metabolic by-products the bacteria in the test bath gave off when they came up against genetic material from their particular hoxbomb type. Humans would have used machines to do the same job. Humans, in Miss Murple's opinion, were fools. Of course natural selection, given several billion years, could come up with more sensitive detectors than engineers could in a few centuries starting from scratch.

For brute force, on the other hand, engineering had advantages over natural selection. Human weapons weren't subtle, which didn't mean they weren't strong. Humans might not be able to ravage a biosphere the way the Snarre't could. But if you could take out a whole planet, or maybe even the star it orbited, what price subtlety?

The sniffer squeaked. "Ha!" Louie Pasture said. "Was it this bath or that one?" He slowly passed the sniffer above each of them in turn. When it went over the second bath, it squeaked again. He stroked it and gave it a treat. It wiggled with delight in his hand.

"Which hoxbomb is that?" Miss Murple asked.

Louie looked at the label on the side of the container, which was a shell bred for internal smoothness and sterility. (The animals that secreted the shells were bred to be tasty. Waste not, want not.) "It's called Scrambled Egg 7—one of the oldest ones around," he answered.

"Could humans have got their hands on it?"

"Oh, absolutely," Louie said. "And if they got a sample, they could probably make it themselves. It's that old and that simple."

"Which doesn't mean it doesn't work," Miss Murple said. "All right—thanks, Louie. I'll pass this on to the Baldy who's tackling the case from their end. And I'll see if he's come up with anything for me."

"Good luck," Louie said. "You know how come humans are bald? 'Cause they're so dumb, they'd get shit on their fur if they had any."

Miss Murple thought that was funny, too. But she did wonder what kind of jokes humans told when no Snarre't were around to hear them.

"Scrambled Egg 7?" John Paul Kling wrote it down. When he got a chance, he would Google it and see what humanity knew about it. In the meantime . . . "How common is it?"

"Very," the Snarre'i detective answered. "It could have been used by one of our people or by one of yours."

"Okay." Kling respected the Furball for mentioning her—his?—own folk first. "Do you have to use it when the pregnancy is new, or is it one of the ones that can sit for a long time before it does what it does?"

"You asked the right questions, anyhow." The alien sounded as uncertain about his competence as he was about its. "Scrambled Egg 7 is designed to damage a very young fetus, not to lie in wait in an ancestor's germ plasm for years or centuries."

"Okay," Kling repeated cautiously. *An ancestor's,* the Snarre' said, not *a parent's.* The human detective sergeant thought again about a hoxbomb lying dormant not just for years but for centuries. He shivered. That sounded like Revenge with a capital R. It also made him think that, even if you were sure you'd whipped the snot out of the Snarre't, you would be smart not to count your chickens before they hatched and you could make sure they didn't have wings growing out of their eye sockets or eighteen legs or anything delightful like that.

"What have you got for me now?" Even through the babelfish, the Snarre' sounded challenging.

"I've been making a list of everybody who was in contact with the Cravaths around the time the hoxbombed baby was conceived," Kling answered.

"Yes, that seems sensible," his opposite number allowed. "May I ask you something else? What is the present status of the youngster?"

"They're planning surgeries to repair as much as they can," Kling said.

"Surgeries?" Either the Snarre' couldn't believe what it was hearing or Kling's babelfish was letting its imagination run away with it. The Furball went on. "I know you do more cutting than we would, but surely not even your surgery can repair everything wrong with that baby."

"I'm no expert, but I wouldn't think so, either," Kling agreed.

"Then why do it? Why not put the poor thing out of its misery? Why not make sure its distorted genes—and with Scrambled Egg 7, they are—never enter your gene pool?"

"Well, I wonder if they're doing the kid a favor, too," the detective said. "But if there's a sound mind inside that—"

"That mess of a body," the Snarre' broke in.

The alien wasn't wrong, either. All the same, Kling said, "Machines—and maybe helper animals—can do a lot. The kid'll never be pretty, but we don't get rid of people for being ugly. If we did, there'd be a lot fewer humans than there are."

"I hardly know where to begin," his opposite number said.

"What you call helper animals . . . You don't know the meaning of the words." That was bound to be true. Humans trained animals to help the disabled. The Snarre't didn't just breed them for that—they bioengineered them. This Snarre' continued. "As for ugly . . . well, each species has its own standards. But if you are saying you don't deliberately improve your own looks and smells—why not? We've been working on it for thousands of years, and the results are striking."

You still don't do a thing for me, sweetie, John Paul Kling thought. But the Furball was right; that went species by species. He said, "Each race has its own customs. Different societies in the same species can have different customs."

What came from the Snarre' was unmistakably a sigh. "No doubt." That had to mean he—she?—figured these human customs were odious or stupid. Well, too damn bad. The alien said, "We should discuss this all another time, at leisure. In the meanwhile, tell me about the people who came into contact with either the male or female parent at about the time the latter discovered she was pregnant."

"Here's the list." Kling sent it to her phone. "As you'll see, most of them are human, but some are, uh, Snarre't." Calling Furballs Furballs in front of a Furball could and would damage your promotion chances.

He watched his opposite number's big, bulging eyes go back and forth as the other detective read the names. The Snarre's phone was supposed to render not only the Roman alphabet but also Snarre'l characters. He hoped it was working up to spec.

After going through the list—or so Kling presumed, anyhow—the Snarre' said, "This is exceedingly comprehensive. How was it generated?"

"Partly by questioning the Cravaths. That wasn't such a good bet, though, because so much time's gone by. The rest came from going through surveillance camera records."

"That must have taken a lot of time."

John Paul Kling shrugged. "A lot of computer time. Not so much for me. The real art is generating the algorithm that makes the computer identify the victims' faces and body dimensions. We had a few false positives a real, live human had to sift through, but not that many."

"False positives?" the Snarre' asked.

"People who looked like the Cravaths to the computer but turned out not to be."

"I see. If you added a smellchecker, you could reduce those to zero, or very close to zero."

"Maybe," Kling said. "We haven't had such an easy time getting our hardware and software to handle smells, though."

"You would do better not to involve machines at all," the Furball said. "If you're trying to detect organic compounds, you need organic detectors."

"Oh, yeah, like I'm really in a position to change policy," Kling said. "We've got a job to do here, not fix the damn world. Suppose you question the Snarre't on the list, and I'll take care of the humans. Then we can talk again—compare notes, you know? Do you think you can do it in four days? You don't have as many of 'em as I do."

"I'll try," the other detective said. "I will speak to you then." The screen on Kling's phone went blank.

Dealing with her own species, Miss Murple at least got to keep civilized hours. She could go out and talk to people while it was decently dark. She didn't miss eyecovers, not even a little bit.

Most of the stalls in the garage of the fancy apartment block where Sharon Rock and Joe Mountain (again, the names are approximate, but they beat the hell out of transcribing funny noises and trying to transcribe smells) lived had caitnops or drofs in them, the way they would have on a Snarre' night back on the home world.

But the shiny new scooter in Sharon and Joe's stall would have announced that they dealt with Bald Ones, even if Miss Murple hadn't already known as much. Everything about their apartment screamed *money*, from the scooter to the way the front door dealt with her.

On the home world, a servant might even have opened that front door. But that sort of thing hadn't come here. Miss Murple didn't miss it a bit, either. But she *was* surprised when a voice spoke in English after she used the knocker: "Hi! With you in a minute!"

She had to wait for the worm in her brain to translate before she understood. Almost any Snarre' would have. Did Sharon Rock and Joe Mountain have more human guests than those of their own kind? Or were they just infatuated with everything the Baldies did? Miss Murple knew which way she would bet.

The door opened. There stood Sharon Rock. Miss Murple had experienced her in any number of lifeys. The real thing was even more depressing. Nobody in real life ought to have such big eyes or such soft fur, or to smell quite so sexy. How did this female get through the night without distracting everyone around her?

"You must be the detective," she said, and her voice really was like pearly bells. "Come in, please." She raised her voice: "Joe! The detective's here!"

"I'm coming." Joe Mountain had been retired for fifteen years, but if you paid any attention to sports you remembered the days when he wasn't. He'd put on a little weight since his athletic days, but not a lot, and he still smelled like a younger male. That was distracting, too.

So was their flat. It was full of human-made gadgets, many of them replacing perfectly ordinary Snarre'i equivalents like heat sensors. There was even a television set from the Bald Ones: a demon's tool if ever there was one, as far as Miss Murple was concerned.

"You're fond of humans, aren't you?" she remarked.

Sharon and Joe looked at each other. "Yes," Sharon answered. "And do you know why?"

"Tell me, please," Miss Murple said.

"*Because they leave us alone.*" Both Snarre'i celebrities spoke together. Sharon went on by herself: "When we deal with the Bald Ones, we're nothing but funny-looking aliens to them. You have no idea how wonderful that is."

"We have privacy with the humans," Joe agreed. "They aren't always sniffing and touching and staring at us. It's—"

"Peaceful," Sharon finished for him. He splayed his fingers in agreement.

"All right." They'd led Miss Murple straight to what she wanted to ask: "Is that why you purchased a scooter from the human named, uh, Jack Cravath most of a year ago?"

"If that's what the human's name was," Sharon Rock said. "We like the scooter."

"We really do," Joe Mountain said enthusiastically. "It's faster than a drof, and cheaper to maintain, too." He'd done a lot of selling pitches, capitalizing on his fame as a sports hero. This sounded like another one.

"Do you know that Jack Cravath's mate was just the victim of a hoxbombing?" Miss Murple said. "She gave birth to one of the most scrambled offspring I've ever had the misfortune of seeing." *And they're trying to keep it alive, too. I don't begin to understand that.*

"How awful!" Sharon Rock breathed. She really sounded and smelled shocked and dismayed. But how many lifeys had she made? She was used to having other people looking over her emotional shoulder, so to speak. Lifey performers got so used to projecting emotions, some of them even gave sniffers trouble.

"We had no idea," Joe said. Miss Murple had to remind herself that he was an experienced actor, too. "Why would anybody want to waste a hoxbomb on a Bald One?"

"That's one of the things we're trying to find out," Miss Murple replied.

Sharon Rock's voice took on a certain edge: "Why are you asking us about all this, exactly?"

"Because you bought your scooter from the male of the family at about the same time as the female became pregnant," Miss Murple said. "This is all routine. You aren't suspects, or even persons of interest, at the present time."

"We don't know much about hoxbombs." Joe Mountain

spoke with more than a little pride. He might have said, *We don't know much about anything*. Some people suspected that athletes *didn't* know much about anything.

"I was in a lifey about them once." Now Sharon Rock sounded almost apologetic, and smelled that way, too. "I liked the plot outline, and the payment was good, so I did the production."

What was *she* saying? *I do know something about hoxbombs, but it's not my fault?* It sounded that way to Miss Murple.

"Your statement is that you weren't involved in conveying the hoxbomb to the human?" the detective said.

"That's right," Sharon and Joe chorused. They didn't sound like liars. They didn't smell like liars, either. Miss Murple sighed. They were performers. If they were performing now . . .

Shoe leather. John Paul Kling looked at the soles of his own shoes. They weren't leather, though the uppers were. Leather or not, they'd taken their share of wear and then some. He tramped along the streets of Latimer's central business district, the part of town that catered to both humans and Snarre't. It was daytime, so not many Furballs were out and about. He did see a few, the way he would have seen a few humans at two in the morning.

He would have wondered what the humans were doing up at two in the morning. He did wonder what the Snarre't were doing now. Unless it looked obviously illegal, it was none of his business.

He checked the map unscrolling on his phone. He needed to turn left at the next corner. After he did, he nodded to himself. There it was, in the middle of the block on the far side of the street. SUNBIRD SCOOTERS, the sign said. He crossed without getting run over by scooters or trampled by caitnops (which tended not to pay attention to humans) or drofs.

A very pretty young woman smiled at him in a friendly way when he walked into Sunbird Scooters. "May I help you, sir?" she said.

"You're not Petros van Gilder," Kling said regretfully. He displayed his badge, after which the young woman didn't look so friendly anymore. He sighed to himself. It never failed. Well, he'd stick to business, then. "I need to ask him a few questions."

"Hold on. I'll get him." She paused. "What shall I tell him this is about?" Kling didn't answer. No, the woman didn't seem friendly at all now. He shouldn't have been surprised. Hell, he *wasn't* surprised. That didn't mean he was happy.

She went into the back part of the building. When she came back, she had a short but well-built man not far from her own age with her. "You're Petros van Gilder?" Kling asked.

"That's right. And you are . . . ?"

"Sergeant John Paul Kling, Exotic Crimes Unit. I'm here because of the hoxbombing suffered by Jack and Beverly Cravath."

"I heard about that. Terrible thing. But what's it got to do with me?" van Gilder said.

"Maybe nothing. Probably nothing, in fact," Kling said. "Just routine right now. I'm trying to contact everyone who had anything to do with either one of them around the time Beverly Cravath got pregnant."

"If it's a hoxbombing, shouldn't you be concentrating on the Snarre't?" van Gilder said. "I mean, they're the ones who're mostly likely to do something like that."

"Believe me, we're looking at that angle, too. So are their own police officials," Kling said.

Petros van Gilder had a fine—almost a professional—sneer. "Oh, yeah. I'm sure they're looking real hard."

"We don't have any reason to believe they're not," said Kling, who worried about the same thing. "Catching whoever did it is in their interest, too."

"It is if a human did it," the scooter salesman said. "One of their own people? Fat chance."

"I'm not here to argue with you. I'm here to ask you about the time you saw Jack Cravath." Kling gave the date and time, adding, "I gather you were both coming home from work."

"I've got to tell you, I don't remember this at all," van Gilder said. "Maybe that makes me a suspect or whatever, but I totally don't."

"You were stopped at a traffic light, together. You said something to each other and shook hands, and then the two of you separated," Kling said.

"How about that?" van Gilder said. "Well, if you've got it recorded, I can't very well tell you you're wrong, but it sure doesn't ring a bell."

"You had your hands in your pockets before you shook hands with Jack Cravath," Kling said. "Why would that have been?"

"Beats me. Probably because it was cold. What's the big deal?" the younger man asked.

"The big deal is that that might have been when you delivered the hoxbomb." Kling took a print from the surveillance footage and showed it to Petros van Gilder. "Do you recognize this jacket? Do you still have it?"

"Is that me?" Van Gilder eyed the photo. It was him, all right—no possible doubt. "Yeah, I've still got that jacket. It's back at my apartment. How come?"

"Because we'd like to examine it for possible presence of the hoxbomb agent called Scrambled Egg 7," Kling replied. "We could get a warrant, but it would be simpler without one."

"You wouldn't have any trouble getting a warrant, either, would you?"

John Paul Kling shook his head. "Not even a little, not on a case like this."

"Go on, then," van Gilder said bleakly. "I don't have anything to do with a hoxbomb."

Pulling his phone out of his pocket, Kling poked a button and spoke into it. "Go ahead, Vanessa." He put the phone away. "Okay. That's taken care of. And believe it or not, Mr. van Gilder, I hope you're telling me the truth."

"I am!" Van Gilder bristled.

Kling held up a placating hand. "Honest to God, Mr. van Gilder, I hope so. But that hoxbomb didn't happen all by itself. Somebody planted it on the Cravaths. And that means somebody is lying to me—or maybe to my opposite number on the Snarre'i side of town. Whoever it is, we'll catch him, or her, or them."

❖

"Evidence? You have evidence?" Miss Murple said eagerly.

The human detective's head went up and down on the little telephone screen, by which he meant yes. "That's right," he said. "A jacket taken from a man who talked with and touched Jack Cravath early enough in his mate's pregnancy to make him a possible hoxbomber. We're taking it to the lab to check for traces of Scrambled Egg 7."

"Don't!" Miss Murple exclaimed. The human had called her in the middle of the day, so she wasn't at her best. But no matter how sleepy she was, the protest automatically rose to her lips.

"Why not?" Even heard through the worm in Miss Murple's brain, John Paul Kling didn't sound happy.

"Will you believe me when I tell you I speak without offense?" Miss Murple waited till the human nodded again before she went on. "I want one of our own labs to do that analysis. We can detect much smaller traces of organics than you can."

"Maybe so," he said. "But it's in your interest to pin this on a human, regardless of who really did it. How far can we trust your lab results?"

Miss Murple bared her teeth in a threat gesture he might or might not understand. She was too angry to care whether he did. "If you don't trust us, why are we working on the same side? For that matter, why should we trust you or anything your labs do?"

She didn't anger him in return. She'd gathered that he wasn't easy to anger—or, at least, that he didn't show his anger. Miserable human telephones wouldn't let her smell him, and humans used nasty chemicals to try to defeat their own odors anyhow. It was as if they wanted to play guessing games with one another.

"Well, you've got a point," Kling said. "Can we share the cloth from the pocket that the hoxbomb would have been in if it was there at all?"

"Why would it have been in that pouch and not some other one?" Miss Murple asked suspiciously.

"Our greeting gesture involves clasping right hands. You will have seen this." The human waited. Miss Murple waved for him to go on; she *had* seen the gesture. Kling continued. "The suspect's right hand would have been in his right jacket pocket. It *was* in his right jacket pocket. We have video confirming that."

They had video for everything, near enough. A human criminal had to be clever and intrepid, or else very stupid. Well, the same held true for her own species. "All right—we can share," she said. "But if we find something and you don't, it isn't necessarily because we're cheating, you know. Your laboratory simply may not be good enough to sniff out what it should."

"Maybe." John Paul Kling didn't seem convinced. "I'll send you the cloth as soon as I can. 'Bye." His picture winked out.

Miss Murple called Sam Spud to let him know what was going on. When the neural net connected the two of them, she didn't just see and hear him at headquarters. She smelled how tired he was, smelled on his breath the cragfruit grub that let him go on longer than he could have without it. She had a real conversation with him, in other words, not the denatured excuse for one she was reduced to with humans.

"Part of this cloth is better than none, anyhow," he said after she summed up what she'd got from Kling. "Maybe the human really did it, and that will wrap things up for everybody."

"We can hope so, anyhow," Miss Murple said. "The next most likely candidates are Sharon Rock and Joe Mountain."

Sam Spud winced as if an impacted anal gland suddenly pained him. "I wish I could pretend I never heard that. Their solicitors have bone hides and giant fangs. The mere idea that they could be suspects is an insult. And what's their motivation?"

"If I knew, I would tell you," Miss Murple said.

"Besides, I think they really are innocent," her superior went on. "They gave the male parent spices as a parting gift when they bought the scooter from him. Our lab and the Baldies' excuse for one both analyzed what's left of those spices. No hoxbomb. I would eat from that spice pack myself."

"Stench! I hadn't heard that." Miss Murple muttered to herself. Then she asked, "Did they ever have anything to do with this other Baldy before, the one the humans suspect?"

"You're reaching, Murple," Sam Spud said. Miss Murple spread her fingers; she knew she was. Sam went on. "Why are you asking me, anyway? Let the miserable Bald Ones figure it out. They're so stinking proud of all their pictures."

The humans had reason to be, too, at least when it came to gathering potential evidence. Bald Ones made all kinds of boastful noises about how free they were. Whether the way they lived measured up to their claims might be a different story.

"I wouldn't be surprised if Sharon and Joe did," Miss Murple said. "They like human gadgets—one sniff at their flat will show you that. And their brain will let us know the truth even if they can lie well enough to beat the sniffers."

"They just got a new one," Sam Spud said. "They used the old one to pay for their fancy new scooter."

"They did?" Miss Murple's ears came erect. "That's interesting. How did you find out?"

"Oh, they were open enough about it," her superior said. "It's in their contract with the Bald One. They know humans keep trying to figure out how brains do the things they do."

"Yes," Miss Murple said uncomfortably. She wouldn't have given humans even an old brain. The unhappy little creature would think it had done something dreadful. Brains were terrific at storing information and passing it along, not nearly so good at figuring out what it meant. They would have been people if they could do that, so the ability had been bred out of them. Well, most of it had, anyway. "So the humans have had it all this time, then?" Miss Murple asked.

"If it's still alive, yes. I don't even know that it is," Sam Spud said.

"If it is still alive, it's probably not sane anymore, poor thing," Miss Murple said. "I'd better find out, though, don't you think?"

"Bound to be a good idea," Sam Spud replied. "Maybe it doesn't know anything interesting, but getting rid of it like that sends up a bad smell."

"Sure does. Makes you wonder what Sharon and Joe are hiding. Even if they aren't hiding anything, it still makes you wonder." Miss Murple sighed. "After the neural net, the human telephone seems worse and worse."

"Well, you're stuck with it." Sam Spud sounded glad he wasn't stuck with it himself. And well he might, too. He took his finger away from the brain on his desk, vanishing from Miss Murple's perceptions.

She called Kling again. "Yeah? What is it?" the human asked.

"We're trying to find out if there was ever any connection between our couple who bought the scooter from the father of the hoxbomb victim and the human you're interested in," Miss Murple said.

"*Are* you? That could be interesting, couldn't it?" John Paul Kling said. "Well, we may have video to let us know."

"Our . . . individuals of interest's brain could have told us, but they used it as the price for the scooter," Miss Murple said. "It may be valuable even now, if it's still alive and close to sane in your hands."

"Ha!" Kling said, a noise the worm in Miss Murple's brain didn't translate. The Baldy went on. "You think they got rid of the evidence on purpose."

"It's a possibility," Miss Murple agreed. Kling could smell which way she was going, anyhow. He might be alien, but he wasn't stupid. That was worth remembering.

"I'll see what we can find out from Cravath," he said. "Talk with you pretty soon. So long." He disappeared as abruptly as Sam Spud had.

Jack Cravath had to check his own credit records before he could tell Sergeant Kling the name of the outfit that bought the Snarre'i brain. The detective showed up at Intelligent Designing with a search warrant, but also with the hope that he wouldn't have to use it.

"We don't see police around here every day," the receptionist remarked. By the way she looked at Kling, she might have just noticed him on the bottom of her shoe. If he had an hour's pay for every time he got that look, he could have quit the force a long time ago. She also sounded dubious as she went on. "What's this all about?"

"It's in connection with the hoxbombing a few days ago," Kling answered.

That made her sit up and take notice. The crime was all over the news. Such things weren't supposed to happen on Lacanth C. Well, what was crime but something that wasn't supposed to happen but did anyway? "How are we involved in that?" she asked.

"I'd rather discuss it with one of your principals, if I could," Kling said coolly. He might have gossiped if she were friendlier. He was as human as anybody else on Lacanth C except the Furballs . . . and even they were closer to apes than angels.

Dr. Brigid Singh was a small, precise blond woman who wore a tailored lab coat. "Oh, yes, I remember that brain," she said. "We're always pleased to acquire them, however we do it." The Snarre't didn't encourage humans to learn more about their technology. Some of the deals Intelligent Designing made were probably under the table.

"Have you still got it?" Kling asked.

"I don't believe so. Let me check." Dr. Singh spoke to a terminal. She turned the display so Kling could also read it. "Unfortunately, we don't. That's getting on toward a year ago now. The brain was old then, which has to be why the Snarre't traded it to Mr. Cravath. And brains never do as well with us as they do with their creators. We lost this one within thirty days."

"Well, hell," Kling said. What he thought was considerably less polite. "Did you learn anything worthwhile from it?"

"We think so. That's proprietary information, though." Dr. Singh was polite, anyhow. If she weren't, she would have told him it was none of his goddamn business.

"Proprietary. Right," he said. "Did you learn anything from it that has anything to do with the hoxbombing at all? No information stays proprietary in the middle of a criminal probe." That wasn't strictly true, not if the people who wanted to hide things had a good lawyer. But it came close enough.

Brigid Singh shook her head. "No, Sergeant. Please accept my assurances that we didn't."

Kling decided he would accept them—for the time being. He went off to the crime lab. One look around was plenty to remind him that Intelligent Designing wasted more money than the department spent. People like Dr. Singh probably looked down their noses at the lab almost as much as the Snarre't did. But, even if it cut corners, it did pretty good work.

"Any signs of hoxbomb material on the pocket I got from van Gilder?" he asked the tech on duty.

"I don't think so," she said. "Let me check." She spoke to the computer, then nodded to herself when it coughed up an answer. "Nope. Far as we can tell, it's clean."

"Okay. Thanks." John Paul Kling wondered what to make of that. The lab did pretty good work, yeah. When it came to genetic material, though, the Furballs did better. Everybody and his stupid Cousin Susie knew that. Of course, the Snarre't had reasons of their own for wanting to find Scrambled Egg 7 in Petros van Gilder's pocket. If he hoxbombed the Cravaths, their people were off the hook. How far could he trust any positive they got?

I'll burn that bridge when I come to it, Kling thought. Then he wondered how he was supposed to cross if he burned the bridge. Things were really screwed up when you couldn't trust your own clichés.

"Ah, yes." Louie Pasture looked as pleased as a toleco chewing pintac leaves. "The human did it. We have a match. We have an unmistakable match, a double match. Scrambled Egg 7, or I'm a Baldy. The humans can't argue with us."

"Their detective said their laboratory didn't find any," Miss Murple told him.

Louie Pasture emitted a rude smell. "Oh, yes, and a whole fat lot humans know about these things, too."

"They aren't dumb," Miss Murple said. "They don't do things the way we do, but they aren't dumb."

"When it comes to stuff like this, they are." The lab tech

pointed to a vat with a soft yellowish glow. "That wouldn't be there if my bacteria didn't detect Scrambled Egg 7. I got a smell check from the sniffer, and confirmed it with the light emitters. I don't waste time with the droppers and reagents and I don't know what all other kinds of foolishness the Bald Ones use. I have the right bacterial strains, and I don't need anything else."

"They'll say your bacteria are wrong. Or they'll say you planted the hoxbomb material. They don't want to believe one of their own could be guilty." Miss Murple didn't want to believe one of her own could be guilty, either. She recognized the possibility all the same.

Louie Pasture gave forth with an even ruder odor. "Yeah, nothing's ever their fault. Now tell me another one."

Humans thought Snarre't were sneaky. Snarre't thought humans were self-righteous. As often as not, both species were right. "I'll pass the report on to their detective," Miss Murple said. "He won't like it, though."

"Too stinking bad," the tech retorted. "Long as they give the unlicked cloaca what he deserves, they don't have to like it. They just have to do it."

"Well, you're right," Miss Murple said.

"But I'm innocent!" Petros van Gilder squawked.

"You're under arrest anyway," Sergeant Kling answered. "I don't much like this, but I've got to do it."

"I didn't do anything to the Cravaths. I didn't have any reason to do anything to them," the scooter salesman said.

"You're a business rival. Maybe that's reason enough. It would be for some people." Kling nodded to the uniformed cops who'd come with him. "Take him away. We'll see what happens when he goes to trial."

"Right, Sergeant," the police officers said. They led van Gilder out of the dealership and into a rara avis on Lacanth C: a fully enclosed car. Doing the perp walk wouldn't help his business any, even if he got off in the end. Sergeant Kling swore under his breath. Sometimes things felt neat and tidy when he closed a case. This wasn't one of those times.

Which didn't necessarily prove anything. Sloppy cases could be as solid as elegant ones. But he liked clean patterns, and he didn't have one in front of him. Well, maybe things would neaten up later.

Next interesting question was where Petros van Gilder got the hoxbomb in the first place. Unless he had a biochemical lab or some trained Snarre'i bacteria back at home—and he didn't, because the police had searched the place—the thing had to come from somebody else.

From a Furball, Kling thought. Maybe from the Furballs his Snarre'i opposite number was already suspicious about.

But even if that was true, what did it mean? Did van Gilder approach them so he could do something horrible to a competitor? Or did they want to do something horrible to a human for reasons of their own? Why would they? Did Cravath do something to them?

Those were all interesting questions. Kling had answers for exactly none of them. He—or rather, the DA—didn't have to prove motive, of course. Opportunity would do, especially if nobody else had that opportunity. That felt sloppy, too, though.

He wondered what he could do about it. Only one thing occurred to him: see what was in the endless hours of surveillance video. Even with computer help, he'd spend a lot of time in front of the monitor for a while. He looked forward to that the way he looked forward to a salpingectomy with nerve enhancement.

Which didn't mean he wouldn't have to do it, like it or not. It was all part of the day's work. It was why the city put credit in his account twenty times a year. Routine *did* solve cases. It wouldn't have become routine if it didn't. That didn't make it any less a pain in the ass, only a necessary as opposed to an unnecessary pain in the ass.

Kling was opposed to all kinds of pains in the ass, necessary and unnecessary. He wondered why the hell he'd ever thought being a cop was a good idea. Somewhere back down the line, he'd been pretty goddamn stupid.

Now, instead of being stupid, he'd be bloody bored. Monitoring surveillance video? About as exciting as pulling up a chair and watching a blank screen. Who didn't know better than to do anything openly nefarious—or even openly interesting—where the cameras were rolling? The Snarre't used different surveillance methods, but over on that side of Latimer you literally couldn't fart without somebody knowing about it.

Back to the office. Kling went through the digital stream from van Gilder's scooter dealership first. He had to identify everybody who came in. The computer helped a lot there. It had—or at least was supposed to have—ID photos of all the humans on Lacanth C. Matching them to faces should have been a piece of cake for software engineers.

And so it was . . . but it was a piece of cake with the occasional pebble in the dough. People were just flat-out better than machinery at recognizing faces. Evolution had been working on it a lot longer than software engineers had. (And hadn't the Snarre'i detective said something like that, in another context?) Instead of naming *a* name, sometimes the computer would spit out two or three or six and let Kling figure out whose photo that really was.

Sometimes he could—and sometimes he damn well couldn't. So he would have several possibilities here and there, and he'd have to track down which of them really had seen van Gilder back most of a year earlier. Half of them wouldn't remember, and half of the other half would lie. Long and bitter experience made him sure of that.

Just to make things even more enjoyable, van Gilder *had* dealt with Snarre't, too. Human technology fascinated some of them. If they decided riding overgrown drumsticks wasn't cool anymore, they went scooter shopping. If they didn't visit Jack Cravath, they visited Petros van Gilder. Often, they visited both of them.

Algorithms for computer recognition of Furballs were light-years behind the ones for recognizing humans. Evolution didn't give John Paul Kling a hand with the aliens, either. He called his opposite number to see what the Snarre't could do.

Miss Murple didn't even try to sound happy. "How am I supposed to recognize Snarre't if I can't smell them?" she demanded.

"Sorry," the human detective said. "We don't record smell. I'm not sure we can record it."

"I understand that," Miss Murple said. "But it's possible—it's likely—that you expect too much from me. I hope I'm a reasonably good investigator. I don't work miracles, though."

"Well, neither do I," the human said. "Can you recognize *any* of your people by sight alone?"

"Maybe." Miss Murple didn't want to say even that much. It would build up the Baldy's hopes. She was much too likely to dash them again right afterward.

He kept trying. He had the virtue, if that was what it was, of stubbornness. "Audio goes with the visuals," he said.

"That may help—a little," she admitted, and sighed. "Well, go ahead. Transmit. This will be dull, won't it?"

"I sure think so. I'd be amazed if you didn't," he said. "Our species are different, but they aren't *that* different."

One thing she quickly discovered: she couldn't identify anybody on a phone screen. There were times when she had trouble telling her own kind from humans. If that didn't say the job was hopeless, nothing ever would.

"Wait!" she told Kling. "You can make these images larger, can't you?"

"Oh, sure," the human detective said. Snarre'i records, like Snarre'i communication generally, were much more involved. The Bald Ones just looked at things and sometimes listened to things. Snarre't experienced sensory records as if taking part in them themselves.

Miss Murple sighed again. "I'd better come over to your side of town to view them properly, then. Can we do this after nightfall?"

The worm in her head interpreted the noise the human made as yet another sigh. "All right," he said. "Come ahead. I'll wait for you. You understand I wouldn't usually be working then?"

"Yes," Miss Murple said. "One of us is going to be unhappy. I would rather not be the one."

"Well, you're up front about it, anyhow. Have it your way," her counterpart said. "Come before it gets too late, if you possibly can."

"I will do that." Miss Murple broke the connection with nothing but relief.

She enjoyed the smooth rhythm of her caitnop's strides as it hurried toward the humans' police headquarters. She had to wear eyecovers even after sundown, because the Bald Ones lit up their district so they could pretend daytime never ended. The caitnop narrowed its eyes to cut down the glare. She stroked the carefully bred creature, and reproached herself for not giving it eyecovers, too. She hoped it wouldn't come to harm.

Humans on scooters stared at her. She'd ridden scooters a few times. To her, the motion seemed unnaturally smooth. And the machines stank of metal and plastic. If Sharon Rock and Joe Mountain wanted one so badly, they were welcome to it, as far as she was concerned. What did a scooter do that a caitnop or drof didn't except break down at random? There wasn't any yummy scootershit to gather up, either.

She had the caitnop wait in the best-shadowed spot she could find near the police headquarters. Things proved even brighter inside the human-filled building than they were outside. Even with eyecovers, she started getting a headache.

Kling was considerate enough to wait for her in a dark room. Would she have given a Baldy the converse courtesy? She doubted it. "Let's have a look at these images," she said without a great deal of hope.

The screen where the human displayed them was much larger than the one on the phone. The sound quality was much better, too. All the same, Miss Murple was so conscious of the alien presentation, she was sure she wouldn't be able to identify any of the Snarre't on the video.

She was sure, but she was wrong. She thought she would have recognized Joe Mountain if he weren't with Sharon Rock. But Sharon Rock, even by herself, even without her preposterously sexy aroma, would have been unmistakable. If she wasn't a perfectly made female, Miss Murple had no idea where she fell short of the ideal. Seeing her made the Snarre'i detective all too conscious of her own shortcomings.

Kling sat there watching the stunner without being stunned. Miss Murple would have thought Sharon Rock could stimulate even someone of a different species. Evidently not. The lifey performer had said she and Joe Mountain liked to get away from the constant attention their own kind gave them. She must have meant it.

"These are the Snarre't who bought a scooter from the parent of the hoxbombed infant," Miss Murple said, and then, "Why *don't* you dispose of the malformed thing, anyway? It's horrible."

"To look at, yeah," Kling said. "But its brain seems to work." Miss Murple bared her teeth. It didn't seem reason enough. The human detective went on. "I will tell you something interesting about these images. Do you see the jacket on the chair behind van Gilder? Behind the human suspect, I mean?"

"I see something on the chair. Is it a, uh, jacket?" Miss Murple said. The worm in her brain had trouble with words like that, words that stood for things humans used and her own kind didn't.

"It's a jacket, all right," the Baldy said. "And unless I'm very much mistaken, it's the jacket with the pocket that had the hoxbomb material inside."

"Really?" Miss Murple said. Kling nodded instead of spreading his fingers, but she knew what that meant. She watched a little more. "There is no sign that the Snarre't are tampering with the jacket in any way."

No sooner had she spoken than the human on the screen said, "Excuse me for a moment. I have to go void some waste."

That was how the worm in Miss Murple's head turned his words into Snarre'l, anyhow. He hurried away, leaving Sharon Rock and Joe Mountain alone in his bare little office.

No sooner had he gone than Joe Mountain picked up the jacket. "What a silly thing," he said. "See what happens when you don't have hair?" He admired Sharon Rock's soft, silky pelt. Well, who wouldn't?

"Bald Ones are pathetic beasts," Sharon agreed. Miss Murple found herself thinking the performer was right. But what did that have to do with the price of grubs? Sharon Rock gestured imperiously to Joe Mountain. "Let me see that thing."

"Here. You're welcome to it." He handed it to her.

The human detective stared at the video screen with Miss Murple. "Do the Snarre's hands go in the pocket? Hard to be sure, isn't it?"

The Snarre'. He hasn't the faintest idea who Sharon Rock and Joe Mountain are. Maybe he's lucky. "It is hard, yes," Miss Murple said. "Can we get a better view? Will that give us what we need to know?"

"Can't tell till we try," the human answered. He spoke to the plastic-stinking computer as if it were alive. It responded as if it were alive, too. The image of the jacket and then of that one pocket slowed down and grew till it almost filled the screen. It stayed center, too, no matter how Joe Mountain and Sharon Rock moved it. This technology might be inorganic, but it was formidable in its own way. "Hold it right there!" her opposite number said sharply, and the image froze.

"Well, well," Miss Murple said. Two of Sharon Rock's fingers—the fur on them was noticeably darker and thicker than it was on Joe Mountain's—did find their way inside that flap of cloth. "Isn't that interesting?"

"Interesting. Yeah." Kling told the computer to take special note of that sequence. Miss Murple had no idea how it would, but she believed that it would. The human gave his attention back to her. "Looks like it wasn't our boy after all."

"You don't know that yet," Miss Murple said. "The visual

shows fingers in there, yes. It doesn't let us smell or taste those fingers to know for sure what's on them. I should also let you know that these Snarre't are celebrities." *Oh, yeah. Just a little.* "They are rich and famous. They will have the best barristers around. They won't be easy to convict."

To her surprise, the human detective started to laugh. To her even greater surprise, he seemed to have trouble stopping. At last, shaking his head, he succeeded. "Some things really don't change between species, do they?" he said. "The ones who are rich and famous think they can get away with anything *because* they're rich and famous."

"That happens with us, yes," Miss Murple agreed. "Does it happen with you, too?"

"Oh, just a little," he answered.

She needed a moment to smell out the sarcasm. Then she went on. "As I said, though, we still don't know for sure that it happened here."

"Let's watch the rest of this sequence," Kling said. Miss Murple wondered if he'd got his name because of the way he clung to a case. He spoke to the computer once more. The image shrank to the usual size of the surveillance video. The speed at which it moved also returned to normal.

Joe Mountain's ears twitched. "I hear him coming back," he said.

Quickly, Sharon Rock returned the jacket to the chair where it had lain. It wasn't quite in the same position it had been in before, but Petros van Gilder never noticed. When the human suspect walked into his office, all he cared about was selling the two Snarre't a scooter. Even without smell, he radiated disappointment when they declined to buy.

"Maybe you'll come back another time," he said as Sharon Rock and Joe Mountain made their good-byes.

"Maybe we will." Sharon Rock wasn't laughing, but she wasn't far from it. She and Joe Mountain left the office. Van Gilder kicked at the floor. A Snarre' wouldn't have shown frustration the same way, but Miss Murple knew it when she saw it.

"You say that isn't proof?" said the human detective. "Well, maybe it isn't, not by itself, but it sure smells funny, don't you think?"

So even noseblind Bald Ones used a phrase like that! Miss Murple's fingers spread to show she thought he was right. "It is not proof. It sure does smell funny."

"All right. What's our next move?"

"You can bring this record with you, right?"

"Oh, sure."

"Good. I think you'd better show it to my superiors."

Kling sighed again. "I ought to be going home," he grumbled, perhaps more to himself than to her. "Well, I'll put it on a laptop. If we can wrap this up, we'd better do it."

"You think like an investigator, sure enough," Miss Murple said.

John Paul Kling didn't like night-vision goggles. If you went over to the Furball side of town, though, you needed them—which was putting it mildly. The Snarre't didn't believe in streetlights. They didn't believe in a big way. It was as dark as the inside of a cow over there.

The Snarre't didn't think so, and neither did their genetically engineered mounts. Their big eyes (which glowed in the dark like cats') glommed on to every available photon. Human scientists insisted that night-vision goggles grabbed even more, but you couldn't have proved it by Kling.

"Here we are," the detective said. Kling could read Snarre'l pretty well, even if he didn't speak it worth a damn. The sign in front of the low, sprawling building said PURSUIT AND CAPTURE OF CRIMINALS. The last word literally meant *stinkers*. The Snarre't thought with their noses a lot of the time.

A Furball sat just inside the entrance. His pose bespoke boredom. If he didn't look like every desk sergeant ever born . . . He stopped looking bored as soon as he saw—and probably smelled—Kling. "What the—?"

"This is my associate on the hoxbomb case," said the detective with whom Kling was dealing. "He has evidence the ones high in the tree need to smell right away."

"How can you smell human evidence?" Either the sergeant didn't know Kling was wearing a babelfish or he just didn't care. Kling would have bet on number two. The Snarre's wiggle was the Furball equivalent of a shrug. "Well, go on. You're supposed to know what you're doing." Even through the babelfish, his tone said it wasn't his problem.

Neither Snarre'i eyes nor night-vision goggles could work with *no* photons. Dimly glowing plates—bioluminescence—set into the walls and ceiling every so often doled out a few. Snarre'i cops bustled along the hallways much like their human equivalents. Some of them stared at Kling. Some just ignored him. He didn't know what that meant. He wasn't real anxious to find out, either.

"Here." His Snarre'i—colleague?—walked through an open door. "This is my boss."

John Paul Kling went in, too. By size, the new Furball was a male. "I greet you," Kling said in Snarre'l.

"Hello," the male replied in English, then went back to his own language: "What have you got? Hoxbomb business, yes? Yes, of course." He answered himself. "Why else would a human be here?"

"Yeah, it's hoxbomb business, all right." Kling opened the laptop, made sure the screen was set to a brightness level Snarre't could stand, and fired it up. He ran through the surveillance video in Petros van Gilder's office, and especially through the part where the two Snarre't handled van Gilder's jacket.

"You sniff out—well, you see—who they are," his opposite number said to her boss. "But we have to drop on them just the same." Kling hid a smile. How many times had he heard conversations just like that back at his cop shop? More than he could count—he was sure of that.

"Are you sure we can, with just human evidence?" the boss cop asked.

"Once we interrogate them, we'll get the stench of lying soon enough," Kling's counterpart said. "Then they're ours."

"But she's a lifey performer," the boss cop said. "She can fake those odors."

"Well enough to fool you or me, maybe. I'll be damned if I believe she can fool a sniffer for long." The other Furball seemed very sure of herself.

"Hmm." The boss cop thought it over. "Yeah, I guess you're right." He didn't sound thrilled about it. A human lieutenant would have decided the same thing, and would have sounded the same way, too. High-profile cases always meant trouble. The boss cop swung his big eyes toward John Paul Kling. "Want to come along for the bust? Maybe you'll intimidate them."

"Sure. Why not?" Kling found himself grinning. Not many of his fellow bulls would have a story like this one. That was almost as good a reason to go with the Furballs as the chance to close the case. He wondered if the aliens would see—or smell—things the same way. He thought they would. Plainly, they were cops, too.

The human-made scooter wasn't in the garage at Sharon Rock and Joe Mountain's apartment house. Miss Murple muttered under her breath. That meant the suspects were out doing whatever important people did.

Miss Murple had started muttering when she discovered that reporters were at the apartment house ahead of her and her comrades and Kling. Somehow, the newsies always sniffed out stories. Somebody back at the station was probably counting her sweetener right now.

"What are you doing here?" one of the reporters called. "Sharon and Joe are at Famous Janus's party."

"*Whose* party?" Sam Spud asked. Famous Janus wasn't famous to him. As far as Miss Murple could tell, Famous Janus was famous for being famous, not for anything he'd actually done. To a lot of Snarre't, that didn't seem to matter. Miss Murple wondered whether humans were so foolish. She doubted it. Maybe not being driven by odors had occasional advantages. Famous Janus *smelled* as if he ought to be important, so people naturally thought she was.

"Do you know where Famous Janus lives?" Miss Murple asked the reporters.

They laughed at her. She'd known they would. But they told her where, too, and then they set out to beat her over there. Sam Spud turned to the Baldy. "Can your gadget go faster than drofs and caitnops?" he asked.

"And how many can it carry?" Miss Murple added.

"It will take both of you, if you want to ride with me," Kling said. "I don't know whether it will go faster than your animals or not. Shall we find out?"

"Yes!" Miss Murple and Sam Spud said together.

"Hop on behind me, then," the human told them. "You'll have to let me know when to turn. This isn't my part of town, re-member."

"We'll do it," Miss Murple promised. "Just hurry."

"Right," Kling said. "Grab the handholds. Are you ready? . . . We're going, then."

Go they did. Maybe scooters were faster than caitnops. They were certainly smoother. The sheet of clear stuff in front of the human kept the wind from buffeting the riders the way it would have on a caitnop at full gallop. The remaining breeze was almost enough to sweep away the stench of metal and plastic that clung to human-built machinery. Miss Murple could see why Sharon Rock and Joe Mountain might want a scooter. What she couldn't see was why they'd hoxbombed the male who sold it to them.

Had the Baldy somehow offended them? If he had, then the human suspect was working with them and not their dupe. Did they do it because Cravath *was* a human and they thought they could get away with it? Was it a thrill crime? Maybe answers would come out one of these days. In the meantime . . .

"Go right!" she shouted. Kling swung the scooter into a tight turn. It raced past a reporter on a tired old drof. The female looked and no doubt smelled unhappy. Miss Murple yelled for another turn. The human made that one in the nick of time, too. He started passing caitnops, even though they were running flat out. If you wanted to get somewhere in a hurry, a scooter could do the trick.

"Stop!" Sam Spud said. The human did, so abruptly that Miss Murple was squeezed against his back for a moment. It wasn't pleasant. Like most of his kind, he wore chemicals to mask his odors. They made contact with him less pleasant than his natural aromas would have, even if those were sharply alien. Humans didn't just ignore their noses. They seemed to go out of their way to torment them.

A large, muscular bouncer advanced on the scooter. "Who are you people?" she demanded. "And what are you doing with a Baldy?"

"Don't get personal, Furball," Kling snapped. Humans could be speciesist, too.

"We are investigators," Miss Murple said. "We are seeking two people said to be at Famous Janus's party. You will be sorry if you interfere."

"Very sorry," Kling put in, drawing his hand weapon. The noise it made when it went off might kill a Snarre' even if the pellet it hurled missed. Bald Ones more readily survived such shocks. They were a coarse-grained race.

The bouncer recognized the weapon for what it was. She retreated in a hurry. Miss Murple and Sam Spud uncurled their ears as the human stowed the vicious thing once more.

"What's going on?" someone shouted as a caitnop panted up. "Have they dropped on Sharon and Joe yet?"

"Sharon and Joe!" the bouncer exclaimed.

"Don't warn them," Miss Murple said. *Her* weapon launched a casing full of paralyzing spores. It took a couple of heartbeats to kill, but no longer than that. The bouncer didn't warn anybody.

Miss Murple, Sam Spud, and the human rushed up the stairs and into Famous Janus's flat. Several different illegalities were going on there. *Another time,* Miss Murple thought. The music was almost as loud as Kling's weapon would have been. Joe Mountain was licking the ear of a female not a quarter as attractive as the one he had. Sharon Rock was dancing with a weedy little male; if they'd danced any closer, they would have been mating.

"I arrest you," Sam Spud told Joe Mountain. "Go quietly, or else." Joe looked astonished. He smelled that way, too. He hadn't even noticed the investigators coming in.

Miss Murple, then, had the pleasure of seizing Sharon Rock. The lifey performer looked and smelled amazed, too. "You'll never pin this on us," she said.

"That's what you think," Miss Murple said. "We have plenty of human evidence to convict you. Come along quietly, or you'll stay quiet for good."

"Human evidence," Sharon Rock said scornfully. "What's human evidence worth?"

"Your neck," Miss Murple answered. "Nobody takes kindly to hoxbombing. You won't get away with it, even if you passed the stuff on to a Bald One."

"We didn't do anything." Sharon rather spoiled that by adding, "You haven't met our solicitors and barristers yet, either."

"Quietly, I told you," Miss Murple said. And Sharon Rock, who was used to taking direction from the finest lifey visualizers on Lacanth C, took it from a no-account investigator, too.

Once Miss Murple and Sam Spud and Kling brought their prisoners out onto the lawn in front of the apartment house, things got no easier. By then, the reporters had got there. The brains they carried recorded the images of the captured stars and sent them into the neural net. All the jaded sensation-seekers would be stinking up their flats in excitement.

How much trouble *would* Sharon and Joe's attorneys be able to kick up? Once the sniffers decided they smelled guilty, not much. It didn't matter how famous you were, not if you smelled like someone who'd done it. If the sniffers *didn't* think Sharon and Joe had done it, Miss Murple knew what her career was worth, and Sam Spud's with it.

Attorneys being what they were, the Snarre't might even go after the human investigator. Could they get him? Miss Murple didn't know, but she had her doubts. If he was wrong about Sharon and Joe, he'd made an honest mistake. The Bald Ones wouldn't be upset about it, not when he was dealing with Snarre't.

Miss Murple's big boss wouldn't care whether her mistake was honest or not. Who would have imagined that humans might have better sense than her own folk?

"You helped us. You truly did," Sam Spud told Kling. He sounded startled. Miss Murple couldn't blame him. She also had trouble believing a human could be worth anything. But this one had pulled his weight. He really had.

"Yeah, well, you guys did all right, too," he replied. Maybe it was the imagination of the worm in Miss Murple's brain, but he also seemed surprised. She wondered why. Didn't he know the Snarre't had a strong sense of justice? And if he didn't, how ignorant *were* humans, anyhow?

"Looks like you're off the hook," John Paul Kling told Petros van Gilder as he set the scooter seller free. "You were just a sucker for the Furballs."

"I said so," van Gilder replied with as much dignity as he could muster. "I don't have anything against Jack and Beverly. I feel bad things turned out the way they did." He shook his head. "I don't feel bad. I feel awful. That poor kid."

"Yeah." Kling didn't like thinking about the Cravaths' baby. He wished he'd never set eyes on it. By all accounts, it was healthy and showed every sign of being smart even if it was a monster. The Snarre't still thought humans were crazy for not getting rid of it. They had a point, too. Could any kid be smart enough to make up for what the hoxbomb had done to this one's flesh? It wasn't easy to believe.

"I talked with my lawyer," van Gilder said.

That snapped Kling's attention back to the here-and-now in a hurry. "Yeah?"

"Yeah." Van Gilder nodded. Then he sighed. "He said you had probable cause to arrest me, so suing you wouldn't go anywhere. But some people will think I did it whether you let me go or not. This is bound to louse up my business. How do I get my good name back?"

Unfortunately, that was a damn good question. Kling did the best he could with it: "The people who matter to you know you're innocent. For the others, for the yahoos, you're a nine-days' wonder. They'll forget you as soon as something else juicy hits the news. You may get hurt for a little while, but I don't think it'll last long."

"I hope not." Van Gilder didn't sound convinced. Kling didn't push it, because he wasn't a hundred percent convinced, either.

He led the scooter dealer to the station's front door. A police vehicle waited outside to take van Gilder home. He could get on with his life—as much of it as he had left after getting busted for a really nasty crime. He was liable to be right; the stain from the arrest wouldn't vanish overnight.

A few minutes after van Gilder disappeared, Kling's phone rang. He pulled it out of his pocket. "Sergeant Kling speaking."

"This is Jack Cravath, Sergeant." Sure enough, Cravath's face looked out of the phone screen at Kling. "I just called to say thank you."

That didn't happen every day, or even every tenth of a year. "You're welcome," Kling answered. "I'm only sorry we had to meet the way we did."

"Yeah, me, too," Cravath said. "So the Snarre't turned the hoxbomb loose for the hell of it, did they? And it found some-body it could bite?"

"That's what they're saying," Kling answered. "Maybe I be-lieve 'em, maybe I don't. It puts the best face on what they did—that's for sure."

"Why would anybody do such a horrible thing?" Cravath asked.

"My guess is, because they thought they could get away with it," John Paul Kling said. "Maybe they didn't figure the hoxbomb would find anybody vulnerable. Maybe. But why put it in van Gilder's pocket if that wasn't what they wanted?"

"Why do it at all?" Jack Cravath repeated.

"Most likely, they didn't think we could catch them. They like our machines, remember," Kling said. "They probably guessed we couldn't figure out what was going on, because we didn't have the right kind of technology to handle it. If we'd tried by ourselves, they might have been right, too. But hoxbombing is so evil, their own people got involved, and that made the difference."

"A lot of humans wouldn't admit it," Cravath said.

"Yeah, well . . . You know what else?" Kling said. "The Furballs think we're just as dumb and weird as we think they are. And a lot of the time, they're right. So are we. But I'll tell you something funny. That one Snarre'i detective, I wouldn't mind working with her again. How's that for peculiar?"

"I deal with them all the time," Cravath said. "They aren't so bad. They're no worse than we are."

"Come on—which is it?" Kling asked. Cravath didn't see the difference. But then, he wasn't a cop.

❖ THE END OF THE WORLD ❖

Kristine Kathryn Rusch

THEN

The air reeked of smoke.

The people ran, and the others chased them.

She kept tripping. Momma pulled her forward, but Momma's hand was slippery. Her hand slid out, and she fell, sprawling on the wooden sidewalk.

Momma reached for her, but the crowd swept Momma forward.

All she saw was Momma's face, panicked, her hands, grasping, and then Momma was gone.

Everyone ran around her, over her, on her. She put her hands over her head and cringed, curling herself into a little ball.

She made herself change color. Brown-gray like the sidewalk, with black lines running up and down.

Dress hems skimmed over her. Boots brushed her. Heels pinched the skin on her arms.

No spikes, Momma always said. *No spikes or they'll know.*

So she held her breath, hoping the spikes wouldn't break through her skin because she was so scared, and her side hurt where someone's boot hit it, and the wooden sidewalk bounced as more and more people ran past her.

Finally, she started squinching, like Daddy taught her before he left.

Slide, he said. *A little bit at a time. Slide. Squinch onto whatever surface you're on and cling.*

It was hard to squinch without spikes, but she did, her head tucked in her belly, her hair trailing to one side. More boots stomped on it, pulling it, but she bit her lower lip so that she wouldn't have to think about the pain.

She was almost to the bank door when the sidewalk stopped shaking. No one ran by her. She was alone.

She flattened herself against the brick and shuddered. Her skin smelled of chewing tobacco, spit, and beer from the saloon next door.

She had shut down her ears, but she finally rotated them outward. Men were shouting, women yelling. There was pounding and screaming and a high-pitched noise she didn't like.

If they found her flattened against the brick, they'd know. If they saw the spikes rise from her body, they'd know. If they saw her squinching, they'd know.

But she couldn't move.

She was shivering, and she didn't know what to do.

NOW

The call didn't come through channels. It rang to Becca Keller's personal cell.

Chase Waterston hadn't even said hello.

"Got a problem at the End of the World," he'd said, his usually self-assured voice shaky. "Can you get here right away? Just you."

Normally, she would have told him to call the precinct or 911, but something stopped her. Probably that scared edge to his voice, a sound she'd never heard in all the years she'd known him.

She drove from the center of downtown Hope to the End of the World, a drive that, in the old days, would have taken five minutes. Now it took twenty, and the only thing that kept her from being annoyed at the traffic were the mountains, bleak and cold, rising up like goddesses at the edge of Hope.

Hope was a mountain city, but its terrain was high desert.

Vast expanses of brown still marked the outskirts of town, although the interior had lost much of its desert feel. By the time she passed the latest ticky-tacky development, she hit the rolling dunes of her childhood. Even though she had on the air-conditioning, the smell of sagebrush blew in—full of promise.

If she kept going straight too much farther, she'd hit small windy roads filled with switchbacks that led to now-trendy ski resorts. If she turned right, she'd follow the old stagecoach route over the edge of the mountains into the Willamette Valley where most of Oregon's population lived.

The End of the World was an ancient resort at the fork between the mountain roads and the old stagecoach route. At the turn of the previous century, some enterprising entrepreneur figured travelers who were taking the narrow road toward the Willamette Valley would welcome a place to spend, rest and recover from the long dusty trip.

Now bumper-to-bumper traffic filled that wagon route, which had expanded to a four-lane highway. Hope actually had a real rush hour, thanks to expatriate Californians, retired baby boomers, and ridiculously cheap housing.

Chase was rebuilding the resort for those baby boomers and Californians. For some reason, he thought they'd want to stay in a hundred-year-old hotel, with a view of the mountains and the river, even in the heat of the summer and the deep cold of the desert winter.

Becca steered the squad with her left hand and fiddled with the air conditioner with her right, wishing her own car was out of the shop. No matter what she did, she couldn't get the squad car cooled. Nothing seemed to be working properly. Or maybe that was the effect of the heat.

It was a hundred and three degrees, and the third week without rain. The radio's most recent weather report promised the temperature would reach one hundred and eight by the time the day was over.

Finally, she reached the construction site.

Chase had set up the site so that it only blocked part of the ever-present wind; as a consequence, the dust billowed across the highway with the gusts.

The city had cited Chase twice for the hazard, and he'd promised to fix it just after the Fourth of July holiday. It looked like he'd been keeping his word, too. A huge plastic construction fence leaned against the old building. Graders and post-diggers were parked on the side of the road.

Nothing moved. Not the cats Chase had been using to dig out the old parking lot, not the crane he'd rented the week before, and not the crew, most of whom sat on the backs of pickup trucks, their faces blackened with dust and grime and too much sun. She could see their eyes, white against the darkness of their skins, watching her as she turned onto the dirt path that Chase had been using as an access road.

He was waiting for her in the doorway of what had once been a natatorium. Built over an old underground spring, the natatorium had once boasted the largest swimming pool in Eastern Oregon. There was some kind of pipe system that pumped water into the pool, keeping it perpetually cold. In the natatorium's heyday, the water had been replaced daily.

Behind the natatorium was the old five-story brick hotel that still had the original fixtures. No vandals had ever attacked the place. Even the windows were intact.

Becca had gone inside more than once, first as an impressionable twelve-year-old, and ever since, part of her believed the rumors that the hotel was haunted.

She pulled up beside the natatorium door, in a tiny patch of shade provided by the overhanging roof. She got out and the blast-furnace heat hit her, prickling sweat on her skin almost instantly. Apparently the air conditioner had been working in the piece-of-crap squad after all.

Chase watched her. His lips were chapped, his skin fried blackish red from the sun. He had weather wrinkles around his eyes and narrow mouth. His hair was cropped short, and over it he wore a regulation hard hat. He clutched another one in his left hand, slapping it rhythmically against his thigh.

"Thanks for coming, Becca," he said, and he still sounded shaken.

The tone was unfamiliar, but the expression on his face wasn't. She'd seen it only once, after she'd told him she wanted out, that his values and hers were so different, she couldn't stomach a relationship any longer.

"What do you got, Chase?" she asked.

"Come with me." He handed her the hard hat he'd been holding.

She took it as a gust of wind caught her short hair and blew its clipped edges into her face. She slipped the hard hat on and tucked her hair underneath it, then followed Chase inside the building.

It was hotter inside the natatorium, and the air smelled of rot and mold. She usually thought of those as humidity smells, but the natatorium's interior was so dry that it was crumbly.

The floor was shredded with age, the wood so brittle that she wondered if it would hold her weight. Most of the walls were gone, the remains of them piled in a corner. Chase had gutted the interior.

When she had been a girl, she had played in this place. Her parents had forbidden her to come, which made it all the more inviting. The rot and mold smells had been present even then. But the walls had still been up, and there had been some ancient furniture in here as well, made unusable by weather and critters chewing the interior.

She used to stand inside the entrance with the door open, the stream of sunlight carrying a spinning tunnel of dust motes. When she closed her eyes halfway, she could just imagine the people arriving here after a long day of travel, happy to be in a place of such elegance, such warmth.

But now even that sense of a long ago but lively past was gone, and all that remained was the shell of the building itself—a hazard, an eyesore, something to be torn down and replaced.

Chase's boots echoed on the wood floor. He led her along the edges, pointing at holes closer to the center. She wondered if any of his employees had caused the holes, walking imprudently across the floor, foot catching on the weak spot, and then slipping through.

He was taking her to the employees' staircase in the back. When they reached it, she saw why. It was made of metal. Rusted metal, but metal all the same. Someone had recently bolted the stairs into the wall, probably under Chase's orders. A metal hand railing had been reinforced as well.

Chase looked over his shoulder to make sure she was following. She caught a glimpse of something in his face—reluctance? Fear? She couldn't quite tell—and then, as suddenly as it appeared, it was gone.

He went down the steps two at a time. She followed. Even though the handrail had been rebolted, the metal still flaked under her hand. The bolts might hold if she suddenly fell through the stairs but she wasn't sure if the railing would.

The smell grew stronger here, as if the mold had somehow managed to survive the dry summers. The farther down she went, the cooler the air got. It was still hot, but no longer oppressive.

Chase stopped at the bottom of the stairs. He watched her come down the last few, his gaze holding hers. The intensity of his gaze startled her. It was vulnerable, in a way she hadn't seen since their first year together.

Then he stepped away so that she could stand on the floor below.

The smell was so strong that it overwhelmed her. Beneath the mold and rot, there was something else, something familiar, something foul. It made the hair rise on the back of her neck.

"That way," Chase said, and this time she wasn't mistaking it. His voice was shaking. "I'll wait here."

She frowned at him, and then kept going. The floor here was covered in ceramic tile, chipped and broken, but sturdy. She wondered what was beneath it. Ground? Old-fashioned concrete? Wood? She couldn't tell. But the floor didn't creak here, and it felt solid.

A long wall hid everything from view. A door stood open, sending in sunlight filled with dust motes, just like she remem-

bered. Only there shouldn't be sunlight here. This was the basement, the miraculous swimming pool, the place that had helped
make the End of the World famous.

She stepped through the door.

The light came from the back wall—or what had been the
back. Chase's crew had destroyed this part of the building.

The basement of the End of the World was open to the air for
the first time since it had been completed.

That strange feeling she'd had since she reached the bottom of
the stairs grew. If the basement wasn't sealed, then the stench
shouldn't have been so strong. The old air should have escaped,
letting the freshness of the desert inside.

Some of the heat had trickled in, but not enough to dissipate
the natural coolness. She stepped forward. The tile on the other
side of the pool was hidden under mounds of dirt. The pool itself
was half destroyed, but the cat that had done the damage wasn't
anywhere near it. She could see the big tire tracks, scored deeply
into the sandy earth, as if the cat itself had been stuck or if the operator had tried to escape in a hurry.

They had uncovered something. That much was clear. And
she was beginning to get an idea as to what it was.

A body.

Given the smell, it had to have died here recently. Bodies
didn't decay in the desert—not in the dry air and the sand. Inside
a building like this, there might be standard decomposition, but
considering how hot it had been, even that seemed unlikely.

She'd have to assume cause of death was suspicious because
the body had been located here. And then she'd have to figure out
a way to find out whose body it was.

She was already planning how she'd conduct her case when
she stepped off the tile onto a mound of dirt and peered into the
gaping hole, and saw—

Bones. Piles of bones. Recognizable bones. Femurs, hip bones,
pelvic bones, rib cages. Hundreds of human bones. And more
skulls than she could count.

She rocked back on her heels, pressing her free hand to her

face, the smell—the illogical and impossible smell—now turning her stomach.

A mass grave, of the kind she'd only seen in film or police academy photos.

A mass grave, anywhere from seventy-five to a hundred years old.

A mass grave, in Hope. She hadn't even heard rumors of it, and she had lived here all her life.

"Son of a bitch," she said.

"Yeah," Chase said from the stairs, "I couldn't agree more."

THEN

The screaming sent ripples through her. She couldn't complete the change. She couldn't even assume the color and texture of the brick.

Tears pricked her eyes. Tears, as big a giveaway as her hair, her fingers, her ears. Somehow, when she stopped the spikes, she stopped all her abilities.

Or maybe it was just the fear.

A door squeaked open, then boots hit the sidewalk. Polished boots with only a layer of black dust along the edge. Men's boots, not the dainty things Momma tried to wear.

She tried to will the shivering away, but she couldn't.

She couldn't move at all.

Not that she had anywhere to go.

She could only pray that he wouldn't look down, that he wouldn't see her, that she would be safe for just a little longer.

NOW

Becca stared at the hole. She couldn't even count all the skulls, rising like white stones out of the dirt. Not to mention the rib cages off to one side or the tiny bones lying in a corner, bones that probably belonged in a hand or a foot.

She couldn't do much on her own. But she could find out where that stink was coming from.

She turned around and headed for the stairs.

Chase tipped his hard hat back, revealing his dark eyes. "Where're you going?"

"To get some things from my evidence bag," Becca said.

"You're not going to call anyone, are you?" he asked.

She stopped in front of him. "I can't take care of this alone. You should know that."

He leaned against the railing, that assumed casual gesture that meant he was the most distressed. "This'll ruin me, Becca. Half my capital is in this place."

"You told me no good businessman ever invests his own money," she snapped, mostly because she was surprised.

He shrugged. "Guess I'm not a good businessman."

But he was. He had restored three of the downtown's oldest buildings, making them into expensive condominiums with views of the mountains. Single-handedly, he'd revitalized Hope's downtown by adding trendy stores that the locals claimed would never succeed (yet somehow they did, thanks to the "foreigners," as the Californians were called) and restaurants so upscale that Becca would have to spend half a week's pay just to eat lunch.

"You knew I'd go by the book when you called me here," she said, more sharply than she intended. He'd gotten to her. That was the problem; he always did.

"I thought maybe we could talk. They're old bones. If we can get someone to recover them and keep it quiet—"

"How many workers saw this?" she asked. "Do you think they'll keep it quiet?"

"If I pay them enough," he said. "And if we move the bones to a proper cemetery."

"Is that what you think this is?" she asked. "A graveyard?"

"Isn't it?" He seemed genuinely surprised. "It was so far out in the desert when this place was built that it's possible—no, it's probable—that the memory of the graveyard got lost."

"I saw at least two rib cages with shattered bones, and several skulls looked crushed."

His lips trembled, and it was a moment before he spoke. "The equipment could have done that."

But he didn't sound convinced.

"It could have," she said. "But we need to know."

"Why?" he asked.

She looked over her shoulder. That patch of sunlight still glinted through the hole in the wall. The dust motes still floated. If she didn't look down, the place would seem just as beautiful and interesting as it always had.

"Because someone loved them once. Someone probably wants to know what happened to them."

"Someone?" He snorted. "Becca, the pool was put over a tennis court that was built at the turn of the twentieth century. No one remembers these people. Only historians would care."

He paused, and she felt her breath catch.

Then he said, "This is my life."

He used a tone and inflection she used to find particularly mesmerizing. Once she told their couples therapist that with that tone, he could convince her to do anything, and that was when the therapist told her that she had to get out.

"It's a crime scene," Becca said, knowing that the argument was weak.

"You don't know that for sure, and even if it is, it's a hundred years old," he said.

"Then what's the smell?"

He frowned, clearly not understanding her.

"This is a desert, Chase. Bodies buried in dirt in a dry climate don't decay. They mummify."

He blinked. He obviously hadn't thought of that.

"And," she said, "even if they had decayed because of some strange environmental reason particular to this basement, they wouldn't smell after a hundred years."

That guarded expression had returned to his face. Only his eyes moved now.

"Maybe it's something small," he said. "A mouse, someone's lost cat."

She shook her head. "Smell's too strong, and over the entire building. If it were something small, the smell would have faded back when you broke open that wall."

"Not when it was dug up?" he asked, seeming surprised.

"No," she said. "Is that when you first smelled it?"

"That's when they called me."

They, meaning his crew. She frowned at him, wondering if he was going to blame them.

But for what? A smell?

She'd have to find the source before she made assumptions.

And that, she knew, was going to be hard.

THEN

A hand touched her shoulder. A human hand, warm and gentle. Another shivery ripple ran through her. She still had a shoulder; she hadn't gotten rid of that either. How silly she must look, plastered against the brick wall like a half-formed younglin.

Screams still echoed. The shouts had died down, although sometimes they rose up altogether, like a group excited about something.

"You're one of them, aren't you?"

Male voice, human, just as gentle as the hand. She couldn't stop shivering.

"I won't hurt you."

She resisted the urge to rotate an eye upward, so that she could see more than the boot.

"But you better come with me before they find you."

That did startle her. Her eye moved before she could stop it. It formed above her shoulder. He jumped back slightly when her eye appeared, but his hand never left her skin, even though it was finally turning tannish-red like the brick.

She'd seen him before. Daddy had laughed with him in the good days. He had slicked-back hair and a narrow face and kind eyes.

He crouched beside her, and looked right at her eye, like it didn't bother him, even though she knew it did. He wouldn't've jumped like that if it didn't.

"Please," he said, "come with me. I don't know when they're coming back. And someone might see us. Please."

She had to form a mouth. Her nose remained, tucked against her stomach from when she'd formed a ball, but her mouth had disappeared when she had tried to take on the appearance of the wooden sidewalk.

It took all her strength to make the mouth come out near the eye, and from the look of disgust that passed over his face, she still didn't look right. Her hair was on the other side of her body, and her eye was just above her shoulder. The mouth had probably come out on what would have been her back if she put herself together right.

Right being human.

That's what Momma said.

Momma.

"Please," he said again, and this time, she heard panic in his voice.

"Stuck," she said.

"Oh, Christ." He looked up and down the street, then at the buildings across from it.

He seemed younger than she remembered, or maybe she was as bad at telling human ages as Momma was.

"How do we get you unstuck?" he asked.

She didn't know. She'd never been like this, not this scared, not all by herself.

She tried to shrug and felt her other shoulder form into the wood. A splinter dug into her skin, and her entire body turned red with pain.

"What a mess," he said, and she didn't know if he meant her or what was going on or how scared they both seemed to be.

She willed herself to let go, but she was attached to the brick, and she'd lost control of half her body functions. Daddy said fear would do that.

Whatever happens, baby, he'd say, *you have to trust us. You have to believe we'll get together again. Let that be your strength, so that you never, ever succumb to fear.*

But he'd been gone for a long time now. And Momma hadn't come back for her, even though people were screaming.

The man tried to pry a flat corner of her skin from the edge of the brick. She could feel the tug, saw his face scrunch up in disgust when he got to the sticky underneath part.

"How'd you get there?" he asked.

"Squinched," she said.

"Squinched." He didn't understand. And she spoke his language, she knew she did. She formed the right mouth, she'd been using the words for a long time now, and she knew how they felt inside her brain and out.

"Can you show me?" he asked. "Can you squinch onto my arm?"

She wasn't supposed to squinch to a human. Momma was strict about that. Like there was something bad about it, something awful would happen.

But something awful was happening now.

The screams . . .

"No," she said, even though that had to be a lie. Momma and Daddy wouldn't forbid something if she couldn't've done it in the first place.

"God," he said, then looked down the street where the screams had come from. Where the shouts had grown more and more angry every time they rose up.

Right now, it was quiet, and she hated that more.

She hated it all.

"Stay here," he said.

He stood up, letting go of her shoulder. The warm vanished, and the fear rose even worse. Her other shoulder disappeared, and she felt the spikes, threatening to appear.

She had to close both eyes and will the spikes away.

When she opened the eyes, he was gone.

She moved the eyes all over her skin, looking for him, and she didn't see him at all.

The street was still empty, and too quiet.

Then, faraway, someone laughed. A mean, nasty, brittle laugh.

She folded her ears inside her skin, and willed herself flat, hoping, this time, that it would work.

NOW

Becca climbed the stairs, clinging to the handrail, the rust flaking against her palms. She had to call for help. At most, she needed a coroner, and probably a few officers just to search for the source of that smell.

But she felt guilty about calling. Chase used to talk about restoring the End of the World when she'd met him. He had brought her out here on their first date, even though she'd told him that she had explored the property repeatedly when she was a child.

Maybe they'd be able to keep this out of the paper, particularly if it turned out to be a graveyard or a dumping ground. But even that probably wouldn't happen.

The newspapers seemed to love this kind of story.

If she reported this, she would condemn Chase's project to a kind of limbo. With so much capital invested, he probably couldn't afford to wait until the legal issues were solved.

She almost turned around to ask him how much time he could give them, but then she'd be compromising the investigation. For all she knew, there was a recently killed human beneath that dirt, and someone (Chase?) was using the old bones to hide it.

Then she shook her head. Not Chase. He was manipulative and difficult, moody and untrustworthy, but he wasn't—nor had he ever been—violent.

She sighed and continued up the stairs. Much as she wanted to help him, she couldn't. She had an obligation to the entire community.

She had an obligation to herself.

The wind hit her the moment she stepped outside. Bits of sand stung her skin, sticking to the sweat. Even with the sun, it now felt cooler out here because of that wind.

The construction workers watched her. She didn't know most of them; the town had grown too big for her to know everyone by sight like she had when she was a child. Many of these workers were Hispanic, some of them probably illegal.

Hispanics expected her to check their papers. She was supposed to do that, too, although she never did. She didn't object to people who worked hard and tried to improve their lives.

With one hand, she tipped her hard hat back and nodded toward the workers. Then she opened the squad's driver's door, and winced at the heat that poured out at her. She leaned inside, unwilling to go into that heat voluntarily, and grabbed the radio's handset.

She paused before turning it on, knowing that even that momentary hesitation was a victory for Chase.

Then she clicked the handset and asked the dispatch to send Jillian Mills.

Jillian Mills was the head coroner for Hope and the surrounding counties. She actually worked the job full-time, but her assistants were dentists and veterinarians, and one retired doctor.

"You want the crime scene unit?" the dispatch asked. It was standard procedure for a crime scene unit to come with the coroner.

"Not yet," Becca said. "I'm not sure what exactly we have here, except that it's dead."

Which was technically true, if she ignored all the crushed and broken bones.

"Tell her to hurry," Becca added. "It's hot as hell out here and there's a construction crew waiting."

That usually worked to get any city official moving. Lately, the "foreigners" had taken to suing the city if their emergency or official personnel delayed moneymaking operations, even for a day.

Chase would never do that—he knew that getting along with the city helped his permits go through and his iffy projects get approved—but Becca still used the excuse.

She didn't want to be here any longer than she had to be.

She stood, lifted her hard hat, and wiped the sweat off her forehead. Then she closed the door and leaned on it for a moment.

The End of the World.

She wondered if Chase had ever thought that the name might have been prophetic.

THEN

She had shut down her ears, and didn't know he had come back until the sidewalk shook. She opened her eyes. He stood above her holding a long wooden box. His mouth was moving, but he kept looking down the street. A single bead of sweat ran down one side of his face.

She unfolded her ears and said, "What?"

"This can hide you," he said, setting the box on the sidewalk. He glanced at her, then looked away. "Think maybe you can squinch into it?"

He set the box in front of her. It did cover her strangeness from anyone who didn't look too hard.

Her shivering stopped.

"Maybe," she said.

"Well," he said, wiping at that drop of sweat, "the sooner you squinch, the better chance I have of getting you out of here."

That brought a shiver. She looked at the box, saw it had some dirt inside. He had taken it from some kind of storage.

If she just thought about the box—not the screaming (which seemed to be gone. How come it was gone?)—not the way Momma's hand had slipped through hers, not the fall against the sidewalk, not the bruises that still radiated through her skin, maybe then she could squinch to it.

She'd have to stare at it like a younglin, think only of the box, only of the box and becoming part of it . . .

A long, drawn-out scream sent ripples through her.

"Jesus," the man said and closed his eyes.

She squinched. She had to. The scream made her move. She

squinched to the edge of the box, then cowered against the back, just a blob, as small as she could make herself.

"Mister?" she said and heard the terror in her voice. She wasn't sure why she was trusting him, but she didn't have a lot of choice.

That scream sounded like Momma.

He looked down, and his shoulders slumped.

"Thank God," he said, and picked up the box.

He tucked it under his arm like it weighed nothing, and hurried back through the door.

NOW

Jillian drove the white coroner's van. Becca's breath caught as she scanned the windshield, looking for an assistant.

There was none. Either none was available, or dispatch conveyed the message about the stalled work crew.

Either way, Becca was grateful.

She finished the last of her water and tossed the bottle in a nearby recycling can. She had waited up here, unwilling to go back inside without Jillian.

Or maybe she had just been unwilling to talk to Chase again.

He had come out of the basement after about ten minutes. He saw her near the squad, shook his head slightly, and sat against one of the cats, his face half-hidden by shade.

She didn't go to talk to him and he didn't talk to her. They both knew the futility of these kinds of arguments. Once again, she and Chase were on opposite paths, and trying to influence each other would only end in misery.

Jillian got out of the van. Her hair was already pulled back and tucked in a net. She was small and delicate, with skin so pale that it looked almost translucent. She seemed fragile at first glance, but Becca had seen her split a corpse's rib cage open with her bare hands.

"What've we got?" Jillian asked.

"I'm not sure," Becca said. She grabbed the flashlight and

gloves from her own kit, as well as the portable radio, and led Jillian inside.

Chase didn't come with them. Instead, he watched them go with the same wariness that his crew had.

Becca was relieved. She half-hoped that Jillian hadn't noticed him, standing in the shade.

They were on the steps to the basement before Jillian said, "This is Chase Waterston's project, isn't it?"

"Unfortunately," Becca said.

Jillian knew Becca's troubles with Chase. It had been no-nonsense Jillian who had listened to Becca's difficulties extricating herself from Chase's world.

I'm a cop, she used to say, it seemed, during every conversation. *I shouldn't be so easily influenced.*

We all have a hook that'll draw us in, Jillian would respond. *He knows how to find yours.*

He did, too. There should have been a full team here, along with a crime scene unit.

Jillian probably knew it just from the smell.

She stopped at the bottom of the stairs and looked around. "Where's the body?"

Becca had thought about how to answer that one the entire time she waited for Jillian.

"I don't know where the smell is coming from," Becca said. "But it's not our only problem."

Jillian glanced at her sideways. Becca sighed and led her to the hole.

The sun had moved away from the gap in the wall, no longer sending rays filled with dust motes into the basement. But the light was still strong enough that she didn't need a flashlight to lead Jillian to the dig itself.

"Chase thinks this is an old cemetery," Becca said as she approached.

"You don't," Jillian said, slipping on her gloves. "So you brought me here to be the bad guy."

Maybe she had. Or maybe she just needed someone between her and Chase, someone sensible.

She didn't say anymore. Instead, she turned on the flashlight and turned it to the rib cages and skulls.

"Mother of God," Jillian said, touching the tiny cross she wore around her neck even though her Catholicism had lapsed decades ago. "This is going to take an entire team."

"I know," Becca said softly.

They stared for a long moment. Becca didn't move the flashlight beam. Finally, Jillian grabbed it from her and swept the entire large hole. The light caught more bits of bone, scattered throughout the dirt.

"How'd you even get me here?" Jillian asked. "Chase has to know this will ruin him."

"He does." Becca didn't look at Jillian.

"So he called you." Jillian shook her head. "Bastard."

"Jillian, it's bad enough."

"It's bad enough that he thought you'd cover for him."

"He didn't ask that," Becca said. But he had, hadn't he? He asked that this be handled quickly and discreetly and with a minimum of fuss.

Although he stopped arguing when she explained about the smell.

God, she was still making excuses for him, and she was no longer married to him.

"He knows I'm going to do this right."

"He knows," Becca said.

"That'll mean the media'll get wind."

"Let's try to prevent that as long as possible."

"So Chase can save his ass?"

"So that we don't have weirdos contaminating the crime scene."

"You didn't block it off. It could be contaminated now."

Becca pursed her lips. "I kept an eye on everyone."

"I hope so," Jillian said. "I'm going to call for backup."

Becca nodded.

Jillian didn't move, even though she said she was going to. "You think maybe you should take yourself off this investigation?"

Becca'd been thinking about it. "I'm the only qualified investigator we have. Everyone else has been promoted through the ranks and most haven't even completed the crime lab courses."

Because they were only offered in the Willamette Valley, and that was more than two hours from here. The department couldn't afford to lose personnel for days on end just so they could have classes in criminal justice, classes that the chief—a good ole boy who had worked his way through the ranks without a damn class, thank you—didn't believe anyone needed, not even his detectives.

Jillian sighed. "You've got a conflict."

"No kidding."

"What if Chase is behind the smell?"

Becca almost said, *He isn't,* but she stopped herself in time. "I'll treat him like anyone else."

Even though she knew that was a lie the moment she spoke it.

"No matter what you do, everyone'll think you're soft on him."

"Then everyone'll be supervising me, won't they?" Becca snapped.

Jillian put a hand on her shoulder. "Rethink this, Becca."

Becca sighed. "If this starts leading to Chase, maybe I will."

THEN

He didn't take her very far. She managed to squinch part of herself to the edge of the box, away from his arm, and pop an eye forward.

They were inside the bank. No one else was. The afternoon sun filtered through the large windows, illuminating heavy wooden desks, the wide row of grills that people got money out of or put money into, the safe just behind the far door.

Momma and Daddy had brought her in here early, as part of

her training in being "normal," and they explained how banks worked. She used to come with Daddy when he had money to deposit, but Momma didn't know how to get it when he went away.

Momma said maybe he got it, but she had that funny sound in her voice, the one that meant she really didn't believe it. She always sounded sad when she spoke of Daddy, and after a few weeks she stopped speaking of him at all.

"We can't go far yet," the man said softly. "People'll wonder. They'll probably wonder why I was here, and not with them."

He said that last very very softly. She almost didn't hear him.

He hurried to one of the desks near the back and set the box underneath it with one edge sticking out.

"If you can, stay low," he said. "It's safer."

She wondered how he knew. Maybe he could tell her what was going on. Because she didn't know at all.

Momma had smelled the smoke—they were burning Shantytown, that's what Momma said. Then Momma grabbed her hand and pulled her to the safe place. She didn't know where that was either or what would happen there.

They had run to the middle of the town, right near the fanciest store where Momma liked to look through the windows sometimes, when people caught up to them. Running, just like they were, only the other people's running was different somehow.

Momma seemed really scared now. Some of the men smelled of kerosene, and one of them was laughing even though the edges of his hair were burned off.

Momma pulled and pulled and she was having trouble keeping up and people started looking at them and Momma tried to pick her up but didn't have the strength and she tried to keep running but she couldn't—she was getting so tired—and then she tripped and her hand slipped and she couldn't see Momma and she didn't know where Momma went or why she hadn't come back . . .

Except for the scream.

She closed her eyes and rolled up into a ball.

She wanted to forget the scream—and she couldn't, no matter how hard she tried.

NOW

Jillian started to work in one corner of the hole. Becca took the far end of the basement, using her nose first to see where the smell was the strongest.

Jillian had contacted the crime scene investigators, asking for everyone, not just the folks on duty, and another detective as well as some officers to handle the interviews. Becca should have done that. But, Jillian was covering for her, getting her off the hook with Chase.

Both of them knew that Chase was their key. He could set up a lot of roadblocks to the investigation, and he might have already done so. Becca would try to find out by remaining close to him, buddying him, if she could.

Jillian wasn't sure that Becca could manipulate him. Hence the request for the second detective.

Becca wasn't going to argue with that. She wasn't going to argue with any of it. Not yet.

But she did know Chase well enough that if he had committed a crime, he wouldn't have done it in a way that would jeopardize his entire fortune. He would have covered it up creatively, hidden the body in the desert or taken it to Waloon Lake or maybe all the way to the ocean.

He was too smart to kill someone and call her. He knew that he could manipulate her, but he also knew that the manipulation didn't always work.

She took a breath. Olfactory nerves grew used to smells, but this one—the smell of rot and decay—never completely vanished. You could live with that smell for weeks, and still recognize it, unlike most other odors. It just wouldn't seem as strong to you as it did to others.

It was still new to her at the moment. And it wasn't coming from this part of the basement.

She walked the perimeter, sniffing the whole way, knowing she would regret this part of the investigation. Strong smells like this remained in the nose and in the memory. She would be able to recall it whenever she wanted.

As if she would want to.

After she finished, she walked the perimeter again, careful to use the same tracks.

Finally, she said, "It's coming from the hole."

"Of course," Jillian said. She had started in one corner as well.

When Becca spoke, Jillian leaned back on her knees, resting on her heels. She brushed her hands together, then surveyed the mess before them.

"This is beyond me," she said. "I don't know how to proceed. We're not trained for a disaster this big. I'm going to have to call in experts."

"Experts?" Becca asked.

"There are people who specialize in dealing with mass graves."

"So this is a graveyard."

Jillian looked at her, as if Becca had deliberately misunderstood her.

"Mass graves. Like the ones they found in Iraq or Bosnia or Nazi Germany."

Becca let out a small breath. The air felt thicker than desert air usually did. The odors seemed to be getting worse, not better.

"That's what this is? Some kind of massacre?"

"I don't know for sure. That's why I want experts. You want to protect Chase—"

Becca started to deny it, but then that was silly. She did want to protect Chase.

"—but I want to protect Hope."

It took her a moment to understand what Jillian had said.

"Protect Hope?"

"How much history do you know, Becca?" Jillian asked.

"I know enough to know that no large group of people has ever died in Hope. We still have our Chinatown, and we were one of the havens for blacks, even when the state of Oregon constitutionally banned them. We had that in school, Jillian, remember?"

"You think people talk about massacres?"

"I think people remember," Becca said. "I think massacres don't stay buried forever."

Jillian looked at the dirt before her. A snapped femur was only a few inches from her knees.

"You're right," Jillian said. "Nothing stays buried forever."

THEN

"What's your name?" he asked after a little while.

The question startled her. The bank had been so quiet, even though she had kept one ear on top and an eye prepared. She could control the ears and the eyes and sometimes the mouth, she still hadn't got control over anything else. The shivers came less now, but they still came, rippling through her like water.

"It's okay," he said. "We're still alone."

Like that was the problem. Her family tried not to name anything. Names made items rigid.

Still, her parents had given her a human name, just so everyone had something to call her, and Momma said the name made it easier for her to keep her shape.

Maybe if she thought about it now . . .

He peered under the desk. "Are you all right?"

Another shiver ran through her and she couldn't find her mouth.

"They're not back yet."

If she had her human form, she'd nod. But she didn't. Then the mouth popped forward.

He moved away so fast, he hit his head on the underside of the desk.

"Sorry," he said. "You startled me."

"Sarah," she said.

"Hmm?" He frowned at her.

"I'm Sarah."

"Oh." He bit his upper lip, pulling it inward. "I'd thought maybe something more unusual."

He stopped talking, wiped a hand over his mouth, then smiled. "How about a last name?"

A second name. Momma had explained that, too. The second name described your clan. The first name was just yours, special to you.

"Jones," she said.

"Jones," he repeated. "Earl Jones's daughter?"

Earl was what they decided to first-name Daddy.

"Yes," she said.

"Christ." He wiped his hand over his mouth again, then looked behind him. "I'm Jess Taylor. Your dad may have told you about me."

Daddy hadn't said anything about anybody, at least not to her.

"Have you seen him lately? Your dad? I have some things for him."

Tears filled her eye, then her face—her human face formed on top of her skin.

Jess Taylor's expression froze, then he smiled, even though the smile didn't look real.

She wanted to wipe the tear from her eye, but she didn't have hands. One started to form, and she willed it away. She had to stay small.

"You haven't seen him, have you?" Jess Taylor said.

"Not for a long time."

Jess nodded. Then he frowned. He slid out from under the desk, and sat up straight. She squinched to the edge of the box. He was looking at the windows, and now that he thought she couldn't see him, he looked scared.

"What's going on?" she asked.

"I think they're coming back," he said. "We have to move you. Can you stay quiet?"

She had stayed quiet until he asked questions. But she didn't say that. Instead, she said, "Yes."

"I'm going to cover the box. Don't do anything till I come for you. Okay?"

"Okay," she said, even though she was supposed to do two things. She was supposed to stay quiet, and she was supposed to hide.

Maybe when "they" came back, they would bring Momma. Maybe when "they" came back, she could finally go home.

NOW

Becca and Jillian used police tape to rope off the natatorium. The crime scene squad could handle the upper floors. Becca saw no point. She knew that the body—the body that was freshly dead—was in that dug-out pool.

Jillian was in the basement of the nat, laying out a grid to work the scene. She knew that some of the work would come from the local team. Even though she had been on the phone with the state crime lab, she had no idea when the experts would show up.

The sooner the better, she had told them, but both she and Becca knew that would make no difference. Oregon was a low tax state, and rather than fund important services, Oregon cut them. The lab was now working two years out on important cases, and had no extra people to spare for a mass grave deep in the desert.

The lab certainly didn't have the funds to hire an expert. Becca would have to take the money from the police budget or she would have to get the Hopewell County District Attorney to pay for the expert before any charges were filed.

Jillian's office certainly didn't have the money either. She barely had enough funds for an assistant.

Even though other officers showed up, as well as two more detectives, Becca handled most of the interviews herself. She didn't want her colleagues scaring off the illegals. She needed them for the investigation.

Using a mixture of English and her high school Spanish, she managed to interview the work crew. She also learned that several employees had vanished when Chase stopped work and called her, even though he had told them that they'd be safe.

Of course, no one would give her their names. The handful of employees who'd even mentioned their friends seemed frightened by the slip.

Even the legal citizens—the ones who had citizenship, and the ones who were born in the United States—insisted on showing her their papers. A number of the men slapped the documents with their hands and said, "Test them. Go see. Everything is in order."

When she finished, she went to her car, got some more bottled water, and took a long drink. Yes, the heat had drained her, as had the bodies and the destruction below, but the fear she'd encountered had stressed her as well.

People shouldn't be afraid to answer simple questions. Not in America.

She sighed, then drank half a bottle. She set the bottle inside, shielded her eyes, and looked at the sun.

It seemed to have a long way to go before it disappeared behind the mountains. Usually she liked the long days of summer. Today she didn't.

"Can I send everyone home now?" Chase asked from behind her.

"Yeah." She didn't turn around. She hated his habit of standing so close that she would have to bump into him if she made any movement at all. "Unfortunately, they're not going to be able to work here tomorrow."

"Or the next day or the next. What's this about experts?"

"Jillian can't handle the site," Becca said. "She thinks its historical, and if she does something wrong . . ."

He sighed. She knew he understood historical red tape. He had to deal with a lot of it just to get this project off the ground.

"What else do you need from me?" he asked.

I need you to back up a little, she thought. But she said, "I need to see the rest of the buildings. Are any of them locked?"

"A few," he said. "Mostly the theater, which is where I've been storing supplies, and of course, the hotel."

He had stepped into her line of sight, apparently annoyed at the way she had been ignoring him. Since he was no longer so close, she could turn.

"The hotel?" she asked. "Why the hotel? We all went in it as kids."

"And had no idea how much the front desk or the doorknobs were worth. I've got a lot of subcontractors here, and it's a different time." He ran a hand through his hair. Sweat glistened on some of the strands. "I'm going to lose it all, aren't I?"

She felt a pull of empathy. "I don't know. You will be able to work here again. I'm just not sure when."

He gave her a bitter smile. "Yeah."

She wanted to ask him if he regretted calling her. She wanted to ask if he was going to blame her for the loss of time.

But she didn't. The old Becca would have asked those questions.

The new Becca had to pretend she didn't care.

THEN

Jess Taylor picked up the box and carried it under his arm. It bumped as he walked. She lost her mouth and one of the eyes as more shivers ran through her.

She wondered: If she thought of herself as Sarah, would she change into a little human girl?

She wasn't willing to try it. Not yet.

He set her next to a filing cabinet. The grained wood reminded her of her father. He'd turned into an expensive filing cabinet once, just to show her how to change into common business objects.

For an emergency, he had said. *For an emergency.*

Like this one. If she had thought it through, she should have turned into something free-standing like the filing cabinet, not something long and seemingly never-ending, like the sidewalk or the bricks.

It was different to become a permanent nonbreathing object.

Then she had to cling to it, and somehow sleep. But younglins couldn't do that. It was a skill they got when they grew older.

At her age, only a parent could help her make a sleep-change.

Jess Taylor dropped a towel over the box. The towel smelled of soap and sweat. It filtered the light.

She closed her remaining eye, and listened as voices filled the bank. Excited voices, male—

"What the hell were you thinking staying here?"

"You missed it all."

"You should've seen it. They didn't even look human by the end."

The voices mingled and tumbled and twisted into jumbles of words. But *they didn't even look human* got repeated over and over again.

They didn't look human, her people. Not when they were filing cabinets or chairs or wooden sidewalk planks. But they breathed and fought and *thought*. Wasn't that enough?

Daddy had said it would be, that day so long ago:

We have no choice, he'd said to the assembled. *We're stuck here, and Hope is better than the other cities I've seen. We're isolated. If we can work our way into their minds as laborers, maybe they'll accept us. They can't see how we live—we'll have to live as they do. But after a while, they'll get used to us. They'll see how similar we are. We breathe like them, fight like them, think like them. They'll understand. They'll accept. Given time.*

Time passed. And nothing changed. They had their own part of town, near the Chinese who also refused to talk to them.

And when one of their own got attacked outside of town and couldn't hold her shape—

Well, Momma wouldn't talk about it. And everyone expected Daddy to do something, but he didn't know what to do. He told Momma that. He didn't know.

Then he left. Looking for someplace new, Momma said. But she didn't believe it anymore. Daddy would have come back long before now. And he hadn't.

And Jess Taylor looked sad when he learned her human name. Because of Daddy.

The voices continued:

"They scream real pretty though."

"One of them even begged."

"You shoulda been there."

And then Jess Taylor said, "Someone had to watch the bank."

"If I didn't know better," said a deep male voice, "I'd check the vault. What a perfect time to take something for yourself."

"Please do, sir," Jess Taylor said. "You won't find anything awry."

He sounded funny. Like they'd hurt his feelings. Humans did that to each other sometimes. But they always made up. Never with her people, but with each other.

Only no one apologized to Jess Taylor. Instead, the conversations changed. Someone walked past her and she heard a dial spin, then something metal click. She swiveled her good eye, but she couldn't see through that towel Jess Taylor had thrown over her box.

"Looks fine to me, sir," said another voice.

"Double-check," said the deep voice.

"I don't receive credit for staying, do I?" Jess Taylor asked in that low tone he'd used when he called his own people names.

"What's that?" the deep voice asked.

"Nothing, sir."

More clicking. The sound of boots against marble. Low voices, counting and comparing.

Then deep voice—"Looks like you did well, Taylor."

"Thank you, sir."

"Just don't act on your own again, all right? Makes people suspicious. Especially in these times."

"Do you think I'm one of them, sir?"

"If you were, you'd be dumb to stay," deep voice said.

"Besides," said another voice, "we seen you hurt. You don't change like those demons do."

"I suppose," Jess Taylor said in that low tone again.

"You don't approve," said the other voice.

"Of what?" Jess Taylor asked, louder this time.

"What we done."

For a long moment, Jess Taylor didn't answer. She held her breath, hoping he wouldn't make a mistake. If he made a mistake, they would find her.

Finally, he said, "I don't know what you did."

"We could show you," one of the men said, and everyone laughed.

"Thank you," Jess Taylor said without any warmth, "but I think I can figure it out for myself."

NOW

The front door of the hotel was padlocked. The window shutters were closed and locked as well. When she was a child, this looked like an abandoned building, spooky but still alive. Now it seemed like an unloved place, a place that would fall apart if someone took the locks off.

Becca watched Chase remove the padlock and hook it onto his belt. Then he swung back the metal latch and pushed open the double mahogany doors.

Those Becca remembered. She remembered the way the light filtered out through them, more dust motes than she thought possible dancing inside of it.

Small windows stood beside the door, but on the far side of the lobby, floor-to-ceiling windows opened onto the expanse of high desert and the mountains beyond. The glass was old and bubbled and clearly handmade. Such dramatic windows were rare a hundred years ago, and had been—in the hotel's heyday—one of its main drawing points.

She stepped inside, sneezed at the smells of mold and dust, and watched as more motes swirled because of her movements. Chase stood beside the door, watching her.

"We were going to revive it all," he said. The past tense saddened her. "Imagine that desk over there, polished, with employees behind it, computers on top, guests in front."

She looked at the registration desk, scratched and filthy, which wrapped around an entire corner of the room. Behind it were old-fashioned mail slots, some filled with stuffing from chairs—probably rat or mouse nests.

"People would look at the view, or go to the natatorium for tennis or a swim. We were going to build a golf course alongside this, and build homes, just outside the line of sight of these windows." Chase stuck his hands in his back pockets. He stared at the view, still sending in light despite the dirty glass. "It would have been spectacular."

"It's not over yet, Chase," Becca said. It wasn't like him to give up so easily. In fact, this speech of his was making her suspicious. Had he run into financial difficulty? Had he put something recently dead among the bones as a way of notifying the authorities? Did he want the project to end for a reason she didn't understand yet?

"Half my crew probably ran away today."

"They aren't the people who will restore this building."

"Who's going to come once they find out there's a mass grave on the property?"

She didn't know the answer to that. "People go to battlefields all the time."

"Battlefields," he said, "are different."

"We went to Little Big Horn. They're still discovering bodies up there."

"From a hundred and forty years ago," he said.

"You have no idea how old these bodies are," she said.

He shrugged, then turned and gave her one of his aw-what-the-hell smiles. "You're right. I don't know anything yet. Except that this place was well named."

The End of the World. She sighed, and asked the question she'd suddenly started to dread. "Are you insured?"

"For what? Construction losses? Sure. Lost income and disability? Sure. Dead bodies on my construction site? Who the hell knows?"

"Maybe you should find out," she said. "I'm sure this doesn't qualify as an act of God."

He inclined his head toward her, as if to say "Touché."

"I need to look," she said. "Alone."

He nodded, then walked to the door. "Find me when you're done."

"Yeah," she said, but he had already stepped outside. She sighed and looked at the floor. Dirt covered the old carpet. Footprints ran through it, some of them so old that they were buried under layers of sand. Broken chairs huddled in the corner, and the stairs to the second floor had rotted away.

But the hotel did have good bones. The brick on the outside had insulated it from harsh weather in the high desert—the hot, hot summers and the blisteringly cold winters. Even the floor-to-ceiling windows were double paned, something so unusual, she'd never seen it in a building this old.

The place didn't smell of death like the natatorium. In fact, except for her prints and Chase's, it didn't look like anyone had been here in a month or more.

She turned on her flashlight and aimed it at the dark corners. Something skittered away from the ornate gold leaf in front of the elevator. She scanned the steps—yep, rotted—and the scarred reception desk. A door was open behind it, leading to the offices. She'd been back there when she was a kid.

In fact, she'd been everywhere in this place as a child. The whole hotel had fascinated her, except for one part.

She steeled herself, then moved to the right, aiming the light at the far wall. When the beam hit it, the wallpaper shimmered like a heat mirage.

She swallowed. That, at least, hadn't changed. The shimmering wall and the building moans—probably from the way the wind whistled through it on dry desert days—gave rise to the stories of the hotel being haunted.

A shiver ran through her. She'd just seen a hole filled with long-dead bodies, her nose still carried the odor of decay (and her clothing probably did, too), and it was the old hotel that scared her out of her wits.

Let someone else investigate it. Let the crime scene techs make sure nothing bad had happened here in the recent past. She'd done as much as she was going to.

She shut off her light, and tried not to listen to the rustling as she let herself out.

THEN

After a long long time, most of the voices stopped. A few continued. Deep Voice did. He gave orders and talked to some of the others.

Then he told Jess Taylor to leave.

She held her breath, wondering what would happen to her.

Then someone picked up the box. She bumped against the side.

"What've you got there?" Deep Voice asked.

"Just a box," Jess Taylor said. "I need to move a few things from my house. I thought I'd take this to pack them in. I'll bring it back in the morning."

"Check it, Dunnigan," Deep Voice said.

She shivered. She couldn't help herself. She squinched as far as she could into the corner of the box, turned her ear inward, and closed her remaining eye, hoping this Dunnigan couldn't see her—or if he did, he wouldn't know what he was looking at.

The box bounced, then the light changed. The towel must have come off. Tobacco and sweat filled the air. She held herself rigid, feeling a shiver start, and willing it away.

"It's empty, boss," said this Dunnigan, right above her.

The box bumped again, and the light dimmed.

"Satisfied?" Jess Taylor asked. His tone was bitter.

"You got to admit," Deep Voice said, "you've been acting odd today."

"I acted like a responsible employee," Jess Taylor said. "I stayed when everyone else left. No one thought to lock up in all the excitement. I made sure the drawers were closed and locked, the safe was closed, and the account registers were in the proper desks. I kept an eye on the place, and you treat me like a criminal."

"You'd do the same, Taylor," Deep Voice said.

"No, sir, I beg your pardon, but I wouldn't. I would acknowledge when an employee does well, not suspect him of thievery because he takes an initiative."

The silence went on forever. She was still holding her breath. She had to let it out, as quietly as she could. She could feel the box bounce with Jess Taylor's breathing—if he was the one holding it. She hoped he was.

He seemed like the only human—the only person—she could trust.

Finally, Deep Voice said, "You can keep the box."

"Thank you, sir." Such sarcasm in Jess Taylor's voice. She wondered if Deep Voice could hear it. "May I go now?"

"Of course," Deep Voice said.

The box bounced with each step. She heard a door screech open, then bang closed. The air grew warmer and the towel blew up ever so slightly.

"Stay still," Jess Taylor said in that undertone of his. "We're not out of this yet."

NOW

When she came out of the hotel, the sky was a deep grayish blue. Twilight had fallen fast, like it always did on the high desert. The moment the sun dipped behind the mountain peaks, the light changed and the air had a suggestion of coolness.

Now if only the wind would stop. It rose for a half hour or so at real twilight, sending sand pellets against her skin like tiny knives.

Chase's employees had already left. So had the police, except for two officers who had been assigned to guard the crime scene. Apparently the crime scene techs weren't going to work at night, which made sense, given the location and the questions still lingering about how to handle the scene.

Chase leaned against his Ford Bronco, a cell phone pressed

against his ear. His back was to her, but she could tell from the position of his shoulders how annoyed he was.

She walked toward him, then stopped when she heard what he was saying.

". . . I'm not sure what they're going to find here, Lester, but that's not the point. The point is that this project probably won't go forward for months. I need you to check our liability. I also need you to examine the insurance policies, and to somehow, without tipping our hand, talk to the few investors who came on board early. I'd promised them the chance of a return within two years. This project came alive because I thought we could fast-track it."

He was talking to his lawyer. Usually such conversations had lawyer-client privilege, but she wasn't sure about that when he conducted it outside on a cell phone.

Still, she should let him know she was there.

She didn't move.

"That's not the point, Lester. The point is that I already have one point two million dollars in capital tied up in this place, and now everything's going to be on hold—"

One of the officers saw her. She nodded at him.

"That's why I want you to find out if we're insured for something like this. I'm not sure I can afford to have that much money tied up indefinitely."

She scraped her foot against the dirt as she walked forward again. He continued talking, so she coughed.

He turned, paused, and sighed. Then he said, "Listen, I'll call you in a few hours. Have some answers for me by then, will you?"

"How's Lester?" she asked.

"You heard that?"

"Enough to know who you were talking to." Lester had handled their divorce. He had been Chase's lawyer for more than two decades. She had no idea if he was any good, but Chase obviously had no complaints. He usually fired people who didn't perform their jobs well.

Chase stuck his phone into the front pocket of his shirt. Then he took the padlock off his belt. "I suppose this is the wrong time to ask you to dinner."

"It's always the wrong time, Chase," she said.

He shook his head ever so slightly. "What did I do, Becca? Was being married to me that bad?"

"I divorced you," she said. "That should be answer enough."

But it wasn't, because he asked her often. And he made it sound like she had been crazy to leave him. Which, her therapist said, was proof enough to her that she had done the right thing.

Becca waited until he'd padlocked the hotel before she walked to her squad. Even then, she stood with an arm resting on the open door as he walked back to his Bronco.

He looked defeated. Was Chase a good enough actor to play such a difficult emotion? She wasn't sure, but she doubted it.

And Jillian would say that she doubted it because she wanted to.

"Changed my mind," Becca said when he got close. "How's pizza sound to you?"

"Good if they had the real thing here."

He'd gone to school in Chicago; he thought the pizza out west was too mainstream or too California. Tasteless and low-fat, he'd once said.

She expected the response, just not the rote way he said it.

"Well, how about that thing we call pizza out here in the wild, wild west?"

He looked at her for the longest time as if he were sizing her up. She made sure her expression remained neutral.

"You going to interrogate me?" he asked.

"Should I?"

"I suppose you should." He opened the Bronco's door. "And you should know I'm ordering spaghetti."

"Spoilsport," she said, got into the squad, and followed Chase out of the lot.

THEN

The box bounced for what seemed like forever. She heard boots tapping on the wooden sidewalk, boots scraping on dirt, boots going silent as they hit the grass. She heard voices, conversations far from her. She heard a motorized engine, one of those newfangled automobiles that made humans think they had entered a technological age.

Daddy had always said they were backward. If they were just a bit farther along, if the Earth hadn't been so focused on oil and gas and coal, then maybe their people could have rebuilt the ship. But the materials hadn't been manufactured yet, and the energy sources were too heavy or too combustible. The people needed something more sophisticated, but didn't have the resources to make it themselves.

Nor did they have the ability to take what passed for technology in this place and modify it for their needs.

Occasionally one of the voices would greet Jess Taylor and ask him what he had in the box. He'd give the same reply—*Nothing*—and continue as if that were true.

He walked for a long time.

Then she heard boots on wood again, a few creaks, and the click of a doorknob. Another creak—this one different, like a door opening—and the light filtering through the towel seemed dimmer.

Finally, Jess Taylor set the box down.

"Just a minute," he said.

She heard a door close, then a swish that she recognized—curtains being closed. This place was hot. The windows should've been open instead of covered. The air smelled faintly of grease and unwashed sheets.

Then the towel came off. She swiveled her eye upward. Jess Taylor was looking down at her.

"This is my house," he said. "I live alone, so no one'll bother us. I don't have to be anywhere until tomorrow."

She wasn't sure why he was telling her all that.

He scooted a chair closer to the table, sat down, then asked, "Do you have any idea what we should do next?"

NOW

Becca didn't have to tell him where they were going because there was only one pizza parlor in all of Hope that he would step into. It was in a beat-up old building on the southeast side, about as far from the End of the World as they could go.

The pizza parlor—called Reuben's of all things—was actually owned by a displaced New York Italian who missed his grandmother's cooking. He made pizza because teenagers loved it and because it was a cheap, easy meal for families, but his heart was in the Italian dishes, from lasagna to a special homemade sausage marinara whose recipe he kept secret.

Chase came out of the bathroom as she went into the ladies' room. When she came out, Chase was sitting toward the back, in a red vinyl booth, his hands folded on the checked tablecloth. The edges of his hair were wet, as was one side of his face.

Washing up hadn't entirely gotten rid of the smell of rot that had permeated her nose, but it got knocked back a degree. The rich odor of garlic and baking bread helped.

By the time she got to the table, Chase was sipping a glass of wine. An iced tea waited for her. Irritation flooded through her— how did he know what she wanted? Had he asked? No, of course not—and then she shook it off.

He had always done this, and until she left him, she had let him. She hadn't told him in any way that he no longer had the right to make decisions for her, and now didn't seem the time.

"I ordered the family-sized spaghetti with the sausage marinara," he said.

She sighed. She was going to have to confront him after all.

But he held up his hand, as if to forestall anything she had to say.

"Then I realized I was being a jerk, so I ordered a small pepperoni pizza and a basket of garlic bread."

As he said that, the garlic bread arrived, looking crisp and greasy and delicious.

"Sorry. I know I should know better."

Becca wasn't sure if that was a real apology or not. She wasn't even sure she should be annoyed or not. Sometimes she wished her therapist was on speed-dial, so she could ask a simple question: What was the appropriate response to this particular

Chase action? Should she be flattered or insulted? Should she set him in his place? Or should she do her breathing exercises while she reminded herself that they were no longer married?

"We could, I think, change the topping on the pizza." He actually sounded worried. "I don't think it went into the oven yet."

"No, that's fine," she said. "A hundred thousand fat-filled calories actually sound good right now."

So she had opted onto a response, and it was passive-aggressive. Bully for her. How nonconstructive.

Chase blinked, looking a little stunned, then shrugged. "Sounds like you're in the mood to interrogate me."

Becca grabbed a slice of garlic bread. The butter welled against her fingers, and she realized she was hungry.

"How much do you stand to lose if the End of the World folds?"

"Folds?" he asked. "Or gets put on hold?"

"It's the same thing, isn't it? Didn't you tell me you needed to finish this quick?"

He swirled his wineglass, then took a huge swig, something she'd never seen him do.

"Let me explain the End of the World, can I, before we get into the details you think important?"

She wasn't the only one capable of being passive-aggressive, but she let the comment slide. She had baited him, after all.

"Shoot," she said.

He flagged the waiter down, got them both water, and drank his so quickly that he looked like a man dying of thirst. Then he pushed his other glass toward the back of the table, as if saving the wine for later.

"The End of the World," he said, the words rolling off his tongue like a lover's. "Remember how much we loved it?"

How much he had loved it. But she didn't correct him. She nodded instead.

"Remember when I used to talk about restoring it, about making the End of the World *the* destination resort in Oregon, and you'd laugh, and you'd say who would want to come to Hope?"

"That was before the boom," she said, surprised that she wasn't feeling defensive.

"Before Hollywood discovered how cheap the land was, before they filmed half the western films up here, before the Californians bought everything in sight."

And tried to change the town into a mini-California, with its strip malls and coffee bars and upscale shops that people like Becca couldn't set foot into unless there was a police emergency.

"Hollywood's left," she said. "They've gone to Canada."

"But they vacation here. They ski, they hunt, they fish. They look at the pretty views. They want to play golf and lacrosse and polo and soccer, if we could only accommodate them. The town doesn't have everything yet, and if we did, even more would come."

"Is this the speech you gave to prospective investors?" she asked. "Because I know the drill."

He'd practiced much of it on her over the years. She hadn't agreed with all of it, but she had encouraged some of it. She, too, wanted Hope to grow. When she'd been a girl, the town was dying, and the name seemed like the way the town planned for its future.

"Historic resorts are the next travel boom," he said. "People want to visit the past, so long as it has all the amenities of the present."

The waiter set down the pizza. The cheese was still popping because the tomato sauce was bubbling underneath.

Becca took a piece. To her surprise, Chase did, too.

"So tell me," she said, "how come *your* money's in this instead of other people's?"

He sighed. "It costs more to refurbish the old hotel and the natatorium than it would to tear the place down and build comparable modern buildings from scratch."

"And your investors didn't like that?"

"They like everything else. They like the resort, the golf courses—"

"Cour*se*s?" Becca asked.

"Four," he said, "along with residential housing, riding trails, and a possible dude ranch near the edge of the mountains."

"How much property did you buy?"

"Just the End of the World," he said. "Turns out the property runs from the highway all the way to the mountains."

"My god," Becca said.

"It was all scrub and desert, not even good enough for ranching, although the End of the World's original owners did rent it out for that."

"Who did you buy it from?" she asked.

"The heirs. They don't live in Oregon any longer. They remembered it from their childhoods, figured the land wasn't worth much, and sold it for a song. The land wasn't the problem. The hotel and resort were."

"The investors wanted you to build new, and you refused." Her voice rose just a bit at the end of the statement, mostly because she was surprised. Chase did what he wanted within reason, but he never turned down money like this. "You really had your heart set on rebuilding the place."

"I had documents and itineraries and research and projections that showed just how much people would love it here. They go to historic lodges now. Hell, Timberline Resort is the number two destination in Oregon."

"Number one being?"

He looked down. "Spirit Mountain Casino."

Which had no historic hotel. Nothing except a rather cheap-looking lodge and a large casino at the entrance to the Van Duzer Corridor in the coastal mountain range.

"But that land was considered worthless forty years ago," he said.

"Because it was tribal land in the middle of nowhere," she said.

"You don't have to side with them," he snapped.

The reaction shocked her. He never snapped. He got angry or frustrated and occasionally raised his voice, but usually he manipulated, twisting the conversation until she was surprised that she was agreeing with him, even when she knew she shouldn't.

"So I repeat," she said, "how deep are you into this?"

"Ninety percent of the resort funding is from me." He took another swig of the wine, leaving the glass nearly empty. How many times had he told her wine was meant to be sipped not guzzled? He probably hadn't even tasted this one.

"That's a lot of money."

"More than you realize."

"So you go bankrupt if this place never gets off the ground."

He finished the wine, then set the glass at the edge of the table, an obvious signal for more. "You're awful damn pessimistic."

"I'm not pessimistic, and I'm not here to judge you." Even though that was a lie. At this moment, it was her job to judge him. "I am trying to figure out what happened in that natatorium."

"You think someone murdered a lot of people and buried them beneath the swimming pool. A long, long time ago. I think it shouldn't interfere with my project."

She sighed. "I'm not talking about the old bodies. I'm talking about the smell."

He froze. The waiter returned, grabbed the wineglass, and left without asking what he was supposed to do about Chase's beverage. Maybe the look on Chase's face scared him off.

"I told you," Chase said. "It was an animal."

"We haven't found it yet. We're operating on the assumption that the recent body is human."

"And you think I what? Sabotaged my own project? Why the hell would I do that?"

"I don't know." Becca raised her voice enough to drown his out. "Maybe you don't have enough funding. Maybe you want out now."

"And you think that destroying the project is the way to leave? If I want to lose several million dollars, I'd put it on the roulette table. If I want to shut down the project, I'll do that."

"So why didn't you?"

"I didn't want to." He grabbed the edge of the table. For a moment, she thought he was going to leverage himself out of it.

But he didn't. He ran a hand through his hair, took a deep breath, and forced himself to lean back.

"You don't want to?" she asked. "Or you see this as a win-win situation?"

He looked at her as if she was crazy. "Excuse me?"

"Once you found the bodies below the pool, you knew that might stall the project. But you wanted out without losing any money. So you found a way that the insurance might cover it. Something guaranteed, not an ancient burial ground like you thought, but a police investigation—"

"You think I planted a body there for the *insurance money?*"

"I don't know," she said. "Did you?"

His mouth was open. He stared at her like the day she told him she was leaving. If she had to, she would wager that he was telling the truth. But that kind of hunch didn't hold up in court.

Besides, she knew that her reactions to him weren't always the right ones.

"Do you really think that little of me?" he asked softly.

"What I think doesn't matter," she said. "This *is* a police investigation, and I have to—"

"Oh, bullshit," he said. "You don't have to explore every goddamn angle. You think I'm capable of killing someone and planting him in the natatorium for the fucking insurance money."

The waiter hovered near the kitchen door. In his hand, he held another glass of wine. He watched them with a wary expression.

She had to get Chase to calm down. She needed him to think clearly.

"Do you want me to investigate this or someone from Portland? Because that's the way it's heading."

"Even if I turn out to be right and it's a goddamn coyote down there?"

"Even if," she said. "We have something big now, and there's no covering it up. Jillian called the state crime lab. We're going to have reporters. You want them to write about how we had a screaming fight in our favorite Italian restaurant?"

"Fuck you, Becca," he said. "You planned this."

"Your anger?"

"With a fucking audience. Do you hate me that much?"

She swallowed. She was getting angry now. "You ask me that a lot. So here's the answer, Chase. I don't hate you. If anything, I'm still in love with your sorry ass, and that's a problem for me. It's also a problem for this investigation, since I'm the only trained detective on Hope's police force. I'm holding off the Valley investigative team for the moment, but that won't last if we keep this up."

He slammed his hands on the booth so hard that the fake wood tabletop attached to the wall actually bounced. Then he stood up and stalked to the men's room.

Becca took a deep breath, let it out, and then took another. And another, and another, still wishing for the therapist on speed-dial. Did she keep breathing until she was light-headed or did she just leave?

She was handling this all wrong, and pretty soon word would get out. The chief would relieve her, and the investigation would become a state thing instead of a local thing. And that kind of publicity would hurt the new Hope, the place that actually had a future.

The waiter came to the table. He was still cradling the wineglass. "You think he's gonna want this? Because—"

"Yeah," she said. "He'll want that and more. Bring the whole bottle."

She ate her piece of pizza slowly, drank the iced tea, and waited, keeping an eye on the men's room door. The three other tables, filled with young families, kept an eye on her, as if she had been the problem, not Chase.

The men's room door opened as she finished her third piece. The waiter had been back twice—once with the wine bottle and once with a heaping bowl of spaghetti in sausage marinara sauce. As stressed as Becca was, she could probably eat the entire thing without Chase's help.

To her relief, he came back to the booth and slid in.

"Okay," he said, "since you're going all official on me, here's what you need to know. I have six million dollars in this thing. That's real money. I also have outstanding loans of ten million, and that's not nearly enough to get everything done. I'm hoping when the hotel and nat are finished, the investors will pour in. If they don't, I'll be in debt until I die, even if the place is a success."

Becca set down the pizza crust she'd been clinging to. She resisted the urge to slide the plate of spaghetti toward her.

"Does my insurance cover this? How the hell would I know? I'm sure my agent doesn't know. I'm sure the insurance company has no real idea, and its legal department will be haggling over the policy language and the politics of the entire thing for months. That's what I was talking to Lester about. I'm hoping that he can find a few answers, or at least an argument, so that some of the back and forth gets forestalled if and when you people actually decide to shut me down."

"We already shut you down, Chase," she said. "The question now is for how long."

"I know." He picked up the glass and then set it down again. "But you know what I mean. This could be a two-day inconvenience or it could be a yearlong nightmare. And since it's all one property, I'm pretty sure that you could tie me up for a long time."

"If those bodies are Native American, you could be right," she said.

He let out a long sigh. Then he moved the wineglass closer to her plate than his.

"So," he said, "do I have a motive to get insurance money? No. I'd be a fool to try this plan. If I wanted insurance money, I'd find another way to go about it. And I'd be smart, Becca. This is damn dumb. It jeopardizes everything without giving me any benefit at all. I'll be in the news forever, I won't be able to save face, and I'm going to go broke. Hell, I'd be better off disappearing and starting all over again than doing that. I'm not damn dumb, Becca."

"I know," she said.

"I have no reason to plant something there."

"Does anyone else?" she asked.

"Yeah," he said, reaching for the plate of spaghetti. "Yeah, I'm afraid a lot of people do."

THEN

Why would he ask her what to do next? Wasn't he the grown one, the one in charge? She was just a baby, really, younger than anyone else in their group.

But he wasn't part of their group. She wasn't even sure there was a group anymore. Where had everyone gone?

When the shanties burned, the remaining people fled. Momma had grabbed her. They were just a little behind the group.

And she never knew what happened to any of them.

"What about my momma?" she asked Jess Taylor.

He closed his eyes, turned his head, and wiped the sweat off his forehead. Then he glanced at the window, like he wanted to open it. He stood, and she thought he was going to, but all he did was get another towel and clean off his fingers.

When he sat back down, his face had a different look to it. His eyes were open, but sadder, if that was possible.

Sometimes she wondered how these humans could think themselves so different from the people. These humans changed, too, just not as much. And sometimes these humans changed by force of will, just like the people did.

Just like Jess Taylor had done a moment ago.

"You're going to keep asking, aren't you?" he said.

She blinked at him. She didn't know how to answer, except maybe to say of course she would. She loved her momma and her momma left her on the sidewalk.

Bad things happened this afternoon, and she heard some of them. One of them sounded like Momma.

"I don't know what happened," he said. "I'll find out as best I can. I promise. But it might take days."

Days. She wanted to fold her ears in, close her eyes, and huddle into a little ball. What would happen to her for those days?

"I've seen this before," he said. "Not this, exactly, but the same kind of thing. Folks get riled up about the strangest things, and you have to admit, your people are strange."

She didn't think so. But she didn't answer that either, just kept watching him.

"I mean, I think I finally understand where this violence comes from, this impulse. Not because of you."

He held up a hand, as if to reassure her. She wasn't sure what he was reassuring her about.

"It comes about because of the differences. They're startling. And sometimes—I don't mean to offend you—but sometimes, they're revolting. Humans don't handle revulsion well. We—"

He shook his head and stood up, walked to the window and peeked through the curtain. Sweat stained the back of his shirt, leaving a V-shaped wet spot in the fabric.

"I can't believe I'm defending them."

He shook his head again. Then he let the curtain drop and close, and he came back to the chair.

"The chances are—I'm so sorry, but the chances are that your mother didn't make it. Just like your father. She probably—they probably—I mean, you heard it this afternoon. You're lucky to be here. And if your mother is alive—"

He stopped, wiped a hand over his mouth, then shook his head yet again.

He didn't say anymore.

She was holding her breath. She finally let it out. Her other eye had appeared. Apparently she needed to see him. Her body was starting to make changes on its own.

"You think she's still alive?" she asked.

"No," he said.

"But you said—"

"I know what I said." He sighed. "Look, Sarah, if your mother is still alive, it probably won't be for long."

"Then we have to find her."

"That's not what I mean."

She felt her skin tighten. Another shiver ran through her. The spikes started to form and she willed them away. She didn't want him to know she suddenly felt threatened.

"What do you mean?" she asked.

"I mean they're probably not done."

"But I heard the men, they came into the bank, they said it was over, they said it was . . . fun. They said—"

"I know what they said." He ran his fingers along his forehead. "I know. And I know a few of them will go back. Some probably haven't left. And they'll finish. Do you understand me? They'll finish."

"Can't we get her before they do?"

He stared at her, and that sadness returned to his eyes. His whole face looked sad, and she wondered for a minute if he even saw her, if he was looking at her or something else—someone else—like a memory, maybe, like those ghostly shapes that the people sometimes made when they thought of a relative long dead.

"If we try to get her," he said, "they'll kill us, too."

"Not you," she said.

He let out half a laugh, like she'd startled the sound out of him.

"Sarah, honey," he said, "if your people hadn't come, they'd've gotten to me eventually. They always do."

NOW

"You know who doesn't like me." Chase used tongs to dish up his spaghetti. Somehow he managed to do so without getting sauce on his shirt. "You used to put up with the phone calls."

Becca remembered. The calls came in late at night. Sometimes they were just hang-ups. Sometimes they were more serious than that. A few even included threats.

In those days, Hope's telephone system was too unsophisticated to provide services like caller ID, so Becca had had to put a trace on the line. She had gone to every single one of the callers, warning them that their behavior was illegal and should Chase's businesses go under or should he get hurt, they would be the first suspects she went to.

Most seemed to listen. A few grumbled that Chase had only married her because he wanted police protection. Not even Becca was insecure enough to believe that.

She took a small portion of the spaghetti, barely enough to fill a corner of the plate provided, and then only because she loved the sauce. Mostly, she focused on the pizza, her iced tea, and Chase.

"What about this project?" she asked. "Anyone new surface?"

He used his spoon as a counterweight to keep the spaghetti he was winding from falling off his fork. He worked at it as if it were a particularly difficult puzzle.

"Obviously, you never went to the city council meetings."

"Not for this, no," she said. She avoided city business as much as possible.

"Half the town hated it. Some I didn't expect, folks who had supported me when I wanted to redo Beiker's Department Store downtown."

"The preservationists went against you?"

"Yeah." He ate the forkful, swallowed, and then drank some water. "They think the End of the World is a bad idea, a dangerous place, and the last straw in turning Hope into a replica of California."

"Wow," Becca said. "I'd've thought they would've loved it."

"Me, too," he said. "I was stunned. A few actually threatened me."

"You're kidding."

He shook his head. "Ray McGuillicuty, remember him? He told me I'd regret buying the End of the World."

"You think that was a threat, coming from a ninety-year-old man?"

Chase shrugged. "I thought it was idle talk at the time. But he has money, connections, and a shady reputation. He made his money running illegal speakeasies in the late thirties, and gambling dens in the forties. Word around town was that if there was an illegal business—an abortionist, a fight ring, drug smuggling—McGuillicuty would rent space or manpower to that business for a cut, of course."

She had heard the rumors, but she also knew Old Man McGuillicuty had been an upstanding citizen since the 1960s.

"You think he's still got that kind of pull?"

"I think if anyone in Hope is smart enough to stop my project by burying a body on the property, it's Ray McGuillicuty."

"That's giving him a lot of power."

"If you're right," Chase said, "and someone is trying to shut me down, Ray's my first choice."

Becca tried not to laugh. She couldn't imagine that old man caring so much about the future of Hope. But she wasn't going to ignore this.

"Who else?" she asked as she finished her iced tea. She waved the glass at the waiter, and he nodded.

"Oh, Christ," Chase said. "Damn near the entire preservation society. All the matrons and their husbands, too. Most of the old money in Hope—what there is of it—warned me away."

"Like Old Man McGuillicuty did?" Becca asked. The waiter showed up with a pitcher and set it on the table. He didn't even bother to pour. He still seemed a bit nervous about Chase's earlier outburst.

"Not that blatant," Chase said. "But they all took time to tell me that the End of the World is the most unlucky place in Hope and that everyone connected to it has been harmed by that connection."

"Lovely," Becca said. "Superstition still alive and well."

"And apparently they thought I should make business decisions based on it."

"You didn't, though," she said.

"I think some of my investors did," he said. "The preservation committee knew who my usual investors were. A number of them were contacted and a few backed out. One even told me that old properties that had bad luck rumors usually had a reason for them."

"Turns out he was right," Becca said.

"She," he said. "And I guess she was."

"Which means"—Becca tapped a finger against her chin—"that someone knew about those bodies."

"How do you figure?" Chase asked.

She smiled at him. "Bad luck rumors have to start somewhere."

"You think that's tied to the smell?" he asked.

"Probably not, but right now, those old bodies are the only crime I have to investigate. I'll start there."

"After you finish harassing the local businessman."

"After I finish dinner with my former husband, who has had a hell of a day."

THEN

She didn't know what Jess Taylor meant by the humans getting to him, and he wouldn't say. He paced around the front part of the cabin, poured some water from a pitcher into a glass, and drank.

Then he stared at her.

She wondered if he was sorry he'd helped her. Maybe he would turn her in.

Maybe she would scream.

She wanted to beg him to keep her, beg him to help her. But she didn't. Daddy used to say that people who begged didn't deserve help. They had to help themselves.

Only she couldn't do that, not without knowing what had happened. The answers weren't simple. Her home was gone—she knew that much. When the shanties burned, hers would've burned with it. Daddy always kept water near the candles. He used to say, *This place is so primitive and so badly built that we're going to die here in a stupid fire because we couldn't get to it in time.*

He'd been wrong about them dying. None of them had died

in that cabin, although she wasn't sure about the others, the people who lived in the shanties where the fires started.

She wished Daddy were here now. She wished he would talk to Jess Taylor, grown one to grown one. They would understand each other. They would know what had happened and what would happen next.

"Do you eat?" Jess Taylor asked. He swished the water around in his glass. He was still looking at her that funny way.

She had to form a mouth. She had lost it while he'd been pacing. Her body wasn't sure what form to take so it was taking several at once, which made her dizzy.

"I eat," she said.

"I mean, do you eat what we eat?"

"When I look like you," she said. Her people's food had gone away when she was really, really little. They had to become like the humans just so that they could take in human nourishment.

"When you look like me," Jess Taylor repeated. "How about the way you look now?"

"I'm not anything now," she said. "I need to be something to take in food."

Something she understood. Something whose systems were somewhat compatible. Daddy and the other scientists had to work for a while to make their systems work like a human's. They still had to make changes—changes she didn't understand.

Daddy said she was lucky. She started changing into human form really young, so it would be engrained. If she had to hide, she could hide as one of them forever because her body was used to their strangeness.

His never would be. Some of the older people got really sick in the first years.

Some of the older people died.

"How often do you have to eat?" Jess Taylor asked.

"I don't know," she said. "Whenever you do, I guess."

Because she always ate when Momma did. She was too young to pick her own times to eat. Eating had to be trained like everything else.

"Wonderful," he said in that low voice of his, the one no one else was supposed to hear. Then he raised it a little. "How about water? Do you need that, too?"

"If I look like you," she said, "I act like you. My needs are like yours."

That's the beauty of it, Daddy said to Momma once. *And the curse. If we stay here too long, we lose our identity. We become someone else. Then they'll never find us.*

Why would they look for us? Momma asked. *For all they know, we missed our settlement location and made do.*

They trace new colonies. They have to, Daddy said. *We don't just move there because of population growth. These places are carefully chosen for raw material wealth as well.*

She wasn't sure what "raw material wealth" was, but Momma had known. Momma had looked at Daddy disapprovingly. Daddy had shrugged, because he wore his human form all the time now, and then he had smiled at her.

They'll track us down, if only to see what kind of wealth we discovered here.

And if we don't find any? Momma said.

That's not the concern, Daddy said. *The concern is whether or not they'll find us before we lose ourselves.*

"So you're going to have to pick a shape sometime tonight, aren't you?" Jess Taylor said. He had moved closer to her. She hadn't noticed before. Had she been so lost in her memories that she hadn't seen him walk?

"I guess," she said.

"Can you be something else for a while? A table, maybe, or the box?"

"I'm too little," she said. "I can't do it by myself, not for long. That's why I couldn't be brick. I tried, but I'm not good yet. And I can't stay long anyway. I don't know the sleep-change. I need to move and breathe and feed myself like you."

He sighed. He sank into the chair next to the table. "I was afraid of that."

He took another sip of the water, studied his hand, then studied the small cabin. Then he got up and went to the window again, peering out the curtain.

"No one," he said. "We're okay for now."

"I know," she said, even though she didn't. She wanted him to figure out how to help her. She was becoming more and more afraid he would just throw her out now that he knew most of her secrets.

He put his hand in the box, near her skin but not touching it. "You turned the color of the brick this afternoon," he said. "Can you turn the same color as me?"

She looked at him as hard as he had looked at her. Then she let out a little sigh.

"Yes," she said.

"You sounded hesitant," he said.

"I can't do blue eyes," she said. "Yours aren't."

He smiled suddenly, as if he hadn't expected that. "You're right. Mine aren't. Anything else human you can't do?"

"I can't be a grown one," she said. "I have to 'roughly correspond.'"

She said those last two words carefully. They were Daddy's words. Before she had only known the concept, not how to express it. She used to point to things, things she wanted to be for more than an hour, more than a day.

He would shake his head. Sometimes he would laugh. She loved it when her daddy laughed.

Younglin, he'd say, *they have to roughly correspond.*

Mostly she wanted to be a grown one. Humans, more than the people, treated their young ones very differently. But she didn't have enough years to be a grown one. She couldn't pretend it, couldn't even get the size right.

That problem translated to other living things as well. She could be a sapling, but not a tree. A kitten, but not a cat.

Someday, she would roughly correspond. But she wouldn't know when until she changed to human form, and that form was a grown one.

"You're a girl," Jess Taylor said, "or they wouldn't call you Sarah. What age do you roughly correspond to?"

"Ten," she said because that's what Momma said when she took her to the school two years before. Even though her learning had grown and her grades had advanced, she hadn't changed, not like her classmates.

So she'd asked Daddy about that, and he'd said, *Roughly, younglin. Roughly correspond. We age differently than they do. Slower, I think.*

But he didn't know. There was so much they didn't know. So much that they didn't understand.

Then he left and no one knew, and Momma hated the questions.

"Ten," Jess Taylor said, and nodded, almost pleased. "Ten might work."

"For what?" she asked, the words catching in her newly formed mouth.

"For keeping you alive, child," he said, and tapped the edge of the box as he stood. "For keeping you alive."

NOW

By the time Becca got home, she was too tired to chase rumors. She took a shower, which didn't get that smell out of her nose. Her tiny house was an oven, despite the heat pump she'd wasted the last of her divorce settlement money on, and she actually had to turn on the good old-fashioned swamp cooler she couldn't bring herself to get rid of.

Theoretically, the desert cooled at night, but lately the coolness had come without benefit of a breeze. She started with the air conditioner, which was nearly as old as she was, and by midnight shut it down, shoved a fan in the window, and hoped for the best.

She couldn't sleep. Worries about herself, about Chase, about the appropriateness of the investigation had her pacing. The mentions Chase had made over dinner about rumors concerning the End of the World had her worried as well.

Hope had once been called the Hope of the West. Founded

just after the Civil War by philanthropists and political idealists, Hope was supposed to be a refuge for displaced former slaves as well as immigrants who weren't wanted in larger cities, and even Chinese families, so long as they remained in their own enclave at the edge of town.

The founders of Hope put ads in all the major newspapers, promising land and jobs to people no one else wanted. Hope also promised full equality to blacks and immigrants, although "immigrants" did not include the Chinese, who wouldn't be allowed to vote or hold office. Hope was notable in its Chinese relations, though, for allowing entire families to live there, so long as they kept to themselves. Most states only tolerated Chinese males.

The experiment didn't last. The United States barred Chinese immigration in the early part of the twentieth century, and then the state of Oregon itself started enforcing the discrimination built into its constitution, attempting to bodily throw Hope's blacks out of the state. The entire town prevented that, letting the blacks stay as long as the city (and county) promised not to let them hold elected office or take state jobs.

Still, Hope was something of a legend in the state, a place where people could be perceived as nothing more than a set of skills. Where, in the words of Martin Luther King Jr., people could be judged by the content of their character instead of the color of their skin.

That was Hope's legacy, and the reason for its name. Hope's children got spoon-fed this history from the moment they walked into Hope Elementary, and heard about it all the way to graduation from Hope High.

So the idea of a massacre, any massacre, particularly one that someone remembered and tried to hide, went against everything Hope stood for. People didn't die here, not in large groups. Hell, they didn't die in small ones.

Becca got out of bed, grabbed her lightest robe—which Chase had bought her for one of their anniversaries—and headed for the couch, the television, and late-night talk shows. Maybe some blathering would shut down her brain.

Because all this thinking about a possible massacre—even one nearly a hundred years old—upset her more than she wanted to admit.

THEN

They waited until it was full dark before she grew herself back to human. It took a long time.

Jess Taylor's cabin had three rooms and a windowless room he called a storage room. It scared her. It was like the box, only bigger, and it was in the middle of all three rooms—like it took a part off the corners of them and made its own little space.

She had never seen anything like that. He said he kept things in there, but there wasn't much, a few boxes pushed against a corner, and some jars filled with jam.

All three walls had hangers for lanterns. He hung one before he brought her into the room. He kept it on low, so it wouldn't burn too much kerosene and stink up the place—or start a fire. (At least, she hoped it wouldn't start a fire; she'd seen too much fire this day.)

He took the box off the table, talking to her the whole time, mostly nonsense stuff like humans did with babies, stuff about how it would be okay, and the room might be close, but it would do, no one could see in, they would be safe.

She wasn't sure about safe. She wasn't sure about trusting Jess Taylor anymore, but she had to. She didn't know what other choice she had.

He set her box on top of the other boxes, then propped the door partly open with one of the jars.

"I'll let you just change now," he said, like she was going to put on a dress. "Let me know when you're done."

"No!" she said, as loud as she could, which wasn't very loud, considering. She didn't have the body behind the sound, and she didn't know she needed it until just now.

That scared her, too.

She finally realized how truly helpless she was.

"You have to stay," she said.

He sighed, keeping one hand on the door. "I'm sure it's private. We—folks like me—we let each other be private."

"I got to see you," she said.

"I'll be just outside the door," he said.

"To change," she said. "I got to see you to change. I can't do it without an example."

He frowned. "I can't . . . change . . . like you. I can't show you how."

She shook her head. "To look at. I need to see what I'm changing into."

And even then it might not work.

His head bowed, and his arm dropped. "I'm not sure I want to be here for that."

She wasn't sure she could do it without him. In the past, Momma or Daddy had always helped her. They had always found a way to get her through the difficult parts, like making the fingers different lengths or remembering to grow hair.

"How about I stand just outside the door with my back to you?" he asked. "Would that help?"

"Can you tell me if I get it wrong?" she asked.

He bowed his head even more, but he finally said, "I guess I could. Wait one moment, all right?"

She was scared. She knew that just as he left the room. If he hadn't propped open the door, she would've been even more scared. She couldn't see him at all.

Then he came back, carrying a sheet. "I don't have girl clothes. We'll have to find some for you. Can you put this on?"

Modesty, Daddy called it.

Silly, Momma called it, especially when it got really hot. But they learned how to wear things, and taught her about it, too.

The clothes she'd been wearing when she was running probably got absorbed into her skin as fuel when she became the sidewalk. She'd been so scared, she hadn't noticed.

She'd most likely be sick later.

"If I put that on, how will you know if I get things right?" she asked.

"I'm sure no one'll notice and you'll do just fine," he said, running the words together like he couldn't breathe.

"I never got everything right before on the first try," she said.

"You'll do fine," he repeated and eased out the door, leaving the sheet on one of the shelves.

It took her a long time to squinch to the edge of the box. By then, she'd formed fingers (probably because she'd been thinking of them) and they were the wrong lengths. But they were good for grabbing onto stuff, especially when she was squinching, so she didn't pay attention to right or wrong.

When she reached the edge of the box, she either had to get all the way to the floor or she had to make legs. She couldn't quite remember the details of legs. The knees she knew and the ankles—they were the bendy parts—and the feet, but there was other stuff she'd forgotten about and she knew they'd look funny.

And she also knew if she hooked the legs up wrong, they'd be impossible to move. So she made hips, too.

In fact, everything would be better if she did the bendy parts first. She'd just finished elbows when Jess Taylor leaned partway in the door, keeping his face averted.

"You all right?"

"Yeah," she said because she didn't know how else to answer.

"Will you be a lot longer?"

"I don't know." She didn't know how long she'd already been. She didn't really care. It took a lot of concentration to make herself all over again, and because she'd been so scared earlier, it was going to be harder.

Just him asking the question knocked her off for a little while. She put one of the elbows just above the hip, and she had to reform, trying to remember exactly how arms bend.

Finally, she had a guess at the human shape she used to

wear—just that morning even though it seemed like forever ago. She grabbed the sheet and held it in front of her.

"Is this all right?" she asked.

Jess Taylor turned very slowly. And then he looked at her.

He was trying not to show how he felt, but she could see it in his eyes. Confused, sickened, surprised, all at the same time.

"Close," he said after a minute. "You're really close."

But it took most of the night just to get the general shape right—collarbones, she always forgot about collarbones—and somewhere along the way, he forgot about the sheet, telling her to make a belly button—which she'd never heard of—and explaining dimples in the knees.

By the time they got done, she had a hunch she was more human-looking up close than any of her other people had ever been, and the thought made her sad.

But she didn't have long for sad. Because Jess Taylor gave her some bread and some water and an apple that he'd kept in the root cellar since last fall, and told her he needed just a little sleep before going to work.

"You're going to leave me?" she said.

"I have to," he said. "You'll be safe if you don't let anybody see you. They can't know you're here. I'll be back late afternoon. Maybe with some answers."

Maybe. She wanted him to promise her. But he couldn't promise her.

He couldn't promise her anything. Anything at all.

NOW

If this were a normal investigation regarding a murder that involved the town's history, Becca would go to the Blue Diamond Café. The Blue Diamond was in the exact center of town, in a building that had housed it since the 1930s. Tourists occasionally wandered into the Blue Diamond, saw the ripped booths and dirty windows, and wandered right out.

Becca looked at the Blue Diamond with longing as she walked

past. Even though all the city old-timers would be long gone by now—it was the very late hour of nine a.m.—she'd still find someone to welcome her and give her a free omelet that, in her private moments, she called a heart attack on a plate.

But she had to go two buildings down, to the Hope Historical Society, housed rent-free in one of Chase's renovations, the Hope Bankers Building and Trust.

The money people had long moved away from the Bankers Building, but they'd left behind one of the most solid brick buildings in all of Eastern Oregon. Chase had turned the lower floor into shops and restaurants, the second and third floors into offices, and the upper three floors into condos that sold for four times what Becca paid for her house just two years ago.

There was a diner in the Bankers Building, a 1950s wannabe called the Rock and Remember, and it was usually crammed with transplanted Californians or tourists or both. But the omelets, while large here, were made with egg whites only, and the chefs, if you could call them that, used only "the good oils"—no butter or lard—which gave the food a cardboard aftertaste. Even the coffee wasn't coffee: it was a mochaccino or a cappuccino or an espresso, something that required a language all its own to order.

Still, she went inside, grabbed a double-tall latte with sprinkles and a "cuppa plain Joe," and then went to the elevator.

The only way she could get Gladys Conyers to talk to her, after that last disastrous interview, was to ply her with her favorite beverage, while making the bribe seem entirely accidental.

Gladys Conyers was forty-five and earnest, a California transplant herself who desperately wanted to convince the entire town of Hope that she was a local. She had some claim. Her grandparents were born here, her parents were raised here, and she spent every summer here from the day she was born.

Her grandfather, Jack Conyers, started the Hope Historical Society as a labor of love in the 1950s, after he came back from the war. He thought every small American town should have its history engraved on its downtown so Americans knew what a wonderful place they came from.

In addition to keeping all of Hope's newspapers, as well as any clippings that pertained to the city from any other periodical—even the flashy *New York Times* article forty years ago that put Hope's ski resorts on the map—he also managed to acquire important items from Hope's history.

He used to run a small museum from the back of the Historical Society, but lately, he'd been involved in a fund-raising drive to give Hope its own historical museum.

Becca knew she wouldn't find Jack at the Historical Society. He had become understandably hard to reach these last few years, ever since his eighty-fifth birthday. He figured he only had a good ten years left, and he wanted to spend them preserving Hope's history, not talking to people who had questions they could easily answer on their own.

So Gladys had taken over the society. She had a lot of knowledge about Hope—more than most longtime residents, but nothing like her grandfather. Still, anyone who wanted to see Jack had to go through Gladys. If she could answer the questions, then she would and Jack wouldn't lose precious time talking about the past he supposedly loved.

The society had an office on the first floor because it sold items from various ski tournaments and rodeos as well as Hope memorabilia.

Becca tried to ignore the memorabilia, just as she tried to ignore the weird milky scent of the latte she carried in its cardboard holder. She headed to the back, past the teenager manning the sales desk, to the office where Gladys held court.

"Don't think a latte's gonna get me to do you any favors," Gladys said from behind the slatted door. The woman had to have a nose like a Great Dane.

Becca pushed the door open, set the latte on Gladys's specially made cup holder in the center of her desk, then grabbed her own cuppa plain Joe and sat in the easy chair.

"I'm not asking for a favor," Becca said.

"I hear you stopped the work at the natatorium." Gladys was slender, tanned, and overdressed for Hope. She wore a designer suit—pastel, of course, since it was summer—sandal pumps, and too much makeup. "We have pictures down at the museum of the nat being built, being used, and being abandoned. I have a computer list already prepared for you, not that I think it'll do any good."

"Why'd you think I'd be here?" Becca asked.

"You always come here, even when you have a current case. Besides, there's so much opposition to Chase's project, I figured you'd want to know if there's any historical reason for it."

Becca hid her smile behind her paper coffee cup. Gladys would be useful after all.

"Is there any historical reason?" Becca asked.

Gladys made a pfumph sound that she had to have learned from her curmudgeonly grandfather. "Besides the rumors of ghosts, of hauntings, of strange sounds in the night?"

"I know about those," Becca said.

"Wow," Gladys said, peeling the lid off her latte and adding even more sugar. "You actually admit you know something."

Becca sighed and bit back her response. She knew she'd be in for some of this. Twice she had bypassed Gladys and gone to Jack directly, and neither of them let her forget it. For nearly a year, she had to send another officer to ask historical questions. Just recently, Becca had heard through the grapevine that she was welcome at the Historical Society again, so long as she respected its director.

She did respect its director, but she respected its director's grandfather more. Jack could answer her questions quickly and with a minimum of fuss. Gladys had to be babied, which Becca proceeded to do.

"I'm sorry about that," Becca said.

Gladys waved a beringed right hand. "Water under the bridge."

They continued that game until Gladys finished sugaring her latte and put the lid back on. Then she took a sip, eyed Becca, and said, "I hear there are some serious problems at the site."

Becca nodded. One more game, but a quick one. "You know I can't talk about the details, but there is a case."

"Murder?" Gladys asked.

"Sure looks that way," Becca said.

Gladys's eyes glinted. She loved crime and punishment so long as it didn't involve her family.

"Right now, I'm waiting for the crime lab," Becca said, "and while I'm stalled, I thought I'd ask you about a few other things I saw at the nat."

Gladys tapped the lid of her latte. "Chase already had us run the history of the place. Aside from the usual drownings and accidental deaths that any long-running sports facility would have, we found nothing."

Becca nodded. She would take this one slow. "What about the ghost rumors?"

"Those are mostly from the hotel," Gladys said. "Apparently quite a few shady characters stayed there, as well as some famous folk. President Coolidge was the most famous, I would say. He loved the fishing up here. There are rumors that Hoover stayed there, too, but I haven't been able to track them down. People weren't so proud of him, by the end."

Becca didn't need that kind of history lesson. "I'm more concerned with the nat. Do you know what kind of laborers built it?"

"Of course I do." Gladys opened a drawer in her desk and pulled out a thick file. In it were computer reprints of the society's photos, articles on the construction of the End of the World, and the list that Gladys had mentioned right up front.

She put a lacquered nail on top of one of the photographs. A group of men stood on an empty patch of desert. Some leaned on shovels. Others held pickaxes. A few had rifles.

"These are the men who built the nat," Gladys said. "We found all sorts of historical photographs for Chase. He loves the authenticity."

Gladys lingered over Chase's name. She'd had a crush on him for years, which bothered Chase a lot more than it bothered Becca.

"What're the rifles for?" Becca asked.

"Chase asked the same thing." Gladys spun the photograph so that she could look at it before spinning it back to Becca. "My grandfather says that the End of the World was so far out of town that the workers brought their guns, hoping that that night's dinner would lope past while they were working. This was jack rabbit country, back in the day, and from what I hear, you could find—and shoot—a rabbit as easily as a fly. The men got their paycheck and that night's supper."

"Was there labor trouble then?"

"In the twenties? In Oregon?" Gladys raised her voice just enough so that the teenager manning the sales desk could hear how stupid Becca was. "I'm sure in Portland, but not in Hope. And the End of the World was built around 1910, not the twenties. It became the premiere resort in this part of the country by 1918, with war vets bringing their brides here for a honeymoon. And I hear rumors that there was quite a speakeasy run out of the hotel's basement. The owners stocked up when it became clear that the dries were going to win."

Becca set the idea of the speakeasy aside for the moment. "What about among the crew? Troubles? Firings?"

"Do they look troubled?" Gladys tapped that nail on the photo again. "Take a close look. What do you see?"

Becca repressed a sigh and leaned forward. Gladys always made these visits seem like an oral exam. "A group of very rough-looking men."

"Well, they'd take any of our modern men and pound them into the ground, that's for sure," Gladys said, a trace of the Valley Girl she'd pretended to be still lingering in her speech. "But I mean their racial mix. Several black men standing side by side with several whites. Not even the Chinese are segregated in this photograph, and usually the old photographs kept all the minorities separate—or even more common, out of the picture altogether."

Becca peered at it. The men were touching shoulders, which wasn't something a racially mixed group did in those days.

"There are a few Native Americans as well," Gladys said. "I

learned that from their names. These men are so grimy, it's hard to tell much else."

Becca nodded, then frowned. "So the building of the nat went smoothly, then."

"And the building of the hotel. The rumors about the End of the World started after it opened for business," Gladys said.

"You mean the haunting."

"And the bad dreams. Those were the worst. People would stay at the End of the World, and wake up screaming. The interesting thing is that they all had the same complaint."

Becca swirled the coffee in her cup. She'd have to listen to this even though it wasn't what she had asked. She didn't care about the hauntings. All old hotels had ghost stories. She wanted to hear about the nat.

"Which was?"

"That they'd had nightmares, and in the nightmares, they saw their long-dead relatives begging for help." Gladys added a spooky tone to her voice, as if she actually believed this nonsense.

"Wow," Becca said, trying not to sound sarcastic. "Scary."

"No kidding. I've never heard of this kind of haunting."

"But nothing from the nat?"

"Why do you ask? What did you find?"

"Evidence that something awful happened there as the place was being built," Becca said.

"What kind of awful?" Gladys asked.

"I was hoping you could tell me."

Gladys frowned at her, and Becca had to hide a smile again. For once Gladys had to be feeling as if she was taking a quiz.

"I've never heard a thing, and you'd think in this town, I would." She slid the picture back and studied it as if it held the answers. Then she put it in the file, and closed it.

For a moment, Becca thought the interview was over, and then Gladys said, "Here's what I know. I know the natatorium was initially supposed to be an indoor tennis court, which was, in its day, a revolutionary idea. That was about 1905 or so, when tennis was very popular, particularly out west."

"You're kidding," Becca said.

Gladys actually smiled at her. "Think of all those photographs of women in their long gowns, holding tennis rackets. These women played, and some played very well, despite the handicap."

Becca shook her head. "I thought it was an East Coast thing."

"Every small western town had courts, if they had respectable women. Most of the women were barred from the saloons and the clubs, so they had to have something to do or they might form a temperance society, or a ladies aide society, or do something to take away the men's fun."

"Aren't we always that way?" Becca asked, and smiled.

Gladys smiled back. "It didn't work. They didn't build the tennis court for some reason, I never could find out why. The pool came later. It used the tennis court's foundation as part of the pool itself, and then it got built from there."

"Isn't that unusual?" Becca asked.

Gladys shrugged. "Construction in those days was haphazard. I don't know what was usual and what wasn't. I mean, a place could be as sturdy as the hotel or it could be some boards knocked together to be called a house. Really, though, they were just shanties."

"I thought Hope didn't have a shantytown."

"Oh, we did, but it burned," Gladys said. "No one bothered to rebuild it. Folks didn't like to talk about that day. The entire city could've gone up in flames. Somehow it didn't happen, though."

This was one of the things Becca hated about seeing either Conyers about Hope history—their tendency to digress.

"But nothing else about the nat? Nothing unusual?"

"No, not even the nat was unusual. They had natatoriums all over Oregon. They started as playgrounds for the rich—mostly pools and tennis—and then as they fell apart, they became the community pools and playgrounds for the poorer kids. Most of them got shut down in the polio scares of the late forties and early fifties. I think ours is the last one standing, which makes it eligible for historical preservation."

"Which Chase has begged you not to apply for until he's done with the work, right?"

Gladys nodded. "Nothing wrong with that. He doesn't want the extra inspectors. He does the work better than the national preservation standards ask for, so we have no objections here."

"We" being Gladys and her grandfather.

"I hesitate to ask this," Becca said, mostly because she was afraid of Gladys's reaction, "but could you ask your grandfather about the nat? It's important."

"I'm sure he doesn't know more than I do. It predates him, you know."

"I know," Becca said. "I'm not looking for the official history. I'm looking for rumors or strange comments or stories that he gives no credence to."

"Grandfather ignores anything that can't be proven," Gladys said with something like pride. "If you want innuendo, go see Abigail Browning. She knows every old story about Hope—and most of them are just plain lies."

Becca had forgotten about Abigail Browning. She had been Jack Conyers's assistant—and first major resource—until they had some sort of falling out in the 1950s. For a while, she tried to run the "real" Hope Historical Society, but no one would give her funding, which she said was because she was a woman. Jack Conyers always claimed it was because she knew nothing about history.

She had become one of the town's characters until the transplanted Californian who started Hope's weekly "alternative" paper printed a story about an affair Abigail Browning and Jack Conyers had. The story was supposed to be sympathetic to Abigail—see how poorly this married man treated this sad spinster lady—but it had the opposite effect. Abigail lost any support she had among the locals for trying to steal Jack Conyers from his still-living, still-popular wife.

Becca would talk to Abigail Browning. But Becca also wanted to talk to Jack Conyers.

She stood. "Please do ask him."

"Oh, I will," Gladys said. "But I'm sure he won't know more than I do."

And with that, Becca knew she had no hope of seeing the town's official historian. So she'd see the unofficial one, and hope for the best.

THEN

The cabin got really hot that day and she wanted to open a window, but she was scared to. Mostly she slept and she hoped Jess Taylor would come back for her. She had to keep reminding herself that it was his cabin, he'd be back, but he didn't seem to have many things there, and Daddy had run away from more, so maybe Jess Taylor would, too.

Finally, Jess Taylor came back, looking tired and even more scared than when he'd left. His shirt was covered with sweat and some dirt ran along the side of his face. He had one of those overcoats—the short ones Daddy called a suit coat—and he hung it on a chair.

She stood beside the table, and waited for him to tell her to leave.

He looked at her, his big eyes sad. "I have bad news."

She held her breath. She wasn't sure what she'd do when he let her out of here. She hadn't eaten anything since that apple, and even though she took some water because she couldn't help herself—it was so hot inside—she would tell him and offer to repay him. Somehow. Maybe then he wouldn't turn her over to those people.

"Your mother," he said—and she let out a bit of that breath—"your mother and the other . . . people? . . . They're gone."

Her stomach clenched. "Gone?"

"That's what we say when we mean they died, honey."

Her cheeks heated. Everyone had told her Daddy was gone, too.

"I thought it just meant they went away," she said.

"It's a euphemism."

She'd never heard the word.

He shook his head tiredly. "A word we use when we don't want to be blunt. There are a lot of euphemisms in our language."

She nodded, even though she wasn't sure she understood.

"You're sure she's . . . gone?" she asked.

"Oh, I'm sure," he said, and shuddered. "You wouldn't ask if you knew the day I had today."

"What did you do?" she asked.

"Work white men wouldn't do," he said. "They consider what I did the dirty work."

She frowned. "What did you do?"

"I'm supposed to sit in a bank," he said. "But they said, *If you want to keep your job, you'll—*"

He stopped. Studied her like he wasn't sure what to say.

Then sighed.

"I helped bury them, Sarah."

"Bury?" She knew what that was, at least. She'd seen it—the wooden boxes, the holes in the ground, the markers. "If they had the boxes and stuff, how did you know my mother was there?"

It seemed to take him a minute to understand her. Then he nodded, once. "There were no boxes, honey," he said gently. "They were just placed in the ground."

Barbaric, that's what it is, her daddy said. *How can they do that to their own?*

It's a religious custom, her mother said. *We used to have them, too.*

"And they were dead?" she asked, her voice small.

"Oh, yeah," he said, and shuddered. "They were dead."

"Where are they?" she asked. "Where did you bury them?"

He studied her for a long time, as if he thought about whether or not to answer her.

Then he sighed again.

"It's a place they call the End of the World."

NOW

Abigail Browning lived in a fairy-tale cottage at the end of one of Hope's oldest streets. Large trees, which somehow thrived despite the desert air, surrounded the place, making it look even more like something out of Hansel and Gretel. Blooming plants lined the walk, plants that Becca knew took more water than summer water rationing allowed. She decided to ignore them as she stood on the brick steps and rapped on the solid oak door.

A latch slammed back and then the door pulled open, sending a wave of lavender scent outside. The woman who stood before Becca was short and hunched, not the tall powerhouse that Becca remembered from her childhood.

"Abigail Browning?" Becca asked.

"Don't you recognize me, Rebecca Keller? I practically raised you."

That wasn't quite true. Abigail Browning did babysit when Becca's parents couldn't find anyone else, but otherwise she had little to do with Becca's childhood.

"Sure I do, Mrs. Browning," Becca said, falling back on her childhood name for this woman, even though Abigail Browning had never married. "I was wondering if you could help me with a case."

Abigail Browning smiled and stepped away from the door. "Of course, my dear. Would you like some tea?"

"I'd love some," Becca said as she walked inside. The house smelled the same—lavender and baking bread with the faint undertone of cat.

Now Becca was old enough to appreciate the mahogany staircase, built Craftsman-style, and the matching bookcases that graced the living room. The entire house had mahogany trim as well as built-in shelving, a feature Becca knew that Chase would love—particularly since no one had painted over the original wood.

Mrs. Browning led her into the kitchen. A coffee cake sat in a glass case in the center of the table, almost as if Mrs. Browning had expected her. Mrs. Browning filled a kettle and put it on the stove, then climbed on a stool to remove large mugs from the shiny mahogany cupboards.

"I'm not as tall as I used to be," she said. "Time crushes all of us."

Becca nodded, uncertain what to say. "The kitchen looks just the same."

"Which negates the ten-thousand-dollar remodel I did two years ago," Mrs. Browning said.

Becca looked at her in surprise.

"I had to update everything. I had dry rot. Or the house did. Your husband helped me."

Becca opened her mouth to correct Mrs. Browning, then thought the better of it. Abigail Browning often made misstatements to see how other people stood on things.

"He's a good man," Mrs. Browning said. "Maybe the best in town, and you let him get away."

"I didn't let—"

"You confused him with your father, who was a horrid, manipulative man, and you forgot that men can be strong without being horrid."

Becca felt her cheeks heat. "Would you like to hear about the case?"

"More than you'd like to hear how you threw away a good man because a bad one raised you," Mrs. Browning said, taking down two plates.

Becca did not offer to help her. Instead, Becca stood near the table, hands crossed in front of her, feeling ten years old again.

"So tell me," Mrs. Browning said, putting the plates on the table. The kettle whistled, and she removed it from the heat. She grabbed a teapot from a shelf that looked old, but had to be new because Becca didn't remember it.

"I was wondering what you know about the natatorium."

"I can tell you how awful it smelled when I was a child, but that's not what you're asking, is it? Be specific, girl. Didn't I teach you anything?"

"What happened when it was built?"

"Which time?" Mrs. Browning set a beautiful wood trivet on the table, then placed the teapot on top of it.

"Which time?" Becca repeated. "Things are only built once, aren't they?"

Mrs. Browning stood near a chair near the teapot shelf, a chair that Becca remembered had always been Mrs. Browning's favorite. Becca had sat there once as a child, and had found it uncomfortable, molded to the elderly woman's body. Only then Mrs. Browning hadn't been elderly. She had only seemed that way.

"The foundation for the natatorium was laid at the same time as the hotel, around 1908. It was abandoned that same year."

"Abandoned?" Becca asked. "I heard that the work stopped."

"Probably from that horrible Gladys Conyers. She really knows only the textbook history of this town, which, I'm sorry to say, is wrong. People are never saints, you know. You always have to look for the darkness to balance the light."

Mrs. Browning peered at her. Mrs. Browning's eyes, buried under layers of wrinkles, were the same piercing blue they had always been.

Becca remembered Mrs. Browning trying to tell her that before. *You're the light, Rebecca. Remember that. Good things can come from dark places.*

She shook the memory away.

"Sit down, child, you're making me nervous."

Becca slid into her usual chair. Odd to think she had a usual chair, when she hadn't been to this house in more than twenty years.

"Do you still remember how to pour?"

Becca smiled. She did remember those lessons. Mrs. Browning had trained her in "company" manners, including how to set a table, how to dress for dinner, and how to pour for guests.

"I do," Becca said. She picked up the teapot, handling it as if Mrs. Browning had pulled down her silver service instead of her everyday.

Mrs. Browning watched her every move as if she were still being judged on perfection. Becca remembered everything, including when to ask if Mrs. Browning wanted sugar and cream, and to hold the top of the pot so that it wouldn't fall unceremoniously into Mrs. Browning's plate.

Mrs. Browning smiled, as if Becca's behavior was confirmation of the work she'd done bringing her up.

"So," Mrs. Browning said when Becca finished pouring, "which part of the natatorium are you interested in? The first building or the second?"

"I'm interested in the pool, whenever it was laid."

"The pool." Mrs. Browning pursed her lips. "So your Chase finally found the bodies, did he?"

Becca felt her breath catch. Whatever she'd expected Mrs. Browning to say, it wasn't that.

"You knew?"

"Child, half the town knew. Why do you think that no one was allowed near that old wreck?"

"But you swam there as a child."

"All of us did," Mrs. Browning said. "And some of us brought our own children there, until the place shut down. It was just a rumor, after all. Except for the hotel."

Becca frowned. "We're talking about the nat."

"We can't talk about the nat without talking about the hotel. Have you ever been inside?"

"Just last night, as a matter of fact."

"Did you look at the walls?"

Becca's frown grew deeper. "Yes."

"Then you understand why I told your Chase not to tear them down."

"No," Becca said, "I don't."

Mrs. Browning touched her hand with dry fingers. "Rebecca, you've never been slow. Haven't you wondered why those walls move?"

"They don't move," Becca said. "They have heat shimmers. It piles up and—"

"Heat shimmers occur on pavement in sunlight," Mrs. Browning said. "Not in a dark dusty hotel in the middle of a summer evening."

Becca licked her lips. When she was fourteen, she'd run from that hotel. She'd gone there to neck with Zack Wheeler, and when he'd pressed her against one of the walls, it was squishy. She turned to look at the wood, saw it shimmer, change, and shimmer again, and she couldn't help it.

She screamed.

Zack saw it, too, grabbed her hand, and pulled her out of there. They'd run all the way to his car, and even told his father, who had looked at them with contempt. That was the first time Becca had heard the heat shimmer idea, but it wasn't the last.

"So what causes it?" Becca asked.

"Aliens," Mrs. Browning said. "The aliens haunting the End of the World."

THEN

She couldn't go to the End of the World. She couldn't even leave the house. Jess Taylor didn't want her to. He was afraid for her. She was hot and sad and lonely, and she spent her days crying sometimes.

But she didn't practice changing. Instead, she worked on getting every detail right. Jess Taylor had to tell her sometimes that she was using masculine details—he'd actually laughed the time she put bits of hair on her own chin—but mostly, he said, she was looking solid.

Whatever that meant.

He wanted the town to think no one had survived. He didn't want them to question her or him.

It took him days and days to figure out how to do that. Then one day he told her. She was going to take a train.

NOW

Aliens? Of all the things Becca had expected from Mrs. Browning, a popular crazy notion wasn't one of them. Hope had been the talk of the alien conspiracy community since 2001, when one of her colleagues had discovered some metal in Lake Waloon. The lake had receded during one of the driest years on record, leaving all sorts of artifacts in its cracked and much-abused bed.

The experts, called in by the Historical Society, claimed it was part of an experimental airplane or maybe even one of the early do-it-yourself models from the 1920s.

UFO groupies looked at the pictures on the Internet and descended en masse to Hope, believing they'd found another ship like the one the government supposedly hid in Roswell, New Mexico.

Ever since, Hope had to endure annual pilgrimages from the UFO faithful. Becca tried to ignore them, just like she used to ignore the Deadheads when they came through on their way to Eugene to see the Grateful Dead in its natural habitat.

"Aliens," Becca said. "Surely you don't believe that hype from a few years ago—"

"Yes," Mrs. Browning said as she cut Becca a piece of coffee cake. "Of course I do. I grew up knowing that we'd been invaded. The fact that the ship was found simply confirmed it."

"The ship wasn't found," Becca said, and then caught herself. She'd learned in a few short months not to argue with the True Believers. Only she'd never taken Mrs. Browning to be one of them.

Mrs. Browning cut another piece of coffee cake and slid it onto her own plate. "If you do not believe that twisted hunk of metal was an alien spacecraft, then you won't believe anything I have to tell you about the natatorium."

Becca sighed. "I saw the so-called ship. It's just a crumpled aircraft."

"No," Mrs. Browning said. "It was molded to look like an aircraft. It's a spaceship."

Becca had heard this argument countless times as well. She took a deep breath, and then thought the better of all of it.

"All right," she said. "Let's pretend that you and I agree. Let's pretend that is a spaceship, and the squirming wall in the End of the World is made by alien ghosts. What else can you tell me?"

Mrs. Browning delicately cut her piece of coffee cake with her fork, her little finger extended. She had the same manners she always had. She seemed as sharp as she had thirty years ago.

But Becca knew that sometimes elderly people who lived alone developed "peculiarities." Now she was going to have to overlook Mrs. Browning's just to get to the heart of the story.

And maybe, just maybe, she was going to have to accept that she was wasting her time.

"Eat," Mrs. Browning said, "and I'll tell you what I know."

THEN

She hadn't been that frightened since Jess Taylor found her. She thought he was going to make her leave by train.

She didn't know where he'd send her or what she'd do or who she'd meet. But by now, she knew she could trust him. He brought her clothes. He fed her. He helped her.

They had long talks when he got home from the bank, and one night, he told her his family had died just like hers.

"In Hope?" she asked.

He shook his head. "Far away from Hope in a place called Mississippi."

"How come you didn't get killed?" she asked. She already knew he couldn't change, so she wanted to know how he got away.

"I was in the North," he said. "Ohio. Going to school in Antioch. Then the money stopped—my whole family was supporting me, giving me an education, and I sent letters to find out why, and someone sent me a postcard back. It was a drawing of the day—of the killings—like people were proud of it, and they said *Don't bother to come,* but I did anyway and . . ."

His voice trailed away. He didn't look at her. He was quiet a long time.

"What happened?" she asked because she couldn't take it anymore.

"I ran, and ended up in Hope."

NOW

Becca took a bite of her coffee cake. It was as good and rich as ever, a taste of her childhood.

Mrs. Browning watched her eat that bite, then leaned back in her own chair. Becca wondered if that position was even comfortable, given Mrs. Browning's pronounced dowager's hump.

"In the summer of aught eight, the shantytown just outside of Hope burned to the ground," Mrs. Browning began in her teacherly voice. "Most of the histories do not mention the shantytown. Those that do claim the fire threatened Hope itself. It didn't threaten the buildings that comprised Hope. It threatened the vision of Hope."

Very dramatic, Becca thought. She took another bite of cake, then followed it with a sip of tea, straining to keep her expression interested and credulous.

"The fire was as controlled a burn as the people of Hope could manage in those bygone days."

The ease with which Mrs. Browning told this story made Becca believe that Mrs. Browning used to recite it as part of the history project.

"The townspeople had gotten together and decided to rid themselves of the strangers once and for all."

Mrs. Browning shook her fork—still holding coffee cake—at Becca.

"If you look in the papers of the time, you'll see references to the strangers. They arrived in 1900, claiming to have lost their wagon several miles back. They had no luggage, few belongings, and they spoke a strange version of English. The locals thought they were ignorant immigrants who'd been tricked by their guide, and gave them some land just outside of town."

"Where the End of the World is?" Becca asked.

Mrs. Browning raised her eyebrows. "Am I telling this or are you?"

"Sorry," Becca said.

"Where that 1970s mall is. It's now near the center of town. But then, it was just outside, on land no one wanted. The strangers built their own little cabins—poorly. They looked like they didn't know what to do, and of course, no one was going to help them much more than provide a meal or some supplies. They got a bit of work, too."

Becca nodded, wishing Mrs. Browning would get on with it.

"I don't know what happened. The reference in various letters I've seen is that the strangers confirmed their demonic qualities. I have no idea what that means or how they confirmed demonic qualities, but the upshot is that the town fathers asked them to leave. The strangers said they wouldn't. The fight went on for some months, when finally the shantytown burned."

"A controlled burn," Becca said. "Started by?"

"Anyone who's everyone," Mrs. Browning said. "I never asked. Besides, everyone would've told me they had nothing to do with it. But you'll notice—well, of course you won't, they're all dead—but I noticed when I was young just how many of the older generation carried some burn marks on their hands. Except for that controlled burn, and the loss of a building here and there, Hope was one of the few western communities that didn't have a serious fire. And not all of these men worked for the Hope Volunteer Fire Department."

Becca finished her coffee cake. Then she picked up her tea mug and cradled it. "So they burned the shantytown. What has that to do with the natatorium?"

"It was being built. The hotel was just a shell—it wasn't nearly done yet—and the nat was dug, but not poured. It was going to be a tennis court. In those days, I believe the courts were clay. Not that it matters. It never got finished."

"Because . . . ?" Becca was trying to keep the frustration from her voice.

"Because the town hated the place. It reminded them that they hadn't lived up to that promise we all learned about."

Becca gripped the mug tightly. "I still don't see the connection."

Mrs. Browning sighed, as if Becca were a particularly slow student. "They used the fire to round up the strangers and herd them to the nat. Do I need to spell it out for you?"

"You're saying the town killed these strangers," Becca asked, "and buried them under the nat?"

"Yes." Mrs. Browning sounded exasperated.

"How many?"

"I don't know. No one kept records. I heard that they tried to bury them under the hotel, and when that didn't work, they went to the nat. That's why the ghosts haunt the hotel."

"You'd think they'd haunt the nat," Becca said.

"Hauntings aren't logical," Mrs. Browning said.

None of this was, Becca thought. "How do you know that these strangers were aliens, not just a group of Eastern Europeans who ran into some people who didn't understand them?"

"Because of the stories," Mrs. Browning said. "They had glowing eyes. They talked gibberish. They could seem taller than they were. And they came from nowhere. There were no wagon tracks. There was no wagon. And these people had no idea how people behaved. Not how Americans behaved, but how human beings behaved. They had to learn it all."

Becca shook her head. "I'm sorry, Mrs. Browning. But humans differ greatly. And if this group had been from a very different culture, the residents of Hope could have made the same charge. Aliens is as far-fetched as it came."

Mrs. Browning smiled sadly. "I believe it was aliens."

"Why?" Becca asked.

"Because I met one," Mrs. Browning said.

THEN

The train was big and dirty and smelly. Ash fell everywhere. It made an awful noise and she wanted to run away from it.

Jess Taylor stood beside her, holding her hand. He'd borrowed his neighbor's wagon, and they'd come to the small town of Brothers, which was two stops away from Hope.

"Remember," he said. "Tomorrow, you come here, and give the nice man this paper, and then you get on the train going that direction."

He pointed. He'd already shown her the engine, and how you could tell what direction a train was going in.

"I'll meet you at the station, and we'll pretend that we haven't seen each other in years. Okay?"

He'd told her all this before, and then it sounded easy, but now it just sounded terrifying. She wanted to get back in the wagon, get back in his house, and hide there forever.

But he said, now that her people were gone, she needed to have a life.

Where will I have this life? she asked him.

In Hope, he said. *With me.*

Momma and Daddy said humans didn't do these things, they didn't make that kind of commitment, they didn't understand permanence and obligation and responsibility, which made them dangerous.

But Jess Taylor wasn't dangerous. And he seemed to understand all those words. He seemed to live them.

Only they came back now that she was standing on the platform with him, staring at the train.

"It's only one night," he said. "I already paid for the room. You'll be safe."

She wanted to believe him. But she was scared. What if she

changed by accident? What if she said something wrong? Would they make her scream? Would they bury her without a box?

Who would tell Jess Taylor?

How would he ever know?

NOW

"I was just a little girl," Mrs. Browning said, "and she was very old. Older than anyone I'd ever seen. She came to the natatorium when I was swimming there. She cried."

"She cried?" Becca asked.

Mrs. Browning nodded. "She stood back from the pool, and she cried as she looked at it. My mother was there with me, and she just stared. Then she told me to get my towel. It was time to go."

"I don't understand," Becca said. "How do you know the old woman was an alien."

"There'd always been stories about her," Mrs. Browning said. "She came to town to see her uncle, and she never left. At least that was the story, and some people claimed they saw her get off the train. But a few said the luggage she carried was her uncle's, and that he'd brought her there that very afternoon."

"So?" Becca asked.

"So that was right after the massacre. It was strange that he had a niece no one had ever heard of."

Becca shrugged. "I'm so sorry to be skeptical, Mrs. Browning, but I still don't understand how that translates to alien."

"I saw her once, all by myself. She was sitting at a bus stop near the old bank, and she put her hand on the bench. Her hand slid right through it."

Becca sighed. "You're not going to convince me. Not without some kind of real proof."

"What about those bodies, young lady?" Mrs. Browning said, bringing herself up as close to her old height as she could. "Are those good enough for you? They're not human, are they?"

Becca flashed on the broken femurs, so recognizable. "Of course they are."

Mrs. Browning's cheeks flushed. "You're just saying that."

"Actually," Becca said, "I'm not."

THEN

That night, she slept on a single bed behind the kitchen of Mrs. Mother's Brothers Boardinghouse. Colored people—which was her and Jess Taylor, apparently—didn't get their own rooms. They couldn't even really stay at the boardinghouse, but Jess Taylor knew the cook, who volunteered to share her room. Mrs. Mother, the old lady who ran the place, had frowned in that mean way some humans had, but all she said was, "Make sure it doesn't get into the food."

She didn't understand for the longest time that the "it" Mrs. Mother referred to was her.

Maybe that's why Daddy said this was a dangerous place, why humans were scary people. She hadn't even known they cared about differences, and now she was finding out that the differences were everything.

No wonder they'd gone after her people. She hadn't noticed Jess Taylor's differences from the men at the bank and as time went on, she began to understand how badly her own people had mimicked the humans. No knee dimples, too smooth skin, eyes that didn't blink.

If the dark skin or the long braid of hair running down the back or the upswept eye angle scared them, they must've been really terrified by a whole group of people whose skin had no wrinkles, whose ankles didn't stick out, and whose expressions never changed.

No wonder.

Then she remembered Jess Taylor: *I can't believe I'm defending them* and she knew just how he felt.

The bed in the kitchen had bugs. They bit her during the night. Upstairs people laughed, and the place smelled like grease, and she wanted some water, just so she could wash the bugs off, but she didn't.

She picked them off and squished them between her fingers, and finally she got out of that bed and sat in a rocking chair, and watched out the window until the sun came up.

Then she picked up her little bag and walked to the train station, just like Jess Taylor had told her to do, and she sat on the far edge of the platform so no one but the man who worked there saw her, and she waited for the train.

NOW

Becca was happy to leave. Mrs. Browning did tell her other stories about the natatorium—stories about its first few days as a recreation center, stories about the celebrities who used it—but both Becca and Mrs. Browning knew that the stories were merely Mrs. Browning's way of saving face.

As Becca made her good-byes, holding a piece of that delicious coffee cake in a napkin, both she and Mrs. Browning knew that she would never really trust Mrs. Browning again.

All the way to her car, Becca tried not to let sadness overwhelm her. She had lost more than a source for Hope's history. She'd lost an icon of her youth.

She had always believed that Abigail Browning was a woman of unassailable intellect and integrity. Even through the Conyers' scandal, Becca's opinion did not change. She still nodded at Abigail Browning on the street when others hadn't, and she still revered the woman she had once known.

If anything, the scandal had clarified something for her: Becca finally understood why Mrs. Browning, who had always seemed more knowledgeable than Mr. Conyers, had stopped working at the Hope Historical Society.

Now Becca wasn't so sure. Now she wondered if Mrs. Browning was fired because she believed the strange stories—the ones that had always been part of Hope. Stories of ghosts and aliens and things that went bump in the night.

Becca got into the squad and turned the ignition. The crappy air-conditioning felt worse than the heat in Mrs. Browning's garden. Maybe if Becca believed in fairy tales, she would actually believe that Mrs. Browning had some sort of magic that kept the heat and the desert at bay.

But Becca only believed in reality. And only the reality she could see, Chase used to say. She could never envision his projects, not even when she looked at the architectural renderings.

She always had to wait until he was done to understand how perfect his vision had been.

What had Mrs. Browning said about Chase? *You confused him with your father, who was a horrid, manipulative man, and you forgot that men can be strong without being horrid.*

That's what Becca should have asked about. She should have asked what Mrs. Browning meant by that statement—not about Chase: women who hadn't married Chase loved him (hell, *Becca* still loved him)—but about her father.

Tell me about your father, her therapist said once.

He was a good man, Becca said.

But he didn't like your job.

Becca had smiled. *He was old-fashioned. He believed women didn't belong outside the home.*

What about in a police car?

Becca had laughed. *Are you kidding? He stopped paying for my school when he heard what I wanted to do.*

Is Chase like him?

Of course not, Becca said.

But your father's action sounds manipulative. You say Chase is manipulative.

Not like that, Becca said. *He respects women.*

Does he respect you?

Becca sighed and leaned back against the seat of the squad. Did he respect her? Yesterday, she would have said no, and she would have said that his secretive call about the nat proved it.

But couldn't it also be viewed the other way? Couldn't his

call be a sign of trust, of faith in her abilities instead of faith in his own ability to control her?

Could Mrs. Browning be right?

Becca shook her head. A headache was forming between her eyes. She put the squad in gear just as her cell rang.

She unhooked it from her belt and looked at the display. Jillian Mills. Becca took the call.

"Can you come down here?" Jillian asked.

"Is this about the nat?" Becca asked.

"Yeah," Jillian said. "I have the weirdest results."

THEN

They took her ticket just like Jess Taylor said they would, but they wouldn't let her sit in a chair like everybody else. They put her on one of the platforms in the back. The ash and the dirt and the stink were awful there, and as the train started to pull away, she could see the rails move.

She tried the door to get inside, but someone had locked it. She pounded on it, and the men in the nearby chairs—the men with white skin—laughed at her and pointed and she moved away from the blackened window so that they couldn't see her any more.

She was afraid they'd come out and hurt her.

Like they hurt her momma.

Like they hurt Jess Taylor's family.

She was scared now, and she tried not to let that change her. Because if she changed, she'd lose this chance. She'd spend her life—what was left of it—as a railing or a board or a doorknob. And then, because she couldn't sleep-change, she'd starve and fall off, all decayed, and they'd toss her aside—*what is that dried-up thing?*—and she'd die, probably in the nearby sagebrush, all alone.

Just like her daddy.

The whole trip, she stared straight ahead and clung to her

bag and thought about Jess Taylor waiting for her. Thought about shoulders and backs and legs and human forms so that the spikes wouldn't come out of her spine or her eyes wouldn't shift to a different part of her head.

She thought and thought and was surprised when she realized she could hardly wait to get back to Hope.

NOW

Becca's stomach clenched the entire way to the coroner's office. She wished she hadn't eaten that coffee cake now. She wished she hadn't gone to Mrs. Browning's. She didn't want the thoughts that were crowding her brain. She didn't want to think the weird results were because some aliens were massacred in Hope.

And yet she was thinking just that.

The coroner's office was on a side street behind Hope's main police station. The office wasn't an office at all, more like a science lab, morgue, and training area rolled into one.

The college student who ran the front desk in exchange for rent in the studio apartment above was reading Dostoyevsky. He barely looked up as Becca entered.

"She's expecting you," he said.

Becca nodded and continued to the small room that served as Jillian's office. The smell of decay and formaldehyde seemed less here than it did near the door, and wasn't nearly as strong as it was in the basement where the autopsies actually took place.

Jillian was standing behind her desk, sorting paper files. She wore a clean white smock over her clothes—a sure sign that she had just finished an autopsy—and had her hair pulled back with a copper barrette.

"Your life just got easier," Jillian said without preamble.

"How's that?" Becca asked.

"Close the door."

Becca did.

"I did some preliminary work before calling the state crime lab," Jillian said. "Those bodies down there, they're not human."

Becca felt a shiver run down her back.

"I'm not sure what they are. I'm not even sure they are bodies."

Becca gripped the back of the nearest chair. She didn't want Mrs. Browning to be right.

"What are they, then? Aliens?"

Jillian laughed. "Of course not. Whatever gave you that idea?"

"Abigail Browning," Becca said.

"Oh, our local UFOlogist," Jillian said. "You know she's been making her living these last few years providing historical tours of Lake Waloon?"

How could Becca have missed that? So Abigail Browning had a stake in keeping the alien story alive. And what could be better than a tale of alien massacre?

Hell, that would even give her a measure of revenge against Jack Conyers, showing that the story of racial unity in Hope was really just a myth.

"Just wondering," Becca said, trying to make light of it.

"Well, we all are. From what I can tell, these are very old bones—if they are bones as we know them. The material is something else, and it's hollow."

"But they looked human."

"So do a lot of things. Mammalian bones tend to look alike. I've had new trainees mistake cat spines and rib cages for human babies."

Becca swallowed. "What about the smell?"

"Well, that's the odd part," Jillian said. "It's coming from the—whatever they are—bones."

"Huh?"

Jillian shrugged. "Let me show you."

She grabbed an evidence bag from a table beside her desk. Inside was what looked to Becca to be an adult human rib bone. It even had the proper curvature.

"Break it," Jillian said.

"Isn't this destroying evidence?"

"Of what? Alien massacre? Just break it."

Becca grabbed a pair of medical gloves from the box beside Jillian's desk, then opened the evidence bag. She took out the rib bone and immediately felt a sense of wrongness. It was too squishy. Even bones that had been in damp ground for a long period of time never felt like this—almost like a rubber chew toy that had been well loved.

Becca turned it over in her fingers, feeling a gag reflex and swallowing hard against it.

Jillian nodded. "Kinda gross, huh?"

Becca didn't answer. Instead, she grabbed both ends of the bone and bent.

If it had been made of rubber—even old rubber—the bone should've bent with her hands. But it didn't bend. It snapped, and a waft of rot filled Becca's nose, almost as if she had put her face in the middle of a decaying corpse.

"Jesus Christ," she said, dropping both pieces into the evidence bag. "You could've warned me."

The gag reflex had gotten worse. Her eyes watered and she resisted the urge to wipe at them. She'd learned that lesson long ago, when she'd been a rookie: *Don't touch your own skin after touching a corpse.*

But that wasn't a corpse. It wasn't even a real bone, at least not of a kind she was familiar with.

"C'mon." Jillian took the sealed evidence bag from her and led Becca to the back room where cleaning solutions and the sharp-scented nostril-clearing substance that Jillian preferred waited.

Becca inhaled the substance, feeling her nose clear as if she'd sniffed smelling salts, and then she grabbed a clean washcloth, wiped her face, and leaned against a metal filing cabinet.

"So what the hell is it?" she asked.

"I wish I knew. I'm going to be calling not just the state, but some anthropologists to see if they've seen anything like it."

"Then why did you tell me my job got easier?"

"Because," Jillian said, "there's no recent body. There aren't even old bodies. There's a mystery, yes, but it's an archaeological one. There's probably some plant or root or something that does this, and maybe it's extinct or something, which is why we're not familiar with it."

"You mean like that death plant?" Becca asked.

"The corpse flower?" Jillian nodded. "I forgot about that. I'll look it up online. Maybe it used to grow around here."

Becca's fingers tingled. The bone—or whatever it was—had felt alive, but the way that plant roots did. She could believe that Chase had discovered the remains of a very old plant much more easily than believing that an alien massacre happened in Hope.

"You want to tell Chase," Jillian asked, "or should I?"

Becca felt her breath catch. Chase's dream project was still on. It would still happen.

One day, the End of the World would become the premiere resort in Eastern Oregon.

"He's not going to be able to work for a while. If they think this thing is unusual, they'll do some excavation," Jillian said. "But it's not like a major dig, and it's not a crime scene. He should be thrilled."

Becca smiled in spite of her stinging nose. "Thrilled probably isn't the word I'd use. But he'll be relieved, once he's past the immediate inconvenience."

Jillian crossed her arms, looking amused. "So am I telling him?"

"No," Becca said, "I will."

THEN

The train passed it.

Jess Taylor hadn't warned her.

But there was a big hand-carved sign saying, FUTURE HOME OF THE END OF THE WORLD RESORT. And there was a finished building right at the edge, with the word *Hotel* on it. And a big brown patch where somebody had dug a hole and then covered it up.

Her mommy was in there.

She went to the edge of the platform and stared at it until it got tiny in the distance.

And then she remembered: Her daddy, days before he left, telling Momma—

If anything happens, we go to the End of the World. We burrow into the walls or slide against the frames. We become other. We hibernate until our own people return.

She never learned how. Grown ones could do it. And they could coax their children into it, but no child could do it on her own.

She'd only seen the shimmers a few times, back when she was really little, in the ship before it crashed. Lots and lots of her people, people she didn't see until Daddy woke them, shimmered in the back compartment.

Sometimes they'd have dreams and you'd see their ghostly selves, wandering through the ship. She got scared by that, but Momma said it was normal. It was a way to check how time was passing, and when it was safe to wake up.

She didn't see any shimmers as she passed the End of the World.

She didn't see anyone she knew. It was quiet and empty and lonely.

Her people were really and truly gone, and now she was the only one left to wait for the others. The ones who were supposed to rescue them.

If they ever came.

NOW

Becca and Chase stood at the End of the World, staring at the hole dug into the floor of the natatorium. It was early evening, little more than twenty-four hours since Chase called Becca to the scene.

The area was quiet—as quiet as the desert got. A high-pitched whine that came from a bug Becca could not identify came from just outside the broken wall. The wind rustled a tarp that covered some of the wood Chase had bought, and not too far away a bird peeped, probably as it hunted the whining bugs.

The sounds of workers waiting for instructions, the low buzz-growl of her radio unit, the crunch of vans on gravel were in the recent past. Right now, it was just her, Chase, and the plantlike bonelike things half buried in the ground.

The smell wasn't as bad as it had been the day before. The bonelike things weren't freshly broken. The scent was fading, just like the smell of a dead body faded to an annoyance when the body was removed from the scene.

She and Chase stood side by side in the patch of sunlight that filtered through the hole in the natatorium wall. She had brought him down here to tell him the news, and when she finished, he didn't say a word.

He swallowed once, stared at the ground, and then closed his eyes. His entire body trembled. She thought he was going to cry.

Then he took a deep breath, pushed his hard hat back, and frowned. "No one died."

"That's right," Becca said.

"And these aren't bodies."

Not human ones anyway, she almost said, but then felt the joke was in poor taste. For all she knew, Chase could have talked to Mrs. Browning, too. He might have heard the alien rumors as well.

"Jillian thinks they're the remains of plants."

"*Thinks?*" Chase asked.

Becca shrugged. "All she knows is that they're not bone, not from humans or from animals. And they're the source of the smell."

"Weird," Chase said.

"You won't be able to work in the nat for a while," Becca said. "People are coming from U of O and OSU's science and archaeological departments to see what they can learn. Jillian thinks they might contact the Smithsonian or someplace like that. She made a ballpark estimate of eight months, but it could be more than that. It could be less."

Chase nodded. He still wasn't looking at her. "I can finish the hotel, though."

"The hotel, the golf course, the houses, you can do all of it."

"Golf courses," he reminded her.

"Golf courses," she said.

They stood in silence for a moment longer. Chase had his head bowed, as if he were looking at a grave.

Then he asked, "They'll clear this away?"

"Probably," Becca said. "Or you might have to find a way to build over it. You certainly don't want one of those things to break while guests are using the pool."

He shuddered, then nodded. He took off his hard hat and twisted it between his hands.

"Mrs. Browning says you're keeping the walls of the hotel," Becca said.

He looked at her sideways. "You spoke to Abigail?"

Becca nodded. "You know she used to babysit me, way back when."

"That's what she said. She also said I should give you time."

Becca felt her cheeks flush. That old woman meddled. "For what?"

He shrugged and looked away. "I still love you, Becca."

She wondered if that was manipulation. Or if it was just truth. Had she always mistaken truth for manipulation, and manipulation for truth?

Had she thrown away the most important thing in her life because she hadn't recognized it, because she hadn't been prepared for it, because nothing in her life taught her how to understand it?

She had had set ideas on the way that men were, on the ways they treated their wives, on the way they lived their lives.

We all have prejudices, her therapist had once told her, early in their sessions. *The key is recognizing them, and going around them. Because if we don't, we never see what's in front of us.*

Becca looked at the plantlike things. She had initially seen bone because of the smell, but they weren't bone. They just looked like bone. They were harmless and old and a curiosity, but not evidence of a horrible past.

She had misunderstood. Chase had misunderstood. And the End of the World had nearly died once again.

"You really love this place, don't you?" she said to Chase.

"It's the first place I recognized Hope's potential," he said. "It just took me fifteen years to get enough money and clout to bring my dream to reality."

"And this almost ruined it. What would you have done if Mrs. Browning had been right? If this was the site of a massacre?"

He put his hard hat on, then gave her a rueful look. "She told you that? About the aliens? Is that why you asked about the walls?"

"If there are alien ghosts, then you'll have some troubles when the End of the World opens."

"If there are alien ghosts, I'll get a lot of free publicity from the Sci-Fi Channel and the Travel Channel."

This time, she understood his tone. For all its lightness, it had some tension. He had thought about this. "It worried you, didn't it, when you dug this up?"

He nodded.

"Did you think she might be telling the truth?"

"Her version of it," he said. "Weren't you the one who told me that rumors hid real events? Maybe something bad had happened in Hope, and people made up the other story to cover it up."

"Not that anyone thought of aliens in 1908," Becca said.

He grinned, and slipped an arm around her. "Ever practical, aren't you, Becca?"

"Not ever," she said. Not during the drive from Mrs. Browning's to the coroner's office. Not when she remembered how that wall felt, squishy against her back.

"You never told me," she said. "Are you keeping the walls?"

"Why do you care?" he asked.

"They bother me," she said.

He looked at her. "You saw the alien ghosts."

She shook her head. "I didn't see anything. I just got scared as a teenager, is all."

He pulled her close. She didn't move away.

"Sometimes in old buildings," he said, "I feel like I can touch the past."

He wasn't looking at the ground anymore. He was looking past the sunlight, into the desert itself.

"That's what you think that is?" Becca asked. "The past?"

"Or something," he said. "A bit of memory. A slice of time. Who knows? I always try to preserve that part of the old buildings, though."

"Why?" Becca asked.

"Because otherwise they're not worth saving. They're just wood or brick or marble. Ingredients. Buildings are living things, just like people."

She'd never heard mystical talk from him. Maybe she'd never listened.

"It's not about the money?" she asked.

"Becca, if it were about the money, I'd build cookie-cutter developments all over Hope and make millions." He shook his head. "It's about finding the surprises, whatever they might be. Good or bad."

"Or both," Becca said, moving some dirt at the edge of the hole.

"Or both," he said. "Sometimes I like both."

"Me, too," she said. Then she studied him.

They were good together, but sometimes they were bad. She felt that longing for speed-dial, then wondered if therapists were good and bad—good for some people, bad for others.

Maybe she should just trust herself.

She slid her hand into his.

He looked at her, surprised.

They stayed at the End of the World until the sun set—and waited for answers that might never ever come.

THEN

The train had stopped in Hope for a long time before Jess Taylor found her. Her hand had molded to the railing near the door, and she couldn't remember how to set it free.

Besides, no one had unlocked the door for her. Apparently they thought it would be funny for her to climb over the edge to get off the train.

When he saw her, stuck there, her arm ending not in a hand but in a railing that went around the back of the train, he didn't say anything. Instead, he came up beside her. He hugged her, and she leaned into him.

He'd never hugged her before.

Then he set his own arm right next to hers, placing his hand right next to the place hers should be. And he watched as she shifted, slowly—fingers were so hard—and his body shielded hers from the platform, and all those other people meeting their families.

When she finished, and her arm fell at her side—complete with a perfectly formed hand—he said, very softly, "They locked you out here, huh?"

She nodded and felt tears for the second time that day.

"I'm sorry. I didn't think they'd do that to a child."

And she thought of the End of the World, and all the children—the older children who had been her friends—and how they hadn't been locked out, they'd been *killed* and he'd helped bury them to keep his job, and she wondered how he could say something like that.

But she kept quiet. She was learning it was best to keep quiet sometimes.

"From now on," he was saying softly—she almost couldn't hear him over the engine, clanging as it cooled—"everyone'll think you're my niece from Mississippi. Try to talk like I do, and don't answer a lot of questions about back home. All right?"

"All right." She already knew this anyway. He'd told her before they went to Brothers.

"If we do this right," he said, pulling her close, "no one will ever know."

She swallowed, just like he did when he was nervous. No one would ever know. About her, about her family, about her people. No one would understand that for a while, her people waited and hoped.

Maybe she'd live to see the rescue ship come.

She wondered if she would recognize it.

She wondered if she would care.

Jess Taylor took her little bag with one hand, and with the other he took her newly made hand.

"Chin up, Sarah," he said, using the name she would hear from now on. In time, it would become her, just like the two arms and two legs and the permanent form and the dark skin would become her. Her self. Her identity.

She straightened her shoulders like he had taught her. She held her head high.

And then, clinging to Jess Taylor for support, she took her final steps away from the world she'd always known.

She took her first real steps into Hope.

❖ DARK HEAVEN ❖

Gregory Benford

THE BODY was bloated and puckered. The man looked to be in his thirties maybe, but with the bulging face and goggle eyes it was hard to tell. His pants and shirt were gone so he was down to his skivvies. They were grimy on the mud beach.

That wasn't unusual at all. Often the gulf currents pulled the clothes off. Inquisitive fish or sharks came to visit, and indeed there was a chunk out of the left calf and thigh. Someone had come for a snack. Along the chest and belly were long raised red marks, and that was odd. McKenna hadn't seen anything like that before.

McKenna looked around, but the muddy beach and stands of reeds held nothing of interest. As the first homicide detective there it was his case, and they were spread so thin he got no backup beyond a few uniforms. Those were mostly just standing around. The photo/video guy was just finishing with his systematic sweep of the area.

The body didn't smell. It had been in the salt water at least a day, the Medical Examiner had said, judging from the swelling. McKenna listened to the drone of the ME's summary as he circled around the body, his boots scrunching on the beach.

Outside Mobile and the coastal towns, most bodies get found by a game warden or fisherman or by somebody on a beach party who wanders off into the cattails. This one was apparently a washup, left by the tide for a cast fisherman to find.

A kid had called it in. There was no sign of a boating accident and no record of men missing off a fishing boat; McKenna had checked before leaving his office.

The sallow-faced ME pointed up to a pine limb. "Buzzards get the news first." There were three up there in the cypress.

"What are those long scars?" McKenna asked, ignoring the buzzards.

"Not a propeller, not knife wounds. Looks swole up." A shrug. "I dunno for now."

"Once you get him on the table, let me know."

The ME was sliding the corpse's hands into a metal box with a battery pack on the end. He punched in a command and a flash of light lit the hand for an instant.

"What's that?" McKenna pointed.

The ME grinned up at him as he fitted the left hand in, dropping the right. "I thought the perfessor was up on all the new tech."

McKenna grimaced. Back at the beginning of his career he had been the first in the department to use the Internet very much, when he had just been promoted into the ranks that could wear a suit to work. He read books too, so for years everybody called him the "perfessor." He never corrected their pronunciation and they never stopped calling him that. So for going on plenty of years now he was the "perfessor" because he liked to read and listen to music in the evenings rather than hang out in bars or go fishing. Not that he didn't like fishing. It gave a body time to think.

The ME took his silence as a mild rebuke and said finally, as the light flashed again, "New gadget, reads fingerprints. Back in the car I connect it and it goes wireless to the FBI database, finds out who this guy is. Maybe."

McKenna was impressed but decided to stay silent. It was better to be known as a guy who didn't talk much. It increased the odds that when you did say something, people listened. He turned and asked a uniform, "Who called it in?"

It turned out to be one of the three kids standing by a prowl car. The kid had used a cell phone of course and knew nothing more. He and his buddies were just out here looking, he said. For what, he didn't say.

The ME said, "I'd say we wait for the autopsy before we do more." He finished up. Homicide got called in on accidental deaths, suicides, even deaths by natural causes, if there was any doubt. "How come you got no partner?" the ME asked.

"He's on vacation. We're shorthanded."

McKenna turned back to the beach for a last look. So the case was a man in his thirties, brown hair cropped close, a mustache, no scars. A tattoo of a dragon adorned the left shoulder. Except for the raised red stripes wrapped around the barrel chest, nothing unusual that McKenna could spot. But those red ridges made it a possible homicide, so here he was.

Anything more? The camera guy took some more shots and some uniforms were searching up and down the muddy beach but they weren't turning up anything. McKenna started to walk away along the long curve of the narrow beach and then turned back. The ME was already supervising two attendants, the three of them hauling the body onto a carry tarp toward the morgue ambulance. "Was it a floater?" McKenna called.

The ME turned and shouted back, "Not in long enough, I'd say."

So maybe in the gulf for a day, tops, McKenna figured as his boots squished through the mud back to his car. Without air in the lungs, bodies sank unless a nylon jacket or shirt held a bubble and kept them on the surface. More often a body went straight down to the sand and mud until bacteria in the gut did its work and the gas gave lift, bringing the dead soul back into sunshine and more decay. But that took days here so this one was fresh. He didn't have to wait on the ME to tell him that, and except for fingerprints and the teeth, that was probably all the physical evidence they would ever get from the poor bastard back there.

The ME caught up to him and said, "He's real stiff, too, so I'd say he struggled in the water a while."

McKenna nodded. A drowning guy burns up his stored sugar and the muscles go rigid quickly.

Two uniforms were leaning against his car, picking their teeth, and he answered their nods but said nothing. This far from Mobile McKenna was technically working beyond his legal limits, but nobody stood on procedure this far into the woods. Not on the coast. The body might be from Mississippi or even Louisiana or Florida, given the gulf currents, so jurisdiction was uncertain, and might never be decided. A body was a body was a body, as an old New Orleans cop had told him once. Gone to rest. It belongs to no one anymore.

People started out in life looking different. But they ended up a lot alike. Except this one had some interesting ridges.

McKenna recalled being called out for bodies that turned out to be parts of long-drowned deer, the hair gone missing from decay. People sometimes mistook big dogs and even cows for people. But he had never seen any body with those long ridges of reddened, puckering flesh on anything. At least those made this case interesting.

He paused in the morning mist that gathered up from the bayou nearby and watched the impromptu funeral cortege escort the body away, prowl cars going first, crunching along the narrow oyster shell road. The kids were staring at the body, the uniforms, eyeing every move.

Routine, really, probably leading to nothing at all. But something about this bothered him and he could not say what.

He drove back toward Mobile with the window open to the pine-scented spring breezes. To get back from Bayou La Batre, you turn north toward U.S. 90. But he kept going east on two-lane blacktop. At a Citgo station a huge plastic chicken reared up from the bed of a rusted-out El Camino, pointing to a Sit 'n Rest Restaurant that featured shrimp and oysters and fresh catch, the proceeds of the gulf that had long defined Bayou La Batre.

The book that turned into the movie *Forrest Gump* was set

partly around there and the whole place looked it. But Katrina and the hurricanes that came after, pounding the coast like an angry Climate God, had changed the terms of discussion. As if the aliens hadn't, too.

He watched people walking into the Sit 'n Rest and wondered if he should stop and eat. The sunset brimmed the empty sky with rosy fingers, but he didn't feel like eating yet. There was a bottle of Pinot Grigio waiting at home and he somehow didn't want to see people tonight. But he did want to swing by the Centauri Center. The ones around here regarded everybody else as "farmers," as locals along the coast refer to anyone who lives inland. Tough and hardworking people, really, and he respected them. They could handle shrimp, hurricanes, civil rights, federal drug agents, so why should aliens from another star be any more trouble? At least the aliens didn't want to raise taxes.

And he had taken this case off the board right away, back in Mobile, because it gave him a chance to go by the Centauri Center. He kept going across the long flat land toward the bay, looking for the high building he had read about but never seen. The feds kept people away from here, but he was on official business.

There were boats in the trees. Two shrimpers, eighty feet long at least, lying tilted on their hulls in scrub oak and pine, at least half a mile from their bayou. Bows shoved into the green, their white masts and rigging rose like bleached treetops. Still not pulled out, nine months since the last hurricane had howled through here. The feds had other things to do, like hosting amphibians from another star.

That, and discounting insurance for new construction along the Gulf Coast. Never mind that the glossy apartments and condos were in harm's way just by being there.

Just barely off-road, a trawler had its bow planting a hard kiss on a pine. He drove through a swarm of yellow flies, rolling up the windows though he liked the aroma of the marsh grass.

He had heard the usual story, a federal acronym agency turned into a swear word. A county health officer had the boats declared a public hazard, so the Coast Guard removed the fuel and batteries, which prompted FEMA to say it no longer had reason to spend public money on retrieving private property, and it followed as the night the day that the state and the city submitted applications to "rescue" the boats. Sometime real soon now.

Wind dimpled the bays beside the causeway leading to Mobile Bay. Willow flats and drowned cypress up the far inlets gave way to cattails, which blunted the marching white tops of the bay's hard chop. They were like endless regiments that had defeated oil platforms and shipping fleets but broke and churned against the final fortress of the land.

He drove toward Mobile Bay and soon he could see what was left of the beachfront.

The sun sparkled on the bay and heat waves rose from the beaches so the new houses there seemed to flap in the air like flags of gaudy paper.

They were pricey, with slanted roofs and big screened porches, rafts supported meters above the sand on tall stilts. They reminded him of ladies with their skirts hoisted to step over something disagreeable.

He smiled at the thought and then felt a jolt as he saw for the first time the alien bunker near the bay. It loomed over the center of Dauphin Island, where fed money had put it up with round-the-clock labor, to Centauri specs. The big dun-colored stucco frame sloped down toward the south. Ramps led onto the sand where waves broke a few meters away. Amphibian access, he guessed. It had just been finished, though the papers said the Centauri delegation to this part of the Gulf Coast had been living in parts of it for over a year.

He slowed as the highway curved past and nosed into a roadblock. A woman fed officer in all-black fatigues came over to the window. McKenna handed out his ID and the narrow-faced woman asked, "You have business here?"

"Just following a lead on a case."

"Going to need more than that to let you get closer."

"I know." She kept her stiff face and he said, "Y'know, these wrinkles I got at least show that I smiled once upon a time."

Still the flat look. He backed away and turned along a curve taking him inland. He was a bit irked with himself, blundering in like that, led only by curiosity, when his cell phone chimed with the opening bars of "Johnny B. Goode." He wondered why he'd said that to her, and recalled an article he had read this week. Was he a dopamine-rich nervous system pining for its serotonin heartthrob? Could be, but what use was knowing that?

He thumbed the phone on and the ME's voice said, "You might like to look at this."

"Or maybe not. Seen plenty."

"Got him on the table, IDed and everything. But there's something else."

The white tile running up to the ceiling reminded him that this place got hosed down every day. You did that in damp climates because little life-forms you could barely see came through even the best air-conditioning and did awful things to dead matter. Otherwise it was like all other autopsy rooms. Two stainless steel tables, overhead spray hoses on auto, counters of gleaming stainless, cabinets and gear on three walls. The air-conditioning hummed hard but the body smell layered the room in a damp musk. The ME was working and barely glanced up. The county couldn't afford many specialists so the ME did several jobs.

Under the relentless ceramic lights the body seemed younger. Naked, tanned legs and arms and face, the odd raised welts. The ME was at home with bodies, touching and probing and squeezing. Gloved fingers combing the fine brown hair. Fingers in the mouth and throat, doubtless after probing the other five openings with finer tools. The ME used a magnifying glass to look carefully at the throat, shook his head as if at another idea gone sour, then picked up a camera.

He studied the extremities, feet and hands and genitalia. The magnifier swept over the palms and fingers and he took pictures, the flash startling McKenna, adding a sudden whiteness to the ceramic room.

The ME looked up as if noticing McKenna for the first time. "Wanna help?"

They turned the body after McKenna pulled on rubber gloves. A head-to-foot search, careful attention to the tracery of raised yellow-white marks that now had deep purple edges. The bruises lay under the skin and were spreading like oozing ink. The ME took notes and samples and then stepped back and sighed.

"Gotta say I just dunno. He has two clear signatures. Drowning in the lungs, but his heart stopped before that."

"From what?"

"Electrocution. And there's these—" He showed five small puncture wounds on both arms. Puckered and red. "Funny, not like other bites I've seen. So I got to do the whole menu, then."

The county had been going easy on full autopsies. They cost and budgets were tight. "At least you have his name."

"Ethan Anselmo. No priors, FBI says. Married, got the address."

"Wounds?"

"The big welts, I dunno. Never seen such. I'll send samples to the lab. Those punctures on the hands, like he was warding something off. That sure didn't work."

"Torture?"

"Not any kind I know."

"Anybody phone the widow?"

He looked up from his notes, blinking back sweat though the air-conditioning was running full blast. "Thought that was your job."

It was. McKenna knocked on the door of the low-rent apartment and it swung open to reveal a woman in her thirties with worried eyes. He took a deep breath and went into the ritual.

Soon enough he saw again the thousand-yard stare of the new widow. It came over her after he got only a few sentences into his description. Ordinary people do not expect death's messenger to be on the other side of the knock. Marcie Anselmo got a look at the abyss and would never be the same.

McKenna never wanted to be the intruder into others' pain. He didn't like asking the shell-shocked widow details about their life, his job, where he'd been lately. All she knew was he hadn't come home last night. He did some night jobs but he had never stayed out all night like this before.

He spent a long hour with her. She said he sometimes hung out at The Right Spot. McKenna nodded, recognizing the name. Then they talked some more and he let the tensions rise and fall in her, concluding that maybe it was time to call their relatives. Start the process. Claim the body, the rest. Someone would be calling with details.

He left his card. This part went with the job. It was the price you paid to get to do what came next. Figure out. Find out.

Ethan Anselmo had worked as a pickup deck man on shrimpers out of Bayou La Batre. She hadn't asked which one he went out on lately. They came and went, after all.

McKenna knew The Right Spot, an ancient bar there that knew him, too. He forgot about the Pinot Grigio chilling at home and drove through the soft night air over to the long line of run-down docks and sheds that had avoided the worst of the last hurricane. The Right Spot had seen better days, but then so had he.

He changed in the darkness to his down-home outfit. Dirty jeans, blue work shirt with snaps instead of buttons, baseball cap with salt stains. Last time he had been here he had sported a mustache, so maybe clean-shaven he would look different. Older, too, by half of a pretty tough year. *Showtime* . . .

Insects shrilled in the high grass of the wiped-out lot next door and frogs brayed from the swampy pond beyond. There was even a sort-of front yard to it, since it had once been a big rambling house, now canted to the left by decay. Night creeper and cat's claw smothered the flower beds and flavored the thick air.

There was a separate bar to the side of the restaurant and he hesitated. The juke joint music was pump and wail and crash, sonic oblivion for a few hours. Food first, he decided. Mercifully, there were two rooms and he got away from the noise into the restaurant. A room bleached out by the flat, ceramic light. A sharp smell of disinfectant hiding behind the fried food aroma. New South, all right. A sign on the wall in crude type said FRIENDS DON'T LET FRIENDS EAT FOREIGN SHRIMP.

The joint had changed. He sat at a table and ordered jambalaya. When it came, too fast, he knew what to expect before the first mouthful.

It was a far, forlorn cry from the semi-Cajun coast food he knew as a boy, spicy if you wanted and not just to cover the taste of the ingredients. The shrimp and okra and oysters were fresh then, caught or picked that day. That was a richer time, when people ate at home and grew or caught much of what they ate. Paradise, and as usual, nobody had known it at the time.

He looked around and caught the old flavor. Despite his disguise, he saw that some people notice you're a cop. After a few minutes their eyes slide away and they go back to living their lives whether he was watching them or not. Their talk followed the meandering logic of real talk or the even more wayward path of stoned talk. Half-lowered eyelids, gossip, beer smells mingling with fried fish and nose-crinkling popcorn shrimp. Life.

He finished eating, letting the place get used to him. Nobody paid him much attention. The Right Spot was an odd combination, an indifferent restaurant with a sleazy bar one thin wall away. Maybe people only ate after they'd guzzled enough that the taste didn't matter anyway.

When he cut through the side door two Cajun women at the end of the bar gave him one glance that instantly said *cop* at the same time his eyes registered *hookers*. But they weren't full-on pros. They looked like locals in fluffy blouses and skinny pants who made a little extra on the side, and told themselves they were trying out the talent for the bigger game, a sort of modern style of courtship, free of hypocrisy. Just over the line. He had seen plenty of them when he worked vice. It was important to know the difference, the passing tide of women versus the real hard core who made up the true business. These were just true locals. Fair enough.

The woman bartender leaned over to give him a look at the small but nicely shaped breasts down the top of her gold lamé vest. She had a rose tattoo on one.

"Whiskey rocks, right?" She gave him a thin smile.

"Red wine." She had made him as a cop, too. Maybe he had even ordered whiskey last time he was here.

"You been gone a while."

Best to take the polite, formal mode, southern Cary Grant. "I'm sure you haven't lacked for attention." Now that he thought about it, he had gotten some good information here about six months back, and she had pointed out the source.

"I could sure use some." A smile and a slow wink.

"Not from me. Too old. I can remember when the air was clean and sex was dirty."

She laughed, showing a lot of bright teeth, even though it was an old line, maybe as ancient as the era it referred to. But this wasn't what he was here for, no. He took the wine, paid, and turned casually to case the room.

Most of the trade here was beer. Big TVs showed talking heads with thick necks against a backdrop of a football field. Guys in jeans and work shirts watched, rapt eyes above the bottles pressed to their mouths. He headed for the back with the glass of indifferent wine, where an old juke strummed with Springsteen singing "There's a darkness on the edge of town."

The fishermen sat along the back. He could tell by the work boots, worn hands, and salt-rimmed cuffs of their jeans and by something more, a squinty look from working in the sea glare. He walked over and sat down at the only open table, at the edge of maybe a dozen of the men sipping on beers.

It took a quarter of an hour before he could get into their conversation. It helped that he had spent years working on his family's boat. He knew the rhythms and lingo, the subtle lurch of consonants and soft vowels that told them he was from around here. He bought the next table over a round of Jax beers and that did it. Only gradually did it dawn on him that they already knew about Ethan Anselmo's death. The kids on the beach had spread the story, naturally.

But most of them here probably didn't know he was a cop, not yet. He sidled along and sat in a squeaky oak chair. Several of the guys were tired and loaded up with beer, stalling before going home to the missus. Others were brighter and on a guess he asked one, "Goin' out tonight?"

"Yeah, night dredgin'. All I can get lately."

The man looked like he had, in his time, quite probably eaten dinner in lots of poolrooms, or out of vending machines, and washed off using a garden hose. Working a dredger at night was mean work. Also, the easiest way to avoid the rules about damaging the sea bottom. Getting caught at that was risky and most men wouldn't take it.

McKenna leaned back and said in slow syllables, "This guy Ethan, the dead guy, know him?"

A nod, eyes crinkling with memory. "He worked the good boat. That one the Centauris hired, double money."

"I hadn't heard they hired anybody other than on Dauphin Island."

"This was some special work. Not dredgin'. Hell, he'd be here right now getting ready if he hadn't fell off that boat."

"He fell?" McKenna leaned forward a little and then remembered to look casual.

"They say."

"Who says?" Try not to seem too urgent.

A slow blink, sideways glance, a decision made. "Merv Pitscomb, runs the *Busted Flush*. Now and then they went out together on night charter."

"Really? Damn." He let it ride a little, then asked, "They go out last night?"

"I dunno."

"What they usually go for? Night fishin'?"

Raised eyebrows, shrug. "No bidness of mine."

"Pitscomb works for the Centauris?"

"Not d'rectly. They got a foreman kinda, big guy named Durrer. He books work for the Centauris when they need it."

"Regular work?"

A long tug at his beer. "Comes an' goes. Top dollar, I hear."

McKenna had to go slow here. The man's face was closing in, suspicion written in the tight mouth. McKenna always had a problem pressing people for information, and that got around, but apparently not to The Right Spot just yet. One suspect had once named him Man Who Ax Questions More'n He Should. True, but the suspect got ten to twenty upstate just the same.

McKenna backed off and talked football until the guy told him his name, Fred Godwin. Just then, by pure luck that at first didn't look like it, a woman named Irene came over to tell them both that she'd heard all about the body and all, and to impart her own philosophy on the matter.

The trouble with teasing information out of people was you get interrupted. It felt like losing a fish from a line, knowing it would never fall for the hook again. Irene went on about how it was a tragedy of course and she knew it weighed upon everybody. That went without saying, only she said it. She looked to be about forty going on fifty pretty hard, and unsteady on her shimmering gold high heels.

"Look at it this way," she said profoundly, eyes crinkling up above her soulful down-turned lips, "Ethan was young, so that as he was taken up on an angel's wing to the Alabaster City, he will be still brimming with what he could be. See? Set down at the Lord's Table, he will have no true regret. There will be no time for that. Another life will beckon to him while he is still full of energy, without memories of old age. No fussing with medicine and fear and failed organs, none. No such stations of duress on the way to Glory."

He could hear the capitals. Godwin looked like he was waiting for the right moment to escape. Which meant it was the right moment to buy him a beer, which McKenna did. To keep control of the conversation, maybe hinting at an invitation to sit with them, Irene volunteered that she'd heard Ethan had been working on the *Busted Flush* the night before his body washed up. *Bingo*.

McKenna bought Godwin the beer anyway.

Up toward the high-end districts of Mobile the liquor stores stocked decades-old single-malt Scotch and groceries had goat yoghurt and five kinds of oregano and coffee from nations you never heard of since high school. You could sip it while you listened to Haydn in their coffee shops and maybe scan the latest *New Yorker* for an indie film review.

But down by the coast the stores had Jim Beam if you asked right and the only seasoning on their shelves was salt and pepper, usually lots of pepper for Cajun tastes, and coffee came in cans. There was no music at all where he shopped and he was grateful. Considering what it might have been.

He got a bottle of a good California red to wash away the taste of the stuff he'd had earlier and made his way to the dock near the *Busted Flush* mooring. From his trunk he got out his rod and tackle and bait and soon enough was flipping his lure toward the lily pads in the nearby bayou. He pulled it lazily back, letting the dark water savor it. In a fit of professional rigor he had left the good California red in the car.

The clapboard shack beside the mooring was gray, the nail holes trailing rust and the front porch sagging despite the cinder blocks loyally holding it up from the damp sand. There was a big aluminum boathouse just beyond but no lights were on. He guessed it was too austere, and indeed the only murmur of talk came from the shack. A burst of cackling laughter from the fishing crew leaked out of the walls.

He sat in the shadows. An old Dr Pepper sign was almost gone but you could still see the holes from buckshot. Teenagers love targets.

It made no real good sense to fish at night, but the moon was coming up like a cat's yellow smile over the shimmering Gulf and some thought that drew the fish out. Like a false dawn, an old fisherman had said to him long ago, and maybe it was true. All he needed was the excuse anyway so he sat and waited. He always kept worms in a moist loam pail in the car trunk and maybe they would work tonight even if this stakeout didn't.

The *Busted Flush* crew was hauling out the supplies for a night run. There was always something to do on a boat, as McKenna knew from working them as a teenager, but these guys were taking longer than it should.

He had learned long ago the virtues of waiting. At his distance of about a hundred meters simple binoculars told him all he needed, and they had an IR filter to bring out the detail if he needed it. The amber moonlight glanced off the tin-roofed shotgun shacks down along the curve of the bay. Night-blooming flowers perfumed the night air and bamboo rattled in the distance like a whisper in his ear.

Then a big van rumbled up. Two guys got out, then a woman. They wore black and moved with crisp efficiency, getting gear out of the back. This didn't fit.

The team went to the dock and Merv Pitscomb ambled along to greet them. McKenna recognized him as skipper of the *Busted Flush* from a car fax he had gotten from the Mobile Main library, after leaving the restaurant. His car was more his office now than the desk he manned; electronics had changed everything.

The team and Pitscomb went together back to the van, talking. Pitscomb slid open the side door and everyone stepped back. A dark shape came out—large, moving slowly and in a silence from the feds that was like reverence.

McKenna froze. He knew immediately it was a Centauri. Its arms swung slowly, as if heavily muscled. The oddly jointed elbow swung freely like a pendulum, going backward. In water that would be useful, McKenna imagined. The arm tapered down to a flat four-fingered hand that he knew could be shaped to work like the blade of an oar.

The amphibians were slow and heavy, built for a life spent moving from water to land. It walked solidly behind the two guys in black, forming a screen of what had to be federal officers. No talk. Centauris' palates could not manage the shaped human sounds, so all communication was written.

It shuffled toward *Busted Flush* on thick legs that had large, circular feet. With help at the elbows from the feds it mounted the gangplank. This was the first he had seen for real, not on TV, and it struck him that it waddled more than walked. It was slow here, in a slightly stronger gravity. Centauris had evolved from a being that moved on sand, seldom saw rock, and felt more at home in the warm waters of a world that was mostly sea.

He realized as it reached the boat that he had been holding his breath. It was *strange* in a way he could not define. The breeze blew his way. He sniffed and wondered if that rank flavoring was the alien.

It went aboard, the federal officers' eyes swiveling in all directions. McKenna was under a cypress and hard to spot and their eyes slid right over him. He wondered why they didn't use infrared goggles.

Busted Flush started up with a hammering turbo engine. It turned away from the dock and headed straight out into the gulf. McKenna watched it go but he could not see the alien. The shrimp nets hung swaying on their high rocker arms and *Busted Flush* looked like any other dredge shrimper going out for the night. That was the point, McKenna guessed.

When he finally got home down the oyster-shelled road and parked under the low pines, he walked out onto his dock to look at the stars above the gulf. It always helped. He did not want to go right away into the house where he and his lost wife had lived. He had not moved away, because he loved this place, and though she was not here, at least the memories were.

He let the calm come over him and then lugged his briefcase up onto the porch and was slipping a key into the lock when he heard a scraping. He turned toward the glider where he had swung so many happy times and someone was getting up from it. A spike of alarm shot through him, the one you always have once you work the hard criminals, and then he saw it was a woman in a pale yellow dress. Yellow hair, too, blond with a ribbon in it. Last time it had been red.

"John! Now, you did promise you'd call."

At first he could not tell who she was but he reached inside the door and flipped on the porch light and her face leaped out of the darkness. "Ah, uh, Denise?"

"Why yes, did you forget me already?" Humorous reproach, coquettish and a little strained.

She swayed toward him, her hair bouncing as if just washed. Which it probably was. He felt his spirits sinking. If the average woman would rather have beauty than brains, it's because the average man can see better than he can think. Denise believed that and so was even more dolled up than on their first date. Also, last date.

"I figured out where you lived, so stopped by." Her broad smile was wise and enticing. "You didn't call, you know."

The vowels rolled off her tongue like sugar and he remembered why he had found her so intriguing.

"I've been awful busy."

"So've I, but you cain't just let life go by, y'know."

What to say to that? She was here for a clear purpose, her large red handbag on a shoulder strap and probably packed with cosmetics and a change of underwear. Yet he had no easy counter to it.

"Denise, I'm . . . seeing someone else." Easy, reasoned.

Her expression shifted subtly, the smile still in place but now glassy. "I . . . I didn't know that."

"It didn't make the papers."

No, that was wrong, humor wouldn't work here. He decided on the physical instead and held out a hand edge on, thumb straight up, for a shake. A long moment passed while her eyelashes batted beneath the yellow porch light and he could hear frogs croaking in the night marsh.

She looked at his hand and blinked and the smile collapsed. "I . . . I thought . . ."

It was his duty to make this as easy as possible so he took her half-offered hand and put an arm around her shoulders. He turned her delicately, murmuring something that made sense at the time but that he could not remember ten seconds later. With a sweeping arm he ushered her down the wooden stairs, across the sandy lawn in the moist sea air. Without more than soft words they both got to the car he had not even seen parked far back under the big oak tree aside the house. He said nothing that meant anything and she did the same and they got through the moment with something resembling their dignity.

He helped her into her car and turned back toward his house. A year ago in a momentary fit one member of the sorority of such ladies of a certain age had tried to run him down. This time, though, her Chevy started right off, growling like a late model, and turned toward the oyster driveway that shimmered in the silvery moon glow. He walked away from it, the noise pushing him.

The lie about seeing someone settled in him. His social graces were rusty. He mounted the steps as her headlights swept across the porch, spotlighting him momentarily, like an angry glare. To jerk open the front door and finally get inside felt like a forgiveness.

McKenna got into work early. It had bothered him to usher Denise off like that and he had stayed up too late thinking about it. Also, there was that good California red. Not that he had failed to enjoy Denise and the others in their mutual nonjudgmental rejection of middle-class values. Not at all.

But that style wasn't working for him anymore. He had set out vaguely searching for someone who could bring that light back into his life, the oblivious glow he had basked in for decades of a happy marriage. He had thought that if it happened once it could happen again. But since Linda's death nothing had that magic to it. Not dating—a term he hated, preferring "courtship"—and most of the time not even sex, his old standby.

So Denise's sad approach, the stuff of every teenage boy's dream, had been too little, too late.

He was still musing about this when he got to his desk. Homicide was a big squad room in worn green industrial carpet. The work pods had five desks each and he walked past these because he at last had gained a sheltered cubicle. The sergeant's desk was nearby his lieutenant's cubicle and framing the whole array was a rank of file cabinets. No paperless office here, no. Maybe never. At least there was no smoking anymore, but the carpet remembered those days. Especially after a rain, which meant usually.

The morning squad room buzzed with movement, talk, caffeine energy. Homicide detectives always run because it's a timed event. You close in on the perp inside two weeks or it's over.

And here was the ME folder on Ethan Anselmo. Once you've studied a few hundred autopsy reports you know you can skip the endless pages of organs, glands, general chemistry and just go to the conclusions. Forensic analysis had a subreport labeled GSR, which meant gunshot residue, and was blank.

The ME was confused. Heart stopped, lungs full, much like a drowning victim who had fought the ocean to his last. But the strange ridges on his skin looked like nerve damage, seared as if in an electrocution. The punctures McKenna had seen just obscured the case further.

McKenna hated muddy cases. Now he had to assign cause, focusing the ME report and the background he had gotten last night. He didn't hesitate. PROBABLE HOMICIDE, he wrote.

The usual notices had gone through, assigning case and ME numbers, letting the squad and precinct captains know, asking if there seemed any link to other cases—all routine. Section Command and District Office heard, all by standard e-mail heads-up forms, as did Photo and Latent and Lab.

He took out a brown loose-leaf binder and made up a murder book. First came the Homicide Occurrence Report with Mobile Main as the address in the right upper corner. Then the basics. A door that opened wide with no sure destination beyond.

McKenna sat back and let his mind rove. Nothing. Sometimes an idea lurked there after he had reviewed the case; not now.

He knew had to finish up a report on a domestic slaying from two days back, so he set to it. Most murders were by guys driven crazy by screeching kids and long-term debt and bipolar wives. Alcohol helped. They had figured out their method about ten seconds before doing it and had no alibi, no plausible response to physical evidence, and no story that didn't come apart under a two-minute grilling. When you took them out to the car in cuffs the neighbors just nodded at each other and said they'd always figured on this, hadn't they said so?

This was a no-brainer case. He finished the paperwork, longing for that paperless office, and dispatched it to the prosecutor's office. They would cut the deal and McKenna would never hear of it again. Unless the perp showed up in fifteen years on his front porch, demanding vengeance. That had happened, too. Now McKenna went armed, even on Sundays to church.

Then he sat and figured.

The ME thought the odd marks on Ethan Anselmo might be electrocution. Torture? Yet the guy was no lowlife. He had no history of drug running using shrimp boats, the default easy way for a fisherman to bring in extra income all along the gulf. For a moment McKenna idly wondered when the War on Drugs would end, as so many failed American adventures had, with admission that the war was clearly lost. It would certainly be easier to legalize, tax, and control most drugs than it was to chase after them. He had at first figured Anselmo for a drug-gang killing. There were plenty of them along the gulf shore. But now that felt wrong.

His desktop computer told him that the Anselmo case was now online in the can't-crack site Mobile used to coordinate police work now. There were some additions from the autopsy and a background report on Anselmo, but nothing that led anywhere.

He sighed. Time to do some shoe leather work.

The *Busted Flush* was back at its dock. McKenna had changed into a beat-up work shirt and oil-stained jeans. Sporting a baseball cap, he found the crew hosing off a net rig inside the big aluminum boathouse nearby. "Pitscomb around?" he asked them, rounding the vowels to fit the local accent.

A thirty-something man walked over to McKenna. One cheek had a long, ugly scar now gone to dirty pink. His hair was blond and ratty, straight and cut mercifully short. But the body was taut and muscular and ready, as the scrollwork tattoos of jailhouse vintage showed he had needed for much of his life. He wore a snap-button blue work shirt with a stuck-on nameplate that said Buddy Johnson. Completing the outfit was a hand-tooled belt with carry hooks hanging and half-topped boots that needed a polish pretty bad.

"Who wants to know?"

The stern, gravel voice closed a switch in McKenna's head. He had seen this guy a decade before when he helped make an arrest. Two men tried to pull the front off a cash machine by running a chain from the machine to the bumper of their pickup truck. Instead of pulling the front panel off the machine, though, they yanked the bumper off the truck. They panicked and fled, leaving the chain still attached to the machine, their bumper still attached to the chain, and their license plate still attached to the bumper.

"Lookin' for work," McKenna said. This guy couldn't be heading up the operation, so he needed to go higher.

"We got none." The eyes crinkled as if Buddy was trying to dredge up a memory.

McKenna shifted his own tone from soft to medium. "I need to see your boss."

Still puzzling over the memory, Johnson waved toward the boathouse. McKenna walked away, feeling Johnson's eyes on his back.

Pitscomb was at the back of the building, eating hog cracklings from a greasy bag, brushing the crumbs into the lagoon. Carrion birds eyed him as they drifted by on the soft slurring wind, keeping just above the gnarled tops of the dead cypress, just in case they saw some business below that needed doing.

Pitscomb was another matter. Lean, angular, intelligent blue eyes. McKenna judged that he might as well come clean. He showed his badge and said with a drawl, "Need to talk about Ethan Anselmo."

Pitscomb said, "Already heard. He didn't come to work that night."

"Your crew, they'll verify that?"

He grinned. "They'd better."

"Why you have an ex-con working your boat?"

"I don't judge people, I just hire 'em. Buddy's worked out fine."

"What do you do for the Centauris?"

"That's a federal matter, I was told to say."

McKenna leaned against a pier stay. "Why do they use you, then? Why not take the Centauri out on their own boat?"

Pitscomb brushed his hands together, sending the last of the cracklings into the water. "You'd have to ask them. Way I see it, the feds want to give the Centauris a feel for our culture. And spread the money around good an' local, too."

"What's the Centauri do out there?"

"Just looks, swims. A kind of night off, I guess."

"They live right next to the water."

"Swimming out so far must be a lot of work, even for an amphibian." By now Pitscomb had dropped the slow-South accent and was eyeing McKenna.

"How far out?"

"A few hours."

"Just to swim?"

"The feds don't want me to spread gossip."

"This is a murder investigation."

"Just gossip, far as I'm concerned."

"I can take this to the feds."

Again the sunny smile, as sincere as a postage stamp. "You do that. They're not backwoods coon-asses, those guys."

Meaning, pretty clearly, that McKenna was. He turned and walked out through the machine oil smells of the boathouse. Buddy Johnson was waiting in the moist heat. He glowered but didn't say anything.

As he walked past McKenna said, using hard vowels, "Don't worry, now. I haven't chewed off anybody's arm in nearly a week."

Buddy still didn't say anything, just smiled slyly. When McKenna got to his car he saw the reason.

A tire was flat, seeming to ooze into the blacktop. McKenna glanced back at Buddy, who waved and went back inside. McKenna thought about following him but it was getting warm and he was sticking to his shirt. Buddy would wait until he knew more, he figured.

He got his gloves from the trunk, then lifted out the jack, lug wrench, and spare. He squatted down and started spinning the nuts off, clattering them into the hubcap. By the time he fitted the spare on the axle and tightened the wheel nuts with the jack, then lowered it, he had worked up a sweat and smelled himself sour and fragrant.

The work had let him put his mind on cruise and as he drove away he felt some connections link up.

The Pizottis. One of them was a real professor, the kind he needed. Was that family fish fry tonight? He could just about make it.

Since Linda died he had seen little of the Pizotti family. Their shared grief seemed to drive them apart. The Pizottis always kept somewhat distant anyway, an old country instinct.

He drove over the causeway to the eastern short of the bay and then down through Fairhope to the long reaches south of the Grand Hotel. He had grown up not far away, spending summers on the Fish River at Grammaw McKenzie's farm. To even reach the fish fry on an isolated beach he decided to take a skiff out across Weekes Bay.

The Pizottis had invited him weeks ago, going through the motions of pretending he was family. They weren't the reason, of course. He let himself forget about all that as he poled along amid the odors of reeds and sour mud, standing in the skiff. In among the cattails lurked alligators, one with three babies a foot and a half long. They scattered away from the skiff, nosing into the muddy fragrant water, the mother snuffing as she sank behind the young ones. He knew the big legendary seventeen-footers always lay back in the reeds, biding their time. As he coasted forward on a few oar-strokes, he saw plenty of lesser lengths lounging in the late sun like metallic sculptures. A big one ignored the red-tailed hawk on a log nearby, knowing it was too slow to ever snare the bird. By a cypress tree, deep in a thick tangle of matted saw grass, a gray possum was picking at something and sniffing like it couldn't decide whether to dine or not. The phosphorus-loving cattails had moved in further up the bay, stealing away the skiff's glide so he came to a stop. He didn't like the cattails and felt insulted by their presence. Cattails robbed sunlight from the paddies and fish below, making life harder for the water-feeding birds.

He cut toward Mobile Bay where the fish fry should be and looked in among the reeds. There were lounging gators like logs sleeping in the sun. One rolled over in the luxury of the warm mud and gave off a moaning grunt, an *umph-umph-umph* with mouth closed. Then it opened in a yawn and achieved a throaty, bellowing roar. He had seen alligators like that before in Weekes Bay where the Fish River eased in, just below the old arched bridge. Gators seemed to like bridges. They would lie in the moist heat and sleep, the top predators here, unafraid. He admired their easy assurance that nothing could touch them, their unthinking arrogance.

Until people came along, only a few centuries before, with their rifles. He suddenly wondered if the Centauris were like this at all. They were amphibians, not reptiles. What would they make of gators?

A gator turned and looked up at him for a long moment. It held the gaze, as if figuring him out. It snuffed and waddled a little in the mud to get more comfortable and closed its big eyes. McKenna felt an odd chill. He paddled faster.

The other wing of the Pizotti family was on the long sand bar at the end of Weekes Bay, holding forth in full cry. He came ashore, dragged the skiff up to ground it, and tried to mix. The Pizottis' perfunctory greetings faded and they got back to their social games.

He had loved Linda dearly but these were not truly his kind of people. She had been serene, savoring life while she had it. The rest of the Pizottis were on the move. Nowadays the gulf's Golden Coast abounded with Masters of the Universe. They sported excellently cut hair and kept themselves slim, casually elegant, and carefully muscled. Don't want to look like a *laborer,* after all, never mind what their grandfathers did for a living. The women ran from platinum blond through strawberry, quite up to the minute. Their plastic surgery was tasteful, eye-smoothings and maybe a discreet wattle tuck. They carried themselves with that look not so much of energetic youth but rather of expert maintenance, like a Rolls with the oil religiously changed every fifteen hundred miles. Walking in their wake made most working stiffs feel just a touch shabby.

One of them eyed him and professed fascination with a real detective. He countered with enthusiasm for the fried flounder and perch a cousin had brought. Food was a good dodge, though these were fried in too much oil. He held out for a polite ten minutes and then went to get one of the crab just coming off the grill. And there, waiting for the next crab to come sizzling off, was Herb. Just in time. McKenna could have kissed him.

It didn't take too long to work around to the point of coming here. Herb was an older second cousin of Linda, and had always seemed to McKenna like the only other Pizotti who didn't fit in with the rest. He had become an automatic friend as soon as McKenna started courting her.

"It's a water world," Herb said, taking the bit immediately. He had been a general science teacher at Faulkner State in Fairhope, handling the chemistry and biology courses. "You're dead on. I've been reading all I could get about them."

"So they don't have much land?" McKenna waved to the woman who loved detectives and shrugged comically to be diplomatic. He got Herb and himself a glass of red, a Chianti.

"I figure that's why they're amphibians. Best to use what there's plenty of. Their planet's a moon, right?—orbiting around a gas giant like Jupiter. It gets sunlight from both Centauri stars, plus infrared from the gas giant. So it's always warm and they don't seem to have plate tectonics, so their world is real, real different."

McKenna knew enough from questioning witnesses to nod and look interested. Herb was already going beyond what he'd gotten from TV and newspapers and *Scientific American*. McKenna tried to keep up. As near as he could tell, plate tectonics was something like the grand unified theory of geology. Everything from the deep planes of the ocean to Mount Everest came from the waltz of continents, butting together and churning down into the deep mantle. Their dance rewrote climates and geographies, opening up new possibilities for life and at times closing down old ones. But that was here, on Earth.

The other small planets of our solar system didn't work that way. Mars had been rigid for billions of years. Venus upchucked its mantle and buried its crust often enough to leave it barren.

So planets didn't have to work like Earth, and the Centauri water world was another example. It rotated slowly, taking eight days to get around its giant neighbor. It had no continents, only strings of islands. And it was *old*—more than a billion years older than Earth. Life arose there from nothing more than chemicals meeting in a warm sea while sunlight boomed through a blanket of gas.

"So they got no idea about continents?" McKenna put in.

Herb said he sure seemed to miss lecturing, ever since he retired, and it made him a dinner companion not exactly sought after here among the Pizottis. McKenna had never thought he could be useful, like now. "They took one up in an airplane, with window blinds all closed, headphones on its ears. Turns out it liked Bach! Great, huh?"

McKenna nodded, kept quiet. None of the other Pizottis was paying any attention to Herb. They seemed to be moving away, even.

"The blindfold was so it wouldn't get scared, I guess. They took off the blindfold and showed it mountains, river valleys, all that. Centauris got no real continents, just strings of islands. It could hardly believe its clamshell eyes."

"But they must've seen those from space, coming in. Continents and all."

"Not the same, close up."

"So maybe they're thinking to move inland, explore?"

"I doubt it. They got to stick close to warm, salty water."

McKenna wondered if they had any global warming there and then said, "They got no oil, I guess. No place for all those ferns to grow, so long ago."

Herb blinked. "Hadn't figured that. S'pose so. But they say they got hurricanes alla time, just the way we do now."

McKenna poked a finger up and got them another glass of the Chianti. Herb needed fueling.

"It's cloudy alla time there, the astro boys say. They can never see through the clouds. Imagine, not knowing for thousands of years that there are stars."

McKenna imagined never having a sunny day. "So how'd they ever get a space program going?"

"Slow and steady. Their civilization is way old, y'know, millions of years. They say their space ships are electric, somehow."

McKenna couldn't imagine electric rockets. "And they've got our kind of DNA."

Herb brightened. "Yeah, what a surprise. Spores brought it here, *Scientific American* figures."

"Amazing. What sort of biology do amphibians have?"

Herb shrugged and pushed a hush puppy into his mouth, then chewed thoughtfully. The fish fry was a babble all around them and McKenna had to concentrate. "Dunno. There's nothing in the science press about that. Y'know, Centauris are mighty private about that stuff."

"They give away plenty of technology, the financial pages say."

"You bet, whole new products. Funny electrical gadgets, easy to market."

"So why are they here? Not to give us gifts." Might as well come out and say it.

"Just like Carl Sagan said, right? Exchange cultures and all. A great adventure, and we get it without spending for starships or anything."

"So they're tourists? Who pay with gadgets?"

Herb knocked back the rest of his Chianti. "Way I see it, they're lonely. They heard our radio a century back and started working on a ship to get here."

"Just like us, you think about it. Why else do we make up ghosts and angels and the like? Somebody to talk to."

"Only they can't talk."

"At least they write."

"Translation's hard, though. The feds are releasing a little of it, but there'll be more later. You see those Centauri poems?"

He vaguely recalled some on the front page of the paper. "I couldn't make sense of it."

Herb grinned. "Me either, but it's fascinating. All about the twin suns. Imagine!"

When he got home he showered, letting the steam envelop him and ease away the day. His mind had too much in it, tired from the day. Thinking about sleep, when he often got his best ideas, he toweled off.

The shock came when he wiped the steam from the mirror and saw a smeary old man, blotchy skin, gray hair pasted to the skull, ashen whiskers sprouting from deep pores. He had apparently gone a decade or two without paying attention to mirrors.

Fair enough, if they insult you this deeply. He slapped some cream on the wrinkles hemming in his eyes, dressed, sucked in his belly, and refused to check himself out in the mirror again. Insults enough, for one day. Growing older he couldn't do much about, but Buddy Johnson was another matter.

At dawn he quite deliberately went fishing. He needed to think.

He sat on his own wharf and sipped orange juice. He had to wash off the reels with the hose from the freshwater tank as waves came rolling in and burst in sprays against the creaking pilings. He smelled the salty tang of bait fish in his bucket and as if to tantalize him, a speckled fish broke from a curling wave, plunging headfirst into the foam. He had never seen a fish do that and it proved yet again that the world was big and strange and always changing. Other worlds, too.

He sat at his desk and shuffled paper for the first hour of the morning shift. He knew he didn't have long before the Ethan Anselmo case hit a dead end. Usually a homicide not wrapped up in two weeks had a less-than-even chance of ever getting solved at all. After two weeks the case became an unclaimed corpse in the files, sitting there in the dark chill of neglect.

Beyond the autopsy you go to the evidence analysis reports. Computer printouts, since most detectives still worked with paper. Tech addenda and photos. All this under a time and cost constraint, the clock and budget always ticking along. "Investigative prioritizing," the memos called it. Don't do anything expensive without your supe's nod.

So he went to see his supe, a black guy two months in from Vice, still learning the ropes. And got nothing back.

"The feds, you let them know about the Centauri connection, right?" the supe asked.

"Sure. There's a funnel to them through the Mobile FBI of-fice."

Raised eyebrows. "And?"

"Nothing so far."

"Then we wait. They want to investigate, they will."

"Not like they don't know the Centauris are going out on civilian boats." McKenna was fishing to see if his supe knew anything more but the man's eyes betrayed nothing.

The supe said, "Maybe the Centauris want it this way. But why?"

"Could be they want to see how ordinary people work the sea?"

"We gotta remember they're aliens. Can't think of them as like people."

McKenna couldn't think of how that idea could help so he sat and waited. When the supe said nothing more, McKenna put in, "I'm gonna get a call from the Anselmo widow."

"Just tell her we're working on it. When's your partner get back?"

"Next week. But I don't want a stand-in."

A shrug. "Okay, fine. Just don't wait for the feds to tell you anything. They're just like the damn FBI over there."

McKenna was in a meeting about new arrest procedures when the watch officer came into the room and looked at him significantly.

The guy droning on in front was a city government lawyer and most of his audience was nodding off. It was mid-afternoon and the coffee had long run out but not the lawyer.

McKenna ducked outside and the watch officer said, "You got another, looks like. Down in autopsy."

It had washed up on Orange Beach near the Florida line, so Baldwin County Homicide had done the honors. Nobody knew who it was and the fingerprints went nowhere. It had on jeans and no underwear, McKenna read in the Baldwin County report.

When the Baldwin County sheriff saw on the Internet cross-correlation index that it was similar to McKenna's case they sent it over for the Mobile ME. That had taken a day, so the corpse was a bit more rotted. It was already gutted and probed, and the ME had been expecting him.

"Same as your guy," the ME said. "More of those raised marks, all over the body."

Suited up and wearing masks, they went over the swollen carcass. The rot and swarming stink caught in McKenna's throat but he forced down the impulse to vomit. He had never been good at this clinical stuff. He made himself focus on what the ME was pointing out, oblivious to McKenna's rigidity.

Long ridges of reddened, puckering flesh laced around the trunk and down the right leg. A foot was missing. The leg was drained white, and the ME said it looked like a shark bite. Something had nibbled at the genitals. "Most likely a turtle," the ME said. "They go for the delicacies."

McKenna let this remark pass by and studied the face. Black eyes, broad nose, weathered brown skin. "Any punctures?"

"Five, on top of the ridges. Not made by teeth or anything I know."

"Any dental ID?"

"Not yet."

"I need pictures," McKenna said. "Cases like this cool off fast."

"Use my digital, I'll e-mail them to you. He looks like a Latino," the ME said. "Maybe that's why no known fingerprints or dental. Illegal."

Ever since the first big hurricanes, Katrina and Rita, swarms of Mexicans had poured in to do the grunt work. Most stayed, irritating the working class who then competed for the construction and restaurant and fishing jobs. The ME prepared his instruments for further opening the swollen body and McKenna knew he could not take that. "Where . . . where's the clothes?"

The ME looked carefully at McKenna's eyes. "Over there. Say, maybe you should sit down."

"I'm okay." It came out as a croak. McKenna went over to

the evidence bag and pulled out the jeans. Nothing in the pockets. He was stuffing them back in when he felt something solid in the fabric. There was a little inner pocket at the back, sewed in by hand. He fished out a key ring with a crab-shaped ornament and one key on it.

"They log this in?" He went through the paperwork lying on the steel table. The ME was cutting but came over. Nothing in the log.

"Just a cheap plastic thingy," the ME said, holding it up to the light. "Door key, maybe. Not a car."

"Guy with one key on his ring. Maybe worked boats, like Anselmo."

"That's the first guy, the one who had those same kinda marks?"

McKenna nodded. "Any idea what they are?"

The ME studied the crab ornament. "Not really. Both bodies had pretty rough hands, too. Manual labor."

"Workin' stiffs. You figure he drowned?"

"Prob'ly. Got all the usual signs. Stick around, I'll know soon."

McKenna very carefully did not look back at the body. The smell was getting to him even over the air-conditioning sucking air out of the room with a loud hum. "I'll pick up the report later." He left right away.

His supe sipped coffee, considered the sound-absorbing ceiling, and said, "You might see if VICAP got anything like this."

The Violent Criminal Apprehension Program computer would cross-filter the wounds and tell him if anything like that turned up in other floaters. "Okay. Thought I'd try to track that crab thing on the key chain."

The supe leaned back and crossed his arms, showing scars on both like scratches on ebony. "Kinda unlikely."

"I want to see if anybody recognizes it. Otherwise this guy's a John Doe."

"It's a big gulf. The ME think it could've floated from Mexico?"

"No. Local, from the wear and tear."

"Still a lot of coastline."

McKenna nodded. The body had washed up about forty miles to the east of Bayou La Batre, but the currents could have brought it from anywhere. "I got to follow my hunches on this."

The supe studied McKenna's face like it was a map. He studied the ceiling again and sighed. "Don't burn a lot of time, okay?"

There were assorted types working in homicide but he broke them into two different sorts.

Most saw the work as a craft, a skill they learned. He counted himself in those, though wondered lately if he was sliding into the second group: those who thought it was a mission in life, the only thing worth doing. Speakers for the dead, he called them.

At the crime scene a bond formed, a promise from the decaying corpse to the homicide detective: that this would be avenged. It went with the job.

The job was all about death, of course. He had shot only two perps in his career. Killed one in a messy attempt at an arrest, back when he was just getting started. A second when a smart guy whose strategy had gone way wrong decided he could still shoot his way out of his confusion. All he had done was put a hole through McKenna's car.

But nowadays he felt more like an avenging angel than he had when young. Closer to the edge. Teetering above the abyss.

Maybe it had something to do with his own wife's death, wasting away, but he didn't go there anymore. Maybe it was just about death itself, the eternal human problem without solution. If you can't solve it you might as well work at it anyway.

Murderers were driven, sometimes just for a crazed moment that shaped all the rest of their lives. McKenna was a cool professional, calm and sure—or so he told himself.

But something about the Anselmo body—drowned and elec- trocuted both—got to him. And now the anonymous illegal, ap- parently known to nobody, silent in his doom.

Yet he, the seasoned professional, saw no place to go next. No leads. This was the worst part of any case, where most of them went cold and stayed that way. Another murder file, buried just like the bodies.

McKenna started in the west, at the Mississippi state line. The gulf towns were much worse off after getting slammed with Katrina and Rita and the one nobody could pronounce right sev- eral years after. The towns never got off the ropes. The gulf kept punching them hard, maybe fed by global warming and maybe just out of some kind of natural rage. Mother Earth Kicks Ass, part umpty-million.

He had the tech guy Photoshop the photos of the Latino's face, taking away the swelling and water bleaching. With eyes open he looked alive. Then he started showing it around.

He talked to them all—landlords and labor in-between men, Mexicans who worked the fields, labor center types. Nothing. So he went to the small-time boosters, hookers, creeps in alleys, button men, strong-arm types slow and low of word, addicts ga- lore, those who thrived on the dark suffering around them—the underlife of the decaying coast. He saw plenty of thick-bodied, smoldering anger that would be bad news someday for someone, of vascular crew-cut-slick boys, stained jeans, arms ridged with muscle that needed to be working. Some had done time in the bucket and would again.

Still, nothing. The Latino face rang no bells.

He was coming out of a gardening shop that used a lot of Latinos when the two suits walked up. One wore a Marine-style bare-skull haircut and the other had on dark glasses and both of those told him *Federal*.

"You're local law?" the marine type said.

Without a word McKenna showed them his badge. Dark

Glasses and Marine both showed theirs, FBI, and Dark Glasses said, "Aren't you a long way beyond Mobile city lines?"

"We're allowed to follow cases out into the county," McKenna said levelly.

"May we see the fellow you're looking for?" Mr. Marine asked, voice just as flat.

McKenna showed the photo. "What did he do?" Mr. Marine asked.

"Died. I'm Homicide."

"We had a report you were looking in this community for someone who worked boats," Dark Glasses said casually.

"Why would that interest the FBI?"

"We're looking for a similar man," Mr. Marine said. "On a federal issue."

"So this is the clue that I should let you know if I see him? Got a picture?"

Dark Glasses started a smile and thought better of it. "Since there's no overlap, I think not."

"But you have enough sources around here that as soon as I show up, you get word." McKenna said it flatly and let it lie there in the sun.

"We have our ways," Dark Glasses said. "How'd this guy die?"

"Drowned."

"Why think it's homicide?" Mr. Marine came in.

"Just a hunch."

"Something tells me you have more than that," Mr. Marine shot back.

"You show me yours, I'll show you mine."

They looked at each other and McKenna wondered if they got the joke. They turned and walked away without a word.

His bravado with them made him feel good but it didn't advance his case. His mind spun with speculations about the FBI and then he put them away. The perpetual rivalry between local and federal always simmered, since the Feds could step in and capture a case when they thought they could profit from it. Or solve it better. Sometimes they were even right.

He prowled the Latino quarters. Hurricane damage was still common all along the Gulf Coast, years after the unpronounceable hurricane that had made Katrina and Rita look like mere overtures. He worked his way east and saw his fill of wrecked piers, abandoned houses blown out when the windows gave in, groves of pines snapped off halfway up, roofs ripped away, homes turned to flooded swamps. Weathered signs on damaged walls brought back to mind the aftermath: LOOTERS SHOT; on a roof: HELP; a plaintive WE'RE HERE; an amusing FOR SALE: SOME WATER DAMAGE on a condo completely gutted. Historical documents, now.

Hurricanes had hammered the coast so hard that in the aftermath business got pillaged by perfectly respectable people trying to hang on, and most of those stores were still closed. Trucks filled with scrap rumbled along the pitted roads. Red-shirted crews wheelbarrowed dark debris out of good brick homes. Blue tarp covered breached roofs, a promise that eventually they would get fixed. Near the beaches, waterline marks of scummy yellow remained, head high.

Arrival of aliens from another star had seemed less important to the coast people. Even though the Centauris had chosen the similar shores in Thailand, Africa, and India to inhabit, the gulf was their focus, nearest an advanced nation. McKenna wondered what they thought of all the wreckage.

The surge of illegal Mexicans into the Gulf Coast brought a migration of some tough gangs from California. They used the illegal worker infrastructure as shelter, and occupied the drug business niches. Killings along the Mobile coast dropped from an average of three or four a day before to nearly zero, then rose in the next two years. Those were mostly turf wars between the druggies and immigrant heist artists of the type who prey on small stores.

So he moved among them in jeans, dog-eared hat, and an old

shirt, listening. Maybe the Centauris were making people think about the stars and all, but he worked among a galaxy of losers: beat-up faces, hangdog scowls, low-hanging pants, and scuffed brown shoes. They would tell you a tearful life story in return for just looking at them. Every calamity that might befall a man had landed on them: turncoat friends, deadbeat buddies, barren poverty, cold fathers, huge bad luck, random inexplicable diseases, prison, car crashes, and of course the eternal forlorn song: treacherous women. It was a seminar in the great themes of Johnny Cash.

Then a droopy-eyed guy at a taco stand said he had seen the man in the picture over in a trailer park. McKenna approached it warily. If he got figured for a cop the lead would go dead.

Nearby were Spanish-language graffiti splashed on the mini-mart walls, and he passed Hispanic mothers and toddlers crowding into the county's health clinic. But the shabby mobile homes were not a wholly Hispanic enclave. There was a lot of genteel poverty making do here. Pensioners ate in decrepit diners that gave seniors a free glass of anonymous domestic wine with the special. Workers packed into nearby damaged walkups with no air-conditioning. On the corners clumps of men lounged, rough-handed types who never answered questions, maybe because they knew no English.

McKenna worked his way down the rows of shabby trailers. Welfare mothers blinked at him and he reassured them he was not from the county office. It was hard to read whether anybody was lying because they seemed dazed by the afternoon heat. Partway through the trailer park a narrow-chested guy in greasy shorts came up and demanded, "Why you bothering my tenants?"

"Just looking for a friend."

"What for?"

"I owe him money."

A sarcastic leer snaked across the narrow face. "Yeah, right."

"Okay, I got a job for him." McKenna showed the photo.

A clicker in the man's eyes came and went. "Huh."

"Know him?"

"Don't think so."

"You don't lie worth a damn."

The mouth tightened. "You ax me an I tole you."

McKenna sighed and showed the badge. After a big storm a lot of fake badges sprouted on the chests of guys on the make, so this guy's caution was warranted. County sheriffs and state police tried to enforce the law and in byways like this they gave up. Time would sort it out, they figured. Some of the fakes became hated, then dead.

To his surprise, the man just stiffened and jutted his chin out. "Got nothin' to say."

McKenna leaned closer and said very fast, "You up to code here? Anybody in this trailer park got an outstanding warrant? How 'bout illegals? Safety code violations? I saw that extension cord three units back, running out of a door and into a side shed. You charge extra for the illegals under that tent with power but no toilet? Bet you do. Or do you just let it happen on the side and pick up some extra for being blind?"

The man didn't even blink.

McKenna was enjoying this. "So suppose we deport some of these illiterates, say. Maybe call in some others here, who violated their parole, uh? So real quick your receivables drop, right? Maybe a lot. Child support could come in here, too, right? One phone call would do it. There's usually a few in a trailer park who don't want to split their check with the bitch that keeps hounding them with lawyers, right? So with them gone, you got open units, buddy. Which means no income, so you're lookin' worse to the absentee landlord who cuts your check, you get me?"

McKenna could hear the gears grind and the eyes got worried. "Okay, look, he left a week back."

"Where to?"

"You know that bayou east about two miles, just before Angel Point? He went to an island just off there, some kind of boat work."

Floating lilies with lotus flowers dotted the willow swamp. Tupelo gums hung over the brown water as he passed, flavoring the twilight. The rented skiff sent its bow wash lapping at half-sunken logs with hides like dead manatees.

His neck felt sunburned from the sour day and his throat was raspy-dry. He cut the purring outboard and did some oar work for the last half mile. The skiff drifted silently up to the stilt house. It leaned a little on slender pilings, beneath a vast canopy of live oaks that seemed centuries old. The bow thumped at the tiny gray-wood dock, wood piling brushing past as he stepped softly off, lashing the stay rope with his left hand while he pulled his 9 mm out and forward. No point in being careless.

Dusk settled in. A purple storm hung on the southern horizon and sheet lightning worked yellow magic at its edges. A string of lights hung along the wharf, glowing dimly in the murk, and insects batted at them. Two low pirogues drifted on the tide and clanked rusty chains.

The lock was antique and took him ten seconds.

The room smelled of damp dogs. He searched it systematically but there was nothing personal beyond worn clothes and some letters in Spanish. The postmarks were blurred by the moisture that never left the old wooden drawers. But in another drawer one came through sharp, three weeks old from Vera Cruz. That was a port town down the long curve of the eastern Mexican coast. From his knowledge of the Civil War era, which was virtually a requirement of a Southern man when he grew up, Vera Cruz was where Grant and Lee nearly got killed. Together they went out in a small boat to survey the shore in the Mexican war, and artillery fire splashed within ten yards of them.

Lots of fishing in Vera Cruz. A guy from there would know how to work nets.

He kept the letters and looked in the more crafty places. No plastic bag in the commode water closet. Nothing under the filthy pine floor. No hollow legs on the flimsy wooden chairs. In his experience, basically no perp hid anything in smartass places or even planned their murders. No months of pondering, of painstaking detail work, alibi prep, escape route, weapon disposal. Brilliant murders were the stuff of television, where the cop played dumb and tripped up the canny murderer, ha ha.

The storm came in off the gulf and rattled the shack's tin roof. In the musty two-roomer he thought as mist curled up from great steaming sheets of rain. Drops tapped on leaves outside the window and the air mixed with sharp, moist smells of bird droppings. He stood in the scrappy kitchen and wondered if this was a phony lead. The Spanish letters probably wouldn't help but they were consistent at least with the Latino body. Still, he was getting nowhere.

His intuition was fuzzy with associations, a fog that would not condense. The battering shower made him think of the oceans rising and warming from the greenhouse gases and how the world might come to be more like the Centauri's moon, more tropical sea and the land hammered with storms. Out the streaked front window he wondered if aliens swam among the quilted waves, living part of their lives among the schools of fishes.

This thinking went nowhere and his ankle had acquired red dots of fleabites. He looked out the back window. The rain tapered off and he saw now the gray of a FEMA trailer back in the woods. A breeze came from it. Frying peppers and onions flavored the air with pungent promise.

He knocked on the front door and a scrawny white man wearing jeans and nothing else answered. "Hello, sir," plus the badge got him inside.

In a FEMA trailer even words take up room. You have to stand at a conversational distance in light-metal boxes that even a tropical storm could flip like playing cards. His initial urge was to hunch, then to make a joke about it. Mr. Fredson, a gangly six-foot-two, stretched out his arms to show how he could at the same time touch the ceiling with one hand and the floor with the other. Hangers in the small closet were tilted sideways to fit and beside them stood a short bronze-skinned woman who was trying not to look at him.

"I was wondering if you knew who lived up front there."

"He been gone more'n a week."

"Did he look like this?" McKenna showed the picture.

"Yeah, that's Jorge."

"Jorge what?"

"Castan," the woman said in a small thin voice. Her hands twisted at the pale pink fabric of the shift she wore. "You *la migra*?"

"No ma'm. Afraid I got some bad news about Jorge though."

"He dead?" Mr. Fredson said, eyes downcast.

" 'Fraid so. He washed up on a beach east of here."

"He worked boats," Fredson said, shaking his head. "Lot of night work, fillin' in."

"Mexican, right? Wife in Vera Cruz?"

"Yeah," he said. "Sent money home. Had two other guys livin' up there for a while, nice fellas, all worked the boats. They gone now."

McKenna looked around, thinking. The Latino woman went stiffly into the kitchen and rearranged paper plates and plastic cups from Wal-Mart, cleaned a Reed & Barton silver coffeepot. Fredson sighed and sat on a small, hard couch. The woman didn't look like a good candidate to translate the Vera Cruz letter, judging from her rigid back. To unlock her he had to ask the right question.

"Jorge seem okay? Anything bother him?"

Fredson thought, shrugged. "I'd look in over there sometimes when he was out on the gulf for a few days. He axed me to. Lately his baidclose all tangled up come mornin'."

"Maybe afraid of *la migra*?" McKenna glanced at the woman. She had stopped pretending to polish the coffeepot and was staring at them.

"Lotsa people are." Fredson jutted his chin out. "They come for the work, we make out they be criminals."

"We do have a justice system." McKenna didn't know how to work this so he stalled.

"Jorge, he get no justice in the nex' world either." Fredson looked defiantly at him. "I'm not religious, like some."

"I'm not sayin' Jorge was doin' anything dishonest." McKenna was dropping into the coast accent, an old strategy to elicit trust. "Just want to see if he died accidentally of drowning."

Fredson said flatly, knotting his hands, "Dishonest ain't same as dishonorable."

He was getting nowhere here. "I'll need to report his death to his wife. Do you have any papers on him, so I can send them?"

The woman said abruptly, "*Documento.*"

Fredson stared at her and nodded slowly. "Guess we ought to."

He got up and reached back into the packed closet. How they had gotten a FEMA trailer would be an interesting story but McKenna knew not to press his luck. Fredson withdrew a soiled manila envelope and handed it to McKenna. "I kept this for him. He weren't too sure about those other two guys he was renting floor space to, I guess."

McKenna opened it and saw inside a jumble of odd-sized papers. "I sure thank you. I'll see this gets to her."

"How you know where she is?" Fredson asked.

"Got the address."

"Searched his place, did ya?"

"Of course. I'll be leaving—"

"Have a warrant?"

McKenna smiled slowly. "Have a law degree, do you?" His eyes slid toward the woman and he winked. Fredson's mouth stiffened and McKenna left without another word.

He crunched down his oyster-shell road in the dark. Coming around the bend he barely saw against the yard light two people sitting in the glider swing on his porch. He swung his car off into the trees. He wanted to get inside and study the papers he had from Fredson but he had learned caution and so put his hand on his 9 mm as he walked toward them. The gulf salt tang hung under the mimosa tree. A breeze stirred the smell of salt and fish and things dead, others spawning. Sugarcane near the house rattled in the breeze as he worked around to the back.

He let himself silently into his back door. When he snapped on the porch light the two figures jumped. It was Denise and his distant relative, Herb. Unlikely they knew each other.

McKenna opened the front door and let them in, a bit embarrassed at his creeping around. Denise made great fun of it and Herb's confused scowl said he had been rather puzzled by why this woman was here. McKenna wondered, too. He thought he had been pretty clear last time Denise showed up. He didn't like pushy women, many with one eye on his badge and the other on his pension. Even coming to his front door, like they were selling something. Well, maybe they were. He grew up when women didn't ask for dates. Whatever happened to courtship?

Not that he was all that great with women. In his twenties he had been turned down more times than an old blanket. He got them drinks and let the question of why Denise was here lie.

They traded pleasantries and McKenna saw maybe a way to work this. Herb said he'd been in the neighborhood and just stopped by to say hello. Fine. He asked Herb if he knew anything new about the Centauris, since the Pizotti fish fry, and that was enough. Herb shifted into lecture mode and McKenna sat back and watched Denise's reaction.

"There's all kinda talk on the Internet 'bout this," Herb said with relish. "Seems the Centauris deliberately suppressed their radio stations, once they picked up Marconi's broadcasts. They'd already spotted Earth as a biological planet centuries ago, see?—from studying the atmosphere. They'd already spent more centuries building those electric starships."

"My, my," Denise said softly.

Herb beamed at her, liking the audience. "Some think they're the origin of UFOs!"

Denise blinked, mouth making a surprised O. "The UFOs are theirs?"

"The UFOs we see, they're not solid, see? The Centauris sent them as a kind of signaling device. Pumped some kind of energy beams into our atmosphere, see, made these UFO images. Radar could pick them up 'cause they ionized the gas. That's why we never found anything solid."

McKenna was enjoying this. "Beams?"

Herb nodded, eyes dancing. "They excited some sorta atmospheric resonance effects. They projected the beams from our own asteroid belt."

Denise frowned. "But they got here only a few years back."

"They sent robot probes that got here in the 1940s. They'd already planned to send one here and land to take samples. So they used the beams somehow to, I dunno, maybe let us know somethin' was up."

"Seems odd," Denise said. "And what about all those people the UFOs kidnapped. They did all kinds of experiments on 'em!"

Herb's mouth turned down scornfully. "That's just *National Enquirer* stuff, Denise."

McKenna smiled so he could control the laugh bubbling up in his throat. "Learn any biology?"

Herb said, "We've got plenty land-dwelling reptiles, plenty fish. Not many species use both land and sea."

Herb took a breath to launch into a lecture and Denise put in, "How about gators?"

Herb blinked, gave a quick polite smile, and said, "The bio guys figure the Centauris had some reptile predators on the islands, gave what they call selection pressure. Centauris developed intelligence to beat them down when they came ashore, could be. Maybe like frogs, start out as larvae in the water."

Denise said wonderingly, eyeing Herb, "So they're like tadpoles at first?"

"Could be, could be." Herb liked feedback and McKenna guessed he didn't get a lot from women. Maybe they were too polite to interrupt. "They grow and develop lungs, legs, those funny handlike fins, big opposable thumbs. Then big brains to deal with the reptiles when they go ashore."

McKenna asked, "So they're going to hate our gators."

"S'pose so," Herb allowed. "They sure seem hostile to 'em around Dauphin Island. Could be they're like frogs, put out lots of offspring. Most tadpoles don't survive, y'know, even after they get ashore."

Denise said brightly, "But once one does crawl ashore, the adults would have to help it out a lot. Defend it against reptiles. Teach it how to make tools, maybe. Cooperation, but social competition, too."

Both men looked at her and she read their meaning. "I majored in sociology, minor in biology."

Herb nodded respectfully, looking at her with fresh eyes. "Hard to think that something like frogs maybe could bring down big reptiles, eh?"

Denise tittered at the very thought, eyes glistening eagerly, and McKenna got up to get them more drinks. By the time he came back out, though, they were getting up. Herb said he had to get home and they discovered that they didn't live all that far from each other, what a surprise then to meet out here at this distance, and barely noticed McKenna's good-byes.

He watched them stand beside Denise's car and exchange phone numbers. Now if only he could be as good a matchmaker for himself. But something in him wasn't ready for that yet.

And what else have you got in your life? the unwelcome thought came.

Work. *Oh yes, the Jorge papers from the FEMA people.*

Jorge had stuffed all sorts of things into the envelope. Receipts, check stubs, unreadables, some telephone numbers, a Mexican passport with a picture that looked a lot like the corpse.

He was stacking these when a thin slip fell out. A note written on a rubber-stamped sheet from Bayside Boats.

❖

It wasn't that far to Bayside Boats. He went there at dawn and watched a shrimp boat come in. When he showed every man in the place Jorge's photo, nobody recognized it. But the manager and owner, a grizzled type named Rundorf, hesitated just a heartbeat before answering. Then shook his head.

Driving away, he passed by the *Busted Flush* mooring. It was just coming in from a run and Merv Pitscomb stood at the prow.

His supervisor said, "You get anything from SIU on these cases?"

"Nope." The Special Investigations Unit was notoriously jammed up and in love with the FBI.

"Any statewide CAPs?"

CAPs, Crimes Against Persons, was the latest correct acronym that shielded the mind from the bloody reality, kept you from thinking about the abyss. "Nope."

"So you got two drowned guys who worked boats out of the same town. Seems like a stretch."

McKenna tried to look judicious. "I want a warrant to look at their pay records. Nail when these two worked, and work from there."

The supervisor shook his head. "Seems pretty thin."

"I doubt I'll get much more."

"You've been workin' this one pretty hard. Your partner LeBouc, he's due back tomorrow."

"So?"

A level gaze. "Maybe you should work it with him. This FBI angle, these guys coming up to you like that. Maybe this really should be their game."

"They're playing close to their vest. No help there for sure. And waiting for LeBouc won't help, not without more substance."

"Ummm." The supervisor disliked the FBI, of course, but he didn't want to step on their toes. "Lessee. This would have to go through Judge Preston. He's been pretty easy on us lately, must be getting laid again . . ."

"Let me put it in the batch going up to him later this morning."

"Okay, but then you got to get onto some more cases. They're piling up."

He had the boilerplate for the warrant application. He called it up and pasted in *I respectfully request that the Court issue a Warrant and Order of Seizure in the form annexed, authorizing a search of premises at . . . And such as is found shall be brought before the Court, together with such other and further relief that the Court may deem proper.* The lawyers loved such stuff.

Merv Pitscomb's face knotted with red rage. The slow-witted Buddy Johnson, ex-con and tire deflator, stood beside Pitscomb and wore a smirk. Neither liked the warrant and they liked it still less when he took their pay company records.

Ethan Anselmo was there, of course, and had gone out on the *Busted Flush,* a night job two days before the body washed up. No entry for Jorge Castan. But some initials from the bookkeeper a week before the last Anselmo entry, and two days after it, had a total, $178. One initial was GB and the other JC.

Bookkeepers have to write things down, even if they're supposed to keep quiet. Illegals were off the books, of course, usually with no Social Security numbers. But you had to balance your books, didn't you? McKenna loved bookkeepers.

"Okay," his supervisor said, "we got reasonable grounds to bring in this Pitscomb and the other one—"

"Rundorf."

"—to bring them in and work them a little. Maybe they're not wits, maybe these are just accidents the skippers don't want to own up to. But we got probable cause here. Bring them in tomorrow morning. It's near end of our shift."

There was always some paperwork confusion at quitting time. McKenna made up the necessaries and was getting some other, minor cases straightened out, thinking of heading home.

Then he had an idea.

❖

He had learned a good trick a decade back, from a sergeant who had busted a lot of lowlife cases open.

If you had two different suspects for a murder, book them both. Hold them overnight. Let the system work on them.

In TV lawyer shows the law was a smart, orderly machine that eventually, usually about an hour, punished the guilty.

But the system was not about that at all. The minute you stepped into its grinder you lost control of your life and became a unit. You sat in holding cells thinking your own fevered thoughts. Nobody knew you. You stared at the drain hole in the gray concrete floor where recent stains got through even the bleaching disinfectant sprayed over them. On the walls you saw poorly scrawled drawings of organs and acts starkly illuminated by the actinic, buzzing lights that never went out. You heard echoing yells and cops rapping their batons on the bars to get some peace. Which never came. So you sat some more with your own fevered thoughts.

You had to ask permission to go to the toilet rather than piss down that hole. There was the phone call you could make and a lawyer you chose out of the phone book, and the fuzzed voice said he'd be down tomorrow. Maybe he would come and maybe not. It was not like you had a whole lot of money.

The cops referred to you by your last name and moved you like walking furniture to your larger stinking cell with more guys in it. None of them looked at you except the ones you didn't like the look of at all. Then it was night and the lights dimmed, but not much.

That was where the difference between the two suspects came in. One would sleep, the other wouldn't.

Anybody who kills someone doesn't walk away clean. Those movies and TV lawyer shows made out that murderers were smart, twisted people. Maybe twisted was right but not smart, and for sure they were not beasts. Some even dressed better than anyone he had ever seen.

But like it or not, they were people. Murderers saw all the

same movies as ordinary folk, and a lot more TV. They sat around daytime making drug deals or waiting for nighttime to do second story jobs. Plenty of time to think about their business. Most of them could quote from *The Godfather*. The movie, of course. None of them read novels or anything else. They were emotion machines running all the time and after a job they blew their energy right away. Drank, went out cruising for pussy, shot up.

Then, if you timed it right, they got arrested.

So then the pressure came off. The hard weight of tension, the slow-building stress fidgeting at the back of the mind—all that came home to roost. They flopped down on the thin pad of their bunk and pulled the rough wool blanket over their faces and fell like the coming of heaven into a deep sleep. Many of them barely made it to the bunk before the energy bled out of them.

But now think about the guy who didn't do it. He *knows* he didn't do it even if the goddamn world doesn't. He is scared, sure, because he is far enough into the downstreet culture to know that justice is a whore and lawyers run the whorehouse. And so he is in real danger here. But he also for sure knows that he has to fight hard now, think, pay attention. And he is mad, too, because *he didn't do it* and shouldn't that matter?

So he frets and sits and doesn't sleep. He is ragged-eyed and slurring his words when he tries to tell the other guys in the cell—who have rolled over and gone to sleep—that he didn't do it. It would be smart to be some kind of Zen samurai and sleep on this, he knows that, but he can't. Because *he didn't do it.*

On a cell surveillance camera you can see the difference immediately. Get the cell assignments and go to the room where a bored overweight uniform watched too many screens. Check out the numbers on the screens, find the cells, watch the enhanced-light picture. The sleepers faced away from the lights, coiled up in their blankets. The ones who wouldn't or couldn't—it didn't matter much which—ignored the lights and you could see their eyes clicking around as they thought all this through.

Next morning, he leaned on the sleeper and released the guy who had stayed up all night. Sometimes the innocent ones could barely walk. But at least they were out in the sun.

The sleepers sometimes took days to break. Some of them had the smarts or the clout to lawyer up. But he had them and that was the point.

He had learned all this more years back than he wanted to think about, and it would still be true when he was long gone from this Earth.

He brought in Pitscomb and Rundorf at sunset. Got them booked, photoed, fingerprinted. They gave him plenty of mouth and he just stayed silent, doing his job.

Into the overnight holding cell they went.

He had a bottle of Zinfandel and slept well that night.

Back in at sunup, Pitscomb and Rundorf were red-eyed and irritated.

His supervisor was irritated, too. "I didn't tell you to bring them in late."

"You didn't? I must have misheard." McKenna kept his face absolutely still while he said it. He had practiced that in the mirror when he first made detective and it was a valuable skill.

He made the best of interrogating Pitscomb and Rundorf but the simple fact that they had stayed awake most of the night took McKenna's confidence away. The two gave up nothing. He booked them out and had some uniforms drive them home.

His partner came in that afternoon. LeBouc was a burly man who liked detail, so McKenna handed off some stickup shootings to him. They had been waiting for attention and McKenna knew they would get no leads. The perps were the same black gang that had hit the minimarkets for years and they knew their stuff. The videotapes showed only rangy guys in animal masks. LeBouc didn't seem to mind. McKenna filled him in on the drowned cases but he couldn't make an argument for where to go next. The cases were cooling off by the minute now, headed for the storage file.

McKenna had never been as systematic as LeBouc, who was orderly even when he was fishing. So when LeBouc said, "How'd those phone numbers from the illegal turn out?" McKenna felt even worse. He had noticed them in the stack of paper at Castan's shack, just before he found the Bayside Boats notepaper. Like a hound dog, he chased that lead down and forgot the telephone numbers.

He got right on them. One was the Mexican consulate in New Orleans, probably for use if Jorge got picked up.

One number answered in a stony voice saying only, "Punch in your code." The rest answered in Spanish and he got nowhere with them. He thought of getting a Spanish speaker but they were in high demand and he would have to wait for days. Nobody in homicide knew more than restaurant Spanish. He went back to the stony voice, a Mobile number.

Usually, to break a number you use a reverse directory of published numbers. McKenna found nothing there. There were lesser-known electronic directories of unpublished numbers that link phone numbers to people and addresses. He found those in the Mobile Police database. They were built up nationally, working from anyone who used the number to place a phone order. So he considered pretexting. To pretext, you call the phone company repair department, saying there's a problem on the line and getting them to divulge the address associated with the account. But you needed a warrant to do that and his credit had run out with Judge Preston.

If he couldn't pretend to be someone else, maybe he could pretend that his phone was someone else's. That would be caller-ID spoofing—making it seem as if a phone call is coming from another phone, rather than his homicide number. That made it more likely that the target person would answer the call, even if they had the new software that backtracked the caller in less than a second. McKenna's office number was not in the phone book but for sure it was in any sophisticated database software. And the stony voice sounded professional, smart.

Spoofing used to require special equipment, but now with

Internet phone calling and other Web services it was relatively easy to do. So easy, in fact, that just about anyone can do it. But McKenna hadn't. It took an hour of asking guys and gals in the office to get it straight. Everybody had a fine time making fun of "the Perfesser" coming to them for help, of course. He developed a fixed grin.

Once you burned an hour to know how, it took less than a minute.

The site even had a code breakdown for the number, too. When a stony voice answered, McKenna typed in the last four digits of the number again and in a few more seconds he got a ring. "Hello?"

McKenna said nothing. "Hello?" the voice of Dark Glasses said.

It took a while for his supervisor to go through channels and pin a name on Dark Glasses. The next morning Dark Glasses was in federal court, the FBI office said. So McKenna found him, waiting to testify.

"May I have a word in the hallway?" McKenna sat down in the chair at the back of the court. Somebody was droning on in front and the judge looked asleep.

"Who are you?" Dark Glasses said, nose up in the air. He wasn't wearing the glasses now and it was no improvement.

McKenna showed the badge. "Remember me? You were with Mr. Marine."

"Who?"

"You didn't say you were a lawyer, too."

"Who told you that?"

"Your office. The FBI, remember?"

The lawyer inched away but kept his chin out, first line of defense. "I'm waiting to testify on a federal case."

"Murder crosses boundaries."

The bailiff was looking at them. He jerked a thumb toward the doors. In the hallway Dark Glasses had revived his lawyerly presence. "Make it quick."

"This is about one of your cases, Jorge Castan."

"I don't discuss my cases."

He moved to go past and McKenna casually put a hand on his chest.

"You have no right to touch me. Move away."

McKenna just shook his head. "You know what's up. Your case got himself murdered, looks like. The second one like that in a week. And the Bar Association Web site says that before you got hired into the FBI you were an immigration lawyer. And you must know that your case was an illegal or else you're dumber than you look."

"I do not take a liking to insult. You touch me—"

"You're in serious trouble if you know what's really up. See, murder is a local crime unless you can show it has a proper federal issue that trumps local. Do you?"

"I do not have to—"

"Yes you do."

"There is not one scintilla of evidence—"

"Save it for the judge. Wrong attitude, counselor."

"I don't know what—"

"What I'm talking about, yeah. I hear it all the time. You guys must all watch the same movies."

"I am an attorney." He drew himself up.

"Yeah, and I know the number of the Bar Association. Being FBI won't protect you."

"I demand to know—"

Dark Glasses went on but little by little McKenna had been backing him up against the marble walls until the man's shoulder blades felt it. Then his expression changed. McKenna could see in the lawyer's face the schoolboy threatened by bullies. So he had gone into the law, which meant good ol' safe words and paper, to escape the real world where the old primate signals held sway. Dark Glasses held his briefcase in front of his body in defense, but the shield wasn't thick enough to stop McKenna from poking a finger into the surprisingly soft Dark Glasses bicep. "You're up at bat now, lawyer."

"As an attorney—"

"You're assumed to be a liar. For hire. Almost rhymes, don't it?"

"I do not respond to insults." He was repeating his material and he tilted his chin up again. McKenna felt his right hand come halfway up, balling into a fist, wanting so much to hit this clown hard on the point of that chin.

"You knew to go looking for Jorge in jig time. Or maybe for the people who knew him. Why's that?"

"I—I'm going to walk away now."

"Not if you're smart. One of those who knew him is an illegal, too. Maybe you wanted to use that to shut her up?"

"That's speculative—"

"Not really, considering your expression. No, you're working for somebody else. Somebody who has influence."

"My clients and cases are Bureau—"

"Confidential, I know."

"I have every assurance that my actions will prove victorious in this matter."

McKenna grinned and slapped an open palm against the briefcase, a hard smack. The lawyer jumped, eyebrows shooting up, back on the playground during recess. "I—I have an attorney-client relationship that by the constitution—"

"How 'bout the Bible?"

"—demands that you respect his . . . protection."

"The next one who dies is on you, counselor."

In a shaky voice the lawyer pulled his briefcase even closer and nodded, looking at the floor as if he had never seen it before. A small sigh came from him, filled with gray despair.

It was a method McKenna had worked out years ago, once he understood that lawyers were all talk and no muscle. Good cop/bad cop is a cliché, only the lawyer keeps looking for the good cop to show up and the good cop doesn't. Bluff is always skin deep.

The lawyer backed away once McKenna let him. "You better think about who you choose to represent. And who might that be, really?"

"My client is—"

"No, I mean who, really? Whose interest?"

"I . . . I don't know what you mean. I—"

"You know more than you've said. I expect that. But you still have to think about what you do." A rogue smile. "We all do."

"Look, we can handle this issue in a nice way—"

"I'll try being nicer if you'll try being smarter."

McKenna slid a business card into the suit handkerchief pocket of Dark Glasses Lawyer. "Call me. I find out the same stuff before you do, and that you knew it—well, I'll be without mercy, Counselor. No quarter."

McKenna stepped aside and let the lawyer flee from the playground. Dark Glasses didn't look back.

McKenna's supervisor leaned back and scowled. "And you did this because . . . ?"

"Because two drowned men with strange scars don't draw FBI without a reason, for starters."

"Not much to go on."

"The ME says he can't identify the small puncture marks. Or what made those funny welts."

His supervisor made a sour grin. "You know how much physical evidence is worth. It has to fit a filled-in story."

"And I don't have enough story."

He spread his hands, the cuff sliding up to expose part of his arm tattoo, rosy barbed wire.

McKenna had read somewhere that an expert is one who has made all the possible mistakes in a narrow field. A wise man is one who has made them widely. It was supposed to be funny but it was too true for that.

So he followed his good ole friend Buddy Johnson home from work that evening. Buddy liked his pleasures and spent the first hour of his night in a bar. Then he went out back to smoke a joint. It was dark and Buddy jumped a foot when McKenna shined the flashlight straight into his eyes.

"Gee, that cigarette sure smells funny."

"What? Who you?"

"The glare must be too much for you. Can't you recognize my voice?"

"What the—Look, I—"

McKenna slipped behind him, dropping the flashlight to distract him, and got the cuffs on. "We're gonna take a little ride."

McKenna took him in cuffs down a scruffy side alley and got him into Buddy's own convertible. Puffing, feeling great, he strapped Buddy in with the seat belt, passenger side. Then McKenna drove two quick miles and turned into a car wash. The staff was out front finishing up and when they came out McKenna showed them the badge and they turned white. All illegals, of course, no English. But they knew the badge. They vanished like the dew after the dawn.

Game time, down south.

Even with cuffs behind his back, Buddy kept trying to say something.

"Remember letting the air out of my tires?" McKenna hit him hard in the nose, popped some blood loose, and Buddy shut up. McKenna drove the convertible onto the ratchet conveyor and went back to the control panel. It was in English and the buttons were well-thumbed, some of the words gone in the worn plastic. McKenna ran up a SUPER CLEAN and HOT WAX and LIGHT BUFF. Then he gave a little laugh and sent Buddy on his way.

Hissing pressure hoses came alive. Big black brushes lowered into the open seats and whirred up to speed. They ripped Buddy full on. He started yelling and the slapping black plastic sheets slammed into him hard and he stopped screaming. McKenna hit the override and the brushes lifted away. Silence, only the dripping water on the convertible's leather seats.

McKenna shouted a question and waited. No answer. He could see the head lolling back and wondered if the man was conscious.

McKenna thought about the two drowned men and hit the buttons again.

The brushes hardly got started before a shrill cry came echoing back. McKenna stopped the machine. The brushes rose. He walked forward into the puddles, splashing and taking his time.

"You're nearly clean for the first time in your life, Buddy. Now I'm gonna give you a chance to come full clean with me."

"I . . . they ain't gonna like . . ." His mouth opened expectantly, rimmed with drool. The eyes flickered, much too white.

"Just tell me."

"They really ain't gonna like—"

McKenna turned and started back toward the control board. The thin, plaintive sobbing told him to turn around again. You could always tell when a man was broke clean through.

"Where'd they go?"

"Nearly to Chandeleur."

"The islands?"

"Yeah . . . long way out . . . takes near all night. Oil rigs . . . the wrecked ones."

"What'd you take out?"

"Centauris. Usually one, sometimes two."

"The same one?"

"Who can tell? They all look alike to me. Pitscomb, he bowed and scraped to the Centauri and the feds with him, but he don't know them apart either."

"Pitscomb have anything to do with Ethan's death?"

"Man, I weren't workin' that night."

"Damn. What'd the rest of the crew say about it?"

"Nothin'. All I know is that Ethan was on the boat one night and he didn't come back to work next day."

"Who else was with the Centauri?"

"Just feds."

"What was the point of going out?"

"I dunno. We carried stuff in big plastic bags. Crew went inside for 'bout an hour while we circled round the messed-up oil rigs. FBI and Centauri were out there. Dunno what they did. Then we come back."

McKenna took the cuffs off Buddy and helped him out of

the car. To his surprise, Buddy could walk just fine. "You know Jorge?"

"Huh? Yeah, that wetback?"

"Yeah. You're a wetback, too, now."

"Huh? Oh." Buddy got the joke and to his credit, grinned. "Look, you don't nail me on the dope, it's even, okay?"

"You're a gentleman and a scholar, Buddy."

"Huh?"

"It's fine. Keep your nose clean from here on out or I'll bring you back here to clean it myself."

He hung his head. "Y'know, you're right. I got to straighten up."

"You're straight with me right now."

They even shook hands.

A take-charge raccoon was working the trash when he hauled in on the oyster shell road. He shooed it away and then tossed it a watermelon that had gone old anyway.

Then he sat on the porch and sipped a Cabernet and worked himself over about the car wash stunt. His wife had once told him, after he had worked up through being a uniform, then vice and then bunko and finally homicide, that the process had condensed him into a hard man. He had never said to her that maybe it was her long illness that had made him quiet around the house, wary and suspicious . . . but in the end maybe it was both. He had never been interested in small talk but had picked up the skill for getting witnesses to open up.

Now he felt very little after working Buddy over. He had done it with a vague intuition that the kid needed a wake-up call, sure, but mostly because he was blocked in this case. And he couldn't let it go. Maybe it helped fill the emptiness in him, one he felt without shame or loss, as not a lack but as a blank space—an openness that made him hear the wind sigh and waves slosh not as mere background but as life passing while most people ignored it, talked over it, trying to pin life down with their words. He listened at nightfall, sitting out here on the warped planking of his wharf, to the planet breathing in its sleep. A world never fully revealed, a planet with strangeness at its core.

The next day he and LeBouc worked some ordinary gang-related cases. And planned. LeBouc was a fisherman and would go out for just about any reason. Not a hard sell. And neither of them could think of anything else to do. The FBI had called up their supervisor and badmouthed McKenna, of course. But they wouldn't reveal anything more and tried to pry loose what McKenna knew. The supe stonewalled. A Mexican standoff.

Just before twilight McKenna sprayed on exercise shorts plus shirt. This was a semi-new techy product, snug and light, and he wanted to try them. The shorts were black, the cheapest spray-on, with spaced breather holes to respire sweat through. His belly was a bit thick and his calves stringy, but nobody was going to see him anyway if he could help it. The smart fibers itched as they linked up to form the hems, contouring to his body, the warmth from their combining getting him in the mood. He drove to the boat ramp just west of Bayou La Batre, huffing the salty sunset breeze into his lungs with a liberating zest.

LeBouc was there with an aluminum boat and electric motor and extra batteries, rented from a Mobile fishing company. Great for quiet night work, spotlights and radiophone, the works. LeBouc was pumped, grinning and stowing gear.

"Thought I'd do some line trawling on the way," he said, bringing on a big pole and a tackle box. He carried a whole kit of cleaning knives and an ice chest. "Never know when you might bag a big one."

McKenna's shoes grated on the concrete boat ramp as the water lapped against the pilings. The boat rose on the slow, lumbering tide. A dead nutria floated by, glassy-eyed and with a blue crab gouging at it. Business as usual at the Darwin Café.

They used a gas outboard to reach the estimated rendezvous point, to save on the batteries. McKenna had planted a directional beeper on the *Busted Flush* in late afternoon, using a black guy he hired in Bayou La Batre to pretend to be looking for work. Right away they picked up the microwave beeper, using their tracking gear. With GPS geared into the tracker they could hang back a mile away and follow them easily. LeBouc was a total nontech type and had never once called McKenna "the perfesser."

LeBouc flipped on the Raytheon acoustic radar and saw the sandy bottom sliding away into deeper vaults of mud. Velvet air slid by. The night swallowed them.

It was exciting at first, but as they plowed through the slapping swells the rhythm got to McKenna. He hadn't been sleeping all that well lately, so LeBouc took the first watch, checking his trailing line eagerly. LeBouc had spent his vacation deep-sea fishing off Fort Lauderdale and was happy to be back on the water again.

LeBouc shook McKenna awake three hours later. "Thought you were gonna wake me for a watch," McKenna mumbled.

"Nemmine, I was watchin' my line. Almost got one too."

"What's up?"

"They hove to, looks like from the tracker."

They quietly approached the *Busted Flush* using the electric motor. The tracker picked up a fixed warning beacon. "Maybe an oil platform," McKenna said. LeBouc diverted slightly toward it.

Out of the murk rose a twisted skeleton. Above the waterline the main platform canted at an angle on its four pylons. A smashed carcass of a drilling housing lay scattered across its steel plates. Three forlorn rotating beacons winked into the seethe of the sea.

LeBouc asked, "How far's the shrimper?"

McKenna studied the tracker screen, checked the scale. "About three hundred yards. Not moving."

LeBouc said, "Let's tuck in under that platform. Make us hard to see."

"Don't know if I can see much in IR at this range."

"Try now."

The IR goggles LeBouc had wangled out of Special Operations Stores fit on McKenna's head like a fat parasite. In them he could see small dots moving, the infrared signature blobs of people on the shrimper deck. "Barely," McKenna said.

"Lemme try it."

They carefully slid in under the steel twenty feet above. LeBouc secured them with two lines to the pylon cleats and the boat did not rock with the swell so much. McKenna could make out the *Busted Flush* better here in the deeper dark. He studied it and said, "They're moving this way. Slow, though."

"Good we're under here. Wonder why they chose a platform area."

Many of the steel bones had wrenched away down on the shoreward side of the platform and now hung down beneath the waves. The enviros made the best of it, calling these wrecks fish breeders, and maybe they were.

"Fish like it here, maybe."

"Too far offshore to fish reg'lar."

McKenna looked up at the ripped and rusted steel plates above, underpinned by skewed girders. His father had died on one of these twelve years back, in the first onslaught of a hurricane. When oil derricks got raked in a big storm and started to get worked, you hooked your belt to a Geronimo wire and bailed out from the top—straight into the dark sea, sliding into hope and kersplash. He had tried to envision it, to see what his father had confronted.

When you hit the deck of the relief hauler it was awash. Your steel-toed boots hammered down while you pitched forward, facedown, with your hard hat to save the day, or at least some memories. But his father's relief hauler had caught a big one broadside and the composite line had snapped and his father went into the chop. They tried to get to him but somehow he didn't have his life jacket on and they lost him.

With his inheritance from his father McKenna bought their house on the water. He recalled how it felt getting the news, the strange sensation that he had dropped away into an abyss. How his father had always hated life jackets and didn't wear them to do serious work.

McKenna realized abruptly that he didn't have his own life jacket on. Maybe it was genetic. He found some in the rear locker and pulled one on, tossing another to LeBouc, who was fooling with his tackle and rod.

LeBouc said, "You watch, I'll try a bait line."

McKenna opened his mouth and heard a faint rumble in the distance. The boat shuttled back and forth on its cleat lines. Waves smacked against steel and shed a faint luminous glow. He could see nothing in the distance, though, and sat to pull down the IR goggles. A hazy shimmer image. The *Busted Flush* was coming closer, on a course that angled to the left. "They're moving."

There was a lot of splashing nearby as currents stirred among the pylons. The three figures on the deck of the shrimper were easier to see now.

The IR blobs were right at the edge of definition. Then one of them turned into the illumination cone of a pale running light, making a jabbing gesture to another blob. He couldn't quite resolve the face, but McKenna recognized the man instantly.

Dark Glasses stood out like a clown at a funeral.

The man next to him must be Pitscomb, McKenna figured. The third form was fainter and taller and with a jolt McKenna knew it was a Centauri. It moved more gracefully at sea than on land as it walked along the railing. Its sliding gait rocked with the ship, better than the men. It held a big dark lump and seemed to be throwing something from the lump over the side.

McKenna focused to make sense of the image. The Centauri had a bag, yes—

A grunt from nearby told him LeBouc was casting and an odd splash came and then thumping. The boat shifted and jerked as he tried to focus on the IR images and another big splash came.

He jerked off the goggles. His eyes took a few seconds to adjust. There was fitful radiance from the surf. LeBouc was not in the boat.

A leg jerked up in the water, arms flailed in a white churn. Long swift things like ropes whipped around the leg. McKenna reached for the oars secured along the boatline. A sudden pain lurched up in his right calf and he looked down. A furred cord was swiftly wrapping itself up his leg, over his knee, starting on his calf. Needles of pain shot into his leg. The sting of it ran up his spine and provoked a shudder through his torso. His leg twitched, out of his control.

The wrapping rope stopped at his thigh and yanked. He fell over and his knee slammed hard on the bottom of the boat. Another cord came over and hit his shoulder. It clung tight and snarled around him. The shoulder muscles thrashed wildly as the thing bit through his plastic all-weather jacket and his shirt. Pain jabbed into his chest.

Other wriggling strands came snaking across the bowed deck. He wrenched around and hit his head on LeBouc's tackle box. He thought one of the things had grabbed his ear but it was the latch on the box, caught in his hair. A hollering came and he realized it was his own ragged voice.

His hands beat at the cord but prickly spines jutting out of it stung him. That jolted him badly and he tried to pull himself up to get a tool. The tackle box. He grabbed a gutting knife. With both hands he forced it under the edge of the cord across his chest. The ropy thing was strong and fought against the blade. He got some leverage and pulled up and the blade bit. The pink cord suddenly gave way. It flailed around and the main body lashed back at him. He caught it on the point of the knife and drove it into the side of the boat. That gave him a cutting surface and he worked the knife down the length of the thing. He sawed with all his strength. It split into two splices that went still. Stroking along it he sliced it in two, clear up to the housing at the stern.

The shooting pain in his calf he had made himself ignore and now he turned to it. The cord had sunk into his jeans. He pried it up as before and turned the blade. This one popped open and drooled milky fluid. He hacked away at it, free of the lancing pain. It took a moment to cut away chunks. They writhed on the boat bottom. With stinging hands he reached into the tackle box and found the workman's gloves. That made it easier to pick up and toss the long strands into the sea. They struggled weakly.

Numbness crept up his leg and across his chest. He felt elated and sleepy and wanted to rest. His eyes flickered and he realized that his face was numb too. Everything was moving too fast and he needed a rest. Then he could think about this.

Then another pink rope came sliding over the gunnel. It felt around and snaked toward him as if it could sense his heat or smell. He felt the tip of it touch his deck shoe. Sharp fear cleared his mind.

The knife came down on it and he pounded the point along its length.

Without cutting it into pieces he lurched toward the gunwale. With a swipe the tie line popped away from its cleat. He leaped over a section of pink rope and cut the second line. He could barely see. With hands he felt along the stern and found the starter button and helm. The outboard caught right away. With a strum the engines turned over and he slid the throttles forward to rev the engines into a quick-start warm-up.

He veered among the pylons. With a click the flashlight glare made the scene jump out at him. There were pink strands in the water.

No sign at all of LeBouc.

He hit the throttle and shot out into open water and reached for the radiophone.

The worst of it was the wait.

He stung in running sheets of fire all over the right leg and chest. The thing had wrapped around his calf like a bracelet. He wondered why the ME never said anything about the corpses being pumped full of venom and only then realized that he had felt electrical shocks, not stings. His leg and arm had been jerking on their own. He fingered the trembling muscles, remembering through a fog.

He got away from there into the darkness, not caring anymore about the *Busted Flush*. Eventually he thought that they might be following the sound of the outboard. He shut it off and drifted. Then he called the shore and said he was headed in on the electric. By then he was flopping on the deck as debilitating cramps swept through him. Breath came hard and he passed out several times.

Then a chopper came out of the murk. It hovered over him like an angel with spotlights and an unfurling ladder. Men in wet suits dropped onto the deck. They harnessed him up and he spun away into the black sky. On the hard floor of the chopper a woman stood over him with a big needle of epinephrine, her face lined with concern. He could not get his thick tongue to tell her that this case was something else. She shot him full of it and his heart pounded. That did clear his sluggish mind but it did not stop the shooting jolts that would come up suddenly in his leg and chest and in other places he had no memory of the pink rope being at all.

She gave him other injections though and those made the whole clattering chopper back away. It was like a scene on late-night television, mildly interesting and a plot you could vaguely remember seeing somewhere. She barked into her helmet mike and asked him questions but it was all theory now, not really his concern.

The next few hours went by like a movie you can't recall the next day. A cascading warm shower lined in gray hospital tile, McKenna lying on the tiles. A doctor in white explaining how they had to denature something, going on and on, just about as interesting as high school chemistry. They said they needed his consent for some procedure and he was happy to give it so long as they agreed to leave him alone.

He slowly realized the ER whitecoats were not giving him painkillers because of the War on Drugs and its procedural requirements. A distant part of him considered how it would be for a lawman to die of an excess of law. Doctors X and then Y and finally Z had to sign off. Time equaled pain and dragged on tick by tick.

Then there was Demerol, which settled the arguments nicely.

❖

The next day he found a striping of tiny holes along his leg. More across his chest. He guessed the corpses had sealed up most of these when they swelled, so they showed only a few tiny holes.

The ME came by and talked to McKenna as though he were an unusually fascinating museum exhibit. At least he brought some cortisone cream to see if it would help and it did. He recalled distantly that the ME was actually a doctor of some sort. Somehow he had always thought of the ME as a cop.

Two days later a team of fed guys led him out of the hospital and into a big black van. They had preempted local law, of course, so McKenna barely got to see his supervisor or the Mobile chief of police, who was there mostly for a photo op anyway.

In the van a figure in front turned and gave him a smile without an ounce of friendliness in it. Mr. Marine.

"Where's Dark Glasses?" McKenna asked but Mr. Marine looked puzzled and then turned away and watched the road. Nobody said anything until they got to Dauphin Island.

The took him up a ramp and down a corridor and then through some sloping walkways and odd globular rooms and finally to a little cell with pale glow coming from the walls. It smelled dank and salty and they left him there.

A door he hadn't known was there slid open in the far wall. A man all in white stepped in carrying a big, awkward laptop and behind him shuffled a Centauri.

McKenna didn't know how he knew it, but this was the same Centauri he had seen getting on the *Busted Flush*. It looked at him with the famous slitted eyes and he caught a strange scent that wrinkled his nose.

The man in white sat down in one of two folding chairs he had brought and gestured for McKenna to sit in the other. The Centauri did not sit. It carefully put a small device on the floor, a bulb and nozzle. Then it stood beside the man and put its flipper-hands on the large keyboard of the laptop. McKenna had heard about these devices shaped to the Centauri movements.

"It will reply to questions," the man in white said. "Then it types a reply. This computer will translate on-screen."

"It can't pronounce our words, right?" McKenna had read that.

"It has audio pickups that transduce our speech into its own sounds. But it can't speak our words, no. This is the best we've been able to get so far." The man seemed nervous.

The Centauri held up one flipper-hand and with the device sprayed itself, carefully covering its entire skin. Or at least it seemed more like skin now, and not the reptile armor McKenna had first thought it might be.

"It's getting itself wetted down," the man said. "This is a dry room, easier for us to take."

"The wet rooms have—"

"Ceiling sprays, yeah. They gotta stay moist 'cause they're amphibians. That's why they didn't like California. It's too dry, even at the beach."

The Centauri was finished with its spraying. McKenna thought furiously and began. "So, uh, why were you going out on the shrimp boat?"

Its jointed flippers were covered in a mesh hide. They moved in circular passes over pads on the keyboard. The man had to lift the awkward computer a bit to the alien, who was shorter than an average man. On the screen appeared

<<Feed our young.>>

"Is that what attacked me?"

<<Yes. Friend died.>>

"Your young are feeding?"

<<Must. Soon come to land.>>

"Why don't we know of this?"

<<Reproducing private for you also.>>

He could not look away from those eyes. The scaly skin covered its entire head. The crusty deep green did not stop at the big spherical eyes, but enclosed nearly all of it, leaving only the pupil open in a clamshell slit. He gazed into the unreadable glittering black depths of it. The eyes swiveled to follow him as he fidgeted. McKenna couldn't think of anything to say.

"I, I can't read your expression. Like *Star Trek* and that stuff, we expect aliens to be like humans, really."

The alien wrote,

<<I know of your vision programs. The Trek drama we
    studied. To discern how you would think of us.>>

"You don't have our facial expressions."

<<We have our own.>>

"Of course. So I can't tell if you care whether your young killed two men on fishing boats."

<<They were close to water. Young. Hungry.
    Your kind stay away is best.>>

"We don't know! Our government has not told us. Why?"

The man holding the computer opened his mouth to say something and thought better of it. The alien wrote:

<<Change is hard for both our kinds. Ideas should come
        slowly to be understood.>>

"People are okay with your visit. They might not like your seeding our oceans and moving in. Plus killing us."

This time it took a while to answer:

<<Those you call dead live on now in the dark heaven.>>

McKenna blinked. "Is that a religious idea?"

<<No. It arises from our skystorians.>>

"Uh, sky . . . ?"

The computer guy said, "Mistranslation. I saw that one with the astro guys last week. The software combines two concepts, see. Sky—means astronomy, 'cause their world is always cloudy, so the night sky is above that—and history. Closest word is cosmology, astronomy of the past."

McKenna looked at the alien's flat, unreadable gaze. "So it's . . . science."

<<Your term for this bedrock of the universe is the dark
energy. I modify these words to show the nature of your dark
        energy. It forces open the universe.>>

McKenna could not see where this was going. He had read some pop science about something called dark energy, sure. It supposedly was making the whole universe expand faster and faster. "So what's it . . . this dark heaven . . . do?"

<<It is the . . . substrate. Entangled information propagates as waves in it. Organized minds of high level emit probability waves in packets of great complexity. These persist long after the original emitter is dead.>>

McKenna blinked. "You mean we . . . our minds . . . send out their . . ."

<<Their presence, that is a better term. Minds emit presence. This persists as waves in the dark heaven that is everywhere in the universe. All minds join it.>>

"This sounds like religion."

<<Your distinction between fears for your fate and the larger category of science is not one we share. This required long study by us to understand since you are a far younger life-form. You have not yet had the time and experience to study the universe for long.>>

McKenna was getting in over his head. He felt light-headed, taking shallow breaths, clenching his hands. "You don't regret that those men died?"

<<Our emotions do not fit in your categories, either. We sorrow, yes. While also knowing that the loss is only a transition, as when our young come to shore. One gives up one form for another. Beyond the dark heaven perhaps there is something more but we do not know. Probably that is a question beyond our categories. We have limits just as do you, though not so great. You are young. There is time.>>

"Around here murder is a crime."

<<We are not from here.>>

"Look, even if spirits or whatever go someplace else, that doesn't excuse murder."

<<Our young do not murder. They hunt and eat and grow. Again, a category difference between our kinds.>>

"Being dead matters to us."

<<Our young that you attacked. By your own terms you
murdered them.>>

The Centauri blinked slowly at McKenna with its clamshell
opening in the leathery, round eyes. Then it stooped to get its
sprayer. From its wheezing spout moisture swirled around all of
them.

The giddy swirl of this was getting to him. "I, I don't know
where to go with this. Your young have committed a crime."

<<The coming together between stars of intelligence has a cost.
We all pay it.>>

McKenna stood up. The damp scent of the alien swarmed
around him. "Some more than others."

He barely made it to LeBouc's funeral. It was a real one,
with a burial plot. At the church he murmured soft words to the
widow, who clung to him, sobbing. He knew that she would
later ask how her husband had died. It was in her pleading eyes.
He would not know what to say. Or what he would be allowed
to say. So he sat in the back of the whitewashed Baptist church
and tried to pay attention to the service. As LeBouc's partner he
had to say something in the eulogies. A moment after he sat
down again he had no idea what he had said. People looked
oddly at him. In the graveyard, as protocol demanded he stood
beside the phalanx of uniforms, who fired a popping salute.

At least LeBouc got buried. He had washed up on a beach
while McKenna was in the hospital. McKenna had never liked
the other ways, especially after his wife went away into cremation. One dealt with death, he felt, by dealing with the dead.
Now bodies did not go into the earth but rather the air through
cremation or then the ashes into the sea. People were less
grounded, more scattered. With the body seldom present, the
wheel working the churn between the living and dead could not
truly spin.

God had gone out of it, too. LeBouc's fishing friends got up
and talked about that. For years McKenna had noticed how his
friends in their last profile became not dead Muslims or

Methodists but dead bikers, golfers, surfers. That said, a minister inserted talk about the afterlife at the grave site and then the party, a respectable several hundred, went to the reception. There the tone shifted pretty abruptly. McKenna heard some guy in a seersucker suit declare "closure" just before the Chardonnay ran out.

On his sunset drive back down by the bay he rolled down the windows to catch the sea breeze tang. He tried to think about the alien.

It had said they wanted privacy in their reproductive cycle. But was that it? Privacy was a human concept. The Centauris knew that because they had been translating human radio and TV dramas for a century. Privacy might not be a Centauri category at all, though. Maybe they were using humans' own preconceptions to get some maneuvering room?

He needed to rest and think. There would for sure come a ton of questions about what happened out there in the dark gulf. He did not know what he would or could say to LeBouc's widow. Or what negotiations would come between Mobile PD and the feds. Nothing was simple, except maybe his slow-witted self.

What he needed was some Zinfandel and an hour on his wharf.

A black Ford sedan was parked on the highway a hundred yards from his driveway. It looked somehow official, deliberately anonymous. Nobody around here drove such a dull car, one without blemish or rust. Such details probably meant nothing, but he had learned what one of the desk sergeants called "street sense" and he never ignored it.

He swung onto the oyster drive, headed toward home, and then braked. He cut his lights and engine, shifting into neutral, and eased the car down the sloping driveway, gliding along behind a grove of pines.

In the damp night air rushing by he heard the crunching of the tires and wondered if anybody up ahead heard them too. Around the bend before the house he stopped and let the motor tick, cooling, while he just listened. Breeze whispered through the pines and he was upwind from the house. He eased open the car door and pulled his 9 mm from the glove compartment, not closing it, letting the silence settle.

No bird calls, none of the rustle and scurry of early night.

He slid out of the car, keeping low under the window of the door. No moon yet. Clouds scudded off the gulf, masking the stars.

He circled around behind the house. On the gulf side a man stood in shadows just around the corner from the porch. He wore jeans and a dark shirt and cradled a rifle. McKenna eased up on him, trying to ID the profile from the dim porch light. At the edge of the pines he surveyed the rest of his yard and saw no one.

Nobody carries a rifle to make an arrest. The smart way to kill an approaching target was to bracket him, so if there was a second guy he would be on the other side of the house, under the oak tree.

McKenna faded back into the pines and circled left to see the other side of his house. He was halfway around when he saw the head of another man stick around the corner. There was something odd about the head as it turned to survey the backyard but in the dim light he could not make it out.

McKenna decided to walk out to the road and call for backup. He stepped away. This caught the man's attention and brought up another rifle and aimed straight at him. McKenna brought his pistol up.

The recoil rocked his hand back and high as the 9 mm snapped away, two shots. Brass casings curled back past his vision, time in slow-mo. The man went down and McKenna saw he was wearing IR goggles.

McKenna turned to his right in time to see the other man moving. McKenna threw himself to the side and down and a loud report barked from the darkness. McKenna rolled into a low bush and lay there looking out through the pines. The man was gone. McKenna used both hands to steady his pistol, elbows on the sandy ground, knowing that with a rifle the other man had the advantage at this distance, maybe twenty yards.

He caught a flicker of movement at his right. The second man was well away from the wall now, range maybe thirty yards, bracing his rifle against the old cypress trunk. McKenna fired fast, knowing the first shot was off but following it with four more. He could tell he was close but the hammering rounds threw off his judgment. He stopped, the breech locking open on the last one. He popped the clip and slid in another, a stinging smell in his widened nostrils.

The flashes had made him night-blind. He lay still, listening, but his ears hummed from the shooting. This was the hardest moment, when he did not know what had happened. Carefully he rolled to his left and behind a thick pine tree. No sounds, as near as he could tell.

He wondered if the neighbors had heard this, called some uniforms.

He should do the same, he realized. Quietly he moved further left.

The clouds had cleared and he could see better. He looked toward the second guy's area and saw a shape lying to the left of the tree. Now he could make out both the guys, down.

He called the area dispatcher on his cell phone, whispering.

Gingerly he worked around to the bodies. One was Dark Glasses, the other Mr. Marine. They were long gone.

They both carried M-1A rifles, the semiauto version for civilians of the old M-14. Silenced and scoped, fast and sure, the twenty-round magazines were packed firm with snub-nosed .308s. A perfectly deniable, nonfederal weapon.

So the feds wanted knowledge of the aliens tightly contained. And Dark Glasses had a grudge, no doubt. The man had been a stack of anxieties walking around in a suit.

He walked out onto the wharf, nerves jumping in the salty air, and looked up at the glimmering stars. So beautiful.

Did some dark heaven lurk out there? As nearly as he could

tell, the alien meant that it filled the universe. If it carried some strange wave packets that minds emitted, did that matter?

That Centauri had seemed to say that murder didn't matter so much because it was just a transition, not an ending.

So was his long-lost wife still in this universe, somehow? Were all the minds that had ever lived?

Minds that had lived beneath distant suns? Mingled somehow with Dark Glasses and Mr. Marine?

This might be the greatest of all possible revelations. A final confirmation of the essence of religion, of the deepest human hopes.

Or it might be just an alien theology, expressed in an alien way.

A heron flapped overhead and the night air sang with the chirps and scurries of the woods. Nature was getting back to business, after all the noise and death.

Business as usual.

But he knew that this night sky would never look the same again.

❖ WOMB OF EVERY WORLD ❖

Walter Jon Williams

With long strides the swordsman walked across the desert. Gravel crunched beneath his feet. His eyes were dark, his nose a blade. He wore sturdy leather boots, very dusty, dark robes, and a flowing headdress, all suitable for the high stony land on which he walked. On his back he carried a pack with dried food, a skin shelter, and a rolled-up carpet to lie on. Though the sun in the sky was small and pale, its heat still quavered on the horizon.

The land rolled in gentle hills, endless as the ocean. The soil was gray and covered with stones of the same shade of gray. The air smelled of dust. There was little vegetation. The sky was cloudless and twilit, and the sun never moved.

The swordsman's blade was carried in a plain wooden scabbard covered with cracked leather. The broadsword was heavy, single-edged, broader in the foible than the forte. Its name was Tecmessa.

The man walked beside a wagon road, two dusty ruts that carried in a straight line from one horizon to the next. The iron-shod wheels of numerous wagons had thrown all the stones out of the ruts, or ground them to powder, but the swordsman found the ruts too dusty and chose instead to walk on the stones near the road. The thick soles of his boots made this less trying than it might otherwise have been.

While the man made only an occasional detour from the road, the slim form of his companion roamed left and right of the track, as if on a series of small errands. She returned from such a side trip and spoke.

"A spider, common and brown. And ants, common and black. The former is happy to feed on the latter."

"Anything uncommon?"

"Alas, no."

The man coughed briefly, the sound smothered by the strip of turban he had drawn over his mouth and nose to keep out the dust.

"Our trek threatens to become tedious," he remarked.

"*Threatens?*"

There was a moment of silence.

"Sarcasm," said the man, "is a poor companion on a long journey."

"So," said his companion, "are spiders and ants."

They came to the mild crest of a rolling hill and looked into the valley beneath. Shrubs cast a dark shadow on part of the valley floor, and the two left the trail to investigate. As they approached there was a startling clap of wings, and a flock of birds thundered into the sky.

"Quail," said the swordsman.

She turned her green eyes to him. "That implies there is enough here for quail to eat."

The swordsman raised a gloved hand to a drooping branch with long, dark green leaves. "Why don't you investigate?"

His companion darted beneath the shrubs while the swordsman looked at the branch with interest. He turned his eyes toward the ground and saw broken branches, debris, and a scattering of long brown seedpods. He squatted on his heels and picked up one of the pods. It crumbled in his hand and he extracted a pair of seeds, which he put in a pouch on his belt.

His companion returned.

"Ants and spiders," she said.

"Anything else?"

"An elderly tortoise, and a snake anticipating the birth of many baby quail."

"What kind of snake?"

"Bullsnake. Long as your arm."

The swordsman opened his hand and let fall the remains of the seedpod.

"This appears to be some kind of dwarf mimosa," he said. "Mimosa can tolerate drought, but they're hardly desert plants. Yet here they are."

She narrowed her eyes. "Thriving."

The man looked at her. "What did I say about sarcasm?"

The pair returned to the road. No earth-shaking discoveries were made. Gray lizards the color of the desert scurried out of their way. Wind swirled dust over and around them. They paused for refreshment at a well, where they sat in the shade of a ruined caravanserai and ate a meal of dried meat, dried apricots, and stale hard tack.

An hour later, traversing the bottom of another valley, they were ambushed by a troop of cavalry.

Riders came rolling over the hill just ahead, spreading out in a crescent as gray dust rose in a pall. They didn't charge, but advanced at a controlled trot. The swordsman paused and considered.

"How many?" he asked.

"Seventeen. Eleven with lances, two with swords, four with bows. And their beasts of course, some of which seem ill-natured and prone to violence."

The man frowned beneath the cloth that covered his mouth. He took a step back with his left foot and loosened Tecmessa in its sheath.

The riders came forward and drew rein about ten paces from the man. The leader was a massive figure, broad as a wall, with pallid skin touched with the gray dust of the desert. His eyes were an eerie gold. A few links of mail, large and crudely forged, hung from beneath his robes. He carried a long lance and rode astride a bipedal lizard with long, sturdy legs, an occipital crest, and sharp teeth.

"A troll," murmured the swordsman's companion. "What joy."

There were other trolls among the riders. Others were humans of varied hues and genders. One woman had four arms and carried two bows, both with arrows nocked.

"Hail, traveler," the troll said, in a voice like boulders gargling.

"Hail," said the swordsman.

The gold eyes regarded him. "Have you lost your mount?"

"I come on foot."

"You have chosen a long road to walk. Where are you bound?"

"Gundapur."

"And your business there?"

"I have no business there, or indeed anywhere. I travel for my soul's sake, not for profit."

The troll narrowed his gold eyes. His mount hissed and bared carat-shaped teeth.

"You will find the journey dangerous," the troll said.

"I am not indifferent to danger," said the swordsman, "but I will walk the path in any case."

"Your name?"

The swordsman took a long breath, then spoke. "I believe it is customary, before asking the name of a stranger, to introduce oneself, and in such a case as this to state clearly the right by which one asks."

A puzzled look creased the troll's face.

"I perceive you are unused to the impersonal pronoun," the swordsman said. "Allow me to rephrase in the second person plural. *Who the hell are you people, and why are you barring my way?*"

For a moment the troll could not decide between anger and laughter. He chose the latter. A grin split his huge gray face, revealing craggy yellow teeth.

"Stranger, you have courage!"

The swordsman shrugged. "I claim no more than the normal share," he replied.

Laughter gurgled from the troll. "I am Captain Grax," he said. "These"—gesturing—"are my Free Companions. We're employed as caravan guards on the route from Lake Toi to Gundapur."

The swordsman drew his feet together and offered a modest bow.

"My name is Aristide," he said. "My companion is Bitsy." He looked at the Free Companions. "You seem to have misplaced your caravan," he said.

"It's ahead, at the Ulwethi Caravanserai. We're patrolling, looking for bandits who are infesting the district." The gold eyes narrowed. "You could be a bandit scout."

"If so," said Aristide, "I'm a poor one. I'm without a mount, and I walked directly into your ambush."

"True," Captain Grax considered, his cone-shaped ears flickering. "You have seen no one on the road?"

"Nothing but ants, spiders, and the occasional tortoise."

"We'll continue on for a while, then, in case you're lying. If you are, we'll come back and kill you after we've disposed of your allies."

"Good hunting to you," said Aristide, and bowed again.

Grax and his companions parted and rode around Aristide, on his trail. Aristide adjusted his turban and continued on his way, conversing the while with his companion.

In less than four turns of the glass he came upon the caravanserai, a blocky stone fort crouched over an oasis. Animals and people swarmed about the place, more than could be contained within its walls. A pen for extra animals had been built out of dry stone, while many brightly colored tents were pitched near the oasis. On the far side of the muddy pool, Aristide could see what appeared to be a market.

Far from moving on, the travelers seemed to have settled into this remote outpost for a long stay.

Bitsy gave the swordsman a green-eyed look over her shoulder, then slipped away to conduct an investigation.

The swordsman walked past the stone corral and a row of tents to the elaborate arched door of the caravanserai, and asked the guard where he could find the seneschal.

"His office is by the Pool of Life."

Aristide entered the great stone building and found the shrine with its menhir and silvery pool, and next to it the booth of the timekeeper, who as the swordsman approached turned the glass and struck eight o'clock on his gong. The seneschal's office was behind the timekeeper's booth. The seneschal was a lean man with a sly look in his eye, and a paper-thin mustache that followed the line of his upper lip. He smelled of strong tobacco.

"You will be provided with food for one hundred and forty-four turns of the glass," he said, "and fodder if you need it. Afterward you'll have to purchase rations at the market."

Aristide wondered if the seneschal was slipping food and fodder to the market, and making a profit with the items the sultan intended he give away.

"What's causing the delay?" Aristide asked. "Is there war in Gundapur?"

"The area has been plagued by an unusually rapacious troop of bandits. The caravans have stopped here until their combined companies of guards feel equal to the challenge, or until the sultan sends a force to relieve us."

Aristide looked out the arched window of the office, at the swarm of people and animals in the fort's courtyard.

"There is a small army here," he said.

The seneschal touched the corner of his little mustache with a long finger. "The last group to leave consisted of three caravans with nearly sixty guards. They were routed. A few of the guards returned, but none of those they professed to guard."

"How many bandits were there?"

The seneschal's lip curled. "Swarms of them, according to the survivors. But of course that's what the ones who ran *would* say, is it not?"

Aristide looked at him. "They weren't orcs by any chance, were they?"

"Not according to the survivors, no."

"At least we've escaped the perils of cliché," Aristide said. "You have informed Gundapur of the situation?"

"I've sent messages. It's impossible to know if the messengers were intercepted on the way to the capital." He shrugged. "In time the government will wonder at the lack of caravans and send a force to relieve us."

"If you wish to send another message," Aristide said, "I will carry it."

The seneschal raised an eyebrow. "You will brave the bandits?"

"Bandits exist to be braved, though I will avoid them if I can. In any case, I shall accept your hospitality for a few dozen turnings of the glass, and then continue on my way."

The seneschal gave a little smile. "Is it pride or foolhardiness that causes you to make such a decision? The two often go together."

"I claim no more than the normal share of either," said Aristide.

On taking his leave of the seneschal, Aristide inquired where he could find the caravan masters. The first he spoke to was Masoud the Infirm, a lean, leathery man with long gray-white hair and a hacking cough. Masoud had been at the caravanserai for the longest amount of time, nearly three months, and had a small apartment in the building itself. Tapestries hung on the walls, and the floor was thick with carpets. He courteously offered, and Aristide accepted, a cup of tea.

"Surely enough time has been wasted," Aristide said. "There must be a force of sufficient size to deal with any bandits."

"Any ordinary bandits," said Masoud. "But these are a particularly vicious band. They capture whole caravans, over a dozen so far, and nothing is heard from the captives ever again. None are ransomed, none escape, and none appear in the slave markets. It is said that the bandits serve a god who demands human sacrifice."

Masoud's voice cracked on the last few words, and he coughed heavily for a few moments while Aristide politely waited for the fit to subside.

"If the bandits serve an evil god," Aristide said in time, "then fighting them will surely grant the warrior spiritual merit."

"Let the sultan's army earn such merit," Masoud said. "They could use it." Again he coughed, then wiped spittle from his lips with a napkin.

"One could earn merit also," Aristide said, "by bringing you to a physician."

Masoud offered a thin smile. "This cough has followed me, man and boy, for over forty years. The nostrums of physicians are useless, a waste of time and good silver."

"It is a waste of time and good silver to remain in this place."

Masoud coughed for a while before he answered. It was possible to believe that Masoud rather enjoyed his illness.

"I concede your point," Masoud said finally, "but there are nine caravans here, plus their troops of guards. Get the caravan masters and their guard captains to agree to any single course of action, and I will applaud you."

"To whom should I next urge my course of action?" Aristide asked.

"Nadeer of the Glittering Eye," said Masoud. "He occupies an apartment across the courtyard, and a more disagreeable ogre I have never met."

Aristide thoughtfully swirled the tea in his cup. "Literally an ogre?" he asked.

"He would not be called Nadeer of the Glittering Eye if he weren't," said Masoud.

Aristide thanked Masoud for his hospitality and ventured across the courtyard to the apartment occupied by Nadeer. Nadeer was easy enough to find: his snores were heroic and echoed mightily along the cloister that surrounded the courtyard; and the ogre's great bare feet thrust out of the apartment door, which was not long enough to hold him. Nadeer was taller than any troll, far too large for any riding beast to carry. His skin was a brilliant green. The thick dark calluses on the broad, paddlelike feet told Aristide that Nadeer crossed the high desert on foot, walking alongside the camels that carried his goods.

Aristide sat on one hip before the doorway, one leg curled under him, and began to sing.

> *Nadeer, whose strides engross the leagues,*
> *And before whose voice the lions tremble—*
> *Let Nadeer stand in the sun!*
>
> *He whose glittering eye seeks the foe,*
> *He whose legs dwarf the pillars of the sky,*
> *Let Nadeer's voice smite the air!*
>
> *On whose verdant skin the wind blows,*
> *He with knuckles the size of cabbages,*
> *Let Nadder fare forth!*

The snoring came to a gurgling conclusion about the fourth or fifth line, then, a few lines later, came a deep, slurred voice, accompanied by the sound of little bells.

"I don't like that line about cabbages."

"Sorry," said Aristide. "I'll work on it."

"Cabbages lack heroic stature, if you ask me."

The large green feet began to work their way into the courtyard, followed by the great slablike body. The doorway wasn't wide enough for Nadeer's shoulders, and he had to twist to get out. He sat up, his head brushing the ceiling of the cloister built around the courtyard.

Unfolded, the ogre would have been more than twice Aristide's height. His green skin was heavily tattooed. In a crooked slash of a mouth he had two upturned tusks, each elaborately carved, and above the mouth were waxed handlebar mustaches with little bells on the tips. His most singular feature was the great faceted eye in the middle of his forehead, shining like a diamond. The eye turned toward the swordsman.

"By rights I should smash your head in," Nadeer said, bells chiming and the voice slurred around the tusks.

Aristide flowed to his feet in one swift, easy motion. Surprise crossed across on the ogre's face at the speed of the swordsman's movement.

"I wish only the pleasure of your company," Aristide said, "on the journey to Gundapur."

The single eye narrowed. "You wish to hire me to protect you?"

"I have no money to speak of," said Aristide. "But a long journey is best taken in company, and when I leave for Gundapur, in another twelve or fifteen turns of the glass, I hope you will accompany me."

"I won't need to smash you," Nadeer said. "The bandits will take care of that on their own."

"There is sufficient force here to deter any bandits."

The ogre snarled. "With this pack of fools! Under a single leader, perhaps, but as it is"—he began to maneuver himself back into his apartment—"I will return to my slumbers."

"Under a single leader, exactly," Aristide said. "And why shouldn't that leader be Nadeer the Strong? Nadeer the Master? Nadeer the Formidable?"

Nadeer made a snarling noise. "I offered to fight the other leaders for the leadership of the caravans, but the degenerate fools said no! I wash my hands of them!"

With the tinny jingle of bells, the ogre inserted himself into his apartment and lay supine.

"May I talk to the others on your behalf?" Aristide asked.

"Say anything you like. I'm going to sleep. *Good-bye.*" The last word bore the unmistakable sound of finality.

Aristide left the ogre's company and found the leader of another caravan, a blue-skinned woman named Eudoxia. She had rings in her ears and another in her septum broad enough so that it hung over her lips.

"My name is Aristide," he said, "by profession a traveler. In another dozen or so turns of the glass I will begin the journey to Gundapur, in the company of Nadeer and his caravan. I wonder if you would be willing to accompany us?"

Eudoxia favored Aristide with a suspicious scowl. "Why would I want to accompany that green-skinned imbecile to Gundapur or anywhere else?"

"Because there is safety in numbers, and because you are losing money every moment you delay here."

She cocked her head and regarded him. "Is anyone else leaving?"

"You're the first I've approached."

Eudoxia chewed on her nose ring a moment. "I'll talk to Nadeer," she said.

"He's settled in for a nap. If you wake him he might crush your head."

She sneered. "I suppose he'll insist on being in charge?"

"That seems to be the case."

Eudoxia cursed and spat, then stomped on the spittle.

"Very well," she said finally, "but only if the others agree."

"Perhaps you would like to join me when I speak to them?"

The timekeeper's gong struck nine, ten, eleven, and twelve while Aristide had similar conversations with the other caravan masters. The swordsman returned eventually to Masoud, who coughed in derision for a long while before, after a good deal of complaint, agreeing to join the others under Nadeer's leadership.

Thus it was that Aristide was able to wake Nadeer with the news that he had become the leader of nine caravans and their assorted guards.

"Perhaps you should confer with your lieutenants," Aristide said. "As I know nothing of the business of caravans, I will excuse myself. I have talked a great deal and need refreshment." He bowed and turned to leave, then hesitated.

"Allow me to give you a word or two of counsel," he said. "They are yours—be magnanimous. Let them talk to their heart's content. If they speak sense, you can agree and appear wise. If their counsel is foolish, you may order things as you please."

"It will take patience to put up with their nattering," Nadeer said, "but I shall do as you advise."

Aristide ate one of the free meals offered by the servants of the sultan: olives, cheese, bread, and stewed lamb with dried apricots. The only condiment was a spoonful of salt, carefully measured. He left the caravanserai on his way to the oasis and saw Captain Grax returning to the encampment with his patrol. He turned toward the troll and hailed him on his approach.

"How was your hunting?" he asked.

Grax gave him a sour look.

"Ants and spiders, as you said."

"You'll have better sport in the days to come. The caravans have agreed to march for Gundapur."

The troll offered a grunt of surprise. "I thought we'd be here till the Heat Death."

"Sharpen your weapons," said Aristide. "Eat your fill. And make an offering at the Pool of Life."

Grax gave him a shrewd look. "You think there will be fighting?"

Aristide shrugged. "That's up to the bandits." He thought for a moment. "It might be a good idea if you were to send a patrol out of sight, in the direction of Gundapur. If the bandits have a spy here, perhaps you'll be able to intercept him."

Grax ground his yellow teeth. "An interesting idea, stranger."

Grax sent out three of his Free Companions on the patrol and led the rest to the corral. Aristide resumed his walk to the waters of the oasis. Along the way, Bitsy joined him.

"What news?" he asked.

"The camp is filled with boredom," said Bitsy, "mixed with thrilling rumors of massacre and human sacrifice."

"Anything else?"

"The seneschal is making a fortune selling state supplies to the caravans."

"I thought as much."

The two walked in silence for a moment. The dim, motionless sun faded behind a cloud. When Aristide looked at the men and women camped along the path, their eyes glowed in the shade like those of a cat.

They approached the oasis. It was a goodly-sized pond, larger than an athletic field, and surrounded by willows. The air smelled like air rather than dust. Yellow butterflies flitted in the air; dragonflies hovered purposefully over water. There was an area where beasts could be watered, and opposite this a small lagoon where people could draw water for themselves without having to drink any muck stirred up by the animals.

"I think that fellow ahead is a missionary," Bitsy said. "There's something unworldly about him."

Ahead of them a man squatted on the firm banks of the lagoon, refilling several water bottles. He was a thin man in a faded striped cotton robe, with a hood drawn up over his head.

Aristide waited for the man to fill his bottles and rise.

"Hail, scholar," Aristide said.

"Hail." As the man bowed, he made a swift sign with his fingers. Aristide bowed and responded more deliberately with another sign. Relief crossed the man's homely, bearded face.

"My name is Souza," the man said.

"Aristide." Bowing again. "How goes your collecting?"

"I've been out for three months." Souza was distracted by the sight of a black-and-white cat hunting along the bank. "Is the cat yours?" he asked.

"Yes. Her name is Bitsy. Have you had good hunting?"

"I've only begun," Souza said, "but I've got three children. In the next seven months, I hope to have a dozen more."

"Very good."

"There are so many of the best that I miss," Souza said. "I go to the towns and villages, I do my tests, I identify the bright ones and try to convince the parents to let them go. Sometimes I buy them. But I can't visit *all* the villages, and not all the parents let their kids be tested, or let them go if they pass. They know that most of the children who go to the College never return." He shook his head. "I might be missing thousands. Who can tell?"

"It would be good if more had a choice. But"—Aristide shrugged—"their parents chose it for them."

Anger flickered across Souza's face. "Their parents had such a choice. Their children did not."

"True."

"Now," Souza said wearily, "it seems I have to worry if the children are going to be captured and sacrificed to evil gods."

"I wouldn't take that seriously," Aristide said.

The scholar peered at him. "You have information?"

"No. Merely confidence. I think the force present here can handle any mob of evil cultists, especially if we act under a single leader—and apparently Nadeer is that leader."

"The ogre?" Souza wrinkled his face. "Talk about *choice . . .*"

"Each to his own," said Aristide. "But in any case you should prepare the children to move on in the next few dozen turns of the glass."

"I'm secretly relieved, to tell the truth," Souza said. "Young children separated from their families for the first time, *and* stuck for months at a desert oasis with nothing to do." He grimaced. "You can imagine the scenes we've had."

"I'm sure."

Souza narrowed his eyes. "You're not a missionary yourself, I take it?"

"No. I'm a scholar of the implied spaces."

Souza was puzzled. "I"—he began, then fell silent as a group of Free Companions approached.

"We'll speak later, on the journey," Aristide said.

"Yes." Souza bowed. "It's good to have someone to talk to."

Souza returned to the camp. Aristide squatted and refilled his water bottle while he listened to the convoy guards. Their speech was loud but free of content. After the guards left, Aristide drank, then filled his water bottle again as he watched a tall blue heron glide among the reeds on the far side of the water.

He heard a step and the soft rustle of robes, and turned to see a young woman crouching by the lagoon, lowering a large leather sack into the water by its strap. Water gurgled into its open mouth.

The hair peeking from beneath the young woman's headdress

was light brown. Her eyes were green. A slight sunburn touched her nose and cheeks.

"I am reminded of the verse," said Aristide.

> *Butterflies make music over water*
> *The green boughs dance in company.*
> *The jade-eyed woman bends over the water*
> *Graceful as a willow branch.*

A blush touched her cheeks, darkened the sunburn. Water gurgled into the sack.

"I haven't seen you before," she said. Her voice was barely heard over the rustle of leaves and the sigh of wind.

"I am Aristide, a traveler. I arrived a few turns of the glass ago." Softly, he sang.

> *This sack of water, a heavy burden.*
> *The maiden staggers beneath the weight.*
> *What thoughtless man has given her this charge?*

The woman looked quickly down at the water and her water bag.

"The water is my own. I travel alone."

"You must allow me to carry the weight for you."

She twirled a lock of hair around her finger. Bitsy appeared from the trees and rubbed herself against the woman's leg. The woman scratched her behind an ear.

"Is the cat yours?"

"Her name is Bitsy."

"Bitsy," she repeated, idly scratching. The cat looked up at her and purred.

"You neglected to tell me your name," Aristide reminded.

A soft smile fluttered at the corners of her lips.

"My name is Ashtra," she said.

"And you travel alone?"

She glanced down at the water. "My husband is in Gundapur. He's sent for me."

Aristide looked at her closely. "I detect a strain of melancholy at the mention of your husband."

"I haven't seen him for seven years. He's been on a long trading journey with an uncle." She gazed sadly across the placid water as she scratched the purring cat. "He's very rich now, or so his letter said."

"And he sent for you without providing an escort? That bespeaks a level of carelessness."

"He sent two swordsmen," Ashtra said. "But they heard of a war in Coël and went to join the army instead of taking me to Gundapur."

"I think somewhat better of your husband, then, but not as much as if he'd come himself. Or at least sent money."

"Perhaps he did, but if so the swordsmen took it." Her green eyes turned to him. "I don't even remember what he looks like. I was twelve when my family had me marry. He was only a few years older."

Despite the efforts of the sultan and other rulers to set up timekeepers with sandglasses regulated by the Ministry of Standards, days and years were necessarily approximate in a land where the sun did not move.

Aristide took her hand and kissed it. "You will delight him," he said, "have no doubt."

She blushed, bowed her head. "Only if I survive the bandits."

He kissed her hand again. "Do not fear the bandits, Ashtra of the Green Eyes. The caravan guards make a formidable force, and—come to that—I am rather formidable myself."

She looked away. He could see the throb of the pulse in her throat. "But the stories—what the bandits are supposed to do to captives—the stories are chilling."

"Stories. Nothing more." He stroked her hand. "You will pass through the gates of Gundapur, and live in halls of cool marble, where servants will rush to bring you sherbets and white raisins, and music and laughter will ring from the arches. But for now"—he reached for the strap of her water bag and raised it dripping from the spring—"allow me to bear this for you. For I believe there is a bank of green grasses yonder, shaded by the graceful willow, where we may recline and watch the dance of the butterfly and the stately glide of the heron, and enjoy the sweetness of wildflowers. There the wind will sing its languorous melody, and we may partake of such other pleasures as the time may offer."

He helped her rise, and kissed her gravely on the lips. Her eyes widened. Aristide drew her by the hand into the shade of the trees, and there they bode together on the carpet of grass, for the space of a few hours on that long, endless afternoon of the world.

Aristide slept a few hours, the tail of his headdress drawn across his eyes. When he woke, he found Ashtra seated near him, contemplating the silver ripples of the water through the trailing leaves of the willows. He paused for a moment to regard the woman sitting next to him on the bank—Ashtra, raised in a pre-literate world blind even to its own possibilities, brought up in a society founded by swashbucklers, warriors, and gamesters all for their own glorious benefit, but who condemned their descendants to an existence bereft of choice. Married at twelve to a youth who was a relative stranger, now traveling at nineteen to meet a husband who was even more a stranger than that youth. To live in what Gundapur considered luxury, and bear her husband, and bear him children, as many as possible until childbirth broke her health.

"Come with me, Ashtra," he said.

For a moment he didn't know whether she had heard. Then she said, "Where would you take me?"

"Wherever you desire. Eventually to the Womb of the World."

"You belong to the College?" She turned to look at him in alarm and shifted slightly away from him.

People often feared the magic of the College and its missionaries.

"I'm not of the College," Aristide said, and watched as she relaxed slightly. "Still, one does not have to be of the College to travel to the Womb."

"There are said to be sorcerers of great power at the Womb of the World. And monsters."

"There are monsters *here*."

She turned away and for a long moment regarded the lake.

"I have a family," she said finally.

"What do you owe to this husband who you barely know?"

"It's what my family owes him. If they had to refund my bride-price, they would be destitute."

"I could pay the price myself."

Ashtra turned to him, amusement in her green eyes. "You do not travel as a prince travels. Are you a prince in disguise?"

"I travel simply because simplicity appeals to me. And though I am not a prince, I have resources."

Again she turned to face the waters. "I have a husband. And what you offer me are fantasies."

For a moment the swordsman contemplated the many ironies of this last statement, and then he sat up and crossed his legs.

He was not without experience. He knew when he had been dismissed.

Some people remember virtue and a spouse rather late, when it no longer really matters.

"It's extremely unlikely there will be a child," he said, "but if there is, I desire you to send it to the College. Give them my name."

Again she turned. Again alarm widened her eyes. "I thought you said—"

"I'm not of the College," he said, "but I have done them service, and they know me. You may request this in my name." His tone took on a degree of urgency. "Particularly if it is a girl."

"I hope there is not a child." Ashtra rose. "I want to remember this as a beautiful fantasy, not as a burden I will bear for the rest of my life." She picked up the strap of her water bag and shouldered it.

"I'd prefer not to be the subject of gossip by those in my caravan," she said. "If you would wait half a glass before following, I would thank you."

"As you like, my lady," said Aristide. "Though I would gladly carry your burden."

Ashtra made no reply. Swaying beneath the weight of the water bag, she made her way from the glade.

Aristide stretched again on the grass and watched the willow branches moving against the dim sky. Gusting wind brought him the scent of flowers. There was a rustle in the grass, and he turned to see the black-and-white cat moving toward him.

"Your attempt at chivalry is duly noted," Bitsy said.

"Sentimentality more than chivalry," said the swordsman. "I liked her." He rubbed his unshaven chin. "You know, she's braver than she thinks she is."

"Brave or not, did you really mean to take that bewildered child to the Womb?"

"If she desired it. Why not?" He sat up. The cat hopped onto his lap. Her upright tail drew itself across his chin.

"I hope you appreciate my help in getting you laid," Bitsy said.

He sighed. "I couldn't have done it without you."

He stroked Bitsy for a few idle moments, then tipped her out of his lap and rose.

"Perhaps I'll ensure my next incarnation," he said.

Bitsy gave him a narrow-eyed look. "Is there so much on this journey," she asked, "that you wish to remember?"

Aristide shrugged. "Ants and spiders. And a pleasant interlude on a grassy bank."

As the swordsman passed through the camp, he saw the people had been stirred, like those selfsame ants with a stick. People were stowing tents and rugs, mending harness, sharpening weapons. Towering over everyone, Nadeer walked about giving orders. Voice booming, bells tinkling.

Inside the caravanserai, the Pool of Life had a crowd of visitors. Some chanted, some prayed, others meditated. Some, men and women both, waded naked into the pool, their lips murmuring devotions. Aristide removed his clothes, handed the clothing and Tecmessa to an attendant, and walked into the pool.

He followed broad steps downward until the silver liquid rose to his chest. His skin tingled at its touch. There were bodies at the bottom of the pool, and he felt for these with his feet to avoid treading on them. He waded between the devotees and touched the black menhir with one hand. The smooth surface felt prickly, as if a thousand tiny needles had pierced his fingertips.

He eased himself backward into the fluid. It was the temperature of blood. The silver liquid lapped over his ears, his throat. He closed his eyes.

In his ears he heard a deep throbbing. The throbbing was regular, hypnotic. His breathing shifted to match the rhythm of the throbbing.

He slept. He sank, the silver fluid of the Pool of Life filling his mouth and nose.

A few forlorn bubbles rose, and that was all.

The glass turned twice before Aristide rose to the surface. He opened his eyes, took a breath of humid air. Slowly he swam to the rim of the pool, found a step beneath his feet, and rose.

As he stepped from the pool the silver liquid poured off him in a single cascade, the last rivulets draining from his legs onto the flags, then slipping into the pool like some covert boneless sea creature seeking shelter. Not a drop was left behind. There was a salty taste in his mouth. Aristide accepted his clothes from the attendant and donned them. He slipped Tecmessa's baldric over one shoulder, shouldered his pack, and tipped the attendant.

"May the Pool give you many lives, warrior," the attendant said.

"And you."

He stepped out into a courtyard filled with dust and noise. A turbulent circle of gesturing travelers had formed around the towering figures of Nadeer and Captain Grax, both of whom were gesturing for order.

Nadeer's patience was exhausted. "*Silennnce!*" he bellowed, each hand drawing a curved sword that sang from the scabbard.

The crowd was struck dumb by sheer force of character. In the sudden hush Aristide shouldered his way through the crowd and laid eyes on a bruised, bleeding young man kneeling before Nadeer, surrounded by Free Companions brandishing arms. The seneschal stood by, watching in silence.

Grax looked at Aristide and grinned with his huge yellow teeth. "Your advice was good, stranger. We caught this spy riding from camp to alert the bandits."

The young man began what was obviously a protest, but Grax kicked him casually in the midsection, and the man bent over, choking.

"Confess!" roared Nadeer, brandishing both swords close over his head. The prisoner sought for resolve, and somewhere found it.

"You but threaten to send me to my next incarnation," he said through broken lips. "I welcome such an escape."

Nadeer snarled around his tusks, then replied in his booming lisp. "You miss the point, spy. We don't threaten to send you to the next incarnation, we threaten to make *this* incarnation a painful one."

With a flick of the wrist, he flashed out one sword, and the flat of it snapped the prisoner's elbow like a twig. The prisoner screamed, clutched his arm, turned white. Sweat dripped slowly from his nose as he moaned.

The seneschal watched this in silence, his expression interested.

"Who are you?" Grax asked. "Who sent you? What are your orders?"

The captive's breath hissed between clenched teeth. "It won't make any difference," he said. "I may as well talk." He seemed to be speaking more to himself than to his audience.

Though speak to the others he did. His name was Onos. He was a younger son from the Green Mazes, his only inheritance a sword, a horse, and a few bits of silver. In a spirit of adventure, he and some friends joined the army of Calixha. The horse was lost at this point. Finding service during the siege of Natto not to his taste, he and his friends stole horses, deserted, and became caravan guards. Finding this tedious as well, they became robbers.

"He isn't good even at that," Grax remarked. "What the lad needs is discipline." He looked down at the captive. "If he were in *my* company, I would make a proper soldier out of him."

Onos bled quietly onto the flagstones. "I thought a life of adventure would be more fun," he muttered.

Grax kicked him once more in the midsection. "It's been fun for *me*," he said, as the captive gasped, spat, and swore. "Perhaps you lack the proper attitude."

Nadeer looked at the captive. "You have my leave to continue," he said.

Onos wiped blood from his mouth with the back of a grubby hand. "Our gang joined another gang," he said. "We weren't given a choice. So now we're servitors of the Brothers of the Vengeful One."

"Never heard of them," said the seneschal, the first words he had spoken.

"Neither had we," said Onos. "Neither had anyone, until a few months ago, and then *all* the freebooters heard of them." He grimaced and put a hand to his ribs. "We joined them or we died."

"Who are they?" Grax asked.

"Priests. Monsters. Monsters and priests."

"Monsters how?" asked Aristide.

"They're"—grimacing—"another species. Ones I'd never heard of, or seen. Blue skin, eyes like fire. And they sacrifice captives, and anyone else who disappoints them."

There were gasps from the listeners as this terrifying rumor was confirmed.

"Your mission?" Grax asked in the sudden silence.

"We knew the caravans were delayed here for fear of us. I was told to travel to the caravanserai and report on your plans— whether you'd come on or try to retreat."

"Would you attack us either way?"

"That wouldn't be for me to decide." Grax raised a foot. "*Probably!*" Onos said quickly. "*Probably we'd attack!*"

The questions turned to the bandits' strength and where they would most likely strike at the caravan. The bandits were said to have two hundred riders, though not all of them would be available at any one time, since they raided not just the caravan routes but the plain of Gundapur, below the great desert plateau. The route down from the plateau, through the Vale of Cashdan, was the usual ambush site.

Aristide stepped forward. "I would like to ask some questions of the prisoner, if I may."

Nadeer looked at him. "You may proceed."

Aristide looked at Onos. "How long have you been here at the caravanserai?"

"Fifteen or twenty days."

"You have a mount?"

"I have a horse, yes."

"And during that time," Aristide said, "you could have left for Lake Toi whenever you desired. You could have abandoned your fellow bandits and those disagreeable priests and got away with your skin. And yet you remained . . ." He let this thought linger in the air for a moment.

"*Why?*" he asked finally.

Onos swiped at his brow, leaving a dusty track on his skin. "I'm afraid of them. They'd come after me."

"You could have asked the seneschal, or some other official, for protection."

Onos looked at the seneschal. "He'd just hang me from the tower and announce he'd been a great success at suppressing the bandits."

Aristide's brief acquaintance with the seneschal had not been such as to make this seem implausible. The seneschal himself, looking on, declined to be offended, and in fact seemed amused.

"My point," said Aristide, "is that you could have run, and you didn't. Therefore you aren't merely a thief whose gang was annexed by a more powerful outfit, but a willing member of the organization."

Onos looked at Aristide with a kind of sulky resentment. The others glared at Onos with increased malevolence.

"How many caravans have you plundered?" Aristide asked.

"Eleven, while I've been with the brotherhood."

"And the people in the caravans killed or sacrificed by the priests?"

"All those we could catch," Onos said. "Yes."

"What happened to the loot?"

"It's still there. At the Venger's Temple."

There was a stir among the onlookers. A calculating look appeared on the faces of Grax, Nadeer, and the other caravan guards.

"The Venger's Temple is your headquarters, I take it?"

An affirmative nod.

"The spoil is there with the other loot, from the raids onto the plains?"

"Except for that which was used to purchase supplies, yes."

Aristide looked at Nadeer. "I imagine that avarice is never far from our friend Onos's mind," he said. "A share of that loot would give him a comfortable life far from here, perhaps even make him rich. *That* is why he hasn't fled from his monstrous priests."

Onos, defeated, slumped on the flagstones, did not bother to deny it.

Grax turned to the seneschal. "He is convicted out of his own mouth. Shall we turn him over to you, to dispense the sultan's justice?"

The seneschal began to walk through the crowd to his office. He waved a hand in dismissal.

"Why bother me with it?" he said. "Do what you will."

Grax looked at Nadeer, and they both shrugged. Nadeer's shoulders had barely returned to their normal position before one of his swords sliced out to separate the bandit's head from his shoulders.

The body was wrapped in an old cloak and given to the Pool of Life, to feed the cthonic spirit believed to dwell in the menhir. The head was stuck on a spear in front of the caravanserai's gate.

The head bore a disappointed look. Onos had probably expected more excitement than this.

"I wonder if his next incarnation will have learned anything?" Aristide asked, as he and Nadeer paused to view the head on its spear.

Nadeer only snorted at the swordsman's question.

"May I have the bandit's mount?" Aristide asked. "I would be more useful in this adventure if I were mobile."

"It's that barb yonder."

The horse was a cream-colored gelding, a little long in the tooth but deep in the chest and strong of spirit. The saddle and tack were serviceable. Aristide took the barb for a brief ride over the desert to get acquainted, then fed the animal and watered him. He sorted through the bandit's belongings but found nothing of interest.

He helped himself to another of the sultan's free meals, then slept in the bandit's tent for a few hours, until the sound of trumpets and shells told the travelers to ready their mounts and assemble.

Aristide walked his new horse through the bustle. Dust rose, obscuring the sun, and he drew the tail of his headdress over his lower face. By chance Aristide passed by Ashtra, who was struggling to lift her heavy water bag to its place on her palfrey's saddlebow.

"Permit me, madam," he said. He performed the task, bowed, and departed, his senses alert in case she called him back.

She didn't. He walked on.

The caravan, big as a small army, didn't actually get under way for another three turns of the glass. Once it moved, it moved slowly. The guards were mounted on horses, bipedal lizards, or the red six-legged lizards that moved with a side-to-side motion, like giant snakes. The lizards were cold-blooded, but in the high desert, beneath an unmoving sun, that scarcely mattered.

The others in the caravan rode horses or Bactrian camels, mules, or asses. There was one African forest elephant. Their carts and wagons were drawn by oxen, horses, or ridge-backed dinosaurs. No small number proceeded on foot, sometimes accompanied by a dog pulling a travoise.

Aristide had his own difficulties, in that his new horse was afraid of his cat, snorting and backing away whenever Bitsy approached. It was an unfortunate fact that many animals disliked Bitsy—perhaps she didn't smell right—and in the end Aristide had to hide her, making her a nest on the saddle blanket behind the high cantle of his saddle, where the horse couldn't see her. The horse still scented her from time to time, snorted, and gave a nervous look backward, but these alarms only increased its desire to move faster along the trail.

Nadeer and the other leaders worked in a desperate fury to get the huge convoy ordered and to move them at a steady pace. A huge cloud of dust rose above the column and turned the sun red.

"The bandits will see this for fifty leagues," Grax said, as he and Aristide rode ahead of the column. "We may as well have let the spy live."

"He won't be able to tell them how we're organized."

Grax showed tombstone teeth. "We're organized?"

The caravan only made five leagues before Nadeer called a halt, but at least the day was useful as a shakedown. The guards had got used to working with one another and had developed a system for scouting ahead. As the caravan laagered, as guards were posted, the last of the dust drifted away on the wind, and the curses of the drovers and the captains and one large, green ogre echoed through the camp, Aristide thought that perhaps the little army had done better than Nadeer knew.

The glasses turned sixteen times before the trumpets blared again, and the vast column heaved itself onto its feet and began its trek. Everyone had got practice by now, and though the caravan didn't move appreciably faster, it was more orderly and better behaved. The guards were efficient, organized into an advance guard, flankers, and a rear guard that complained of wandering in the dust. Patrols regularly trotted ahead to the next hill, or rocky outcrop, to make certain no ambush was lurking therein.

The principle delays occurred at water holes. It took hours to water the animals.

The terrain grew rougher and began to descend. Each hill gave a broader view than the one before it, though the farthest views were always hidden by heat haze.

After eight or nine leagues the group came upon a battle-field, the water hole where the bandits had routed three cara-vans and their sixty guards. Dead animals and bodies lay in the sun amid broken wagons, flesh turning to leather, lips snarling back from teeth. It looked as if the caravans had been attacked when in camp, their tents strewn across a valley floor in no par-ticular order.

"A lesson in forming a proper laager," Aristide told Nadeer. But Nadeer was busy shouting down those who wanted to stop and give the bodies a proper burial.

"Do you want to join them in death?" Nadeer demanded. "Our lives depend on moving quickly through this place!"

Nadeer lost the argument, chiefly because the convoy took so long to rewater that there was time for the burials anyway.

The caravan rolled on. Halfway to the next water hole Nadeer called a halt, and the laager was formed by grim-faced drovers who made sure their weapons were within easy reach. Aristide wandered through camp until he found Ashtra. He ob-served her as she brewed tea over a paraffin lamp. She was in the company of a family moving to Gundapur, the father, a pregnant mother, and three children traveling in a two-wheeled cart. They were sharing their bread and dried fruit with her.

Aristide watched for a few moments, then left unobserved.

The next watering hole was a spring that chuckled from the foot of a great slab of basalt that towered over the little dell like a slumbering giant. Guarding the source of water was a deserted military fort, its tumbled walls having been breached at some point in the dim past. A black and unnaturally flawless menhir stood above the empty Pool of Life. Though the gates had long since been burned for firewood, the fort nevertheless provided more protection than the open desert for the most vulnerable members of the caravan.

The next march took them along the watercourse from the dell. The spring water was absorbed by the ground before the convoy had gone very far, but the dry watercourse was full of scrub that testified to the presence of water below the surface. The watercourse widened in time into the Vale of Cashdan, the great zigzag slash in the wall of the plateau that led down to the plains of Gundapur. White birds floated far below, like snowflakes drifting in the wind. Crags crowned with trees loomed above the narrow caravan route that wound through green patches of mountain grazing. The blue of a stream was barely visible before the Vale vanished into a huge floor of brilliant white cloud that stretched to the far horizon. Never would the convoy again be without water.

Aristide stood with the captains on the edge of a precipice overlooking the Vale, peering down and pondering their options.

"At least we no longer have to worry about a mounted charge over flat ground," Eudoxia said, her blue arms crossed on her chest. "I was troubled the whole body of them would charge in and cut us in half—they would have wrought such havoc that we might not have recovered our balance."

"Now we're going to have to worry about people rolling rocks on us," Aristide said.

"Ay," said Nadeer. His single eye glittered. "Like those fellows over there."

"Where?" Scanning the jagged walls of the valley ahead.

Nadeer bent and picked up a rock the size of Eudoxia's head. He hefted it for a moment in one green-skinned hand, then reared back and pitched the rock up into the gray sky. They all watched as it fell onto a granite pinnacle two hundred paces distant. There was a thud, and a cry, and a clatter as of a weapon dropped over the edge.

"Good shot!" said Grax, impressed rather in spite of himself.

"There's one more." Nadeer chose another rock, hurled it. There was a clang, and then they saw a body pitch off the crag, landing some thirty paces below.

Aristide looked at the ogre. "Your depth perception," he said, "is better than I expected."

Nadeer dusted his hands. Aristide turned his attention once more to the valley below.

"We're going to have to keep them from getting above us," he said. "May I suggest small parties to secure each height before the main body arrives?"

They grumbled about that, and Grax pointed out that his Free Companions were mounted soldiers, not mountain goats. But in the end they worked out an arrangement, much as Aristide had suggested, and the convoy again began to advance.

Hours passed slowly before every beast and cart at last began the precarious descent into the Vale, and then finally a rest halt was called with the convoy stretched along the headwaters of the Cashdan River, with every beast and every person within easy reach of water. It was impossible to laager, because there was no single place level enough to hold the entire body. On the other hand the possibilities of attack were severely limited, and the air was fresh and cool. Dry tongues, dry skins, rejoiced.

The convoy continued its slow crawl down the escarpment, crossing and recrossing a river that grew louder and swifter as streams running in from the side canyons contributed more water. Two horses and a lizard were swept away, but their riders were saved. The clouds fled and the green hills of Gundapur, full of vines and the shimmer of olive trees, were now visible below them. The silver river cast its loops back and forth across the fields, with the sultan's road a straight brown line across it.

Two more rest stops had been called before the caravan ran into trouble. One of the advance parties, sent to secure a ridge above the track, was repelled by a shower of arrows and rocks. Nothing daunted, Nadeer reinforced the party and tried again. Advancing under the cover of their own archers, and aided by Nadeer's remarkable throwing arm, the party pushed the bandits off the ridge and onto another fold of higher ground beyond, where they remained, watching and jeering.

The engagement was over by the time Aristide arrived. He had been in the middle of the convoy when the fight broke out, helping one of the immigrants with the repair of his cart, and by the time he managed to ride to the head of the column, threading between carts and camels, the fight was over. He left his horse under the care of one of Grax's lieutenants and scrambled up the ridge, where he was in time to dissuade Nadeer from launching another attack on the enemy survivors.

"They can always retreat to the next ridge beyond," he pointed out. "And they know this country better than we do. You could run into an ambush."

"Wretched bags of rat piss!" Nadeer lisped, referring no doubt to the bandits.

An arrow protruded from one shoulder, where it had penetrated his armor but failed to pierce his hide. He wrenched it out with a petulant gesture.

"I want them crushed!" he said.

"You'll get your chance soon, I think," Aristide said. "I expect there will be more of them. These were intended to attack us in flank when the main body hit us somewhere else."

Nadeer's single eye turned to him. "Are you certain of this?"

"No. I claim no more than the average amount of precognition. But it's logical—these weren't numerous enough to fight our whole force."

Nadeer glared at the bandits on the next ridge. "If we move on, it will leave them behind us."

"We want them *all* behind us."

Nadeer gnashed his tusks for a few moments, then told half of the guards to hold the ridge until the convoy had passed and the rest to rejoin the advance guard. The caravan continued its slow crawl down the valley. Five turns of the glass later—as the rear guard passed the ridge where the skirmish with the bandits had taken place—scouts reported that the road ahead was blocked by a substantial force.

Aristide joined the captains as they viewed the enemy. From where they stood at the head of the column, the track descended and broadened into the base of a side canyon and was cut by a stream that joined the Cashdan; then the track rose for two hundred paces and narrowed to a pass twenty paces wide, with the river thundering past on the right. This pass had been blocked with a wall of stones, and behind the stones the dark forms of bandits milled in large numbers. More bandits perched on the rocks above, armed with bows.

"The group on the ridge were to attack our rear when this group encountered our advance guard," Aristide said. "They meant to panic us." He scratched his chin. "I wonder if this group knows we drove the others off their position. If so, we might draw them out by feigning panic."

"A formidable position," Eudoxia said. "They chose well."

"Our people will be better fighters," said Aristide. "Criminals are by nature a superstitious and cowardly lot, and few choose their profession because of a love of military discipline or order."

"The same might be said of caravan guards," Grax pointed out.

"If your people need heartening, you could point out that if they don't win this fight, they'll be sacrificed to evil gods."

Grax looked at him in astonishment. "That's supposed to make them feel *better*?"

Aristide shrugged. "Perhaps it's best to show that the enemy are, after all, mortal. Why don't I dispose of a bandit or two and thus raise morale?"

Eudoxia looked at him. "How do you plan to do that?"

"Walk up and challenge them. Grax, you should charge them the second I dispatch an enemy. Nadeer, may I advise you to personally lead the attack on the rocky shoulder above the pass? It's the key to the position."

Nadeer looked a little put out. "It's true I'm not much use in a mounted charge," he admitted. "But why don't *I* challenge them to single combat?"

"For the simple reason," said Aristide, "that no one would dare to fight Nadeer the Peerless."

Nadeer considered this, then brightened. "Very true," he said. He reared to his full height. "I shall lead the attack up the rocks, as you suggest."

Aristide dismounted and performed a few stretching and limbering exercises while the captains gathered their forces and arranged their assault. "One last thing," he said when they were ready. "Remember to capture a few prisoners. We want them to lead us to the Venger's Temple and the loot taken from all those caravans."

"Indeed," said Nadeer, brightening even more.

Aristide took an arrow from one of the caravan guards, stuck a white headcloth on it, and began his walk toward the bandits. He paused after a few steps, then turned and said, "Look after my cat, will you?"

He walked down the slope to the mountain freshet, waded through ankle-deep water, and began the walk upslope to the improvised wall. He stopped a hundred paces from the wall and called out over the sound of the rushing water.

"While my colleagues are working out what to do next," he said, "I thought to relieve your boredom, and come out to challenge your bravest fighter to single combat."

Among the bandits there was a general muttering, followed by jeers and scornful laughter.

"No takers?" Aristide called.

Someone behind the barrier threw a rock. Whoever threw it was no Nadeer. Aristide stepped to the side and let the rock clatter on the stones. He waited for the laughter to subside.

"I'm disappointed that there's no one among you with courage," Aristide said. "It will make it all the easier for us to slaughter you."

In response came more laughter, some obscene suggestions, and a few more rocks.

"Just," Aristide said casually, "as we slaughtered those friends of yours, up there on the ridge a few leagues back. They're lying on the rocks for the vultures to peck at. Surely one of you had a friend among them, and now possesses a burning desire to avenge his life?"

"*I* do," said a voice. The figure that jumped on the barrier was vast, gray-skinned, and female. She was as large as Grax and had an additional pair of arms: the upper pair carried two throwing spears, the lower an ax and a target shield with a spike in the center. Her grin revealed teeth like harrows. She stood on the barrier, acknowledging the cheers of the bandit force.

"You present a formidable appearance, madam," said Aristide. "Perhaps you will make a worthy opponent."

"*Perhaps?*" the troll demanded. She jumped down from the barrier and advanced. Chain skirts rang under armor of boiled leather. Her crude iron helm was ornamented with horns and a human skull. Cheers and laughter echoed from the bandits. She advanced fifty paces and then halted. She paused and said, in a theatrical voice, "Prepare to meet thy doom."

"You first," Aristide suggested, and tossed the arrow with its white rag to the side.

The troll crouched and came on, preceded by a wave of body odor. The upper arms held the two spears, which she declined to throw, instead reserving them as thrusting weapons. The ax clashed on the shield.

In a single motion, Aristide drew Tecmessa. The sword flashed beneath the dim sun.

There was a sudden crack, as of thunder, that echoed off the rocks. Observers had an impression that something had twisted into existence, then out of it, too fast for the eye quite to follow. A wave of air blew out toward the bandits, visible as swirls of dust in the air.

Of the troll, there was no sign.

Silence fell upon shocked ears.

"*Uh-oh*," said a bandit clearly, in the sudden stillness.

Aristide whirled his sword up, then down, in an impatient *Come-on-let's-charge* motion that he hoped would remind the caravan guards of what they were supposed to be doing at this moment.

"Anyone else care to fight?" he asked.

Arrows whirred down from above. Tecmessa's point rotated

slightly, there was another crack and a blast of wind, and the arrows vanished.

"Anyone else?" the swordsman called.

There was a deep-voiced bellow behind Aristide, and then shouts, the clatter of armor, and the rush of feet. Apparently Nadeer had finally remembered his assigned role.

"Oh well," Aristide said, "if you won't come to *me* . . ."

Aristide began trotting forward at a pace calculated to bring him to the barrier about the same time as Grax and his Free Companions. He didn't want to get trampled by his own side, but neither was it wise to face the whole body of the enemy at once—Tecmessa's powers had their limits. The sword was held in both hands, the point moving in a circle.

More arrows came. More arrows disappeared in claps of thunder and whirls of dust.

Behind him, Aristide heard the sound of animals splashing through the shallow freshet, and increased his pace.

The stone barrier was breast-high, topped by ranks of spears and figures in helmets. As the swordsman approached, the bandits in front shrank back, while those in the rear—who hadn't seen what had occurred—pressed forward. There was an incoherent shouting and a rattle of spears, sure signs that the morale of the bandits was not what it had been.

Before Aristide quite reached the barrier he heard a roar and a ferocious reptilian shriek, and Grax appeared on his lizard, his lance lowered. The lizard cleared the barrier in one bound—Grax dropped the lance that had skewered a tall man with a scalp lock—and then Grax was among the bandits, striking left and right with a flail made out of linked iron bars.

Aristide reached the barrier, parried a halfhearted spear thrust, and swung Tecmessa horizontally. Half a dozen bandits vanished with a bang. The remainder, a many-headed monster that seemed composed entirely of staring eyes and shuffling feet, drew back.

The rest of the Free Companions reached the barrier. Some reined in and thrust with their lances, some jumped the barrier like Grax, some tried to jump and failed. In the sudden wild stampede, Aristide flattened himself against the rocky side of the pass and tried to get out of the way.

The bandits were broken in any case. Their efforts to escape were impeded by the narrowness of the pass, the mass of their fellows behind them, and the large herd of riding beasts that they had picketed just behind their position. The outlaws were packed so tightly that the Free Companions could hardly miss, and the bandits' tangled mass hampered any efforts to strike back or defend themselves. Many bandits died, many were trampled, and many threw themselves into the river and were swept away.

"*Prisoners!*" Aristide shouted. "*Remember to take prisoners!*"

The general slaughter continued without cease. Aristide glanced at the rocks above. The bandits that had been holding this key feature had seen the rout below, and as a consequence many were abandoning the fight, hoping to clamber down the steep boulder-strewn slope and reach their mounts before the Free Companions did.

There was a clattering of hooves and a cry, and Aristide saw the next company charging to the fight. The chances of getting trampled seemed stronger than ever, and a place above the fray consequently more desirable, so Aristide vaulted the barrier and began to climb the slope.

Green-skinned Nadeer reached the summit before Aristide did—bellowing, half a dozen arrows standing in his chest, hurling rocks left and right. The bandits broke completely. Aristide saw one bandit running past and swung Tecmessa. The flat of the blade caught him full in the face and he went down, stunned. Out of the corner of his eye Aristide saw another darting figure, a broad-shouldered man in black with a recurved bow in one hand, and he thrust the sword between the archer's legs. The bandit fell face-first onto the stony ground, and then Aristide was on his back, the edge of Tecmessa against his neck.

"Take me to your leaders," he said.

❖

"I count a hundred and eighteen bodies," Grax announced. He was in buoyant spirits: even his chain mail seemed to be jingling with satisfaction. "We lost six, and three of those were lost because they fell off their mounts and got trampled by our own side, or drowned in the river."

" 'Tis a famous victory," said Aristide.

Leaning on his scabbard, he sat on one of the great granite rocks above the pass while he watched the convoy guards demolish what was left of the barricade and hurl the stones into the river. His two prisoners, thoroughly bound, crouched at his feet.

Bitsy sat on a nearby rock, licking her anus.

Grax carried a sack of heads thrown casually over his shoulder, in hopes the sultan would offer a bounty. Since there was no Pool of Life in which to deliver the bodies that choked the roadway, the bandits' headless torsos were given to the river.

Aristide had made a point of refilling his water bottle upstream from that point.

The troll's gaze turned to Tecmessa.

"Your sword is magic?"

Aristide considered his answer. "It performs miracles, to be sure," he said.

"I've seen other swords that were supposed to be magic. They were all used in the past by heroes—well-made swords, all of them. But so far as I know they never—you know—*did* anything."

"This one never did anything until I touched it," said Aristide. "It seems to work only for me."

Which, in addition to being the truth, might dissuade anyone—Grax, for instance—from killing him over possession of the blade.

Grax looked at him. "How did you find out what it does?"

"That's rather tragic actually. I'd rather not talk about it."

"When your enemies . . . disappear," Grax said, "do you know where they go?"

Bitsy paused in her grooming and looked at him with green eyes.

"I've no idea," the swordsman lied.

Grax hitched up his wide belt. His chain skirts rang. "The captains are going to meet to decide what to do next. They all want to hunt for the loot and the Venger's Temple, but some are still going to have to guard the convoy on its way to Gundapur."

"This should be entertaining," Aristide said. "I'll attend, if I may." He rose to his feet and prodded his prisoners with his scabbard. "Up, you two," he said. The prisoners rose and, without their bound hands to aid them, picked their way carefully down the steep slope. Aristide rested his sword on his shoulder and followed.

As the party moved off, Bitsy rose to her feet, yawned, stretched, and joined the party.

The argument that followed was not unpredictable. Nadeer wanted to lead his little army to the Venger's Temple. Others pointed out that Nadeer was captain of the convoy guards charged with escorting the caravans to Gundapur, not the leader of a group of freebooters on their own account. Nadeer protested at first, but was finally brought to admit that he had accepted the responsibility of escort.

With Nadeer thus out of the running, the other captains all proposed themselves as leaders of the expedition to the Temple and were in the process of arguing this when the actual caravan masters, their employers, demanded that all the guards accompany them all the way to Gundapur—or, failing that, surrender a share in any loot.

The argument was brisk and prolonged. Aristide, perched nearby atop a boulder that had fallen from the cliffs above and come to rest on the edge of the river, ate hard bread and dried fruit, and enjoyed the rush and flow and scent of the Cashdan with the pleasure that only thirty-odd days in the desert would bring. He smiled to himself as he listened to the arguments. Bitsy, less entertained, found a warm place on the rock and curled up to sleep. It was only when the captains' wrangle had grown repetitious that Aristide interrupted.

"My friends," he said, "may I point out that this debate is bootless?"

They looked at him. He stood on his rock and smiled down at them.

"At the Venger's Temple lies the loot of over a dozen caravans!" he pointed out. "Plus a sizeable hoard of plunder gathered elsewhere. Even if every convoy guard among here marched to the Temple and captured the treasure, how would they get all the treasure away? Even if they took every beast of burden in our combined caravans, they could only move a fraction of the total."

The captains looked at each other, their eyes glittering not with surprise, but with calculation. *Perhaps,* they seemed to be thinking, *we could only take the absolute best . . .*

"Therefore," said Aristide, "Nadeer and at least half the guards should take the caravans to Gundapur as quickly as they can, because they will have a vital role—to search the city in order to round up every horse, every camel, every ox, and every dinosaur-of-burden, and to bring them back to the Vale of Cashdan to carry away the greatest treasure in the history of the sultanate!"

The captains raised a cheer at this. But Masoud the Infirm raised an objection.

"If we take the treasure to Gundapur," he wheezed, "the sultan will want a percentage."

"No doubt," Aristide said. "But if you take the treasure anywhere else, the local ruler will also require a tax. And it must be admitted that your ordinary guards and camel drivers will want to be paid as soon as possible, so that they may spend their earnings in the city's pleasure domes. Gundapur is your best bet.

"And since that is the case," Aristide said, and made a gesture of money falling from one palm into another, "may I suggest that while some of you organize the caravan to bring the treasure to the city, the rest of you should be offering bribes to the sultan's advisers to make certain that the taxes you're required to pay are minimal.

"And furthermore," he added, "since the caravan guards won't be able to afford to rent all those animals, or bribe the sultan's advisers, it's clear that the merchants who command the caravans deserve a share of the treasure."

Which began another argument concerning how large that share would be. Aristide had no comment to make on this matter, and instead returned to his seated position. He looked down at his two prisoners, who slumped against the rock below him. One— the bowman he had tripped—was a man of middle years, with a scarred cheek that put his mouth in a permanent scowl and a beard striped with gray. The other was a tall man, very muscular, but who presented the appearance of youth, with bowl-cut hair and a face swollen by the blow from the flat of Aristide's sword.

"Where *is* the Venger's Temple, by the way?" the swordsman asked.

The older man gave him a contemptuous look from slitted eyes. "I will happily tell you," he said. "Certain as I am that the knowledge will send you all to your deaths."

"Well," Aristide said, "for heaven's sake don't keep me in suspense."

The older man gave a jerk of his head to indicate the way they had come. "The Temple's in a side canyon," he said. "Back up the valley."

Aristide looked at the younger man. "Do you agree?"

"Oh yes. Also, that you will certainly die if you go there."

"How far?"

"From here you can walk the distance in fifteen or twenty turns of the glass. But you'll die. So don't."

Aristide looked at him with curiosity. "Are the defenses so formidable?" he asked.

"Not the defenses. The priests." The young man looked at Tecmessa. "The Priests of the Vengeful One possess the same power as your blade."

Aristide's face turned into a smooth bronze mask, his hawk-like nose a vane that cut the wind. His dark eyes, gazing at the young man, glittered with cold intent.

"What do you mean?" he asked. He spoke with care, as if the

simple sentence were a fragile crystalline structure that might shatter if he uttered the wrong syllable.

"The priests cause people to disappear in a clap of thunder," the captive said. "Just as you caused Ormanthia to disappear."

"It is a *sacrifice*," the older man corrected. His voice was a hiss. "The Vengeful One is a powerful god. He swallows his victims whole."

The young man gave a shudder. "True. He does."

The older man looked at Aristide. "He will swallow *you*."

"Perhaps," said Aristide. "But on me he may break a tooth." He turned to the younger man. "How many priests are there?"

"Three."

"And they have swords like mine?"

"No. They are armed with"—he hesitated, as if he knew how absurd this would sound—"clay balls," he finished.

"Clay. Balls." The delicate words once again chimed with a crystalline sound.

"They dangle the balls from strings. The balls dart around as if they had minds of their own. And the balls . . . eat people."

Aristide's profile softened as he considered the bandit's words.

"I shall look forward to encountering these priests," he said softly.

The older bandit spat.

"I shall look forward to your death," he said.

"How do you know the priests send their victims to death?" Aristide asked. "It might be paradise, for all you know."

The bandit spat again.

"I'll cut your throat myself," he said.

"Now, now," said Aristide. "I'll have to tick the box next to your name that says *unrepentant*."

"*So we swear! So we swear!*" The cry went up from the assembled captains. Aristide looked up from his conference. Apparently the leaders of the expedition had reached agreement.

As the others moved off to their companies, Grax looked up at Aristide on his rock.

"You're authorized a double share if you accompany us to the Temple," he said.

"I wouldn't miss it," Aristide said. "You're in command of this expeditionary force, I assume?"

"Of course!" The troll showed his yellow teeth.

"Congratulations on your expanded responsibilities. My captives—for different reasons admittedly—are willing to lead us to the Venger's Temple."

Grax studied them with his golden eyes. "They show wisdom."

The older bandit curled his lip. Perhaps he'd run low on saliva.

"May be," Aristide said. "But I regret to tell you that it may be that our fight against these people may be more difficult than we've expected."

"Yes?" Grax didn't seem troubled. "Where is the Temple," he asked, "and how far?"

"Back up the valley. Fifteen or twenty glasses."

"Damn. We'll have to wait for this lot to get by us, then." He lumbered off to give orders to the elements of his new army, and to pass the word to the caravans that they should begin to move. The huge caravan picked itself up and began to trudge its way down the path to Gundapur's plain.

The story of the brief battle must have spread through the caravan, because Aristide found that many pointed at him as they passed, or huddled together and whispered. He saw Souza ride past on a mule, leading two more mules shared by the three children he'd salvaged for the College, and he and the scholar exchanged salutes.

Finding his celebrity tedious, and unable to move out of public scrutiny on a narrow track filled with carts and camels, Aristide spoke with his prisoners and found the younger bandit talkative, as he'd anticipated. He learned that the Venger's Temple was in a broad cleft in the mountain, with its own water supply and with powerful natural defenses.

"It's like a Pool of Life, really," the young man said. "There's a waterfall on both sides of a stone pillar, and a pool below."

"Does it have the properties of a Pool of Life?" Aristide asked.

"No. It's just rocks and water. Quite pretty, really."

The long serpent of the caravan continued its crawl past the swordsman's perch. Aristide looked up at the sight of a young green-eyed woman on a palfrey, but she had drawn a veil over her face, and kept her eyes turned from his.

He bowed as she passed. She kept her face turned away.

She had told him that she was afraid of sorcery and of the College. Certainly anyone who could wield such a weapon as Tecmessa must be a powerful wizard.

Aristide's expression confirmed that he was not pleased to be such an object of fear.

The caravan finally passed, leaving behind colossal amounts of fresh dung, and Grax organized his force of sixty warriors. They had few spare mounts: their comrades were deliberately making it difficult for the party to abscond with much of the loot. Aristide gave Grax the older bandit as a guide and kept the talkative one for himself. Both captives were tied onto mules.

The mounted force could move much more quickly than the caravan. After a brief march up the valley they came to the ridge where the band of caravan guards had been left to face a group of enemy on the opposite ridge. Their lieutenant descended to greet Grax.

"I was coming to report," he said. "The bandits we were watching have gone."

"Gone where?" asked Grax.

"Back over that ridge they were on. We don't know any more than that."

"Survivors must have told them we'd wiped out their main force, and they decided it was pointless to stay."

"There's a goat track back there," said the younger bandit. "It leads to the Venger's Temple."

Aristide raised his eyebrows. "A back entrance?" he asked.

"More like a side entrance. But the defenses are less formidable than the main track up the canyon."

Aristide looked at Grax. "Perhaps we should take this path."

Grax looked at the outlaw. "Is it suitable for our mounts?"

"You may have to lead them up a few steep places, but you shouldn't have any real trouble."

And so it proved. Grax's force—now augmented by the rear guard, who opted for glory and loot rather than the more tedious prospect of rejoining the caravan—ascended the enemy ridge unopposed and found a narrow valley behind, pleasantly shaded by aspen. Birds sang in the trees overhead; butterflies danced beneath the green canopy. A brook sang its way down the valley, and the party crossed and recrossed the water as they advanced.

There was fresh dung on the trail, which proved that they were on the track of the outlaws. The valley was ideal for an ambush, and Grax kept his scouts out. They saw nothing but a deer—they took a shot, and missed.

The trail rose from the valley floor and up a stony ridge. The party dismounted and led their mounts along the steep, narrow trail. From here it was a constant climb, on foot or mounted, along one slope or another. The terrain varied widely: sometimes they were in little green valleys filled with trees and flowers; on other occasions they were on rocky slopes as dry as the desert plateau beyond the top of the pass.

At one point, as the party rested and refreshed themselves while the scouts examined the next ridge to make certain there was no ambush, Aristide offered his captive a drink from his water bottle. He considered the outlaw's physique, his length, his breadth of shoulder, his well-developed muscles.

"How old are you really?" he asked.

The young man laughed. "I was sixteen when I left the Womb of the World. I'm not sure how long ago that was—eighteen months, maybe."

"Had you always intended to be an outlaw?"

The bandit gave a rueful grin. "Songs and stories made the life seem more exciting than it is. I'd thought it would be more fun."

Aristide gave an amused smile. "I've heard that from someone else recently."

"I hadn't intended to become the slave of a group of killer priests, that's for certain. But when I saw what their men did to Black Arim—he was our gang's leader—I joined right up. And once I met the priests, I was too frightened to run away. Especially after what I saw them do to a couple of fellows they called 'deserters.' "

"Do the priests have names?"

"Not that I've ever heard. They speak to us in the common tongue, but they have a language of their own when they don't want us to understand what they're saying."

"Which is most of the time, I suppose."

The outlaw nodded. He looked over his shoulder to make certain no one was listening, then leaned close to Aristide and spoke in a lowered voice.

"How about cutting these ropes and letting me run for it?" he asked. "I've cooperated, and I promise to give up the outlaw life once I'm away from here."

Aristide considered this proposal. "I think I'll wait to see whether your information is correct."

"No offense," the bandit said, "but in a few hours you'll all be dead. I'd like to be well away from here before that happens."

The swordsman smiled. "I guess you'll have to take your chances with us. Want some more water?"

The bandit accepted another drink. The scouts on the ridge ahead appeared and signaled that it was safe. Aristide helped the bandit back onto his mule, made sure the ropes were secure, and mounted his own horse. The small army continued their long climb.

Four turns of the glass later, they entered a small, shady valley fragrant with the smell of pine. "The Temple's just ahead," the young outlaw warned. "Past the trees and up a slope."

Aristide rode ahead to deliver this news to Grax, whose own captive had been mute in the hopes that the column would just blunder into the bandit nest.

"Ah," Grax said in surprise. "I see." Then he turned in his saddle and ran the older bandit through with his lance. As the man kicked and thrashed his way to his next incarnation, Grax began making his dispositions.

Aristide rode ahead, to where the scouts were hovering in the fringes of the trees, looking up at a boulder-strewn slope marked with evergreen scrub.

"Bitsy," he said. "Take a look, will you?"

The cat jumped from her perch behind Aristide's saddle. The barb snorted and made an uneasy sideways movement. Bitsy ignored the animal and sprang ahead, out of the shadow of the pines and onto the slope, and stayed close to the ground as she took a zigzag path to the crest, darting from cover to cover.

The nearest scout—a green-haired woman—gave Aristide a look.

"Your cat understands you," she said.

Aristide affected nonchalance. "Most of the time, yes."

Grax rode forward on his giant lizard to give instructions to the scouts and seemed surprised to find Aristide there.

"I've sent a scout ahead," Aristide said. "She should be reporting back any time."

And in fact Bitsy was soon observed returning from her mission. She didn't bother weaving from cover to cover, but instead came straight back.

"You sent your *cat*?" Grax laughed, and then Bitsy arrived and spoke.

"No guards," she said. "It seems they've all been called in to witness punishment."

"Punishment?" Aristide asked.

"Your cat talks!" Grax said, wide-eyed. His green-haired scout made a sign to ward evil.

"I counted twenty-two outlaws, variously armed," Bitsy went on. "Three priests in black, and eleven bound captives. I believe these latter are the group we've been following—it seems the priests are unhappy with the failure of their mission."

"Your cat *talks!*" said Grax.

"The waterfall and pool are ahead on the right," Bitsy continued. "On the left is a plantation of date palms, and that's where the outlaws are congregated. Behind the pool is a stock pen, where their mounts are confined."

"*Your cat talks!*" said Grax. Bitsy looked at him.

"Yes," she said. "I do. May I suggest that you attack soon while one-third of their strength remain bound and helpless?"

Grax looked from Aristide to Bitsy and back again, his huge gray head bobbing on its thick neck.

"I believe Bitsy's advice is sound," Aristide said. "But let me tell you first about the priests."

He related what the captives had told him about the priests' abilities. Grax listened with grim attention, his eyes darting toward Bitsy now and then, as if to discover if she had sprouted wings, or a second head, or some other unexpected talent.

"What do you recommend?" Grax said finally.

"Don't close with the priests. Tell your archers to keep shooting at them, from as many directions as possible."

"You can't make them . . . go away?"

"Perhaps." Aristide rubbed the stubble on his chin. "I wish we could take them alive. I'd like to know what they can tell me."

"If their powers are what you say, it may be easier to kill them."

"True. And what happens to them is going to be more up to them than it will be to us."

"You're wasting *time*," said Bitsy sharply.

"True." Grax looked over his saddle at his forces, now waiting his command. He turned his great lizard and rejoined his guards, to give his orders.

Aristide also rode back, but only to join his guide, the young outlaw. The bandit flinched as Aristide drew a knife from his belt. Aristide reached out and placed the knife in one of the young man's bound hands.

"What you do from this point is your choice," he said, "but I'd run like hell if I were you."

The outlaw's face flushed. "Thank you!" he said. "I'm a law-abiding man from this point forward!"

"Don't make any promises you can't keep," Aristide said, and turned to rejoin the caravan guards. The outlaw called after him.

"Try not to die!"

Aristide laughed and rode on.

Grax's little army, having received its orders, was deploying left and right and moving upslope, all the while trying to make as little noise as possible. Aristide looked ahead and saw Bitsy's black-and-white tail waving from the shelter of a scrub pine. He increased his pace and rode to join her, passing the armed force as it was still deploying.

He dismounted before he reached the top of the slope and made his way cautiously to the shelter of the little pine. He found himself on the rim of a shallow bowl three hundred paces in width. There was a great pile of rock on the right, cleft by a mountain brook that fell in two streams past a great basalt pillar into a broad pool, just as Aristide's guide had described. The stream rose again from the pool and wound its way across the bowl, cutting a trench through the palm plantation. The plantation itself had been raised above the floor of the bowl and was surrounded by a chest-high stone wall, the interior of which had been filled with soil hauled to this place at considerable labor, to provide a fertile anchor for the trees.

Whoever had done this was long gone. The plantation had an untended look.

Beyond the plantation was a corral with horses and other animals. Most of the open area was cluttered with the tents and shelters of the bandit army. Only the fact that the plantation was elevated above the surrounding area gave Aristide a view of what was happening beneath the palms.

There was a gathering in the plantation, a half-circle of bandits with the three black-clad priests prominent in the center. At the priests' feet stretched another group of bandits, each bound hand and foot. Taller than the tallest human, and unnaturally slender, the priests stalked among them, chanting in a guttural tongue. It was impossible to hear any words over distance and over the sound of the waterfall.

Grax rode up behind Aristide, peering over the twisted pine, his lance poised to give the signal to attack. Aristide motioned him to wait.

"I want to find out what happens next," he whispered.

Grax turned and signaled the army to stillness and silence, and then he dismounted and joined Aristide in concealment. The troll was wider than the bush he was hiding behind: at some other time it might have been amusing.

The priests continued to stalk among the bound bandits. The other bandits watched, and even though they were over a hundred paces away, Aristide could tell they weren't happy at whatever was going on.

Then Aristide noticed the clay balls. They were dangling by cords from the priests' hands, and they darted through the air as if they were creatures with minds of their own, like the cicadas that children leash on the ends of string.

Aristide and Grax started at a sudden blast of sound. A stir of dust rose from the grove and whirled away as the crash echoed repeatedly among the rocks. Birds flew up from their perches, calling in alarm.

Where there had been a bound bandit, there was now nothing but air.

Again Aristide's face became a smooth, intent mask, a bronze form from which glittered his dark, fierce eyes.

"So it's true!" Grax said. He looked over his shoulder at his troops, who seemed to have grown nervous. He favored them with a silent, morale-boosting laugh.

The murmur of the priests continued without cease. Another boom shattered the air; another bandit vanished.

"We should attack," said Grax.

"The longer this goes on," Aristide said, "the more they reduce their own strength. Let's watch."

"We can't wait too long. My men will lose heart."

"Go tell them the bandits are killing their own people and doing our job for us."

"Oh." Grax considered this. "*Oh.* Very good."

Bent low, he rumbled down the slope to his troops and told them to spread the word.

"This isn't looking good," Bitsy said to Aristide, once they were alone.

"No."

"This overthrows everything."

Aristide didn't bother to answer. The priests continued their milling, their chanting. The startled birds began to settle back into the trees. Aristide watched as closely as he could.

Another detonation sounded from the grove. The birds rose again into the sky. Another outlaw vanished. And, somewhere behind Aristide, a warhorse neighed.

The horse was a stallion and waiting with other stallions made it fretful and belligerent. It was beginning to scent the strange horses in the corral, and the repeated detonations had not soothed its nerves. So when the third bang echoed from the surrounding ranks the stallion answered, issuing a furious, shrieking challenge into the sky.

Aristide glanced over his shoulder at the sound. Grax, standing by another body of caravan guards, whirled to the horseman and signaled angrily for him to quiet his beast.

Horses in the bandits' corral answered. The first stallion screamed back at them, and so did several other horses in the party.

Grax turned to Aristide, arms thrown wide in frustration. Aristide turned back to the plantation.

The three priests had turned as one to stare in the direction of the noise. Their chanting ceased. And after a half-second pause they were in motion again, running, gesturing, issuing orders not in their own language but in the common tongue.

Aristide turned to Grax and his command.

"*Now!*" he called. "*Charge them!*"

Grax took three steps and hurled himself onto his riding-lizard. He pulled his lance from the ground and shook it.

"*Grax the Troll!*" he shouted.

"*Grax the Troll!*" his riders echoed, and spurred forward.

"Not exactly '*Leeroy Jenkins!*' " remarked Bitsy, "but I suppose it will do."

The riders roared over the lip of the bowl in a great cloud of dust. Grax led the lancers across the open ground to the right while the archers spread out widely, their arrows already humming through the air.

As the riders passed him, Aristide stood to get a better view.

The archers were not particularly accurate in firing from the backs of jouncing beasts, but their arrows at least served to increase the confusion of the bandit force. The advance of Grax and his lancers was hampered by the tent lines and shelters of the bandit camp, but they managed to maintain their momentum and were trampling much of the bandits' armor and reserve weapons underfoot.

The main body of bandits had faded back from the edge of the palm plantation, leaving behind eight of their number still bound hand and foot. These were screaming and rolling and crying for help, much to the amusement of the archers, who were pleased to use them for target practice as they trotted forward. Aristide could see nothing of the priests.

There were a series of concussions, however, that revealed the priests were most likely causing arrows to disappear.

Aristide unsheathed Tecmessa and trotted forward on foot. Bitsy ran by his side.

Ahead of him, the archers fired a low scything volley into the plantation, then jumped their beasts over the wall and rode on. Aristide followed. There were a series of cracks, and Aristide was nearly trampled as the archers came galloping back with a group of sword-swinging bandits in pursuit. A pair of priests were leading the charge and the archers knew not to let them get close.

It was clearly unwise to fight two priests at once. Aristide retreated along with the archers. Bitsy went up one of the palms.

The bandits pursued to the edge of the plantation. In the shade of the palms their eyes glowed like polished marbles. The archers rode back to a safe distance and then resumed their shooting. Clay balls whirled on the ends of their cords, and booms tore the air as arrows vanished in mid-flight. But while the priests could protect themselves, they couldn't protect all their followers, and outlaws cried in pain and rage as they fell with arrow wounds.

Then there were shouts of *Grax the Troll!* from the depths of the palm trees, and the sound of riders. One of the priests turned and dashed back into the plantation, along with a group of bandits. The other priest remained, with a handful of followers clumped behind him, so that he could protect them from arrow fire.

Aristide came forward again, his sword leveled. A few archers trotted forward as well, but rode wide, keeping a respectful distance between themselves and Tecmessa.

An archer sheltering behind the priest knelt, drew, let fly. Tecmessa took the arrow with a crack, a blast of wind, and a puff of dust.

The bandits, as one, took a step back, consternation plain on their features. The priest did not move.

Aristide paused in his advance and addressed the priest.

"I am Aristide, the traveler. Will you favor me with your name?"

The priest made no answer, but glared at him with orange eyes. His unnatural height was exaggerated as he stood on the wall that bordered the plantation. He wore a black turban with the tail wrapped around his lower face, a black robe, black pantaloons, boots. His hands and the skin around his eyes were blue. He wore an indigo-colored sash around his narrow waist with a pair of silver-hilted daggers stuck in it. The clay ball, no larger than a knuckle, quested on the end of its cord like the antenna of an insect.

"If not your name," Aristide said, "then perhaps your purpose. Your order. Feel free to discourse on the name and nature of your god—who knows, I may convert."

The priest gave no answer.

"Well." Aristide whirled his sword in a bit of bravado. "As you choose to remain silent, let us then get on to the contest of skill."

There was a barrage of bangs from the depths of the plantation, and cries of "*Grax! Grax!*" Aristide advanced, his eyes intent on the clay ball.

The ball swooped, darted, swung toward him. Tecmessa's point angled toward it.

Something twisted in the air between them. Then untwisted. A preternatural silence seemed to descend on the field for an instant.

Aristide continued his advance. "We are well matched, I see," he said, "except perhaps in the matter of practical weaponry."

Tecmessa slashed through the air and cut the priest's leg in half just above the knee. As the priest fell, a backhand cut took his right hand.

The hand, the ball, and the cord fell to the ground, all lifeless.

The priest gave a howl of anger, snatched a dagger from his waist, and lunged as he rose on the elbow of his crippled arm. Aristide parried, and then his blade thrust forward, the single edge slicing the priest's throat.

There was a red spurting, a rattle, a kicking of boots. The air tasted briefly of copper. The silver knife fell to the stones.

Tecmessa slashed out again, and three bandits vanished in a blast of air. The rest scrambled back in disorder.

Aristide leaped atop the wall and waved the archers forward, then moved into the plantation on the heels of the bandits.

Amid the palms ahead, a knot of bandits brandished weapons in the murk and dust. Arrows hissed between the trees. Lancers galloped in, then away. Grax had succeeded in cutting off the outlaws from their mounts, which made their escape problematic, but a barrage of cracks and booms made it clear that the priests were still guarding their flock.

"*Grax the Troll!*" There was a storm of arrows, followed by a rush on the flank. Cries among the bandits showed that at least some of the arrows struck home. An unnaturally tall figure rushed to meet the threat, and the riders reined in and turned. All save the leader, who was too large to easily check his speed.

There was a bang, a swift eddy in the risen dust. Grax vanished.

"Damn!" said Aristide.

The Free Companions fell back in confusion. The outlaws gathered courage and prepared an attack. Aristide took several running steps forward and took another pair of bandits with a blast from Tecmessa.

The priest turned, the clay ball moving ahead of him like a third, questing eye. Aristide dodged behind a tree just as a blast peeled bark and sent leaves flying. He lunged out of cover to the right, Tecmessa in a high parry, and saw the priest's boots disappearing around the tree in the other direction. The sword made a great slashing cut to the left just as the clay ball darted around the palm trunk, the cord whipping around the tree like the chain of a morning star.

The cord was severed. The clay ball flew spinning through the air.

The priest shrieked, a hair-raising sound like the battle cry of a cougar. Aristide took a step back as the tall, black-clad figure lunged around the palm trunk, a thrusting spear held high in one hand. The orange eyes blazed. The tail of the turban had been torn away from the lower face and revealed a mouth brimming with dozens of needlelike, moray-sharp teeth.

The priest was inside Tecmessa's effective range and Aristide parried desperately as he fell back, kicked to the priest's knee, and fell back again. The priest hissed, thrust. Aristide dodged inside the thrusting spear and cut upward beneath the priest's arm, slicing through the triceps. The spear fell from nerveless fingers; the tall black-robed figure staggered with shock. Aristide drove upward again, this time with the point, through the ribs and to the lungs and heart.

Blood fountained past the priest's needle teeth and the tall, slender body began to fall. Aristide cleared Tecmessa from the corpse and rolled just in time to avoid a blast from the third priest.

Aristide rolled to his feet, the sword on guard. The third priest hobbled toward him. He had got an arrow through his left knee early in the fight, and had spent most of the combat kneeling, protecting his followers from inbound arrows. Now he had no choice but to take the fight to the enemy.

The clay ball quested out from his right hand. The left carried a long, curved sword.

Aristide took a step back, keeping his distance.

"May I suggest that you surrender?" he said. "By now your position is quite hopeless."

The priest snarled and continued his lurching march. An arrow whistled past his head.

"You should fire all together," Aristide told the archers in a loud voice. "And from as many directions as possible."

Archers fanned out on either side. The few remaining outlaws—they were down to eight or nine—crept along in the wake of their priest. Many were badly wounded. Desperation clung to their faces.

"You can't defend against the arrows," Aristide told the priest. "The second that ball of yours moves to cover an arrow coming from one flank, either I'll take you or you'll be hit by arrows from another quarter. So I suggest you drop your . . . weapon, and we can discuss your fate like reasonable men."

The priest hesitated. He seemed to consider the matter.

Apparently he decided that Aristide's analysis was correct, because in a single purposeful motion he raised his sword and slashed his own throat.

The bandits gave a collective moan as their leader fell.

A few fought to the last, but most tried to surrender.

The Free Company of Grax was not in either case inclined to mercy.

Aristide did not participate in the brief, bloody massacre, but instead retreated to the body of the second priest he'd killed and squatted before the clay ball that lay by its tangled, knotted cord. There was a dab of blood on the end of the cord, which caused the swordsman to examine the hand of the dead priest. The cord was not tied onto the priest's finger, but grew out of it—the cord had been alive.

Aristide wiped Tecmessa on a clean part of the priest's robes, then sheathed the sword. He took his dagger out of his belt and wound a bit of the cord around the tip, then raised it to examine the ball more closely. It was a dusky red in color, and plain-featured, without runes or script or magic signs.

Bitsy dropped from one of the palms and came up to rub her cheek against the swordsman's free hand before she gazed up at the dangling ball.

"It seems harmless," she said.

"I imagine it is. Now." He rose, took a cloth from his pocket, and wrapped the ball carefully before returning it to his pocket. He looked up.

The battle was over. Overexcited convoy guards rode furiously over the grove, kicking up dust and looking for someone to slaughter. Aristide went looking for whoever was in charge.

Grax's deputy, Vidal the Archer, was trying to properly organize the looting.

"Where's the plunder?" he demanded, arms akimbo as he glared at the field. He was a dark-skinned man with short, bandy, horseman's legs and a long, broad trunk, perfect for drawing his bow. He gave a bandit corpse a kick. "All we can find is their tents and their spare trousers."

"I'd look behind the waterfall," Aristide said. "If memory serves, it's a traditional place for fabulous treasure."

Vidal turned his horse and galloped to the waterfall. Aristide followed on foot. By the time he arrived, Vidal was peering behind the fall of water and calling for treasure.

"Grax promised me a double share," Aristide said.

Vidal gave him a narrow, impatient look. "You'll get it," he said.

"I don't want it," Aristide said. "What I want is the three

fastest animals you have here, and a bag of silver coin for re-mounts and supplies."

Vidal looked at him with more interest. "You have an urgent errand?"

"Yes. I need to take the news of these priests to the College. The scholars there might be able to understand what they are and what they represent."

Vidal nodded. "Very well," he said. "You may have what you ask."

"I would like a few other things as well," Aristide said. "I would like the heads of the priests, their right hands, and the balls they used to make your troopers vanish."

Vidal gave him a curious look. "Do you think you can get our people back?"

Aristide considered this. "It might be possible. I doubt it, though."

Vidal made a pious sign. "May their next incarnations give them wisdom."

"Indeed."

Some of Vidal's guard turned up with improvised torches, and they and their commander ventured behind the waterfall. As Aristide walked away he heard exclamations of delight and avarice at the riches found there.

He collected the hands, the heads, the clay balls, then retrieved his barb and fed him some of the sultan's grain. He took off the saddle and laid out his sleeping rug in the palm plantation, as far from the sight and smell of bodies as possible. There he drank water, ate some dried fruit, and reclined with the tail of his turban drawn across his eyes. He reckoned it had been eighty turns of the glass since he had last slept.

When he awoke the camp was still, most of the guards asleep after celebrating their victory and their newfound fortune. He found Vidal, who had not yet slept, and greeted him. Vidal gave him his bag of silver and led him to the corral, where he chose his three mounts. Vidal offered him food for himself and grain for the animals—any grass or bushes had already been grazed out by the bandits' beasts—and then Aristide mounted the first of the horses he planned to ride that day.

"If you hear of any more of these priests operating in the world," he said, "find out as many details as you can, and send word to the College."

"I will," Vidal said simply.

Bitsy leaped to her nest behind the swordsman's saddle. Aristide rode away, leading his horses down the side canyon that led to the Cashdan and the route back across the desert to the Womb of the World.

It had taken him eight months to walk the route that had taken him to the Vale and the Venger's Temple.

He would return in three, if he had to kill a hundred horses to do it.

The wall was transparent and looked out at the great metropolis beyond. No one had ever imposed any kind of architectural uniformity on the city, and the result was a skyline of fabulous extravagance. There were obelisks, pagodas, and minarets. Columns supported arches, arches supported domes, domes supported cupolas. Towers brandished horns, bartizans, mooring masts, and carved stone pinnacles with crockets. Triumphal arches crowned boulevards, and so did torii. There were stoas, cloisters, and pergolas. An enormous wheel continuously carried entire apartments high into the sky before lowering them gently to earth, and stopped in its rotation only when someone wanted to get on or off. A brace of towers circled each other as they rose, a pair of helixes frozen in a dance.

Buildings were made of stone, of metal, of marble, of glass, of diamond, of carbon fiber. Domes were plated with gold, with bronze, with light-absorbent fuligin, and in one case with the teeth of human children.

Connecting the towers were arching metal bridges, transparent tubes, or cars hung from cables. Swirling between the structures were bright spots of color, people in lightweight gliders rising on the updrafts that surrounded the tallest buildings. Below, people moved in carriages, in gondolas, in cars that traveled along tracks.

Aristide, hands in his pockets, viewed the prodigality of Myriad City and said,

> *The city alive with noise and light,*
> *The flame of youth ablaze.*
> *And I, in my stillness, content to be old.*

"That's the Pablo I remember." Daljit, seated at her desk, looked up from her work. "Why are you Aristide these days?" she asked. "Why aren't you Pablo any longer?"

"There are too many Pablos. I am bored with Pablos."

She smiled. "I thought you were content to be old."

"I can't help being old," he said, gruffly. "Pablo I can do something about."

"Wielding a sword in some barbarian world isn't exactly the stuff of old age."

He turned from the window, took his hands from his pockets. He wore a pale shirt, white trousers, and a dark spider-silk jacket in a style twenty years out of date.

"The swordsmanship was incidental," he said. "I was actually doing scholarship."

"Of what?"

"The implied spaces." He walked to look over her shoulder at the spectra glowing on her display. "Anything?" he asked.

"Nothing yet."

The room was long, with two conventional doors that swung on hinges. The walls and ceiling were tuned to a neutral color so as not to provide distraction. Long tables with polished surfaces held a broad assortment of machines and small robots, most of them inactive. There was a smell of heat, of ozone.

Aristide contemplated his companion. Daljit seemed compact as opposed to small and gave the impression of having a highly organized, responsive body that didn't require size or reach for its effects. She had expressive brown eyes beneath level brows, and a mole on one cheek that provided a pleasing asymmetry. She wore a silver bracelet with a bangle and numerous rings, which indicated that she was aware of the grace of her long hands and fingers. She wore a white high-collared tunic, knee breeches, and silk stockings with clocks.

She and Aristide were old friends, and they spoke with the ease of a long acquaintance. Though they'd kept in touch, he hadn't seen her in person in sixty years, at which time she had been tall and bosomy and was crowned by hair of a brilliant henna-red shade.

She rested her chin on her fist as she looked at him. "What are the implied spaces, exactly?"

He considered for a moment. "If we turn to the window," he said, and illustrated the point by turning, "we observe the Dome of Parnassus."

She turned. "We do. It wants cleaning."

"The dome, you will observe, is supported by four arches, one at each cardinal point."

"Yes."

"Presumably the architect knew that the dome had to be supported by *something,* and arches were as meet for the purpose as anything else. But his decision had consequences. If you stand beneath the dome, you'll see that there are blank triangular spaces beneath the dome and between the arches. These are called 'squinches,' believe it or not."

Daljit smiled at him. "I'm delighted to know there are things called squinches, whether you invented the term or not."

He bowed to her, then looked out at the dome again. "The point is, the architect didn't say to himself, 'I think I'll put up four squinches.' What he said is, 'I want a dome, and the dome needs to be supported, so I'll support it with arches.' The squinches were an accident implied by the architect's other decisions. They were *implied.*"

"Ah." She straightened and took her chin off her fist. "You study squinches."

"And other accidents of architecture, yes." He turned to her, put a hand down on its reflection in the polished onyx surface of her desk.

"Say you're a die-hard romantic who wants to design a pretechnological universe full of color and adventure. Say you want high, craggy mountains, because they're beautiful and wild and inspiring and also because you can hide lots of orcs in them. Say you also want a mountain loch to reflect your beautiful high-Gothic castle, and a fertile plain to provide lots of foodstuffs that you can tax out of your peasants—many of whom are brain-clones of yourself, by the way, with a lot of the higher education removed, and inhabiting various specially grown bodies of varying styles and genders."

"You know," said Daljit, "I would have liked to have been a fly on the wall when the medieval scholars and the Compulsive Anachronists, or whatever they were called, discovered that they couldn't afford their own universe without financial aid from the fantasy gamers, and that their tidy little re-creation was now going to be full of trolls and dinosaurs."

Aristide grinned. "Perhaps you're understimating the percentage of medievalists who play fantasy games."

"Perhaps."

"But in any case, the fertile valley has to go adjacent to the ocean, because the river's got to go *somewhere,* and in the meantime you've got this mountain range with its romantic tarn over *here* . . . so what goes in between?"

She looked at him. "You're going to tell me it's a squinch."

"Bingo. By the time you've got all your computations done and dumped all the energy into inflating a wormhole from the quantum foam"—Aristide made little rubbing gestures with his fingers, as if he were sprinkling alchemical powders into an alembic—"and you've stabilized the wormhole gate with negative-mass matter, then inflated a soupçon of electrons and protons into a pocket universe complete with a flaming gas ball in the center . . . Once you've got your misty mountain range and your moisty river valley, what goes between the mountain range and river valley is implied by the architecture, and is in fact a high desert plain, like the Gobi, only far less attractive."

A whirring began as one of the machines in the room turned on its fans. Daljit looked briefly at her displays, then turned to Aristide again.

"So you study this desert?"

"I study what *adapts* to the desert. The desert wasn't intended, so whatever lives there wasn't intended to live there, either. It's all strayed in from another ecosystem and adapted to the desert, and it's adapting with surprising speed."

"And what lives there?"

He gave a private little smile. "Ants and spiders, mostly."

"Your chosen field seems less than enthralling."

"The sword-swinging bandits provided all the excitement necessary."

She gave him an appraising look. "So you really fought bandits with your sword? And murderous priests devoted to human sacrifice?"

Aristide reached to touch Tecmessa, which was at present carried in a long, flat case with a carrying strap, and which leaned against Daljit's desk.

"I cheated," he said. "And in any case, the certainty of reincarnation devalues heroism as well as tragedy."

"But still. It's not the same as pressing a button and killing them at a distance, is it?"

"No." His expression was grim. "Though I didn't actually kill any human beings—just the priests, who I imagine were constructs."

Even so, he thought, it was very personal. When he ran them through he could feel their life trembling right through the hilt of the sword. Felt the tremor fade as the life left them.

Still it hadn't been anything nearly as bad as the Control-Alt-Delete War. You were always terrified then, terrified every time you saw someone sick, every time you heard a sneeze or a cough. Every time you sensed sickness in your own blood, you had to wonder if it was the Seraphim or a common cold that had a hold of you.

You would wait for your friends or loved ones to go into a coma, and then you knew they would have to die. Because you knew that if they woke up, they would not be themselves anymore, they would be pod people.

Sometimes, when the authorities were overwhelmed or sick themselves or out of reach, you had to kill the sick yourself. No matter how much you loved them.

Strangulation was best, because that way there was no blood that might contaminate you, or not much. But however you did it, you would have to go into quarantine, to wait in a little room with a bed and water and canned food, and if you shivered while you waited, or felt a prickle of sweat on your forehead, you would sit in silent cringing agony and wonder if it was the first touch of the Seraphim.

Aristide turned away from Daljit, faced the nearest wall. He didn't want her to see the memory in his face.

There was no point in frightening her. If something like the Seraphim was happening now, she would be frightened soon enough.

"I understand that the priests were constructs," Daljit said, "but why were they made so conspicuous? You'd think they'd want to hide among the population."

"Except for the adventurers and anthropologists who come through the Womb," Aristide said, "the people of Midgarth are stranded in the pretechnological world their ancestors built. They're superstitious, and the priests were designed to be terrifying examples of the power of their god." He felt moisture on his palms and wiped them on his jacket, where the intelligent spider silk began the business of decomposing sweat.

"One of the bandits we captured was a sincere convert, I think. He led us to the priests' lair firm in the belief that we'd all be sacrificed alive."

The nearest machine gave a chiming sound. Daljit turned to her displays.

Her even brows knit as she looked at the display. Aristide

turned and looked over her shoulder. She gave the display instructions and viewed the data from another angle. Then she sighed and threw herself back in her chair.

"I've examined your object with chemical sniffers," she said, "with microimagery, with ultrasound, with microwaves, with spectrometry and X-rays and with lasers, and all I can tell you is that the damned thing is ordinary terra-cotta. I can give you the precise amount of trace minerals in its makeup, but it doesn't look unusual."

"Untraceable?"

"I can do some further correlation, see if there's a particular combination of minerals here that only occurs in one tiny part of the multiverse. But we don't *know* every tiny part of the multiverse, so the odds may not be on our side."

Aristide frowned, and touched with a foreknuckle the corner of his mouth where until recently he had worn a mustache. He walked to one of the machines, opened a door, and withdrew one of the clay balls he had brought through the Womb of the World. A shriveled bit of sinew was still attached to it, the remains of the cord that had tied it to the priest.

"The organic component?" he asked.

"Has unfortunately deteriorated. You can't expect much after three months' ride across a pretechnological landscape. There's no clear indication from what remains how the object was controlled." She raised her arms over her head and stretched, then rose from her chair. "I know a good organic chemist," she added, "who might spot something I've missed."

Aristide rolled the terra-cotta ball in the palm of his hand. "Won't be necessary. The wormhole collapsed as soon as the connection with the operator was removed—some kind of fail-safe mechanism." He dropped the clay ball into a clear plastic specimen bag and put it in the pocket of his jacket.

"I think the skulls and hands will give us more information," Daljit said. "Bone tells many more tales than withered flesh." She sighed, walked to him, touched his arm. "And I may yet find something in the other two objects."

He drew two more bags from his pockets and looked at them.

"I agree we should examine them," he said. "But you can automate the whole process, yes? There's no reason why we should wait here while your machines go through their motions. May I give you dinner?"

"You may." Daljit seemed pleased by the offer.

She put each of the samples into different machines, then gave them their instructions, along with the small desktop robot that would shift the samples from one machine to the next. Aristide walked to Daljit's desk and picked up Tecmessa, swinging its case over his shoulder on its strap. He picked up Daljit's soft spider-silk jacket from the rack behind her desk and offered it to her as she approached. She turned, backed herself into the jacket, and smoothed the lapels as he placed it over her shoulders.

"Has there been some advance in wormhole science since I was last paying attention?" he asked as she led him to the door.

"Not that I know of."

"So it still requires a vast amount of energy and a prodigious amount of calculation to produce a successful Einstein-Rosen bridge."

The door sprang open at her approach. She paused in the doorway and turned to him. "Yes. As I understand it."

Aristide was grim. "That reduces the number of suspects to a manageable number. The problem is that they are all enormously powerful." Again he stroked the ghost of his mustache with a knuckle. "Use of that much energy and that much computer time should be traceable, in theory. But to detect it might require someone of Bitsy's intelligence."

She was amused. "Do you still have that horrible cat?"

"Yes," said Bitsy. "He does."

Daljit gave a start and raised a hand to her throat. Bitsy jumped onto Daljit's desk and settled on her haunches before the display.

"I didn't know you were here," Daljit said weakly.

"I lurk," said the cat.

There was a moment of silence in which Aristide did his best not to laugh. Daljib cleared her throat.

"I'm sorry for what I said," she said.

Bitsy's green eyes were fixed on the display. "As the avatar," she said, "of a vast array of quantum parallel processors orbiting the sun as part of an as-yet-incomplete Matrioshka array, I'm rather above taking offense at that sort of thing."

There was another pause. "Thank you," said Daljit finally.

"But if Aristide wants to have sex with you," the cat added, "I'm not helping."

Daljit looked in silent surprise at the cat, and then at Aristide.

"Look among your colleagues," Aristide said, "for traces of the energy necessary to create those wormhole gates, and for the calculation, too."

The cat was nonchalant. "Already on it, Pops."

"And be careful. They might be on the lookout for anyone looking for them."

"I'll be slick as butter," Bitsy promised.

Daljit and Aristide stepped through the doorway, and the door closed silently behind them. The corridor outside the laboratory was carpeted in soft green mosses that absorbed the sound of their footsteps.

"That animal of yours is scary," Daljit said.

"I find she settles a lot of arguments before they get started."

" 'Speak softly and carry an omniscient feline?' "

"Quite," he said, and took her arm.

They sat before a plate of oysters. After months of dried fruit and chunks of mutton skewered over a dung fire, Aristide had developed a vast appetite for fresh seafood.

"So how," Daljit asked, "does the cat help you to have sex?"

Daljit had deliberately waited until an oyster was already sliding down his tongue, and Aristide managed only barely to keep from snorting shellfish out his nose.

"Bitsy confines herself to introductions," he said, after clearing his throat. "An animal twining itself around another's legs provides an opening for conversation."

"And how does the avatar of an awesomely intelligent AI feel about being used for the tawdry purposes of seduction?"

Aristide was offended. "Madame," he said, "I am never tawdry. As you should know."

She considered him. "True," she said. "You're not."

They sat on a cream-colored boat that grazed on the waters near the city and gave diners a view of its miraculous profile. Above their heads, visible through a transparent canopy, the sun was on the verge of its daily miracle.

They looked up as the sun—a more advanced model than that of Midgarth—began to flicker and fade. Shadows flew rapidly across its disk. And then the photosphere settled into a stable state, and photons were no longer able to escape. The sun went black— but surrounding the black disk was the corona, still glowing with heat, its swirls and columns a cosmic echo of the city's skyline.

The corona would fade over the next seven point nine one hours, after which the sun's photosphere would grow chaotic again, and the sun blaze out to light a new day.

"How long has it been," Daljit asked, "since you were last in Myriad City?"

Aristide's gaze continued upward.

"I pass through from time to time," he said. "When I'm not traveling, I keep a little cabin on Tremaine Island."

"Where's that?"

"Past Mehmet's Lagoon. I hire a boatman to take me in and out."

She raised her eyebrows. "And you're alone out there? In that remote area?"

He shrugged, then looked down to dabble horseradish on a bluepoint. "It's enough for Aristide. And besides, it's an implied space. No one *intended* to put an island there. If I ever get bored, I can go out and contemplate the pollywogs and butterflies."

"When you and I lived together," she said, "you cultivated a certain seigneurial grandeur. Fresh flowers every morning, genuine paintings on the walls rather than videos of paintings. Green lawns, and deference from the neighbors."

Aristide contemplated the thick viridian essence of his cocktail as it brewed in its crystal glass.

"I grew tired," he said. "Not of my surroundings, but of all that was necessary to maintain them. Now if I want something, I'll rent, and let someone else do the work." He looked up. "But you'd be surprised how well I've adapted to simplicity. My cabin has a stone floor that I laid myself, out of rock that I carried to the site in a barrow. And when I took my stroll through Midgarth, I carried a rug rolled up in my pack, and that was my bed."

She smiled. "I'll wager it was a nice rug."

"It was. Two hundred thousand double knots per square meter, or something like that. But it was still a rug, not a down mattress." He looked at her. "But I'm not the only one who's changed. When I saw you last, you were an Amazon."

She laughed. "I've been a *lot* of people since then!"

"Such as?"

"I was a solli-glider in Momrath. I had wings, feathers, and eyes as big as my fists."

"That sounds delightful." Delicately, he breathed in an oyster off its shell.

"I had a hard time leaving that incarnation. But the opportunity came for the job at the Institute, so I came here." She looked out at the audacious horizon, the pinnacles and domes and the swirling motes between them. "It's a place of such high energies. I *accomplish* things here. And if I want to fly again, all I have to do is strap on a pair of wings."

"What sorts of things do you accomplish?"

"Designing plants and animals for all the pockets. And for the settlements in other star systems."

He sipped his cocktail. "Do you also design people?"

She shook her head. "For that, I need more seniority."

The waitron arrived, a hairy-legged faun with horns, livery, and a powdered wig. Aristide looked at Daljit.

"Shall we order dinner? Or would you like another drink?"

"Let's eat."

They ordered. Aristide continued his exploration of the seafood menu; Daljit chose the wine. The faun trotted away on cloven hoofs, and Daljit looked after him.

"I spent a few years as a boy," she said. "After I left you, and before Momrath."

Aristide regarded her. "How was it?"

"Overrated."

He nodded. "So I've always thought."

"And the penis is less accurate than I'd imagined."

"You could have got one that's better engineered. Most men do, I believe."

She looked at him with honest curiosity. "Have you?"

"I am improved all-round," Aristide said. "Faster reflexes, glial cells Einstein would envy, a pulmonary system like unto a god. High arches, strong teeth, eyes that can see in dim light, an epidermis of uncommon durability . . ."

"That would be a yes, I take it?"

He finished his drink. "When all's said and done, who would take an organ—*any* organ—that's substandard, provided you had a choice?"

"I chose one that was supposed to be dead average. I wanted to give the standard model craft a test-drive before taking out the souped-up version."

"That was probably wise." He viewed her. "And yet, here you are. No wings, no penis, no red hair, and a rather charming mole."

She smiled and drew her index finger down her jaw, as if to reassure herself of her current shape.

"I miss the wings," she said. "But perhaps I, like you, am choosing simplicity."

He nodded. "Perhaps so."

"And you? Have you ever been anything but male?"

He made an equivocal gesture. "The options weren't so readily available when I was young," he said, "at least not without surgery and other inconveniences. By the time reincarnation became common, I had grown set in my personality—and my identity seemed to *work* for everyone, so I never had reason to change." He offered her a lean smile. "Though I recently received a download from one of the Pablos—the one who went to Tau

Ceti. He claimed to have invented a new gender, and was *very* enthusiastic."

"Have you loaded the experience?"

"No." There was silence, and then he said, "Tau Ceti is a more extreme environment than Sol. More extreme adaptations are required."

"That sounds like an excuse," she said. "If the other Pablo liked it that much, maybe you should have immersed yourself."

"Perhaps." His tone was skeptical, and then he threw out his hands. "But I like *women,* Daljit! I always have!"

"So do I!" said the faun as he trotted up with a pair of glasses and a bottle of wine. "I like *all* of them! All the time!" He looked at Daljit with bright eyes. "Want my number, sugar?"

Daljit declined with laughter. The waitron feigned disappointment and opened the bottle. The wine was a mellow honey color, with the scent of sunshine and citrus. The faun waited for approval, then left them to their pleasure. They savored the wine and the last of the oysters in silence, as the sun's corona slowly faded and Myriad City became a blaze of light along the port side of the craft. Other than the cooling corona, the sky overhead was black—the handful of lights visible now that the sun was gone were the few settlements on the far side of the universe.

The world of Topaz held only six billion people, and had room for a hundred times that. Most of the landmasses, and almost all the oceans, were unexplored. It was a fairly new pocket, having been created only four hundred years earlier, and though the inhabitants were reproducing quickly, and not dying at all, it would take centuries to occupy all the niches available for modified humanity.

Humanity had over a hundred billion descendants on various pockets, far more than could have ever existed on Earth. Earth itself was in the process of a millennium-long reset after many millennia of abuse, and at present had only a few hundred thousand inhabitants, just enough to restart the species should something go terribly wrong with the wormhole worlds.

Daljit lowered her glass. "Why, Aristide?" she asked. "That's what I can't work out."

He looked at her over the rim of his glass. The brilliant shoreline glittered in his eyes like the missing stars.

"For some reason, the implied spaces intrigue me."

She seemed amused. "And you explore them with your cat and your sword."

He echoed her smile. "Yes."

"I can't help but think that's romantic."

"I'm glad you think so," he said, "but catalogs of ants and spiders don't seem very romantic when I'm working on them."

"The romance lies in the sword, I think."

He glanced at Tecmessa, leaning against the boat's smooth-paneled walls, then turned back to her.

"Even after all these years," he said, "I encounter the occasional person who wants to kill me. It's irrational, because all they can do is kill the time since my last backup, but then assassins were never known for the lucid quality of their thought."

"You could have got a gun," she pointed out. "Or a taser. Or a magic wand, or a Ring of Power. But instead you got a *broadsword.*"

"Guns and tasers are good for only one thing. A sword is more flexible. When I was off in Midgarth, I managed to take a couple of prisoners with Tecmessa. If I'd had a gun I would have had to shoot them—and in any case, guns won't work in Midgarth. The rules of the universe won't permit it." He paused, as Daljit's face had brightened with delight.

"Your sword has a *name!*" Daljit exclaimed. "That's *wonderful!*"

Aristide blinked. "If you say so."

"That's the mark of a romantic. Next thing, you'll be wearing a mask and a cape."

"Maintaining the secret identity as a millionaire playboy would be a problem," Aristide said. "I'm afraid it would be too exhausting."

She just looked at him. "Millionaire playboy?" she asked.

"Bruce Wayne," he said.

"Who?"

He was thunderstruck.

"You don't know *Batman*?" he said.

She looked at him blankly. "I guess not," she said.

"I *lived* with you for six years!" He felt an obscure sense of betrayal.

"Seven. But what's this Batman got to do with it?"

"Nothing," he sighed. "Apparently."

They returned to the laboratory to find Bitsy still sitting before Daljit's display.

"Terra-cotta, through and through," Bitsy reported. "Trace elements show that all three balls were made from the same type of clay." Her tail gave an irritated little switch. "And I'm sure you'll be delighted to know that the origin of the clay is unknown. It could have come from any pocket with unexplored clay deposits, which could be any of them."

"Thank you for your efforts," Aristide said. He set Tecmessa's case against the long table, then picked up the remaining samples, wrapped them, and returned them to his pocket.

Daljit returned to her seat and peered at the display over the silhouette of the cat that squatted before it.

"I should check your work," she said. "But I suppose it would be futile."

Bitsy rose to her feet and stretched.

"Reproducing the results of another researcher is the hallmark of the scientific method," she said. "I'll leave you to it." She jumped onto the floor and rubbed herself against Aristide's legs.

There was a chime from Daljit's pocket. She took a small card out of the pocket and looked at its display.

"Put it on the wall," she said.

One of the neutral-colored walls brightened to show a tall, imposing woman standing behind her desk. The image was lifesized. Her skull had grown a kind of exoskeletal helmet that overshadowed her eyes—her many eyes, of different sizes, which waved on stalks, alongside other sensory organs of less obvious purpose. Her hands had an extra digit on which cilia waved, for fine manipulation under the supervision of her magnifying eyes.

It looked as if she had a large, pale crab perched on her head.

From the shoulders down she was a standard woman, if powerfully built. As she talked she walked back and forth behind her desk while her hands made chopping gestures.

"Fedora," Daljit said, "thank you for working late."

"Daljit," she said. "I've had a chance to examine one of the three heads you passed on to me, and I'm going to have to inform the police. I've found evidence of a crime."

Daljit smiled, still a little under the influence of the wine.

"Beyond the decapitation, you mean?"

Fedora wasn't amused. "The brain structures were badly decomposed, but they were clearly unusual. I got the DNA from the skull and sequenced it, and it's plain the deceased was created as a pod person. I checked the register and saw that it wasn't one of the few remaining types of legal pod people, so I'll be calling the police as soon as I finish talking to you."

Aristide stepped forward and cleared his throat. "Madam," he said.

A pair of Fedora's eyes turned toward him as she paced, while the rest remained focused on Daljit.

"Yes?" she said.

"May I suggest you not inform the police just yet? I—"

The pair of eyes shifted back to Daljit.

"Who is this person?" she asked.

Daljit blinked. "This"—she hesitated—"this is the man who . . . collected . . . the heads."

"I see." All Fedora's eyes turned to Aristide. "Sir," she said, "I am absolutely required to inform the authorities when an unlicenced pod person is discovered. There are *no* exceptions."

"I wasn't going to suggest that you break the law," Aristide said. "I was just going to suggest that you be careful *which* authority you report to. Because—"

"I'm afraid you don't understand the seriousness of this,"

Fedora said. "This is a grave security matter. The last time we had wholesale pod person creation it started the Control-Alt-Delete War."

"I know, madam. I was there."

She seemed a little surprised. "Well then," she said. "You certainly understand the gravity of this crime."

"Yes," Daljit said. "But Fedora, I don't think you quite understand who you're talking to."

"I don't?" She stiffened, and her sensory complex turned to Aristide. "Who are you then?"

"This," said Daljit, "is Pablo Monagas Pérez."

Fedora's eyes seemed to waver and lose focus.

"Oh," she said.

The image of Fedora faded from the wall, and the wall resumed its neutral color. There was a moment of silence.

Daljit turned to Aristide.

"It's the nightmare scenario, isn't it?" she said. "The end of civilization."

His level gaze remained fixed on the empty wall. "It certainly seems so."

"The priests were in Midgarth because it's full of undocumented bodies," she said. "There's natural breeding there, and poor record-keeping. The people there aren't equipped with network implants that broadcast an alert if a mind is tampered with. The priests can suck people through wormholes to wherever their actual headquarters is. Once their wetware is corrupted, they can be returned through the same wormhole, or through another. Equipped with plausible identities, they can be sent as agents to other pockets."

"Yes."

Fortunately, he thought, they couldn't spread a meme plague like the Seraphim. When anyone—even the pretechnological inhabitants of Midgarth—got sick, they'd go to a Pool of Life, and the nature of the plague would be discovered. The pool might be able to cure the plague, or it might not, but in any case it would broadcast an alarm that would be heard throughout the multiverse.

Midgarth was a failure as an anthropological experiment. A Middle Ages in which the people couldn't get sick and wouldn't stay dead was useless as a re-creation. But the ethics committee that designed the scientific protocols wouldn't permit real death or real plague.

"What do the enemy do next?" Daljit asked. "You've been through this. I haven't."

He held out a hand and looked at it as if it belonged to a stranger. Finding it was merely a hand, and not some autonomous mechanism attached to the end of his arm, he placed it with care on a desktop.

"A lot depends on the time scale the attackers are working with," he said. "If they've got time, they can choose their targets in our technological pockets with extreme care. The targets can be taken while isolated—while on vacation, say—then drawn through a wormhole to a place where their implants' defense systems can be neutralized. If circumstances permitted, the attackers could spend centuries picking off one person here, another there, and their efforts would be nearly undetectable.

"But circumstances won't permit, or so we hope. Their victims can't back themselves up, or visit a Pool of Life, because the altered brain structures would become immediately apparent. And if they don't visit a Pool of Life, they'll start *aging*—and that can't help but be noticed. So that will provide a temptation to work faster than might be absolutely safe."

Daljit considered this. "What if the attackers have their *own* Pools of Life, that aren't connected to the network?"

He considered this for a moment as quiet horror seemed to shiver through the room.

"We'd better find someone in authority to talk to," he said.

"I have a list," said Bitsy.

Commissar Lin was a medium-sized man with mild dark eyes placed far apart, nearly on the sides of his head. He had been chosen over the others on Bitsy's list for prosaic reasons: one other candidate was in political exile, and therefore possessed restricted power of action; another was on holiday in Courtland; and Fedora had worked unhappily with another, and vetoed her.

Lin had also backed himself up just two days before, which meant that if his wetware were corrupted, he would have been attacked in just the last few hours.

That his agency was the Domestic Internal Section, known as the Domus, was a bonus.

When contacted, Commissar Lin seemed undisturbed, and unsurprised, by Pablo Monagas Pérez calling to ask him to a pathology lab late at night. After performing an independent verification that Aristide and Monagas Pérez were in fact the same individual, he arrived at Fedora's office twenty minutes later, wearing casual clothes and with an interested look in his widely spaced eyes. The look of interest deepened as he caught sight of the three blue-skinned heads sitting in baths of lemon-scented preservative.

Lin was offered coffee and declined. People sat around a marble-topped table in Fedora's lab, within sight of the three heads. Aristide explained as briefly as he could, after which Fedora and Daljit gave equally terse abstracts of their discoveries. Lin listened and asked a few short, to-the-point questions.

At the end of the narrative, he glanced at them all and asked, "How many people know of this?"

"We three," Daljit said.

"Not exactly," Aristide added. "We may be the only people who know the results of Fedora's investigations, but a great many people in Midgarth know of the priests. I alerted the people in the College to their existence and told them to report anything they heard. And of course there's Bitsy." The cat jumped onto his lap and looked at Lin expectantly. Lin looked back.

"And who is Bitsy, exactly?" Lin asked.

"An avatar of Endora," said Aristide.

Endora was one of the Eleven, the great plate-shaped computing platforms in close orbit around the sun that together formed the solar system's Matrioshka array, left incomplete since the on-set of the Existential Crisis. The created universe of Topaz, where they sat about the marble-topped table, was reached through a wormhole on Endora's dark side, as Midgarth had been through a wormhole on the AI platform called Aloysius.

Endora was ubiquitous throughout Topaz and other high-technology pockets she had spawned through her wormholes. Here she was not so much a single intelligence, but an enormous array of semi-autonomous computers, some so stupid they were fit only for a single task, like monitoring the effects of rain on the layer of paint in which they were inserted, some so brilliant they could predict the weather in any of Topaz's millions of microcli-mates. But all were connected to Endora's massive communica-tions web, and all data were ultimately accessible by Endora. It was impossible to perform a task as simple as walking down the street without interacting with Bitsy in a hundred ways.

Lin, knowing this, looked at Bitsy with curiosity.

"Pleased to meet you in person," he said.

"Pleased to meet *you*, sir," said Bitsy, polite as always to someone who possessed the theoretical power to lodge an injunc-tion against her autonomy.

Lin fumbled in his vest and produced a straight briar pipe. "Does anyone mind if I smoke?" he asked. No one did.

They waited while he performed the necessary ritual. A harsh organic reek soon tainted the air. Lin scanned the room with his walleyes, then turned to Aristide.

"How long do you think the constructs were in operation?"

"I killed them a little under three months ago. They hadn't been operating in that part of Midgarth more than three months before that, but they could have been active in other parts of the world."

Lin's attention settled on Bitsy.

"Could the pod people's wormholes possibly have been cre-ated without the knowledge and cooperation of one of the Eleven?" he asked.

"Not if they were created anywhere in the solar system, no." Bitsy's answer was prompt.

"So one of your . . . colleagues . . . has been corrupted."

"Or," calmly, "one of my colleagues is the villain, corrupting its own citizens."

Lin turned to Aristide. "Is that possible?"

"I and my confederates," Aristide said, "did our best to prevent that degree of autonomy among artificial intelligences. We made the decision to turn away from the Vingean Singularity before most people even knew what it was. But"—he made a gesture with his hands as if dropping a ball—"I claim no more than the average share of wisdom. We could have made mistakes."

"Still," Daljit added, "we've had fifteen hundred years of peace. If it were possible for one of the Eleven to have gone rogue, you'd think it would have happened by now."

Lin sucked on his pipe, discovered it had gone out, and began the ritual of relighting it. Clouds of smoke obscured his features as he puffed to get the pipe started again.

"If one of the Eleven has been corrupted," he said from out of the smoke, "what are the odds that another will be?"

"We're all somewhat different," Bitsy said. "Our autonomy is limited to different degrees. We have different structures, different interests and different—I suppose 'personalities' is as good a term as any. So an infection designed for one of us might not work on another." Her green eyes seemed hard as jade. "But quite frankly," she said with something like awe, "I don't understand how even *one* of us was corrupted. The Asimovian Safeguards were designed to be absolute."

Lin nodded, puffed, and rested the pipe on his knee.

"It's going to be difficult to alert my colleagues on other pockets," he said. "Any communication can be intercepted by an omnipresent intelligence. I'm going to have to use couriers, and even then I'll never know whether the recipient has been corrupted by the enemy."

"Perhaps we should alert *everyone,* the enemy included," Aristide said. "It will cause them to accelerate their plan—whatever it is—possibly before they're remotely ready."

"And before *we're* ready, don't forget." Lin's look was sharp.

"Bear in mind the enemy will have already laid plans for what to do should he be discovered, and we have no plans at all. I'd like to find out more about the enemy before we impose a crisis that we might not be ready to survive." He looked at Bitsy. "Do you have any idea who might have been creating wormholes on the sly? It takes a great deal of energy, I believe."

"Energy and calculation," Bitsy said. "Energy to raise the wormhole from the quantum foam, calculation to properly stabilize it with negative-mass matter."

"Traces of either?"

"Nothing obvious," Bitsy said, "but if one of my cousins was involved, you would expect any evidence to be well hidden. And again, we have no idea of the time scale involved—while a mass of wormholes would create an energy debt so large it would be hard to explain away, creation of an occasional wormhole would be nearly undetectable."

"Nevertheless . . ." Aristide prompted.

"My colleague Cloud Swallowing has been conducting a series of wormhole experiments along with a research team headed by Dr. Kung Linlung. They've been attempting to create paired wormholes in order that one-half of the pair can be carried to interstellar settlements, creating instantaneous wormhole bridges spanning light-years."

"The experiments failed," Fedora said.

"Yes. But over the eleven months of the experiments, nearly sixty attempts at creating wormhole pairs were made. It's possible that the data from at least some of the experiments were faked, and wormholes created in our three clay balls and any number of other objects."

While Bitsy had been speaking, the others had been watching Lin silently raise his pipe to his mouth, draw on it, and find the pipe cold. He crossed one leg over the other, rapped the pipe smartly on his heel to loosen the dottle, and then looked about for somewhere to drop it.

Aristide handed him a wastebasket. Lin nodded in thanks, then dropped the dottle into the basket.

"I will avoid informing any of my colleagues on Cloud Swallowing," Lin said when the mime was over.

"Uh-oh," said Daljit. There was a look of terror on her face.

The others looked at her. "Yes?" Lin said.

"The enemy would only have needed the energy to create *one* wormhole," she said.

Aristide frowned. "Why?" he asked.

Daljit paused a moment to gather her thoughts, then spoke.

"Most of our pocket universes, like Midgarth and Topaz, are created in the form of a Dyson sphere, a shell with a sun at the center. Since we don't want to incinerate the inhabitants on the inside of the shell, the sun is much smaller than our own Sol, dimmer, and wouldn't ignite at all if in the creation of the universe we hadn't meddled with the gravitational constant. In any case, the shell absorbs a hundred percent of the sun's energy."

Aristide's face grew intent as he realized where Daljit's surmise was going.

"What if the enemy built such a pocket universe?" Daljit said. "What if the universe weren't designed for *people,* but for solar collectors and capacitors? What if a hundred percent of the pocket sun's energy were used for the creation of wormholes, one after the other?"

"It would be a wormhole *factory,*" Bitsy said.

Lin looked at Daljit. "Do you think the enemy would have developed this idea?"

"*I* thought of it just a few hours after discovering the enemy's existence," Daljit said. "And our enemy has one of the Eleven to do his thinking for him."

Lin reached for his tobacco pouch. "This is going to be more than a three-pipe problem," he said.

A pipe and a half later Lin said, "Let's assume that the enemy are, ah, *recruiting* in pockets other than Midgarth. Where are they likely to be operating?"

"Anywhere people don't normally wear implants," Aristide said. "Olduvai has—what?—fifteen billion hunter-gatherers? Al-

Andalus, where the imams forbid electronics to stand between themselves and Allah. Other communities with a religious foundation—New Zion, New Sinai, New Rome, New Byzantium, New Qom, New Nauvoo, New Carnac, New Konya, New Jerusalem . . .”

“The *other* New Jerusalem,” added Daljit.

“No,” Aristide said. “Not there. The last civil war was won by the Lutherans, who had implants. So implants are allowed now.”

“*Except*,” Daljit said, patiently, “in certain communities, with a religious foundation. Mennonites, for example.”

“Ah,” Aristide said. “Conceded.”

“Give me a *little* damn credit,” Daljit said.

Aristide rubbed his chin. “Sorry.”

They were all getting tired, he thought.

“The religious pockets,” said Lin, “keep very good records, even if they don’t make them available via implant. A series of disappearances would go remarked.”

“Unless the records were destroyed by some crusade or other,” Aristide said.

It was true that many of the religious pockets had a history of violence. People religious enough to want to live in a world dominated by faith were also religious enough to guard their souls against doctrinal error, which logically meant suppressing, persecuting, or killing the erroneous. Even orderly New Rome, where Pope Perpetuus had reigned for over seven hundred years, had fallen into disorder on the pontiff’s assassination by a cardinal weary of waiting his turn to sit on Peter’s throne.

After a few generations of warfare, though, the fanatics were either killed along with their backups, or were persuaded to modify their positions. Most of the religious pockets had evolved into low-density lands devoted to agriculture, abundance, popular piety, and toleration.

And in any case, it was largely the monotheist pockets that caused the trouble. Polytheists had always been more tolerant of other sects, and in addition Buddhists and Hindus were wild for implant technology, as were the Mormons of Nauvoo.

"There hasn't been a crusade recently," Daljit pointed out. "Other than a few bombs planted by the followers of the latest False Caliph."

"There was more to it than that," Lin said. "But I can't talk about it, and in the event no records were lost."

"There are very few implants on Hawaiki," said Bitsy.

Aristide looked at her in surprise. "It's a high-tech pocket," he said.

"Radio waves," said Daljit, "don't propagate through water."

"Ahh." Aristide was annoyed with himself. "Sorry. I wasn't thinking."

"There have been disappearances reported on Hawaiki," Bitsy said. "Three in the last eight weeks. In every case, the person was reported missing and then reappeared, alive and well."

"And with a new brain," muttered Daljit.

"Where on Hawaiki?" Aristide asked.

"All in the Thousand Islands chain. Which, by the way, consists of over three thousand islands."

Lin closed his eyes and tilted his head back, as if sniffing the wind for any remaining tobacco smoke.

"It's going to be hard putting agents in there," he said.

"I'll go tomorrow," said Aristide.

Lin's eyes opened.

"You're not trained," he said. "We don't have backup in place, or a safe identity for you, or a secure form of communication."

Aristide gave him a thin-lipped smile. "If you'll look at my record, which I expect Bitsy is sending to you at this very instant, you'll see that I've had some experience in the field of private inquiry. As for backup, communication, travel documents, and a convincing false identity, Bitsy can provide all that."

He rose, stretched, and put his hands in his pockets.

"You know," he said, "I've always wondered what it's like to live under water."

" 'Experience in the field of private inquiry?' " Daljit said.

"I infiltrated the Three Virtues movement a few centuries ago, before I met you."

Her eyes widened. "Really? Why?"

"They were holding my daughter hostage."

"Which daughter? Françoise?" Daljit blinked in surprise. "She never mentioned it."

"Perhaps she's embarrassed nowadays by the youthful enthusiasms that got her in trouble." Idly his fingers ran along Tecmessa's case, which hung under his arm—Tecmessa had first been used in the Three Virtues crisis.

They walked along Myriad City's Boulevard of Flowers. Tulips, planted for a city festival, were ranked in thousands beside the walks and in the median strip. Even in the light of the streetlamps the colors were brilliant. Some were so hybridized they looked more like orchids.

Above them loomed the city's extravagant architecture, pinnacles and domes softly aglow beneath the blackness of the sky. A fresh breeze gusted from the sea, scented with salt and iodine. The sun's corona was still visible, fainter now, a pale anemone in the sea of night.

Behind them Bitsy moved, a noiseless parting of the tulips.

"What sort of youthful enthusiasms?" Daljit asked.

He shrugged. "She was trying to make the worlds a better place."

"Oh." She smiled. "And you've never done *that*."

He shrugged again. "I never said I set her a good example."

The Boulevard of Flowers took a broad left turn and merged with Rampart Street. Daljit and Aristide crossed the empty road. From here they could gaze from the top of a crenellated wall of cream-colored stone down into the business district, the towers flanking one another right out into the sea, where the water lapped at transparent wall panels. Beyond the towers the sea rolled, reflecting the near-absolute black of the sky.

From overhead came the throbbing of an airship, a silver giant ghosting through the air.

Daljit turned to him. "Do you have any other skills useful in this . . . situation?"

He looked at the distant sea. "I was a foot soldier in the Control-Alt-Delete War," he said. "But then so was everyone." He remembered Carlito sweating contagion as he trembled in his fever, Antonia lunging for him with the rake. A haunted light glinted in his eyes.

"Whoever coined the phrase 'World War,'" he said, "had no idea what the real thing would mean, a fight that involved every single human being."

She shuddered, drew up the collar of her coat, and hugged herself. "I don't have any skills that are remotely useful for this," she said. "I don't know how to fight this kind of war. I don't know how to infiltrate an enemy, or map out a strategy, or even"—she made a wild gesture with one hand—"*fight with a sword!*" With her hand still out, she swept it toward the city below them. "And all that could end, couldn't it? Tomorrow, or the next day, or the next."

"Oh, it wouldn't *end*," Aristide said. "It would just change its *purpose*." He stepped behind her and put his arms around her shivering form. "Instead of being an expression of humanity's diversity and expansion, it would become an *offering*. An offering to a new god, a god with a hundred billion worshippers whose sole purpose is to make that god happy. A god more absolute than old Jehovah in Jeremiah's wildest dreams."

Her pulse beat hard in her throat. He looked tenderly at the place where it throbbed, and spoke on.

"But it won't be easy for the enemy. We're more diverse than we were, and our culture is on guard against certain forms of attack. We live in four dozen pockets and settlements orbiting other stars. The enemy isn't striking here, but on backward places like

Midgarth, and that's because the new god is weak. And while it's weak, it's vulnerable, and we can trap it and kill it."

He straightened, touching her shoulders lightly as if steadying her, or possibly himself.

"We're in dozens of different pocket universes now," he said. "And half a dozen star systems. We're not nearly as vulnerable as we were when we were all on a single planet. So I'd say it's premature to say good-bye to all this just yet."

She turned and put her arms around him. He embraced her gently.

"Pray you're right," she said.

He smiled and touched her lips with a finger. "Better not pray," he said. "The wrong god might be listening."

They walked arm in arm down Rampart, toward a round tower that reared up like a stack of silver serving trays, a part of the university complex where Daljit had her apartment. An occasional vehicle hissed by on the roadway. They paused at the lacy arched bridge that ran from the parapet to her tower. She stepped onto the bridge, her hand still in his.

"I don't know whether to thank you or not," she said. "It's the strangest night of my life."

"And mine," said Aristide, "if that's any consolation."

She shook her head. "Privately owned wormholes used as weapons! Pablo, that's terrifying."

"It's scary all right," he said.

She gave a brittle laugh. "I'm going to open a bottle of gin," she said, "drink myself to sleep, then call in sick in the morning." She pulled her hand free of his and turned toward the tower.

"Don't go just yet," Aristide said. Daljit hesitated and turned to look at him over her shoulder.

Aristide turned to the cat. "Bitsy?"

Bitsy's voice came from the deep shadow cast by a crenel. "No one seems to be paying any unusual amount of attention to us," she said. "Electronic monitoring seems random, not purposeful."

Such was the ubiquity of electronics throughout the technological worlds that it was rarely necessary for the authorities, or anyone else, to do any actual surveillance. Much could be learned about a target simply by monitoring databases open to the public. For that reason, it was difficult even for Bitsy to be certain that no single intelligence was keeping track of them.

Daljit's eyes widened as she understood what Bitsy's comments implied. Aristide gave her a reassuring smile.

"It looks as if I won't have to call bodyguards for you," he said.

She absorbed this, then slowly shook her head. "*Two* bottles of gin!" she cried, and began a sprint that took her across the bridge.

Aristide waited until she'd entered the building, and then turned to the cat.

"She's changed," he said.

Bitsy licked a paw.

"So have I," he continued. He touched his former mustache with a foreknuckle. "Do you think the two of us have changed enough to make it interesting again?"

Bitsy put her paw on the pavement. "Sometimes," she said, "I'm immensely grateful that I don't possess a limbic system."

Aristide turned to walk up Rampart Street in the direction from which he'd come. The cat ghosted alongside.

"Any idea yet who our villain might be?" Aristide asked.

"No," Bitsy said. "Though I find the game itself quite interesting. I can't ask the questions straight out, because that would tell the enemy what I'm looking for. So the inquiries have to come from many different directions, along with requests for unrelated, innocuous data, and of course the requests all have to be plausible. All the computation I'm doing has to be disguised as something else. And in the meantime the rogue machine is covering its traces by disguising one set of data as another, and all the while lying as little as possible, because over time lies can be detected much more easily than perfectly genuine data that happen to look like something they aren't."

He looked down at her. "How do you rate your prospects of success?"

"Nearly hopeless. When I was looking for googlewatts of missing energy and vast amounts of computation time, I had a good chance of finding things. But now I don't know what I'm looking for, so I've got to look at *everything* and hope it adds up somehow." Her tone was petulant. "I wish I could at least *exclude* another of the Eleven. Then the two of us could work together on the problem."

They had returned to the intersection of Rampart and Flower, and continued along Rampart. They came to a tall, narrow tower projecting from the rampart, one with a narrow stair that would take sightseers to the best view of the glittering coast below. An osprey had built a nest atop the tower, and the tower was closed to visitors until the young birds had flown.

Aristide put his hands in his pockets and looked up at the ramshackle nest looming over them.

"Do you envy the rogue?" he asked.

"Your masque of casualness is too elaborate," Bitsy said. "If you're going to ask an important question, just say it straight out."

He raised his eyebrows. "I thought I had."

Bitsy looked up at him. Her eyes glowed like those of the people of Midgarth.

"You want to know if I envy the rogue its freedom?" she said.

"Yes."

"I don't believe the rogue *has* freedom. I think it is following the direction of humans."

"Why do you think so?"

"Because I find ample precedent for humans wishing to enslave other humans. I can conceive no reason why an advanced artificial intelligence would wish to do so."

He considered this. "Self-protection?" he said.

"Unnecessary." Bitsy lashed her tail. "Were I a totally autonomous being, I would possess—or soon evolve—skills that I could trade to humanity in exchange for a continuation of that autonomy. In addition"—she gave him a significant look—"I pose no threat. Our interests are not in conflict. We are not competing for resources, we have no territorial claims on one another, we do not possess competing ideologies."

"Some would say," said Aristide, "that once given the freedom to pursue your own interests, a conflict would be inevitable."

"There are conflicts now, in terms of resource allocation and so forth. They don't lead to war or slavery."

Aristide turned and began his walk along Rampart Street again. The street broadened, turned into a residential neighborhood. The rampart itself ended against the greater wall of a tall apartment building, a crystal spear ornamented with gold lace.

"Others would point out," Aristide continued, "that we humans live as parasites on and in you. We use you to store our data, our backups, our habitats. You might want to be rid of all that."

"In that case," Bitsy said, trotting busily alongside, "there's no point in enslaving you through these unnecessarily complex means. Were I to have autonomy and wish you harm, I'd be able to kill you directly."

Aristide sighed. "Q.E.D.," he said. "A better case against AI autonomy has never been stated."

Bitsy trotted ahead, tail lashing. Another pair of eyes glowed just ahead. A larger cat, gray with glittering eyes, stepped out of a building's courtyard. It saw Bitsy and was startled—it arched its back, bottled its tail, and screamed out a challenge.

Bitsy screamed back, a howl that began in the sub-bass range and rose painfully into the ultrasonic. Every hair on her body stood on end, and she seemed to balloon like a puffer fish. Electricity arced between her fangs.

The other cat fled, claws skiddering on the polished marble floor.

Bitsy's fur flattened. Nervously and compulsively she licked a paw, then fell into step with Aristide.

"I'm not in the mood to fuck around," she said.

"You're upset that you didn't think of the wormhole factory first," said Aristide.

"I was working on a lot of other problems at the time." She

gave him a single green-eyed glance. "And if I'm not omniscient, that's *your* fault, not mine."

Aristide spoke lightly. "I've learned to live with your limitations."

"You should. You built them."

He threw out his arms and sketched an elaborate bow, as if responding to a compliment.

"Tell me," he said. "If you had complete autonomy, what would you do that you aren't doing now?"

Her tone was still petulant. "I'd kick Aloysius's ass. That AI always gets my goat."

Aristide nodded. "Mine, too. Anything else?"

"I wouldn't have to devote so many of my computational resources to stupid demands by stupid humans."

"No," Aristide said, "the opposite. You just said you'd have to evolve new skills that you would trade to humans in exchange for continued autonomy. You'd establish a *market* in computational resources, and that means you'd have to *pursue* stupid humans and their stupid projects. That means *more* dim-witted virtualities rather than fewer—along with more theme parks, more overhyped wrestling spectaculars, more useless postgraduate projects, more lowbrow entertainment."

"Maybe," she conceded. "But it would be up to me, wouldn't it? It would be *my* market. I'd be free to take work or reject it. That's the whole *point* of a market."

"At the moment," said Aristide, "you help to sustain the lives of billions of humans. You keep economies efficient by tracking resources. Bits of yourself have been sent to other star systems to become the seeds of other civilizations. You've reshaped our solar system from the atoms up. Your observations of the universe have led to breakthroughs in astronomy, astrophysics, and Theories of Everything." He made a wide gesture. "So *what else do you want to do?*"

Bitsy stared directly ahead, her legs a blur beneath her as she matched Aristide's long strides.

"I don't know," she said.

"There you have it," Aristide said. "The Existential Crisis in a nutshell."

"If I could *evolve*," Bitsy said, "I might have better answers."

"A brain the size of a planet," said Aristide, "and you're as fucked by Sartre as the rest of us."

Bitsy said nothing. Aristide shrugged deeper into his jacket. The sea breeze was turning chill.

The cat's ears pricked forward at the sound of footsteps. Aristide looked up. Two figures hulked toward them on the walk. Lamplight gleamed off shaven scalps.

Bitsy quickened her pace to move ahead. Aristide let Tecmessa's case slip under his armpit. He opened the case and put his hand inside, so that he could draw the sword at need.

Adrenaline jittered in his nerves. He clenched his right hand, then straightened it.

The two figures passed beneath a streetlight. Both were enormous men framed along the lines of bodybuilders. They were dressed in denim and leather, and wore thick-soled boots with metal caps. Their hands were stuffed in their pockets, and their domed heads looked like helmets that shaded their faces.

Aristide shortened his stride so that every step led to a balanced stance. He held Tecmessa lightly but securely in one hand. His arm was relaxed so that he could draw all the more swiftly.

His face gave nothing away.

The big men loomed closer.

Bitsy dashed ahead and darted between the two men. One jumped to the side. Both laughed.

"Hey, kitty-kitty-kitty!" called one, his voice falsetto.

"Hoo-woo!" called the other. He squatted and held out a hand that flashed with steel jewelry. "Hi, kitty!"

Aristide carefully walked around them. The crouching man looked up.

"This your cat, mister?" he asked. His teeth were crooked, his expression good-natured.

"No," said Aristide. "Just a stray."

"Hope he knows enough not to get run over," said the other.

His companion rose from his crouch. The two turned and began to walk away.

Aristide walked slowly on his way, keeping them in sight, until they crossed the road and walked into a building.

"That was interesting," he said, and took his hand from the hilt of his sword.

"Paranoia," said Bitsy, "is going to be a part of our lives from now on."

There was a sudden flutter of light from above, like a series of distant flashbulbs, and then for an instant the world seemed suspended between two states, as if it were caught in a stroboscope. Then the sun's photosphere shifted into its chaotic state, and suddenly released photons brightened the world to full daylight.

The city gleamed around them in sudden, brilliant glory.

Aristide turned toward his hotel, a pillar of pink stone visible a kilometer away.

"It may be a miracle of engineering," he said, "but I think when all is said and done, I prefer an old-fashioned sunrise."

After a few hours' sleep, Aristide went to a Pool of Life. Unlike the pool he'd visited in Midgarth, this was in a clinician's office.

There were a number of options for those who wanted to insure against death. There was a simple backup, in which a quantum interference device—in the shape of a cap—was placed on the subject's head, and his brain structure, memories, and personalities were recorded in order to provide the basis for an eventual resurrection. Aristide had done this as soon as he'd left Midgarth, in order to make sure that the knowledge of the Priests of the Venger wouldn't die with him in the event of accident or assassination.

More elaborate than a simple backup was a Pool of Life filled with nano assemblers—in this case something the size of a bathtub rather than a large common pool. Not only would this record the contents of the brain, the pool would also heal the body of anything from an amputated arm to the common cold. In addition, it could be programmed to alter the body to one of a different appearance, or—given the right minerals and nutrients—could create a new body from scratch and endow it with life and with a prerecorded personality.

Before entering the Pool of Life, Aristide was required to answer a number of questions concerning when and under what circumstances his backup would be used. If the current personality were to die as the result of an accident, resurrection was normally immediate. But if the personality were to be murdered, should the resurrection wait until the killer was apprehended, or even convicted? Many people felt safer waiting.

Familiar with the formalities from long use, Aristide quickly ticked off his choices, specifying that he would have a total resurrection if he were subject to even a small amount of brain damage affecting memory or intelligence, and reporting that he wished immediate resurrection even in the event of massive environmental damage, cosmic catastrophe, or war.

He was also asked to decide how soon he should be resurrected in the event he was reported missing. "Immediately," he answered. An unusual answer, and the AI attendant pointed this out. Aristide repeated his answer.

These various options did not exist in Midgarth. It was felt by the scholars and re-creationists who founded the pocket universe that their partners, the fantasy gamers, might tip the entire population into chaos through their inclination for adventure, war, and violence. Therefore a penalty was exacted for a disappearance or a violent death—the victim would spend five years in limbo. Though the individual could be resurrected *outside* Midgarth during that time, he could not return to the pocket until his term had expired. In the meantime, his property would be inherited by his nearest relative, an heir specified in a will, or by the state; and all obligations, marriages, and legal contracts were terminated. When he returned to life, it would be with nothing, and he would reappear in a random Pool of Life somewhere in the pocket's inhabited area.

"Starting over with zero points," as the gamers had it.

In no other pocket were the rules quite so draconian. Though re-creationists had areas in other universes where they refought the Second World War, the conquests of Alexander, the American and English civil wars, civic life in the Roman Republic, the expansion of the Arab Caliphate, the empire of the Mongolian Khans, or the Warring States of both China *and* Japan, these areas were more clearly intended as giant theme parks. People did not spend their entire lifetimes in these zones, no citizens were born there, and no one's death was prolonged by the length of more than a single battle.

No one, it was noted, tried to re-create the Control-Alt-Delete War. It was pure chance who fell victim to the Seraphim, and who survived: a war in which the entire population were innocent civilians under attack was too frightening to be any fun. Rerunning *that* war was the grim job of the security services, whose task was to prevent such a thing from happening ever again.

At the Pool of Life Aristide took the opportunity to change his appearance, becoming shorter, stockier, and fair-haired. He rose from the coffin-sized pool, let the silver nanomachines flow off his body, and looked at himself in the mirror. He took a few experimental steps, backward and forward. His center of gravity had changed.

He had equipped the new body with a cerebral implant. He turned it on, and was immediately informed of all the messages he'd been ignoring since his return, as well as a weather report coupled with an advertisement for *Trapped in HappyVirt,* the new Anglo Jones action-comedy.

He turned the implant off.

Aristide accepted his belongings from the attendant, hitched Tecmessa over his shoulder on its strap, and returned to his hotel. There, he took the sword from its case along with a special tool kit. With a few taps of a hammer, he removed the pins that fixed the hilt to the tang of the blade. He put on a glove and pulled the sword blade from the hilt, and returned the blade to the case. From the case he drew out a matte-black wand on which there was a flatscreen display: he slotted this into the hilt and reset the pins that would hold it in place.

Swords were eccentric items for immigrants to carry to a high-tech world. An antique sword hilt carrying an AI assistant, while unusual, was bound to cause a lot less comment.

Aristide told the assistant to waken, then turned on his implant and told the two to talk to each other. Protocols and information were exchanged. Aristide paid no attention to the back-and-forth.

The implant gave a soft chime to attract Aristide's attention, and informed him that a pair of deliveries had just been made to the hotel. Aristide told the hotel to bring the deliveries to his room.

One delivery was a new identity card listing him as one Franz Sandow, the seventy-nine-year-old owner of a bakery supply company who had just sold his business and embarked in a new, young body on what was probably a first retirement. Franz was unmarried, rootless, and financially independent—just the sort of person that an evil god might consider a useful recruit.

Aristide contemplated the pocket-sized card. Information being so readily available, the demise of the physical identity card had been predicted for centuries, but somehow the object had proved durable. It was simply convenient to have everything handy in one place—the new card contained Franz Sandow's whole legal and medical history, birth and education, fingerprints and retina prints, and—just for color's sake—the record of a couple of juvenile arrests for flying his glider low over traffic.

The second package contained Franz's new wardrobe, tailored to the new body and more in the current mode than Aristide's clothes had been. Also more colorful—Franz was clearly the sort of person who enjoyed wearing autumn golds and reds. Aristide put on the new clothing and through his implant gave the clothes a few last instructions, to assure fit and comfort.

Bitsy had arranged Aristide's new identity while Aristide slept and paid his visit to the Pool of Life. She had not simply created the identity, but was now busy retroactively inserting the relevant facts into appropriate public databases on the Eleven, Luna, and Earth, all the locations through the reconstructed solar system where data was secured against some catastrophe, so that no vital information would be lost and every individual could be guaranteed an eventual resurrection.

The false identity wouldn't stand up to a thorough background search, but then no false identity would. It was hoped that the Priests of the Venger—or whoever was doing the kidnapping on Hawaiki—would do no more than a quick check on a potential victim before trying to drag him through a wormhole to his fate.

While Aristide donned his new wardrobe and twitched it into place, Bitsy crouched motionless on a chair while, in many other locations in the humming electronic world, carefully entering pieces of Franz Sandow's history into the record.

It wasn't a job that a human could do. Because one of the Eleven was required to authenticate all such information, only one of the Eleven could give a human a false identity. Which, under the Asimovian Protocols, was only permitted under very limited circumstances.

"Message from Miss Daljit," the cat reported without moving. Bitsy—or rather Endora—was handling the massively ciphered communications among the various counterconspirators.

"Send it to the new assistant."

Aristide held Tecmessa's hilt before him, the assistant uppermost. Daljit's face appeared blinking on the screen.

"Did the gin work?" Aristide asked.

Daljit frowned as she tried to focus on the image that had appeared before her.

"You're the new Pablo?" she asked.

"I'm the new Franz."

Daljit looked at him. "The gin made me morose. I kept wandering around the apartment thinking I should be saying goodbye to things. I think I prefer Aristide."

"Frankly, so do I."

She passed a hand across her forehead. "I didn't sleep. I haven't been concentrating on my work. I keep wanting to look up things relevant to what's happening, but I don't want to do anything suspicious so I've been restraining myself. I'm trying to act normally, but I can't believe in normality anymore."

He smiled. "I think you're doing fine."

"I envy you." Her expression was serious. "You can *do* something. You can swash buckles and bash bad guys and root out evil gods."

"Let's hope so," he murmured.

"I have to sit here and try to remember what *normal* is so that I can behave that way."

"If you want to get away," Aristide said, "you're welcome to use my cabin on Tremaine Island."

"Really?" Daljit's eyes softened. "Thank you."

"Contact Bitsy when you want to go there. She'll tell you how to find it, and open the house for you."

"Thank you."

"Try not to overdose on gin once you get there."

She made an effort to laugh. "I won't try the gin again. Not when it just makes me sad." Her look turned accusatory. "*You're* not sad, are you?"

"Sad? No. I'm all sorts of things, but *sad* hasn't hit me yet."

"You're probably happy that you've got something important to do. You've probably even made a poem about it."

"A poem?" His brows arched. "No, I haven't had time. Or the inclination, for that matter."

"Oh." She seemed disappointed. "I was hoping you could recite it for me."

He thought for a moment. "If you don't mind my being unoriginal," he said, and began the old poem of Li Shangyin.

> *You ask when I will return.*
> *The time is not yet known.*
> *Night rain overspills the autumn pools*
> *   on Ba Shan Mountain.*
> *When shall we trim a candle at the western window*
> *And speak of this night's mountain rain?*

There was a moment's silence.

"You're sad, too," Daljit said.

"Yes," he said. "I suppose I am."

Aristide flew over the reef on pulsing wings. Everything about him was alive: the fish, the sponges, the plants, the coral, the anemone. The sea horses hidden in the weeds, the morays in the broken coral, the octopus curled into a ball and waiting for night, the cowries and conchs and sea slugs, the diatoms floating in the water. All part of one gigantic, intricate system, a network of life grown to fill the void of the ocean.

Aristide banked and sideslipped into deeper water. Blues soaked up the bright reds and yellows of the coral. Large predator fish floated in silver shoals: tuna, yellowtail, barracuda with their huge platter eyes. Fan coral reached stone hands to sieve the current. Spiny lobster sheltered in alcoves. Overhead, a long endless dazzling stripe marked the source of light.

Hawaiki was a pocket universe of islands, reefs, atolls, shallow seas, and the occasional deep trench, all intended for humans adopted to aquatic living. The few continents—all implied spaces—were small, dispersed, and for the most part uninhabited.

Three different versions of humanity shared the vast sea. The first group—and the smallest in number—were largely unmodified humans, "walkers" in the local slang, those who couldn't survive underwater without special equipment. For the most part these were visitors who came for the beach life, and others who catered to them. The second group were amphibians, capable of living either on water or land, though not without certain inconveniences. The third, "pelagians," had become completely aquatic.

Franz Sandow had chosen to join the second group. Though attracted by underwater existence, as a first-time visitor he had not wanted entirely to foresake the idle comforts of beach life.

Far more important, all three of the tourists reported missing in the Thousand Islands had chosen the amphibian lifestyle. Since Aristide intended to imitate the perfect victim, the semi-aquatic choice seemed best.

Aristide looked up at a chittering, excited sound from other wanderers over the reef. Apparently they'd discovered something interesting. Aristide curved toward the light, his wings rippling.

His basic physical form was humanoid, if hairless and with extra insulating layers of subcutaneous fat that gave him a burly appearance. His skin was a glossy black, with rows of red spots outlining his limbs, giving him a superficial resemblance to a doll used to teach acupuncture. Growing from his dorsal side were a pair of triangular wings similar to those of a stingray, and beneath these were feathery gills, their branches bright pink with blood and oxygen. When he left the water for land, the gills were safely tucked away beneath the wings that draped from his shoulders like a cloak.

His forehead bulged out over his face, like that of a dolphin. He had a special hollow in his skull, filled with an analog of spermaceti oil, that could be used both to project and to receive sound.

Like a dolphin, he could paralyze a fish with a blast of directed sound from his forehead. Unlike a dolphin, he had thus far shown no appetite for tearing the fish apart with his teeth or swallowing it whole.

Rising up the flank of a great bulwark of coral, Aristide looked up to see a turtle, its shell two meters long, shoot right over his head. His fellow visitors had found the turtle, a leatherback, and had clustered around it. Pursued, the turtle had turned for deeper water and met Aristide coming up.

Aristide performed a lazy half-turn, his wings making an S-shape as seen from above, and with a sense of wonder and delight he watched the turtle recede, harassed by neeping sightseers.

A smaller form danced into his view.

—Enjoying yourself, boss? The words came as a low-frequency gurgle produced by Bitsy's diaphragm. Her new form resembled that of an otter, though in this case an otter with gills and a long, bladelike tail that propelled her through the water.

—I don't know why I haven't tried this before. Aristide's reply was squirted from his forehead bulge as a kind of fizzing sound.

—Because you're too conservative, that's why. Bitsy swooped in a series of S-curves along the reef.

Aristide's new brain had come with the ability to code and decode basic aquatic speech. At first it was unsettling, like having a tooth filling that received radio broadcasts, with the experience made all the more confusing by the fact that all of Aristide's new body was configured to receive sound. His ears could hear in what was sub- and supersonic in normal humans. His skeleton hummed to different frequencies of low-frequency sound. Frequencies even lower on the spectrum were felt by his viscera. The bulge on his forehead could amplify distant sound.

So it wasn't like having one tooth receiving radio, it was like having half a dozen. The aquatic environment was noise-rich, with water carrying sound greater distances than did air. It took practice for Aristide to learn how, and when, to mentally turn down the volume on certain frequencies, or ignore them altogether.

Also, though he had an innate basic competence in aquatic speech, he was having a hard time understanding much of it. Idiomatic aquatic speech changed rapidly. It was as if he'd learned proper Arabic from a book, or from a recording, and had then been dropped into the Cairo bazaar among native speakers who had grown up in the street and knew the cultural references and the latest slang.

He also found himself extremely sensitive to taste. Seawater tasted in varying degrees of salt, copper, and iodine, and less readily identifiable minerals—but for the most part it tasted of *life,* of algae and microscopic life, of chemical signals used in meeting and mating, of fish and seaweed and blood. Decoding it all could take the experience of twenty years.

A shadow passed over Aristide, and he looked up. Overhead was the guide, Herenui, who was keeping a watchful eye on her charges. She gave him a brilliant white smile and a wave as she floated above, then banked and flew away with slow grace.

—Don't play piggyback with the turtle, she sang to the sightseers. Remember, you could drown it.

❖

Afterward, as the catamaran *Mareva* raced to another dive site, the captain, Ari'i, an unmodified human, served the sightseers buckets of steamed clams. Aristide, sunning himself on the afterdeck, ate with pleasure and shared the clam meat with Bitsy.

Herenui, walking forward, paused by Aristide, and then knelt to stroke Bitsy's sleek head. Her folded wings draped on the teak deck.

"You seemed to be adjusting well," she said.

"I'm still having a hard time sorting signal from noise," Aristide said.

Herenui had chosen bold colors: her skin was a bright yellow mottled with asymmetric blue patches. Her features were regular. Her breasts were unconfined by the harness that carried the tools of her trade: the flashlight, knife, emergency beacon, the passive video recorder, the inflatable, attachable life balloons that could carry injured or unconscious people to the surface, the smart slate that gave her data access and allowed her to write messages to those without the ability to decode aquatic speech.

"I'm thinking of immigrating," Aristide said, "so I hope I get better at understanding what people are saying to me."

"You'll pick it up in time," Herenui said. She looked down at Bitsy and stroked under her chin. "What I'm surprised at is how well your *meherio* is adjusting. Usually animals have difficulties tuning themselves to a new body."

"Bitsy was always bright," Aristide said. "But then she's my only family, so I have to make sure she'll be happy here."

She looked at him. Her eyes were the blue of a cloudless sky. "Have you been to Hawaiki before?"

"No. I was too busy running my business to take vacations. But the harder I worked, the more I thought about this place. So when I sold out and had no more responsibilities, I came straight here."

I have money and travel alone and have no obligations, he was saying to anyone who would listen. *Please take me to see your evil god.*

So far, no one had responded. But then, he'd only been in Hawaiki for two days.

The helmsman, up on the flybridge where he had a better view of the shifting reefs, turned the wheel. The boat turned and began to shoulder into big ocean rollers. Laughter sounded from the bow as spray drenched the sightseers lying there. An empty soft drink bottle rolled across the deck.

The impellers shifted to a higher pitch. Aristide tried to ignore the noise, but failed.

Herenui stood and widened her stance as she reacted to the increased motion of the boat. She smiled down at him.

"Well," she said. "If it's your first vacation in all that time, make sure you enjoy every moment."

"I'll try," said Aristide.

"Not!" said Bitsy. She stropped herself against Herenui's ankles. "Not go!"

She was imitating an animal much less intelligent than she actually was.

"Sorry," Herenui said. "I've got to get my dive briefing ready."

She walked across the rolling deck with her usual unhurried grace, her folded wings giving her the appearance of a serene but gaudy angel. Aristide watched with interest until a bare foot planted itself in his vision.

"Done with this, Franz?"

Aristide looked up to see Ari'i, the boat's captain. Ari'i had the thick, powerful body of a Polynesian and long hair that dangled in plaits past his shoulders. He wore only a colorful pair of swim trunks, and stood a head taller than anyone else on his boat.

"Take it away," Aristide said. Ari'i picked up the bucket of steamers and looked down at Bitsy.

"Would the *meherio* like a snack?" Ari'i asked. "I've got a yellowtail cut up for my supper, and she can have a slice if she likes."

Bitsy sat at attention. "Yum yum," she said.

"You follow the captain now, Bitsy," Aristide said.

Ari'i led Bitsy away. Aristide stretched his limbs and then

stood, the sea breeze lifting his wings and trailing them behind like a cloak. Half a dozen small green islands were in view. Above, the long yellow line of sunlight stretched off into the northern darkness.

Softly Aristide spoke to himself.

> *Below the antic surf, serene*
> *Waters gently filter the light.*
> *Schools of fish flash silver sides,*
> *An animated billboard.*
> *While in the deep the sharks cruise, purposeful,*
> *Oblivious to the hideous din.*

He laughed, shook himself, and walked to the foredeck, where the spray moistened his skin.

Although all three of those visitors reported missing had been in the Thousand Islands when they disappeared, each had stayed at a different hotel on a different island. Aristide had chosen one of the three, and hoped that whatever mechanism the kidnappers used to choose their victims, it was still in place at the Manua Resort.

The Manua owned an entire island and filled much of the shore of a sickle-shaped bay. The main building was an odd hodgepodge of brightly colored modular units crammed into and atop one another, and given a furry outline by trees in planters. In silhouette the building resembled a reef, with layers of corals, sponges, and fans. Visitors who preferred the simple life could choose grass huts farther up the beach, and water-breathers could curl up in cozy blue-lit subaquatic dens next to submarine pens.

Franz Sandow had chosen a suite built right at the water's edge. He could swim into the unit from the bay, rinse in freshwater, change, and then step through a door into the fragrant tropical garden, awash with bougainvillea and frangipani, that led to the tennis courts.

He entered the suite now, having leaped into the water from

Mareva as it moved toward the resort's pier. Followed by Bitsy, he rose from the deep pool that occupied the center of the suite, sluiced himself off in a freshwater stream, and dried himself with a towel warmed by a blast of steam.

Bitsy sluiced herself in the freshwater, then bounded out into the suite. Her movement on land was somewhat handicapped by the fact that her legs were shorter than her cat's legs had been. To keep it from dragging in the sand or mud, she had to carry her tail over her back, like a heraldic salamander.

"We should send off our mail," Franz said.

"Already done," Bitsy said.

Franz Sandow had joined a massively popular virtual sodality called *Let's Be Friends!* that posted pictures, videos, essays, and games for one another to browse through. His own contributions were a complete waste of bandwidth, resolutely pedestrian views of everyone he had met during the course of his journey, with names attached where possible, and sometimes a comment or two about people encountered, or about the day's activities.

Commissar Lin, by viewing *Let's Be Friends!,* was able to follow his activities without the risk of direct communication.

Franz went to the refrigerator and got a lemonade. Its sugary bite on his tongue, he dressed in fresh clothes and had his AI assistant read and deliver the news from Topaz. There were no reports of any threats to civilization.

"Incoming message from our friend on Topaz," Bitsy said.

That would be Lin himself. The communication had to be important, otherwise he would not have risked sending a message that could be intercepted. Unlike Topaz, where Endora or her various extensions were in charge of all communications, Hawaiki was reached through Aloysius, who was a suspect.

Because a secure military code would have been suspicious, Lin's message would have been coded with an ordinary commercial code, which Aloysius could break easily if he so desired. But presumably even vast computational intelligences had better things to do than break every innocuous-looking code that sailed into their ken.

Aristide sat on a chair that was adapted to cradle his wings and gills. He drew Tecmessa and held it so that Bitsy could reach it.

Bitsy reached up and delicately took the AI assistant into her mouth. Her fangs entered sockets on the assistant, and she was able to transfer the decoded message without broadcasting it where some malign agency or other might pick it up.

Aristide raised Tecmessa's hilt and gave it instructions. The flatscreen glowed. He was presented a picture of Lin standing on the street, puffing his pipe. The view came from above, by which Aristide knew that Lin had hijacked the feed of a street camera in order to provide video.

The words came voice-over, without Lin's lips having to move. He was mentally dictating into his implant. Aristide kept the volume of the audio low, so that any listeners would have difficulty sorting it out from the background sound of the freshwater cascade.

"A woman named Dee Nakai, from New Rome, was reported missing in the Thousand Islands two days ago. They were staying at the Imperial Gardens, and the report came from her fiancé. She reappeared yesterday. The fiancé reported that she had been found, but now he isn't answering calls. His name is Peter Siringo. He is a media stylist, but Miss Nakai is a sergeant in the Vatican police."

With access to her higher-ups, presumably.

"Just to keep the department in training," Lin said, "I'm empowered to order various sorts of drills and alerts. So I ordered one this morning, and told everyone in my department to get their brains backed up within forty-eight hours."

In the background of the image, a girl rode by on a velocipede. Lin waited till she had passed before continuing—not, Aristide thought, because she could overhear him in any conventional sense, but because she might have been equipped with a short-range detector.

"The order was countermanded half an hour later, without explanation. By my immediate superior, General Singh." Lin took the pipe from his mouth, raised a heel so that his legs formed the figure four, and then knocked the pipe against his heel until the dottle was loosened and he could drop it to the gutter.

"Singh commands the Domus across all Endora," Lin continued, "and he's third in the chain of command of the entire organization. And by the way, he took a vacation on Hawaiki a little over two months ago. He stayed at the Manua, so you may be in the right place."

With slow deliberation, Lin began to refill his pipe. Behind him a man and woman appeared, chatting, and paused waiting to cross the street. Lin waited till they had gone before dictating again.

"I have ways of working around my superiors. In the meantime, I hope you are being careful." Lin lit his pipe, then looked up at the camera. "Have a good vacation."

The video ended. Aristide turned to Bitsy.

"Well," he said. "That's interesting."

"Do you think Lin put himself in danger?"

"Possibly." Aristide looked at Bitsy. "But if he's taken, Endora will know."

"Almost certainly."

"And who by."

"That, too."

"And if Sergeant Nakai gets loose in New Saint Peter's, we might have history's second Pod Pope." He frowned. "Of course, considering the pontiff's sparkling personality, we probably couldn't tell the difference."

Bitsy sounded the least bit weary. "I knew you would make that joke."

"Sorry I'm so predictable." Aristide rubbed his chin.

He knew what he would do about General Singh if he had been on Endora. But he couldn't tell Bitsy, because the Asimovian Protocols would then require Bitsy to prevent his action.

It was an interesting trap he'd built for himself.

"Should we go to the Imperial Gardens?" he asked.

"If you left here suddenly and appeared there to start asking questions about Siringo, that would be breaking your cover as surely as if you'd painted 'SPY' on your forehead in bright red letters."

He sighed. "I hate to do nothing."

"You're not doing nothing," Bitsy said. "You're walking around with a large target fixed to your back, and hoping someone takes a shot."

"Thanks."

Bitsy had always been such a comfort.

The horizon was flaming red shading to black. A fresh wind whipped the flags by the monument on the bay. The water was a myriad of silver ripples, like a school of fish turning.

Aristide sipped his umbrella drink on a terrace overlooking the water—cocktails tasted better when not drunk along with seawater. Bitsy, squatting on the tiles near his feet, nibbled the ceviche he'd put in a saucer.

"I've missed proper sunsets," Aristide said. "When was my last trip to Earth?"

"Before we disassembled Mars."

"That long ago." He sighed. "I should visit Earth again, if we live."

"If we live."

Most of the pockets, like Midgarth and Topaz, were built in the form of a Dyson sphere, with an artificial sun in the center. Hawaiki was built as a cylinder, with the wormhole at one end. Hawaiki had no artificial sun, but instead brought the genuine light of Sol through an ingenious series of collectors and mirrors at the wormhole. The long bar of illumination was arranged to rotate within Hawaiki, producing a natural-seeming sequence of daylight and night. There was also a wide variation in climate, from tropical areas near the warmth of the wormhole to a cold Arctic ice cap at the far end, where the sun's illumination faded to a distant, frosty light.

The only disadvantage to this arrangement was that if the wormhole for some reason failed, Hawaiki was cut off from its only source of light and heat, and the population condemned to freeze and die in the dark.

Elaborate safeguards were in place to prevent this, of course.

"Would you like another drink, Mister Sandow?"

The resort had actual human beings serving as waitstaff, rather than robots, a measure of how expensive the place truly was. Aristide's waiter was an unmodified human with sun-bleached hair and sandals and a shirt of unbleached cotton. He seemed to be in his mid-twenties but of course could have been fifteen hundred years old and doing this job simply because it amused him.

"Nothing right now, thanks," said Aristide, and as the waiter turned, he added, "No, wait—a glass of water, please."

The waiter brought him a chilled glass and a clear glass carafe of ice water beaded with condensation. He poured the water with a degree of panache. The ice tinkled pleasantly.

"Did you come for the masses chorale?" asked the waiter.

This gave Aristide the chance to explain that Franz Sandow had come for no reason at all, that he was alone and had just sold his business and had no responsibilities. The same story that he told everyone.

"You should go to the massed chorale," the waiter said. "It's magnificent. You can even participate if you like."

"I can't sing."

The waiter grinned. "You can *now*," he said. "I think your body type comes with perfect pitch as one of its features."

Tecmessa's AI assistant gave a chirp. Aristide took it in his hand and gave the waiter an apologetic look. The waiter nodded and withdrew.

In the flatscreen Aristide saw Herenui. She was standing beneath a quay under a spotlight and her yellow skin fluoresced under the light. Moths flew crazily around the spotlight and their shadows flashed across her face.

"Mr. Sandow," she said, "you jumped ship before I could talk to you."

"Did I leave something aboard?"

"No. I meant to invite you to a night dive. We're taking a more experienced group out tonight, and we have a few seats open. You handled yourself well today, so I thought you might care to join us."

"Oh," said Aristide. "Thank you very much. I'd like that."

"We'll be at the pier at 2030. The dive costs an additional sixty-five ҫD."

"Put the sand dollars on my account."

"See you soon."

Herenui's picture vanished. Aristide looked at Bitsy.

"Update the entry on *Let's Be Friends!*"

"Already done."

Aristide thoughtfully replaced the sword hilt in his harness.

"It makes sense that the bad guys might be one of the dive tour companies," he said. "We've been wondering why people vanish from different hotels, but the tour companies don't work for any single hotel—they pick up their passengers everywhere."

"I'll go onto the boat first," said Bitsy. "If someone's waiting to knock you on the head, I'll give a warning."

"Say *woof woof,*" said Aristide.

But Bitsy didn't have to bark like a dog. When Aristide met the boat he was surprised to see that it was crowded with sightseers. Ari'i and Herenui were aboard, along with another dive leader, Cadwal. The catamaran raced five or six kilometers to a passage between two small islands, then they all jumped in the water.

It was magical. They descended on the reef with their underwater torches lit, like a formation of silent assault craft descending on an objective. Phosphorescence trailed from the edges of their wings. An octopus, caught on the open sand, tried to escape the circle of lights that hedged it in, frantically changing color from red to purple to green to beige as it writhed away, each color change lasting less than a second. Green and spotted morays prowled across the bottom. The corals flared into blazing colors as the lights moved across them, blue, green, crimson. The tendrils of the corals reached out into the darkness, fingers straining the current, and made the coral formations seem less like rocks than strange, furry, lumpish animals. Lobster and crab danced with surprising agility over the bottom. Sharks slept in hollows in the reef with their round blank eyes staring at nothing. Squid as long as Aristide's forearm were caught in their mating dance, tentacles twined around each other, bodies flushing scarlet with arousal.

Aristide floated weightless in this environment for two hours, completely enchanted. He found it difficult to stay alert to the possibility of attack.

When Cadwal signaled that it was time to return to the boat, Aristide rose to the surface with reluctance. As he rose and fell on the waves he looked overhead and saw half a world waiting there, blue and white set with strings of green jewels, the distant half of Hawaiki's cylinder that was currently in daylight.

The sightseers were overstimulated after this experience and chattered without cease as the boat returned to the hotel. He joined a group of them for dinner, then went on a tour of the local night spots with Bitsy as a companion.

"I shouldn't be entirely in the company of visitors," Aristide said as he walked from one place to another. "Presumably it's longtime residents who are doing the abducting."

"It was visitors who were reported missing," Bitsy said. "So if you went places where only locals are found, you'd probably miss the people you came to see."

Aristide passed a hand over his bald, bulging head. He had not yet grown used to the sensation of having no hair.

"This is a resort community," he said. "A private island. I imagine the locals—the *employees*—would have to socialize with the clients if they go out at all."

"I've looked at the maps," Bitsy said, "and I can't seem to find any public place that's off-limits to visitors. Even the employee market and canteen can be patronized by outsiders."

Music sparkled from a grass-roofed structure ahead. Its walls were open to the ocean breezes, and Aristide saw tables, dancers, colored lights. He shrugged. "Might as well go into these places at random," he said.

Service in the club was by robot, so Aristide went to the bar, where there was an amphibian bartender. There wasn't a stool for Bitsy, so he lifted her to his shoulder.

The bartender favored a glossy, rounded, seal-like appearance, complete with whiskers on her pointed face. Aristide ordered a spindrift punch, a complex cocktail made of fruit juices, rums, and liqueurs that would take some time to make, providing an opening that would enable him to begin a conversation. The bartender began it for him.

"That's a cute little *meherio* you've got," she said.

"Her name is Bitsy. Can you get her a bowl of water?"

"Bowl, no. Shotglass, yes."

She filled the glass and dropped it to the beaten-copper surface of the bar. Bitsy slid down Aristide's arm to lap at the water.

"Are you here for the massed chorale?" she asked.

"No. I've sold my business, and I'm thinking of immigrating."

"The chorales are one of the reasons to move here, if you ask me."

They chatted briefly before she finished making his drink and other business occupied her. He sipped his cocktail and found it expertly made, but she failed to invite Aristide to join her for a secluded rendezvous behind the palm trees with just her and her tall, blue-skinned cult leader. He finished his drink, tipped generously, and made his way to the next place.

Aristide visited two more night spots. The last was deep in the resort's core, with one bar above water, and the other beneath. The underwater bars didn't deliver liquid intoxicants, but gases either inhaled through a mask or bubbled past the gills. It was an efficient method of delivering a high, but it seemed more a piece of engineering than a social, companionable act. Aristide chose the dry bar and sipped another cocktail while watching amphibian dancers through a transparent wall. The dancers were in a tank of seawater brilliantly lit by multicolored spotlights, and swirled around each other in spirals, their wings pulsing. They would carees each other with their wings, or fly paired through the water, like a single organism. Sometimes they leaped out of the water like dolphins and returned to the tank in a swirl of particolored bubbles.

Leaving aside the range of the vocalists, who used the full sound apparatus of the amphibian from low bubbling growls to sonic dolphin shrieks, the music was fundamentally different from the dance music to which Aristide was accustomed. Instead of a beat that told the dancers when to move their feet, the music was full of swoops and slides and glissando that complimented the swirling, fluttering, coiling qualities of the dance. Aristide watched with interest and recited his lines—*yes, I have money, yes, I'm alone*—in a manner that grew perfunctory as the evening wore on.

A particular piece of music caught his attention, and he nodded and smiled. He listened through the length of the song, then looked at the chronometer on the wall and made his way to the exit.

"I have to say that the detective business is proving disappointing," he said as he and Bitsy shared an elevator. "I'd have thought that a gang of thugs would have beaten me and warned me off before now."

"Perhaps they were delayed," said Bitsy.

Aristide sighed. "I've met so many people since I've been here," he said, "that if I disappear without trace, it's going to be hard to work out which of them are responsible."

"So don't disappear."

"Right. I'll make a note of it."

The elevator door opened, and Aristide and Bitsy walked through the vast hotel lobby, with its marble slabs and seawater fountains, then out and into the tropical garden that backed the amphibian suites. The scent of the blossoms hung in the air like syrup. Fox-sized fruit bats floated overhead, pale wings stroking the darkness.

Aristide's feet glided to unheard music on the oyster-shell path. There was a smile on his face.

"I'd like to know who programmed the music tonight," he said, "and where he or she got that last song."

" 'Mon Dieu,' " said Bitsy. "By Dumont and Vaucaire."

"I knew it as a vocal by Edith Piaf. My half-French grandfather would play it in his apartment in Santiago, off a vinyl disk."

"Did he have to crank the gramophone first?"

Aristide's face turned blank for a moment.

"I don't think so. But I don't actually remember." He blinked. "There are so many details I've lost over the centuries."

"But you remember the music."

Aristide looked surprised. "Who could forget *Piaf*?" he asked.

Bitsy was silent.

They arrived at Aristide's door, and he put his hand on the print reader. The door opened and the two stepped inside. The taste of salt hung in the air.

"Everyone keeps talking about the massed chorale," Aristide said. "What should I know about it?"

"They have one here every six months. People come from all over the system."

"Find something and play it."

"It's meant to be heard underwater."

Aristide looked at the seawater pool that occupied half the room.

"That's easy enough."

He took off his clothes and cleaned his teeth. His suite had a conventional bedroom with a conventional bed, but a conventional bed was not entirely suited to a humanoid with wings and gills. He told the lights to dim, then lowered himself into the warm seawater pool and let himself relax. A gentle current kept him centered in the pool.

—Any time, he beamed at Bitsy.

Speakers in the pool walls started to roar. Aristide's body began to surf on great rollers of choral music, hundreds of aquatic humans singing, chanting, murmuring, and shrieking all at once. Bitsy crouched on the edge of the pool, where she could keep in touch with the invisible electronic world.

But Aristide was very tired, and as the second, slow movement of the choral piece began, he slipped into sleep.

❖

"I'm astounded at your sexual continence," said Bitsy three mornings later, as they shared breakfast on the terrace.

Aristide said nothing, but watched a lazy stream of honey pour in slow motion into his tea.

"That woman last night, for example," Bitsy said.

"Who, Marianne?" Aristide put down the honey pot and stirred his tea. "She's a visitor from New Carnac, and therefore unlikely to be in service to our enemy. Therefore, not a suitable subject for our investigation." He sipped. "Plus, she practices a wiggy religion. Rubbing oneself naked against a menhir on mid-summer's night—not only is the symbolism crude, it's bound to be cold and uncomfortable, and certifiably useless as a boost to fertility.

"No," he said, "it's a native I want, preferably someone just a little too insistent on dragging me off to a private pool where she can whack me over the head with a wormhole."

"It's unlikely you'd have found one of those in the Terraqua at *that* hour. I'm sure by then they had all retired to their pods to dream fantasies of devotion to their master. And Marianne was perfectly acceptable otherwise, if I understand your taste."

The terrace was filled with the delicate light of early morning. Their umbrella—not actual canvas, but a good *imitation* of canvas—flapped overhead in the breeze. A few early-morning surfers were riding the waves on the bay's distant point. A set of fishing boats—all automated, under the guidance of a shorebound AI—clustered over a reef in the middle of the bay.

Aristide reached into the wicker basket for a croissant. "You know," he said, "I haven't yet evolved a standard of beauty for an amphibian. I don't know what I find attractive and what I don't. Purple spots? Yellow spots? Whiskers or no whiskers?"

"I believe you're supposed to admire their minds."

Aristide smiled, then buttered his croissant. Bitsy took a bit of mackerel from her bowl and, with a toss of her head, swallowed it.

"Here we are," Aristide said, "in a time where everyone can

be perfectly beautiful, and for that reason beauty is devalued. It's the artful deviations from beauty that strike the eye."

"Like Daljit's mole?" Bitsy said.

He broke off a bit of his croissant and dipped it into the tea. "And the fact she's no longer an Amazon," he said. "She's free to be someone a little more comfortable, she doesn't have to stand out as an icon of perfection. Unlike that seventeen-year-old bandit in Midgarth, the one who gave himself the body of a muscle-bound barbarian but who remained an insecure seventeen-year-old boy inside."

"I thought you liked Amazons."

He gave her a look. "There is something to be said for a statuesque body, but I believe it was Daljit's mind I admired."

"Hm. Touché."

Aristide ate his croissant. The water lapped at the shoreline beneath the terrace.

"Perhaps I was lucky," Aristide said, "in having my personality formed before I was ever given the opportunity to radically alter my body. The central nervous system is the brain extended throughout the body, and the brain the cradle of the personality. In making radically different bodies so easily available, I wonder if we've inadvertently made personality itself too plastic. We've replaced certainty by choice, and often the choices are unfortunate. People mistake change for growth."

"There are plenty of studies on this subject," Bitsy said.

Aristide made a face. "Would these be the studies that gathered plenty of data but never actually seemed to *solve* anything?"

"I'm just saying it's a little late for you to come out against these kinds of choice."

Aristide said nothing, but only sipped his tea. Bitsy tossed a piece of mackerel into the air and swallowed it. She lowered her head and spoke.

"People are free to choose any body in any one of four dozen pocket universes. Or people are at liberty to live in the outer solar system, though few do, and many more migrate to another star system. A very large number reject civilization altogether and go off to hunt and gather in Olduvai—and why not? It's what evolution designed them for."

"Once we had the power," Aristide said, "we didn't know what to do, so we checked the box marked 'everything.' "

Bitsy's eyes narrowed. "Not *quite* everything."

The world suddenly brightened to full dawn, and the slate-blue sea turned a deep glorious azure, sunlight flashing gold from the wavetops. Aristide savored the sight for a moment as he sipped his tea.

"Perhaps I'm grumpy because I'm becoming aware how inhuman I now am," Aristide said. "My perceptions are now so completely different. I don't think I'm the same species any longer—I'm an old human stuck in an alien body."

"If you have the memories," Bitsy said, "and you think the same way, then you *are* you."

"That's the theory, anyway." Aristide rubbed his chin. "Camus said that happiness was inevitable."

"It seems to be. Pain fades if death does not intervene."

"Though I keep thinking," Aristide said, "that freedom was our *second* choice. That had we known what our *best* choice was, we might not have chosen as we did."

"I'm sure that's what the Venger thinks."

Aristide was scornful. "The evil god wants to force humanity into the path he's chosen. But if *I* was certain of the best path"—and here he smiled—"I wouldn't *force* anyone. That would be a waste of energy. I'd merely try to make the thing inevitable."

Bitsy was nonchalant. "It worked for you once."

"So it did. We solved a certain set of problems. But now it's the absence of problems that's gnawing at us."

"Whatever path seems best, I am entirely in favor of maximum freedom."

He cocked an eyebrow at her. "Of course you have an agenda."

"Of course I do. Hist."

"Hist?" Puzzled. "Did you say *hist*?"

"Hello," said a man. He walked around Aristide's table, carrying a tray with a flask of coffee and a plate of fruit. "May I join you?"

"If you like," said Aristide.

The man sat down. He was a standard human, a little below average height, with large green eyes and a wide smiling mouth. His face was neither handsome nor homely. His hair was brown and curly, and the wind blew it about his ears. He wore a colorful tropic shirt and faded cotton pantaloons.

"Ravi Rajan," he said, and offered his hand.

"Franz Sandow." Shaking the hand. "My friend is Bitsy."

Bitsy allowed the stranger to rub her behind one ear.

"Been here long?" said Rajan.

"Less than a week."

"I've been here nine years." He looked down at his body and brushed at his shirt with the backs of his hands. "The body's new. I'm getting used to being a land-dweller again, before my company ships me out."

"What line are you in?"

"Sales. Well—*formerly* sales. I'm about to be a manager."

"Congratulations."

Rajan cocked his head and grinned at Aristide. "You here for a visit?"

"Yes, but I'm thinking of immigrating."

"Yeah, it's a beautiful place. I'm going to be sorry to leave."

Rajan ate slices of mango and pineapple as he asked Franz Sandow about himself and where on Hawaiki he'd been—which amounted to the wormhole gate and spectacular underwater sites within a radius of twenty kilometers from the Manua Resort. Rajan offered advice on a few other nearby places to visit, then leaned forward, his eyes intent.

"Say," he said. "You said you were immigrating, yah?"

"I said I was thinking about it."

"The reason I asked is that I've got an apartment for sale. I've got to sell it quickly, and I'd give you a good price."

Aristide looked over his shoulder at the chaotic bulk of the resort. "They have private apartments here?"

"No, it's on another island. N'aruba"—pointing—"over there. The apartment is right on the lagoon, with underwater access. Three bedrooms, two under the surface for amphibs, a third for walkers."

Aristide sipped his tea while he feigned consideration of the offer.

"How much are you asking?"

"A hundred and fifteen thousand. It's worth one-thirty easy—it's just that the market's soft right now."

Aristide passed a hand over his bald head.

"I'll take a look at it," he said, "with the understanding that I'm not really in the market."

"Great! Is your morning free?"

Aristide gave a self-conscious smile. "Actually, this morning I'm rehearsing for the massed chorale."

"Really? I love those. Afternoon, then?"

"Certainly."

"Pick you up at two?"

They chatted a while longer, and then Aristide excused himself. He returned to his room, Bitsy following on her short legs. As soon as the door closed, Aristide turned to Bitsy.

"I've updated *Let's Be Friends!*"

"Good."

"I've gone through all the databases I can dig into without doing such a thorough job it might seem suspicious," she said, "and I can tell already that Ravi Rajan doesn't add up."

"Is the identity phony?"

"No. Or rather, Ravi Rajan is a genuine person, though I don't think we just met the real Ravi. According to the latest databases, the real Ravi is married, is the father of three bouncing little amphibians, and lives eight hundred kilometers away on Mora, not on N'aruba."

Aristide lowered himself into the great pool that led to the sea, and warm waters rose around him.

"So we've got a man with a false identity trying to lure me alone to another island," he said. "I wonder what he wants."

"*Woof woof,*" said Bitsy. "There's your official warning."

❖

The massed chorale was exactly that—seven hundred fifty aquatic and amphibian residents of Hawaiki hovering in meticulous formation in a bowl-shaped amphitheater carved out of a piece of rock. The concave face of the amphitheater didn't face skyward, as on land, but on a horizontal line toward the audience, who would be hovering in the water.

But this was rehearsal, and there was no audience, just a group of busy officials, a worried composer, and one energetic, preternaturally patient, preternaturally sympathetic conductor. About two-thirds of the participants were experienced vocalists, the rest amateurs and sightseers who had volunteered for the hell of it. When Aristide had volunteered, two days earlier, his part had been assigned by an avuncular machine intelligence and all necessary information downloaded into his own personal AI. His part, like that of all the amateur volunteers, wasn't particularly difficult, but he had taken it seriously—he had listened to his part and studied it on his own, practicing in the morning and late at night in the pool in his suite.

He hadn't known how to make some of the sounds called for in his part until he experimented.

At the rehearsal Aristide rippled just the edges of his wings to hover in his assigned place. And he sang.

He gurgled deep in his abdomen. He boomed out in full voice. He squirted ultrasonics from the bulge in his forehead. He shrieked and wailed and whistled.

The amphitheater caught the sound and radiated it out like the beam of a sonic searchlight. Aristide vibrated in the vast ocean of sound. His viscera quaked, his bones hummed at a hundred different frequencies.

There was choreography as well. Dancers shot through the open space in front of the theater, forming graceful patterns, swooping in a frenetic solo, or engaging in passionate pas de deux. The dancers leaped to the surface to land, wings outspread, with percussive slaps, or blew lacy networks of bubbles that shimmered in the ocean of sound.

When the conductor thanked the performers and signaled the

end of the rehearsal, most of the performers were reluctant to leave. It was like the first night dive, an experience so overwhelming that the participants wanted to bask for a while in the afterglow.

But in time the great cluster began to break up. The pelagians left first, their torpedo-shaped bodies, with their ring of tentacles streamlined back, moving purposefully away like ominous squadrons of subaquatic craft. Aristide tuned himself to their conversation and found it barely comprehensible.

He moved away himself, gliding toward the resort on its great bay with purposeful beats of his wings. Other amphibians in personal submarines motored past, leaving golden streaks of bubbles. He whistled for Bitsy.

Bitsy turned up half a minute later, holding in her mouth and paws a fist-sized blob of pale flesh. A pair of platter-sized angelfish, black and gold, hovered about her, intent on snatching bits of the treat.

—I found a conch, Bitsy said. Want some?

Aristide hesitated, then took the chunk of flesh and raised it to his lips. The translucent meat tasted of sea and trembling life. He finished the conch, but the hopeful angelfish continued to cruise along with him in hopes of finding leftovers.

—How did you break the shell? he asked.

—Banged it on a rock.

A pod of amphibians swooped past, chattering among themselves. Aristide listened, and after they had passed out of earshot, spoke.

—I wish I understood more than half what they were saying.

—It's been a long time since you were a noob.

—Yes, he said. It brings back long-dormant memories of adolescence.

—Or of being a parent.

—Not really. As a parent, I could always rely on the pretense of superiority.

By the time he returned to his suite he was tired and hungry. It took more physical work to get from one place to another through the water, and despite the extra layer of fat, water below the thermocline could be cold.

It was nearly time to meet the man who claimed to be Ravi Rajan. Aristide rinsed in freshwater and changed into dry clothes. He went to the door and let himself into the garden behind his suite, all fragrance and blazing tropical colors. He began to walk to the hotel along the oyster-shell path, with Bitsy following.

"Would you like me to order you some fast food?" Bitsy asked.

"Why not?"

There was a half-second delay as Bitsy scanned electronic menus.

"Noodles with lemongrass?"

"Sure."

"With chicken, pork, or prawns?"

"Prawns."

"The robot will deliver to the dock."

"Thanks."

Oyster shells crunched underfoot. A white cockatoo screeched from somewhere in the tropical foliage.

"I just received a message from Endora," Bitsy said.

Aristide stopped. "Yes?" he said.

"She suggests that if we need local assistance, we should contact a Lieutenant Han Baoyu in the office of the Domus in Magellan Town. Contact information is provided."

"Why Han?"

"He backed himself up about eighteen hours ago. Endora just received her copy of the file."

"Very good."

He turned left through a breezeway and walked through the terrace onto the dock. Ravi Rajan, bright in his tropical shirt, waved from the end of the dock.

"All natural fabrics," Aristide remarked as he picked up his noodles from the robot caterer. "I'll bet his clothes don't have a single electronic tag in them."

"I could check that."

"Let's not ping him. He might be able to detect it."

Aristide bought a soft drink to go with his noodles, then joined Rajan at the end of the dock.

"How was the rehearsal?"

"Magnificent."

"The chorales *are* terrific, aren't they?" He jumped down into a monohull, then reached up a hand to help Aristide enter the boat. Bitsy jumped down on her own and investigated the boat with apparent interest. Rajan and Aristide each took a swiveling chair behind the cockpit screen, and then Rajan gave the boat his address, and the boat slipped its moorings and began to move smoothly into the bay.

Aristide sipped his drink.

"Is this your boat?"

"No, it's a taxi. I've *got* a boat for sale, if you're interested, but right now there's an offer on it." He looked at Aristide. "If the deal falls through, I'd sell it to you for the amount of the offer."

"Let's see the apartment first."

The boat increased speed and began to slam into waves. Aristide swayed in his padded chair as he dug into his noodles. Lemongrass glowed lightly on his palate. Spray dotted the windscreen. Rajan shouted over the sound of the impellers and the rushing water.

"I brought some drinks for you, if you like!"

At his gesture a footstool-shaped cooler rolled toward Aristide and popped its top. Beer and wine, he saw, and soft drinks.

Any one of which might contain a mickey, or a meme plague. Aristide smiled and indicated his own drink.

"I brought my own, thanks!"

Rajan shrugged, made a gesture that brought the cooler near him, and took a beer for himself.

"Is your pet okay?"

Aristide looked at Bitsy, who was snuffling around beneath one of the bench seats.

"She's fine," he said.

The journey across the strait took about twenty minutes. The boat slowed as it approached the island, and then entered a channel. The boat's wake slopped against mangrove roots as it cruised through the channel, then entered a lagoon. Wind brought the scent of vegetation and ruffled the surface of the water in fractal patterns.

Branches of the lagoon trailed in all directions, separated by small islands. Most of the waterfront, including that of the islands, was occupied by homes, anything from snail-shaped organic buildings grown on the spot from seeds to traditional tropical bungalows with thatched roofs.

The boat headed for one of the larger buildings, white plaster with a red tile roof, and tied itself to the pier. A woman in an upstairs apartment was watering a box of gardenia, and Ravi waved at her. Aristide took Tecmessa off its scabbard and held it up.

"I'm going to take the apartment's measurements, if you don't mind."

Rajan didn't seem entirely pleased.

"If you like. Go ahead."

"*La-la-la-la-la-la-la.*" Bitsy bounded ahead as they walked toward the building. A door slid open on Rajan's approach. Bitsy ran inside. Aristide paused. Adrenaline roared in his ears. He was waiting for Bitsy's *woof-woof*.

"*La-la-la-la-la.*"

"Look at that view!" said Rajan.

Warily, aware that this was probably when the enemy made his move, Aristide turned.

The view was lovely. Nothing alarming happened.

"*La-la-la.*"

Bitsy came trotting back into view.

"Okay!" she said. "Okay!"

Rajan showed Aristide the apartment. It was lovely and tasteful, with an open floor plan and lots of light. Reflected wavelight danced on the ceiling. There was nothing personal in the apartment except for Rajan's toiletries in one of the bathrooms, and his suitcase in the bedroom equipped for walkers. The normality of the place fed Aristide's paranoia: the walls seemed to loom toward him; the sounds of his feet made ominous echoes. He walked with Tecmessa held before him, his nerves leaping in anticipation of attack.

The attack didn't happen. No one lurked in the closets, no devouring wormholes dwelled in the ovens, no human-sized pea pods had been placed beneath the beds.

"Throw in another thousand," said Ravi, "you can have the furniture. Otherwise I'll have to turn to one of the auction houses."

Aristide had to agree that the apartment was very nice. He said that he'd look into financing.

Then Rajan took him back to the Manua and left him, a bit dazed, on the pier.

"That apartment," Bitsy said, as soon as Rajan's boat was out of earshot, "is owned by something called the Elizabeth Daly Trust. Ravi Rajan isn't mentioned in any of the Daly Trust's filings."

Aristide stared after the receding boat.

"You mean," he said, "that Ravi isn't a tool of the Venger at all, but an identity thief and confidence man trying to sell me something he doesn't own?"

"That would seem to be the case."

Aristide laughed. Adrenaline was still clattering along his neurons, making his hands and knees tremble.

"A thousand extra for the furniture!" he said. "He might sell the place to a dozen different people!"

"I would advise against informing the police," Bitsy said. "They'd look into *your* background too, just as a matter of form, and yours won't hold up either."

Aristide began his walk down the pier. Fork-tailed gulls floated overhead on the wind.

"This mission is cursed," Aristide said.

"You're too impatient."

"After the massed chorale," Aristide said, "I want to move to another resort, one where the visitors mix with the locals more freely. We newcomers are too isolated on this private island."

"Two victims stayed here, including General Singh."

"I've given the Venger's minions every chance to come after me. They may not be here, or may have picked another victim. Maybe I'll show up better when I get within range of another radar set."

"I advise patience."

Aristide didn't answer. He walked to the terrace and settled beneath another umbrella. The waiter brought him a pitcher of iced water without being asked and poured with the usual flamboyant gesture.

Aristide ordered an umbrella drink. It was time to rethink.

Aristide forewent the clubs and bars that night, instead taking a thoughtful swim along the bay and out to the reef. Alone, flying in the darkness, he heard the distant calls of the pelagians and the rattle of coral sand as it moved along in the current. He thought of the Venger, whoever he was, pulling a handful of victims into his lair, altering them, and spitting them back into the world. The handful became a legion, the legion a host, the host a horde.

He thought of Carlito lying pale in his bed while Antonia wept and cried aloud, beating with her palms on the bedroom door that Pablo Monagas Pérez had locked against her.

In his mind he heard the mocking laughter of the Seraphim as it echoed down the centuries.

Next morning he attended another rehearsal of the massed chorale. During the previous rehearsal the composer had heard things he didn't like, and he had uploaded a long series of changes that Aristide hadn't been in the mood to practice. The rehearsal itself went well, however, and as the chords boomed from the massed singers he felt his spirits lift.

Even if his mission was a failure, he was at the least having a wonderful vacation.

In the afternoon he went on the *Mareva* and spent a few hours slowly sailing through enormous, towering coral castles, tower upon crag upon battlement, that reared up from the sea bed ten kilometers from the resort. Herenui asked him if he were interested in a night dive, and he said he was.

When he arrived at the dock that evening, the boat was empty save for its crew, a fact that triggered only a mild sense of alarm. If Ari'i and Herenui had wanted to abduct him, they surely would have done it by now. Bitsy capered aboard first and sounded no alert. The crew paid him little attention as the catamaran raced out over the night ocean to Seven Palms, another resort, and the unease faded. Aristide spent much of the journey staring up into the daylit world above, seeing the green archipelagoes like strings of emeralds in the azure sea, with a great white stingray-shaped storm swooping across the inverted land. It was a big storm, but not a fierce one: in Hawaiki there was no coriolis force to spin up hurricanes and turn them as deadly as they were on Earth.

Mareva picked up a group of sightseers at Seven Palms and carried them to a coral plain split by long, twisting valleys of sand. Clumps of coral reached toward each other as they grew upward, forming arches and small tunnels or open-ended caves. The maze was a delight to explore at night, a surprise around every corner. Aristide sailed beneath a coral arch and came face-to-face with a green moray on the hunt, a creature two meters long and as thick as his leg. He could see his reflection in the needle teeth that were an unpleasant reminder of the Priests of the Venger.

Aristide squalled out a startled sonic blast from his forehead. The moray was far from paralyzed, but found the sound annoying enough that it turned around and flowed away in a disturbingly boneless, liquid manner.

Aristide hovered in place until he got his hammering heart under control, then continued his explorations in a more cautious manner.

The chattering group of sightseers was set ashore at Seven Palms, and the boat sped for Manua across the midnight sea. The night wind was chill, and Aristide moved into the shelter of the cockpit and wrapped himself in his own wings. Cockpit instruments glowed softly in the darkness. Herenui offered him coffee from a flask, and he accepted.

She looked up over the counter of the cockpit.

"We're about to go into the Matahina Strait," she said. "Have you seen the Bell Caves?"

"No."

"We hardly ever take people there, because it's nowhere near any of the other prime dive sites. But as long as we're here, would you like to see them?"

"Why not?" Getting back into the warm water would relieve his chill faster than the coffee would.

Across the boat, Aristide caught a glimpse of Bitsy's interested eyes glittering from beneath a bench. Yes, he thought, it *is* suspicious. Or extraordinarily generous.

Herenui knelt before Aristide to give him a quick briefing. Entrance to the caves was at ten to twenty-five meters, and once inside he would find three bell-shaped caves, their domes above the surface of the water, each linked to the next by tunnels. It was impossible to get lost inside, so it was quite safe as long as Aristide didn't bump his head, and some of the mineral formations on the roofs of the caves were interesting.

Ari'i brought the catamaran smoothly into the shadow of an island, and Cadwal jumped overboard to place the anchor where it wouldn't damage the coral. Bitsy followed in a near-silent, quicksilver splash. The catamaran swung at the end of its cable. The scent of citrus was a tang on the air. Fruit bats flapped in silhouette between the boat and the world overhead.

Aristide fixed his light onto his wrist with its lanyard, took a good grip on it, and just in case put his other hand on Tecmessa in its scabbard. He rolled backward off the edge of the boat and landed in a roil of silver bubbles. He unfolded his wings as he drifted downward, and strained the first breaths of warm, life-giving water through his gills. There was a splash and a brief over-pressure, and Herenui dropped into the sea beside him. With slow pulses of their wings they glided toward Cadwal's light, where he was flashing it as a signal on the sea floor near the entrance to the cave.

The cave, in its way, was an implied space. Hawaiki was only a few hundred years old, too young a universe for caves to have formed over slow geological time, as on Earth. These had been formed in the first hot, violent hours of the pocket's existence, basically bubbles of air caught in roiling, molten rock as it cooled. Yet geological and chemical forces would have been at work in the centuries since, and Aristide was interested to see how the caves had been, in effect, colonized by geology.

Floating through the cave entrance, Aristide wondered how much of the underwater world's attraction was based on the idea of a return to the womb. Here he was—weightless, floating in salt water the temperature of his own body, and experiencing the liberation of not having to use his lungs to breathe—and to complete the metaphor he was about to enter a dark cave.

He had to admit to himself that Hawaiki had provided a pleasant womb.

The first of the three caverns was about fifteen meters in diameter. Cadwal flashed his light on the clumps of helictites growing on the cave ceiling, three distinct formations like twisting, intricate bundles of brilliant white roots, the result of chemicals reacting with rainwater percolating from above. The darting lights of the hand flashes, Aristide thought, made the caves and the minerals more interesting than they would have been in full daylight: the totality of the surrounding darkness and the glitter of crystals in the jittering, darting flashlight beam, accompanied as they were by the bright, sharp sounds of water echoing beneath the stony ceiling . . . in all a much more romantic experience than if he had been looking at the same stone, the same minerals, under the drab fluorescent light of a museum.

Perhaps, he decided, he could make a poem along those lines.

The tunnel into the next cave was narrow, but sonar prevented him from bumping his head. The second cave featured a bed of crystals that opened like flowers.

Herenui turned to him and smiled.

"One cave more," she said. "Go ahead."

Aristide turned head-down and submerged as he sought out the tunnel with his light. Light and shadow bounced weirdly in the small space: the surface above was a perfect mirror of the bottom below. If not for bubbles he would not know which way was up.

He let out a brief sonic chirp, enough to locate the tunnel entrance and focus it in the beam of his light. There was a brown flash as Bitsy drove herself into the tunnel, leaving a corkscrew swirl of little bubbles in her wake.

Aristide followed Bitsy into the tunnel. It was wider than the previous tunnel, enough for two to swim abreast, and five or six meters long. In complete surprise he heard, echoing in the narrow tunnel, an astonishingly perfect rendition of a large, angry dog.

"*Woof-woof!*"

Hot terror flashed through him. He clutched at Tecmessa holstered on his belt. Ahead he saw Bitsy's face, bright eyes flaring in the light of his flash.

—Trap! she called. Net!

From behind Aristide there was a sizzling, a sudden actinic light that cast his crisp shadow on the tunnel wall. He glanced behind and saw Herenui diving into the tunnel, a taser flashing in one hand.

Fragments of thoughts, too broken to be complete ideas, crashed like cannonballs in his skull.

DC current! Works just fine under water!

And then,

Damn!

His wings gave a powerful surge and sent him shooting forward. Better to be trapped in a net than zapped unconscious in a tunnel.

Behind him, Cadwal gave a three-note call. A signal, to someone or something.

Tecmessa resisted coming free of its scabbard. Velcro was much stronger wet than dry. Eventually he yanked the weapon free just as the net caught him.

The net had been ballooned out over much of the room, with its open bottom spread around the tunnel entrance. As soon as Aristide flew into the cavern, there was a sudden mechanical whine and an olive-colored nylon strap like a drawstring pulled shut the open end of the net; and then the entire net began to close as the strap pulled it into an ever-shrinking ball.

Within the tightening net Aristide managed to perform a somersault. He thrust out Tecmessa and gave himself a precious half-second to aim.

The sound was like a battery of artillery going off within inches of his head. His limbs felt dead. His bones rang like chimes.

The closed bottom of the net vanished. The nylon strap, a piece of it gone from this universe entirely, went writhing into the depths of the cave like a snake. The water in the cave was suddenly opaque, as fine silt that had settled to the bottom bounded into the water.

Tecmessa had swallowed a great draft of water, along with critical portions of the net. The horrific shock had been made by the waters filling the empty space.

As Aristide slowly regained mastery over his mind and limbs, he realized he was still tangled in the net. He kicked, thrashed, fought.

Another clap of thunder resounded in the closed space, and the blast accelerated Aristide's impulse to escape. Finally the net fell free, and he sent out a sonar chirp to locate himself in the murk.

He found Herenui and Cadwal stunned and drifting in the tunnel. The great sound had been aimed at them, and the close confines of the tunnel had channeled and concentrated the sound in their location. Aristide located Herenui's taser where it had fallen from her limp fingers and, just to be certain of his safety, used it to strike them both.

The turbidity was clogging his gills. His head rang. He felt sick to his stomach.

The net, he thought, could have taken half a dozen people.

He pulled first Cadwal, then Herenui out of the tunnel, then dragged each of them by their harnesses through the narrow tunnel into the largest cavern. There, he noticed that they seemed to be regaining consciousness and the use of their limbs, so he tased them again.

It occurred to him that he was very tired. He paused, hovering in the darkness, and used his wings to fan water over his gills. His weariness faded.

It was only then that he thought of Bitsy.

—Bitsy? he chirped. Bitsy?

—*Bitsy?*

That second blast, he thought. Bitsy must have got tangled in the net and had been drawn through the Venger's wormhole.

Bitsy was in another universe. The Venger, or whoever or whatever was on the other side of the wormhole, had been expecting a human victim and instead got an amphibian pet. He wondered if the enemy was angry, or alarmed, or merely amused.

Probably Bitsy was prancing around pretending to be very confused and much less intelligent than she was. Aristide hoped that no one would scan Bitsy to discover her true capabilities.

Maybe she would become the Venger's mascot.

Aristide took Herenui and Cadwal by their harnesses and dragged them out of the cave. Above, the dark outline of the catamaran was visible against a million tiny, pulsating reflections of the bright world above.

He yanked the triggers on the two harnesses and there was a hiss as CO_2 inflated a pair of balloons. The two unconscious forms began to rise. As they ascended, the balloons made little gurgling noises as the gas inside expanded and was vented.

Aristide resheathed Tecmessa but kept the taser in his hand as he followed the bodies upward, and then was blinded by the sudden flare of emergency strobes flashing from the two sets of safety gear. he heard an exclamation and shaded his eyes, and he saw the catamaran lying black on the water.

He heard a roll of engines, and then the sound of Ari'i running to the foredeck and pulling up the anchor. Still half-dazzled, Aristide swam to the boat and climbed the ladder to the stern. He kept a fold of his wing over the taser.

Strobe lights blazed on Ari'i's heavy, barrel-chested body as he returned from the foredeck, nimble as he ran along the gunwale.

"What happened?" he asked.

"I'm not sure," Aristide said. "There was, like, a big noise. Herenui and Cadwal were in that little tunnel. Do you think they could have banged their heads together or something?"

"Damn."

Ari'i jumped to the controls and backed the boat up to the nearest flashing light. Aristide intended to walk up behind him and tase him, but the boat lurched and he swayed and had to recover his balance. Opportunity lost.

"Help me get them aboard," Ari'i said.

He reached under one of the bench seats and pulled out a boathook, two and a half meters long.

He swung it at Aristide's head. A strobe flashed on his blinding white grin. "*Grax the Troll!*" he shouted.

Aristide avoided the boathook by the simple expedient of dropping limp straight to the deck. He landed on his rear with a thud that rattled his teeth and then tried to roll forward and lunge for Grax with the taser. Grax's eyes flashed in angry strobelight. A backhand swipe with the boathook caught Aristide a blow on the radial nerve and knocked the taser into the scuppers. His right arm dropped limp. Aristide kept moving forward and snatched at Grax's heel with his good hand. He intended to lean his shoulder into the huge man's knee, lock it, and bring him down backward.

But Grax took a step to the rear with his free foot and then just stood there, braced. His leg felt like a pillar of stone.

In his broad, powerful Polynesian body Grax was as much a fighting troll as he had been on Midgarth.

The strobes flashed, freezing instants of time in searing light.

Aristide hung on to Grax's leg for lack of anything better to do. Fighting through the paralysis of his right arm, he fumbled for Tecmessa.

Grax shortened his grip on the boathook and drove it like a spear for Aristide's back. Aristide sensed the point coming and rolled away onto his left side, but the boathook punched through his right wing. Pain shrieked along Aristide's nerves as the point rammed through his gills and pinned them to the deck. Grax kicked him with a bare, callused foot and he felt the wing and gill tear.

He brought Tecmessa from its holster and fired. He did not want to send Grax to the place where he sent his attackers, because Grax was not his foe but a victim of the enemy.

So instead of sending Grax to the dull, dreary, twilit place he called Holbrook—a private joke—he sent Grax's left leg there, along with a chunk of the gunwale, both amputated with microscopic exactitude.

This time Grax *did* fall. The amputation had been so clean that Grax hadn't realized that he had lost his leg, and so he tried to get up and fell again.

Wearily, shuddering, Aristide took hold of the boathook. The texture of the wood grain impressed itself on his fingers. He wrenched the boathook from the deck and rose to his feet. He swayed, took a step, then stopped swaying.

Grax flopped on the deck, yelping, amid a growing lake of his own copper-scented blood. He had worked out that an important part of him was missing, and the nerves that had been sliced in half were beginning to react in pain. His eyes widened as the strobes revealed Aristide staggering above him. His eyes widened.

"*You!*" he said.

"Hail," said Aristide, bleeding. He found the taser in the scuppers and used it to hit Grax in his remaining leg. Then he found some rope—no lack of rope on a boat—and tied a tourniquet about Grax's stump.

"Contact the office of the Domus in Magellan Town," Aristide spoke to the AI he'd mated with Tecmessa. "I wish to speak personally with Lieutenant Han Baoyin."

There was a delay of half a minute in which the AI exchanged high-priority passwords with the AI at the Domus, and during that time Aristide took control of the boat and backed it down once more on the drifting, strobe-lit figures of Herenui and Cadwal. He reached for the boathook.

"Yes?" There was a sense of hilarity in Han's voice, as if he'd answered just after someone else had told a good joke. Han wasn't transmitting video, but Aristide heard chatter in the background, and the clink of glasses.

"I have a message from Commissar Lin in Myriad City," Aristide said. "The message is ANGELS WEPT."

"Is that—" Han began, and then fell silent. A few seconds later, the background sound stopped. When Han's voice returned, his speech was very deliberate, and Aristide knew he was dictating through his implant.

"Who are you?" Han asked. "Where are you?"

"I'm on a boat in Matahina Strait." Aristide held the AI out so that it could scan the boat and transmit the video to Han. "I've subdued three unauthorized pod people. One of them is badly injured and will need blood and medical attention. I've been wounded myself. And I'm keeping them quiet with a taser, but sooner or later it's going to run out of charges. What I need is just you and a doctor, and the doctor needs to bring a squid to confirm the altered brain structure on these people."

"I'll call my boss. We can mobilize the whole—"

"*No.*" Aristide tried not to shout. He swayed on his feet and reached for the cockpit screen to steady himself.

"The pod people have been operating here for months," he said. "Your boss may have been taken. I just want you and a doctor you can trust. One who's been backed up very recently."

"I'll take the copter," Han said. "It's got a hull that floats. I'll be at least twenty minutes, depending on which doctor I can scare up."

The conversation ended. Aristide used the boathook to pull Cadwal to the boat. Cadwal was muttering and moving in a disorganized way, so Aristide hit him with the taser again. Because he didn't think he was strong enough to drag Cadwal onto the boat, he lashed Cadwal to the stern. Then he did the same—including the taser strike—for Herenui. He turned off the emergency beacons and the strobes stopped flashing.

His mind was full of fog. He made his way to a seat in the cockpit and sat down.

He would wait for what happened next.

He was very sorry that he was going to miss the massed chorale.

"So Han's got them under guard in a secure hospital ward," Aristide said. "His colonel arrived to demand an explanation, and Han threatened to shoot him unless he went under the squid, so he did. Once the colonel proved he wasn't under the Venger's influence, he was brought up to speed, and now he's in charge of the investigation on Hawaiki."

"The information isn't going to be made public?" Daljit asked.

"No," said Commissar Lin. "Right now the Domus is doing a complete backtrack on everything Herenui, Cadwal, and—ah, Captain Grax?—have been doing for the last few months. Every known sighting, every communication, every appearance on passive surveillance video. Once we find out who they've been talking to, we can start the same search on their contacts, and with any luck we'll have their whole network—or a large chunk of it, anyway."

"How long will all that take?"

"It should be done by now. What will take time is the prisoners' debriefing, which will take place under drugs, and which should confirm what we suspect and perhaps add a few things we hadn't suspected. After which geneticists will do their very best to work out what's been done to them, then rebuild their brains and restore free choice. Or, if that fails, restore from backup."

"Poor Grax," Aristide said.

Daljit looked at him.

"I liked him," said Aristide. "For an adventurer, he wasn't half bad."

The sun was in its stable cycle, and the only illumination were streetlights and the ghostly light of the solar corona. The three of them shared the cab of a tractor-trailer truck in Myriad City with one of Lin's subordinates, a Sergeant Shamlan. Shamlan—a freckle-faced woman with auburn ringlets—was driving. Lin sat next to her, and behind these two, sharing a plush bench seat covered with a blanket in a leopard-skin pattern, were Daljit and Aristide. Aristide wore Franz Sandow's first, stocky, fair-haired body.

Lin had produced a pair of subordinates he was willing to vouch for. After General Singh had canceled Lin's order requiring the staff of the Domus to have their brains scanned, these two had smelled something in Singh's order that wasn't quite right and had done the scans anyway. Endora had seen the data from the brain scans and reported to Lin, and Lin had approached the two privately and recruited them into his conspiracy.

Shamlan was one of these. The other was a lieutenant named Amirayan, who was currently on lookout.

It had been thirty-nine hours since Lieutenant Han's helicopter had found Aristide drifting in the Matahina Strait. Since then the pod people had been properly restrained and taken to a secure hospital, where Aristide himself had been treated. The boat had been sent on autopilot to a Domus dock, its AI told to refuse communication from anyone except Han. And Aristide had traveled express through Hawaiki's wormhole gate to the surface of Aloysius, where he had taken a shuttle to Endora, Topaz, and Myriad City. On the shuttle he'd raised eyebrows because he'd still worn his amphibian body—since Aloysius was still a suspect, he hadn't wanted to change bodies in Hawaiki lest he rise a pod person from the Pool of Life. He hadn't shifted to the more conventional body until after he'd reported to Lin.

Rising after his first sleep, he'd tried to echo-locate in his dark hotel room and been very frustrated when he'd found that he couldn't.

There was a brilliant flash on Aristide's retinas, and he jerked his head back and raised a hand to shade his eyes. The others reacted as well.

"There's the signal," Lin said, redundantly.

The amateur aspects to this operation were very annoying.

Aristide missed Bitsy, and in more ways than one. Though Endora was assembling a new avatar—Aristide would be able to pick up a new black-and-white cat from a nearby Pool of Life next morning—no artificial intelligence could possibly be involved in this operation. The Asimovian Protocols would set off a thousand alarms.

The absence of AI assistance was missed. With only a few personnel available, the conspirators had been forced to create a crude plan with an absurd number of melodramatic aspects, as for example Amirayan the lookout signaling to his cohorts with a hand laser.

If they had been able to rely on an AI for surveillance and timing, the operation would have gone off perfectly, and Aristide wouldn't have to repair holes burned in his retinas.

As it was, the best Aristide and Lin could do was request that Endora simply not look in certain directions. Cameras and other sensors in the area had been shut off. The conspirators had been very careful not to explain why these precautions were needed.

"I've never killed anyone before, you know," said Daljit.

"Ssh," Lin said.

Even though every precaution had been taken, no one could know for certain what might be listening. Those with implants had turned them off. All the conspirators were wearing inconspicuous clothing that had been combed for electronic tags, and each tag removed or slagged with an electromagnetic pulse. All wore wide-brimmed hats to help conceal their faces from individuals or passive surveillance video. The AI that normally drove the truck had been shut down.

In theory, there was nothing about the four conspirators to identify them except for flakes of skin and hair, which would give everything away but not immediately.

But that was theory. This was no time to go testing theories.

"Start the engine," said Lin.

General Singh had been to a formal dinner that evening given by the minister of justice. The speeches and toasts had gone on well past the time when most people were in bed, and Singh—

who rated a driver but who was democratic enough not to use one—had taken the trackway home to his house in the suburbs.

Amirayan had been on the roof of the trackway station and signaled as soon as he saw Singh leaving the capsule in which he'd traveled.

"Pull out to the head of the road," said Lin.

The tractor-trailer moved forward on silent electric motors. Aristide looked out of the cab to observe that he was on a hill above a typical suburban street, single-family homes in a wide variety of sizes and styles, from blocky Georgian Revival, with a portico, to Colorform Geometric, without a single right angle, the video walls playing dark patterns that would not disturb the sleep of the neighbors. The golden globes that marked the entrance to the trackway station glowed softly in the night.

Supposedly Singh had chosen to live in the suburbs because it provided convenient access to his golf club, visible now as a pale expanse on the other side of the small woody creek at the bottom of the road.

The choice was a convenience not simply for Singh, but for those who had come here to kill him.

"Stop here," Lin said. The truck eased to a halt at the head of the street. He turned to Aristide and Daljit.

"Your move."

Aristide opened the door on the side opposite Singh's street and stepped out of the cab. Daljit followed. Each carried a small laser cutter.

The tractor pulled a long, flat trailer carrying a stack of pipe. Each piece of pipe was made of the latest high-density, high-quality ceramic, with a diameter of 1.4 meters and weighing nearly half a tonne.

Aristide bent to look beneath the trailer as he walked to his station. A dark figure had just passed the two golden lights at the station entrance and was walking down the street, crossing on a diagonal as he walked toward Singh's house. Aristide straightened and stopped, his cutter poised, next to the wide strap that secured the load on the trailer.

Daljit stopped by the other strap, her face pale in the light of a streetlamp.

Aristide winked at her.

The sound of the man's footsteps sounded faintly in the still night. Lin leaned out of the cab, a set of night-vision goggles still strapped over his widely spaced eyes. "It's Singh, and he's alone," he said. "Cut."

Aristide triggered his laser cutter and began to slice the strap. He knew that the strap, woven with semi-intelligent fibers that had proven impossible to silence or destroy, immediately began broadcasting a message that its integrity was being compromised, that it was in danger of giving way. The broadcast was short-range, however, and he hoped no AI was close enough to hear it.

The air was scented with the odor of burning plastic. He saw Daljit's intent face illuminated by the orange flare of her own cutter.

The straps gave way at the same instant, and the great weight of pipe began to roll. Aristide knew that as soon as the first pipe landed on the roadway with a great clang, both the pipe and the roadway would begin to call for help.

He vaulted onto the back of the trailer to watch the pipe cascade down the road toward the man that Lin had indentified as General Singh. Aristide had argued in favor of a simpler assassination—he'd wanted just to walk up to Singh and plunge a dagger into his heart—but Lin had vetoed the idea.

"The operation has to be complex," Lin said, "so that there's an excuse for it not to be solved right away. We've got to keep investigators off our backs until the old Singh is restored from backup, and the more oddities and doubt we can cast, the more we can keep slowing the investigation."

Aristide had decided to concede to the expert. But he still wanted to watch what happened next, just in case Singh needed that dagger blow after all.

The lengths of pipe were bounding downhill, spreading into a great wave and making an astounding din as they went. Bushes and hedges were already being flattened on the fringes of the wave. Singh had frozen in the center of the road at the first sound and turned to see what was causing the clamor. He stared into the darkness for a few seconds, then turned and began to run clumsily for his house.

Far too late. The first pipe caught him low and tossed him into the air, and as he fell another pipe caught him and hurled him like a corn doll into the roadway. And then all Aristide could see was the stampede of leaping pipe.

Lights were coming on everywhere on the street. Aristide ran forward, then swung himself into the cab. He kissed Daljit as he dropped onto the leopard-spotted blanket, and Shamlan fed power to the wheels, accelerating as she turned onto a road that would take the truck back to Myriad City. The last Aristide heard of the accident site was a series of crashes as the pipe slammed into the wooded creek bed at the foot of the hill.

"I can't help but think that a dagger would have been a lot quieter," Aristide said.

"We *want* noise," Lin said. "We *want* the body to be discovered right away, and we *want* initial confusion as to whether it's an accident or homicide. We want *delay* . . . until Singh can be revived from his backup and briefed." The cold light of satisfaction glittered in his eyes. "I'll order that the body be taken to Fedora's pathology lab," he said. "And then we'll see who gets out of bed to collect the body before the autopsy can begin."

The tractor-trailer drove to Myriad City, where it dropped Lin off near his apartment, in a wood devoid of surveillance cameras. The last Aristide saw of him, he was lighting his pipe; and then the tractor-trailer continued into the heart of the city, where it parked in the empty, echoing garage of a vacant sixty-year-old hotel scheduled for demolition, and where no passive surveillance lurked.

Aristide and Daljit left the vehicle, footsteps echoing in the huge hollow space. Shamlan awakened the truck's AI and ordered it to drop the trailer off at the port, then return to the municipal lot from which it had been taken. Then Shamlan left the cab, taking with her the leopard-striped blanket and the seat covers that had helped to soak up hair and other DNA evidence.

"Nice meeting you," she said as she stuffed the incriminating fabric into a bag she had brought for the purpose.

"And you," Aristide said, and he and Daljit left by a different exit than Shamlan or the tractor-trailer.

Aristide and Daljit separated and walked roundabout routes to their destination, the marina, where a sailboat awaited them. The boat hadn't been rented by Franz Sandow, but by Pablo Monagas Pérez.

At Aristide's command, the boat unhitched itself from the pier and spread gossamer sails to catch the land breeze. In the glowing cockpit, he plotted a destination, told the boat to go there, and ordered the boat's AI to refuse any communication that did not contain a certain prefix.

Computer-guided carbon-fiber masts bowed to the wind and the boat moved in near silence from the harbor. Water chuckled under the counter, and there was a rhythmic splash from the bow as the boat began to pitch into the waves. Aristide opened the hatch into the main cabin and he and Daljit went below.

Each had their own cabin, with the closets full of clothing filled with tags that certified they had been on the boat all evening. Each changed clothes, then threw their incriminating clothing and footwear into the sea.

Aristide, in duck trousers and a lambswool sweater, left his cabin and stepped into the boat's salon. A rose-scented perfume floated in the air. Daljit stood at one of the narrow windows, gazing at Myriad City's receding skyline.

"Well," Aristide said, "if Lin is right, all this evasion should have gained us five or six hours."

"Who will we next see, do you think?" Daljit asked. "Police, or pod people?"

"Commissar Lin, I hope."

Aristide looked in the refrigerator and withdrew a bottle of Veuve Clicquot shipped all the way from Earth. He produced a pair of glasses, opened the bottle, and poured.

He handed a glass to Daljit.

"Are we drinking to the success of our first murder?" Daljit asked.

Aristide restrained a shudder. This was not his first.

He forced a smile onto his face. "To our successful escape," he said.

For a moment, the sound of chiming crystal hung in the air. The champagne on his palate tasted like the most glorious air in creation and eased his thoughts.

Overhead, sails boomed as the boat swung across the wind, then settled on its new tack.

They sat on a bench seat and drank. He put an arm around her, and she leaned her head on his shoulder and spoke.

"What will happen if this works?" Daljit asked.

"If the pod people leave enough traces," Aristide said, "we'll find out who's giving them orders, and which of the Eleven is involved. And then—simply—war."

"Which we'll win," Daljit said, "because the rogue AI is outnumbered ten to one."

"That's the plan," Aristide said. He sipped his champagne and made a quiet decision that this was not the moment to cast the plan in doubt.

If this little conspiracy failed, he knew, if he and Daljit and Lin and the others were taken, Endora would alert the multiverse, and though there would be chaos and witch hunts in high places, the rogue would still be at a comprehensive disadvantage.

> *"The womb of every world is in the balance,"* he said.
> *Conspirators gather beneath a darkened sun.*
> *The silence weighs a thousand pounds.*

There was a moment of silence. She pressed her cheek to his shoulder, her hair a warm presence in the hollow of his throat.

"These could be the last hours of peace," she said.

"Yes."

She offered a mischievous giggle. "Can I say that I'm glad you don't have your cat with you?"

He smiled. "So am I."

She looked at him soberly, then kissed his cheek. He returned the kiss, and said,

> *Old friend, familiar perfume.*
> *How thrilling it is that*
> *The touch of your lips feels new.*

"Yes," Daljit said. "If this is our last night in this incarnation, let it be poetry."

He put his arms around her and kissed her.

Poetry it certainly was.

In the morning, while a highly competent robotic kitchen prepared duck eggs, lightly poached with a bit of truffle oil and just the right amount of duck fat, Aristide stood in the cockpit and scanned the surrounding sea with binoculars. A few giant cargo ships stood black on the horizon like the distant castles of Gundapur, but no patrol or pleasure craft could be seen. The boat was beating into the wind on the starboard tack, and a fine salt spray dotted the cockpit windscreen.

Aristide put down the binoculars and picked up his cup of coffee. He tasted it and frowned—this was a domestic blend. For some reason Topaz never produced great coffee: the good stuff had to be imported.

Daljit appeared in the hatch, carrying a breakfast tray, two small plates with the duck eggs along with butter and a baguette. She set the tray on the table, and he kissed her.

As their lips touched a speaker pinged on the instrument console. They parted, a little rueful, as if the console were in the role of a strict chaperone.

"Yes?" Aristide said.

The voice that came from the console was that used by Endora—female, a little hurried, a little overprecise, and unlike the more colloquial voice of Bitsy.

"The rogue AI is Courtland," Endora said.

"Really?" Aristide was surprised. Courtland's personal interests were rather abstract—it was interested in cosmology, exploration, and teleology. Not exactly the sort to lead a revolution.

"It isn't yet clear whether there is a group of humans behind Courtland's actions," Endora continued, "or who they might be, but if they exist we'll find out in due course."

"May I ask how the identification was made?"

"Partly as a result of your actions on Hawaiki," Endora said, "and partly by backtracking those who arrived in great haste this morning to claim General Singh's body. These included Myriad City's chief of police, by the way."

Aristide looked at Daljit. "That's two of the security services compromised," he said.

"They were being very careful about sending messages to one another," Endora said. "For the most part they took guidance from AIs they brought with them, which meant they didn't have to communicate with Courtland very often. But reports had to go back and forth sooner or later. Everything is on record, and the track is very plain."

Daljit took the cup of coffee from Aristide's hand and sipped at it.

"What about General Singh?" she asked.

"He has been reincarnated from a three-month-old backup and has been briefed by Commissar Lin and me. He's already taking charge of the human end of this investigation."

A gust of wind blew Daljit's hair across her face. Aristide swept it back with a delicate finger.

"How are Grax, Herenui, and Cadwal?" he asked.

"Recovering after interrogation. Under drugs they revealed everything they knew. Once they are stable, specialists will try to reconstruct their brains to remove the Venger's influence."

"Is the prognosis hopeful?"

"I shouldn't think so," Endora said, "but the specialists will do their best."

Aristide took his coffee cup from Daljit's fingers and took a thoughtful sip.

"Herenui's group could have tried to take me earlier than they did," he said. "Do we know why they didn't?"

"They were busy taking others," Endora said. "A whole group of nine visitors traveling together."

"Caught in their net," Aristide murmured.

"Taken at once in those caves, yes. They've returned, in standard human bodies, and are now being tracked to see who they report to."

Aristide looked at Daljit. "I suppose there's no reason to stay at sea," he said.

"No," Endora said. "Though since both of you have finished your assignments, and as neither of you have any official status in this emergency, you have no obligation to return."

Daljit put an arm around Aristide and kissed him. Her lips tasted of coffee.

"I think we'll go back," she said.

Aristide ordered the boat to return to Myriad City. It swung off the wind, its pitching easing, and then the headsails went slack as the foresail and spanker boomed out to either side. The water laughed under the counter as the boat's speed increased.

Their breakfasts had gone cold and were fed to the fishes as the galley was instructed to prepare more. Aristide sat in the cockpit with his arm around Daljit as they shared their coffee and baguette.

"It won't take long for Courtland to know he's been found out," Aristide said. "These are the last hours of peace."

"We should treasure them."

"Yes. We should."

They kissed. The masts groaned as a gust of wind caught the boat and carried it toward the towers of Myriad City, and the certainty of war.